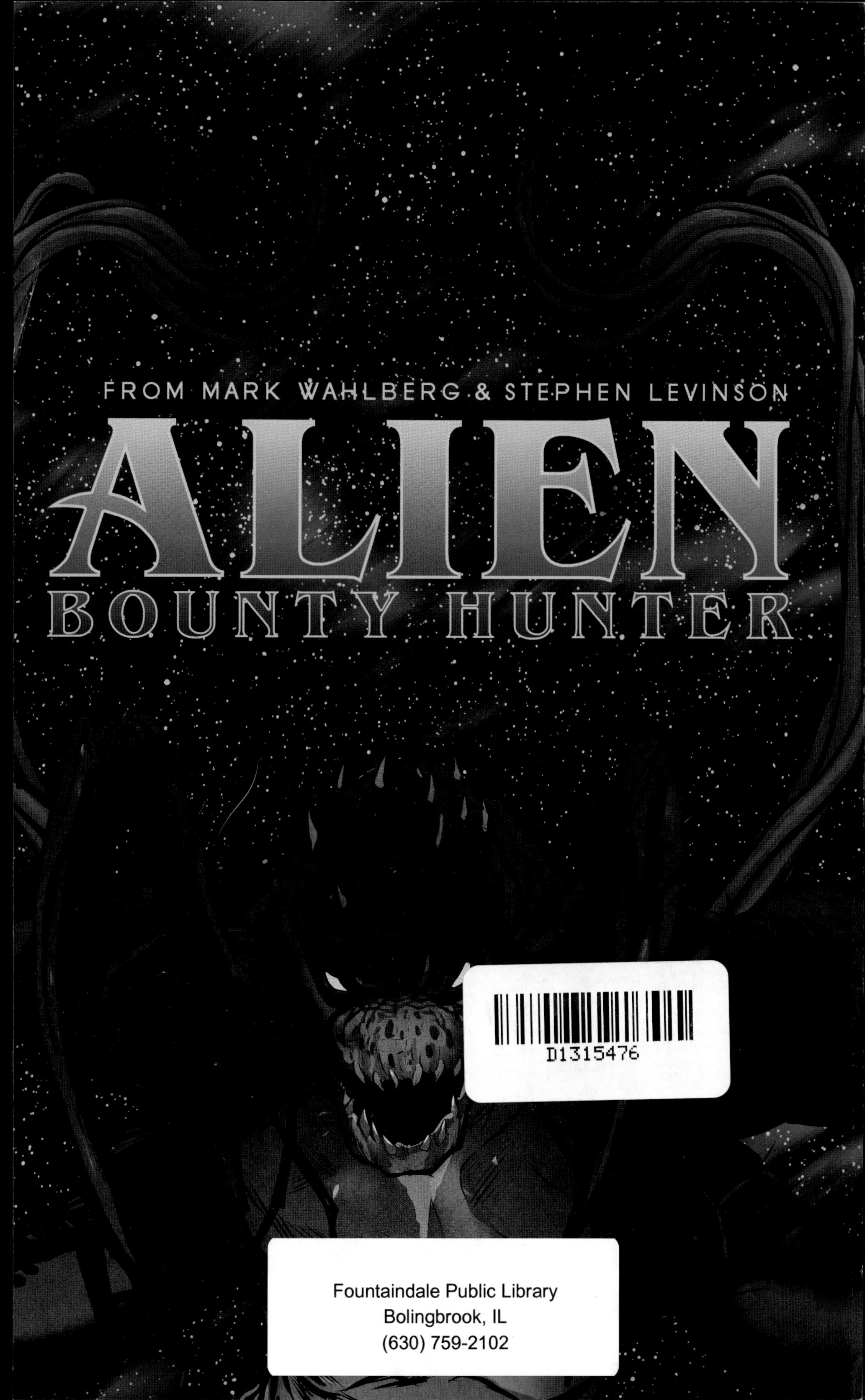
FROM MARK WAHLBERG & STEPHEN LEVINSON
ALIEN
BOUNTY HUNTER

CHAPTER 1

BEN MADSEN
SPECIES: HOMO SAPIEN
PLANET OF ORIGIN: EARTH

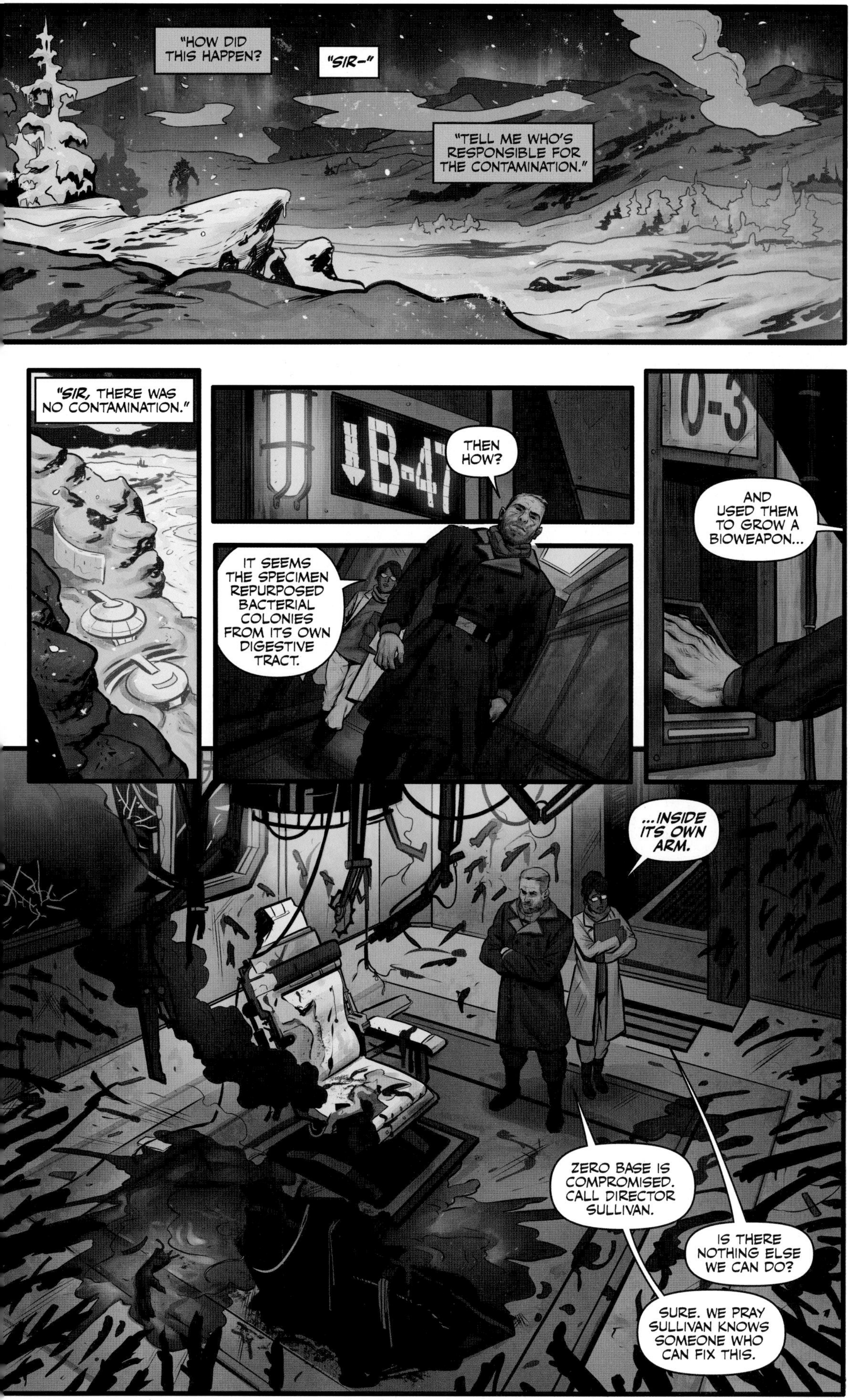
"HOW DID THIS HAPPEN?
"SIR–"
"TELL ME WHO'S RESPONSIBLE FOR THE CONTAMINATION."
"SIR, THERE WAS NO CONTAMINATION."
B-47
THEN HOW?
IT SEEMS THE SPECIMEN REPURPOSED BACTERIAL COLONIES FROM ITS OWN DIGESTIVE TRACT.
AND USED THEM TO GROW A BIOWEAPON...
...INSIDE ITS OWN ARM.
ZERO BASE IS COMPROMISED. CALL DIRECTOR SULLIVAN.
IS THERE NOTHING ELSE WE CAN DO?
SURE. WE PRAY SULLIVAN KNOWS SOMEONE WHO CAN FIX THIS.

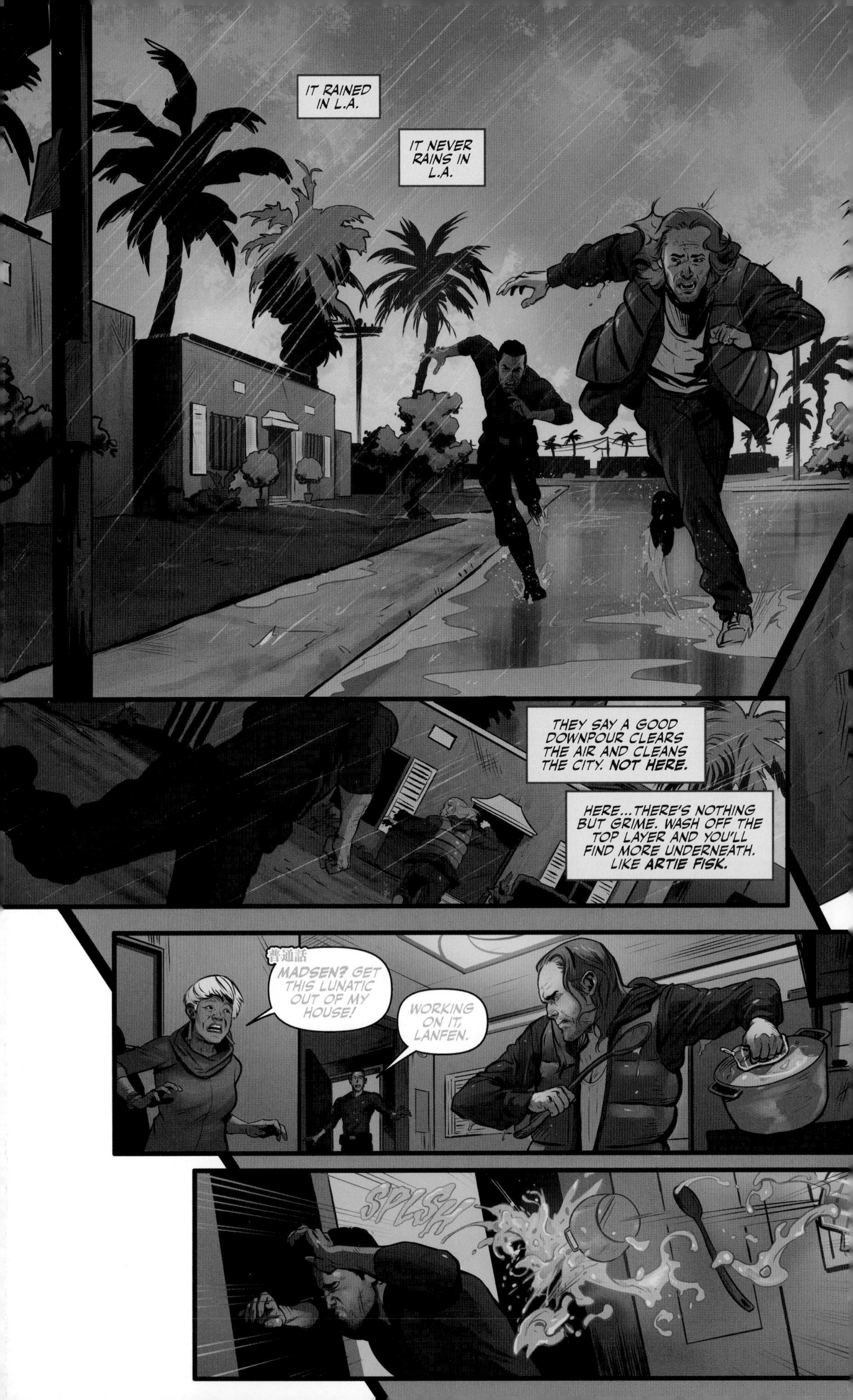

IT RAINED IN L.A.
IT NEVER RAINS IN L.A.
THEY SAY A GOOD DOWNPOUR CLEARS THE AIR AND CLEANS THE CITY. NOT HERE.
HERE...THERE'S NOTHING BUT GRIME. WASH OFF THE TOP LAYER AND YOU'LL FIND MORE UNDERNEATH. LIKE ARTIE FISK.
普通話
MADSEN? GET THIS LUNATIC OUT OF MY HOUSE!
WORKING ON IT, LANFEN.
SPLSH

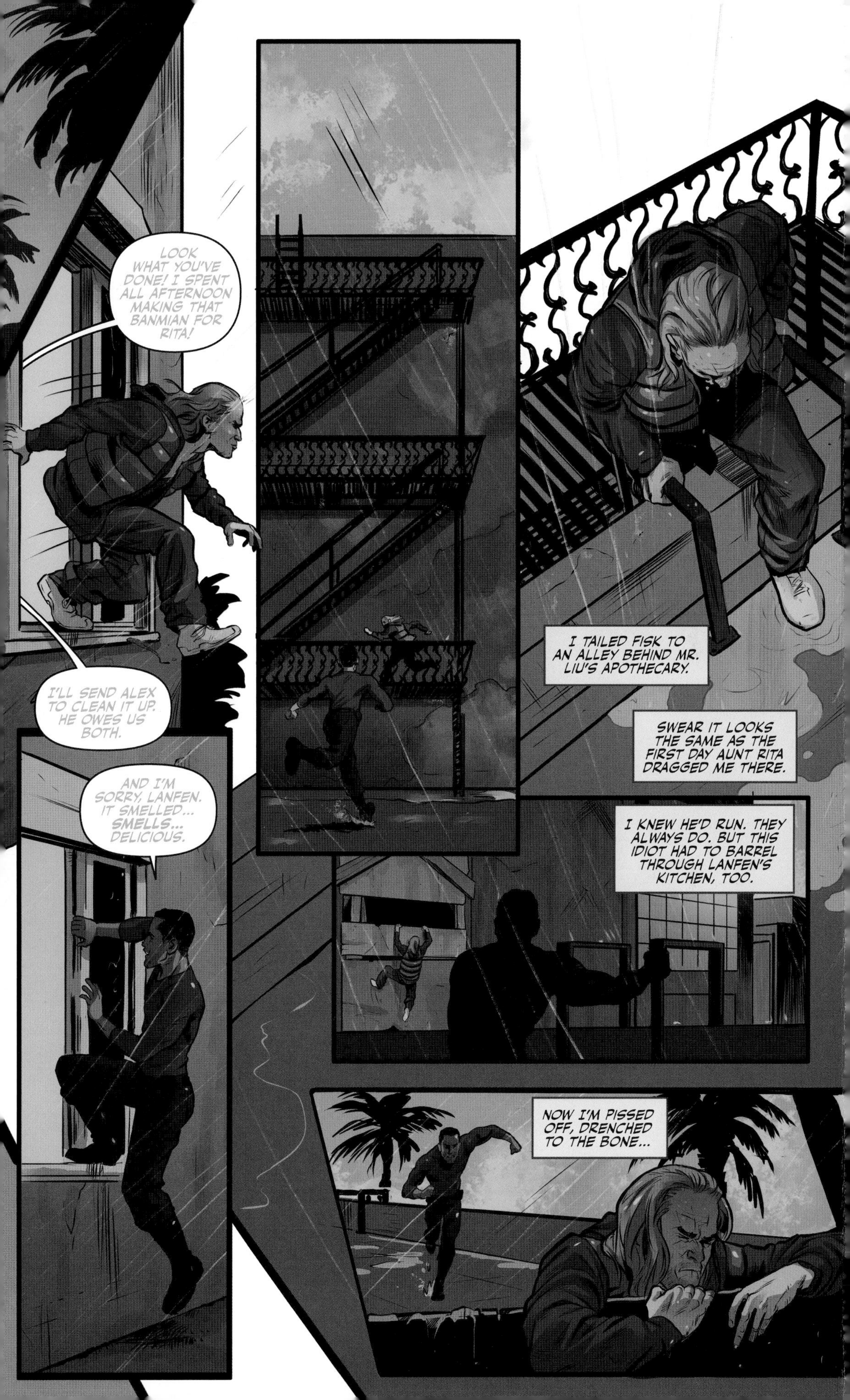
LOOK WHAT YOU'VE DONE! I SPENT ALL AFTERNOON MAKING THAT BANMIAN FOR RITA!
I'LL SEND ALEX TO CLEAN IT UP. HE OWES US BOTH.
AND I'M SORRY, LANFEN. IT SMELLED... SMELLS... DELICIOUS.
I TAILED FISK TO AN ALLEY BEHIND MR. LIU'S APOTHECARY.
SWEAR IT LOOKS THE SAME AS THE FIRST DAY AUNT RITA DRAGGED ME THERE.
I KNEW HE'D RUN. THEY ALWAYS DO. BUT THIS IDIOT HAD TO BARREL THROUGH LANFEN'S KITCHEN, TOO.
NOW I'M PISSED OFF, DRENCHED TO THE BONE...

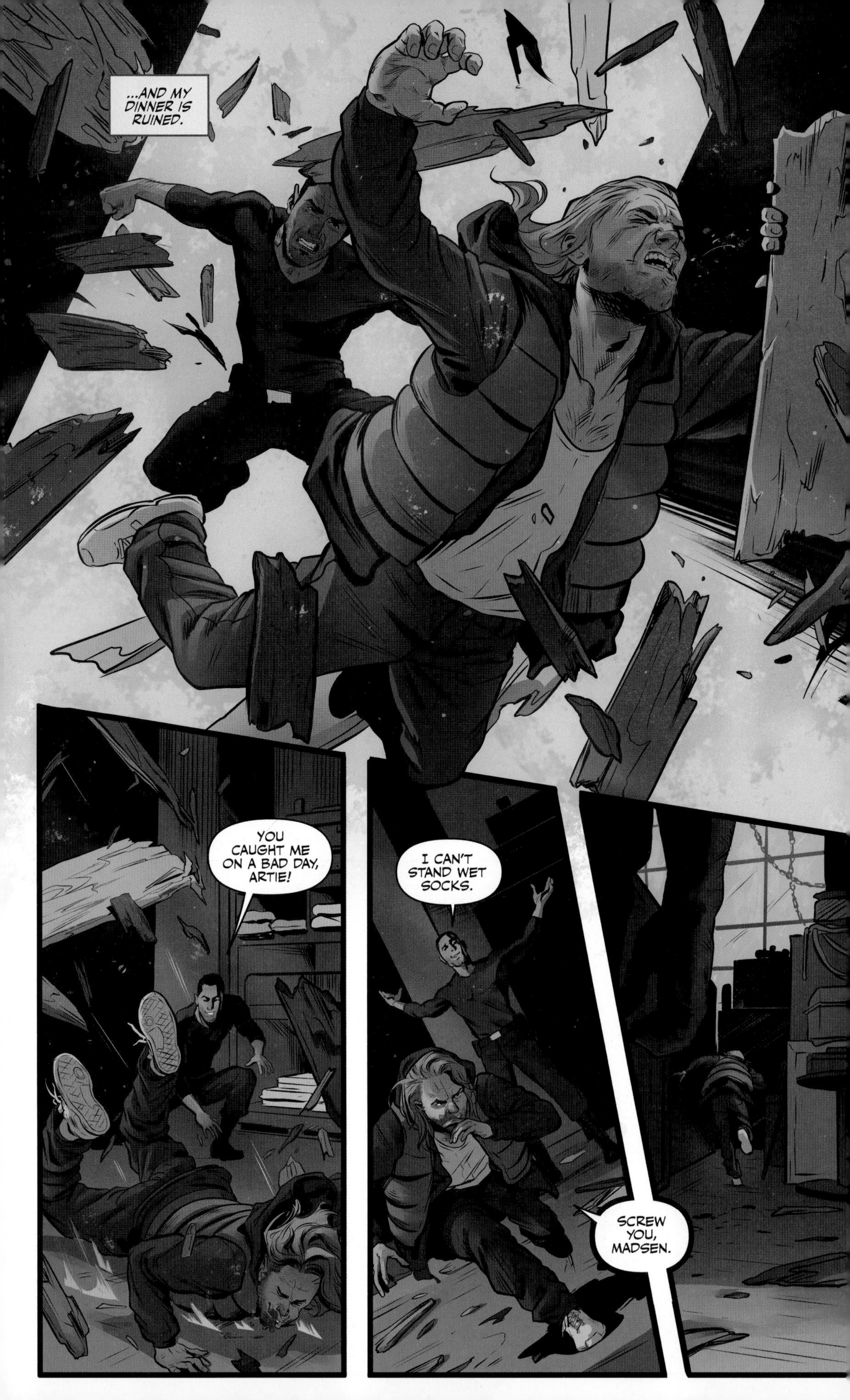
...AND MY DINNER IS RUINED.
YOU CAUGHT ME ON A BAD DAY, ARTIE!
I CAN'T STAND WET SOCKS.
SCREW YOU, MADSEN.

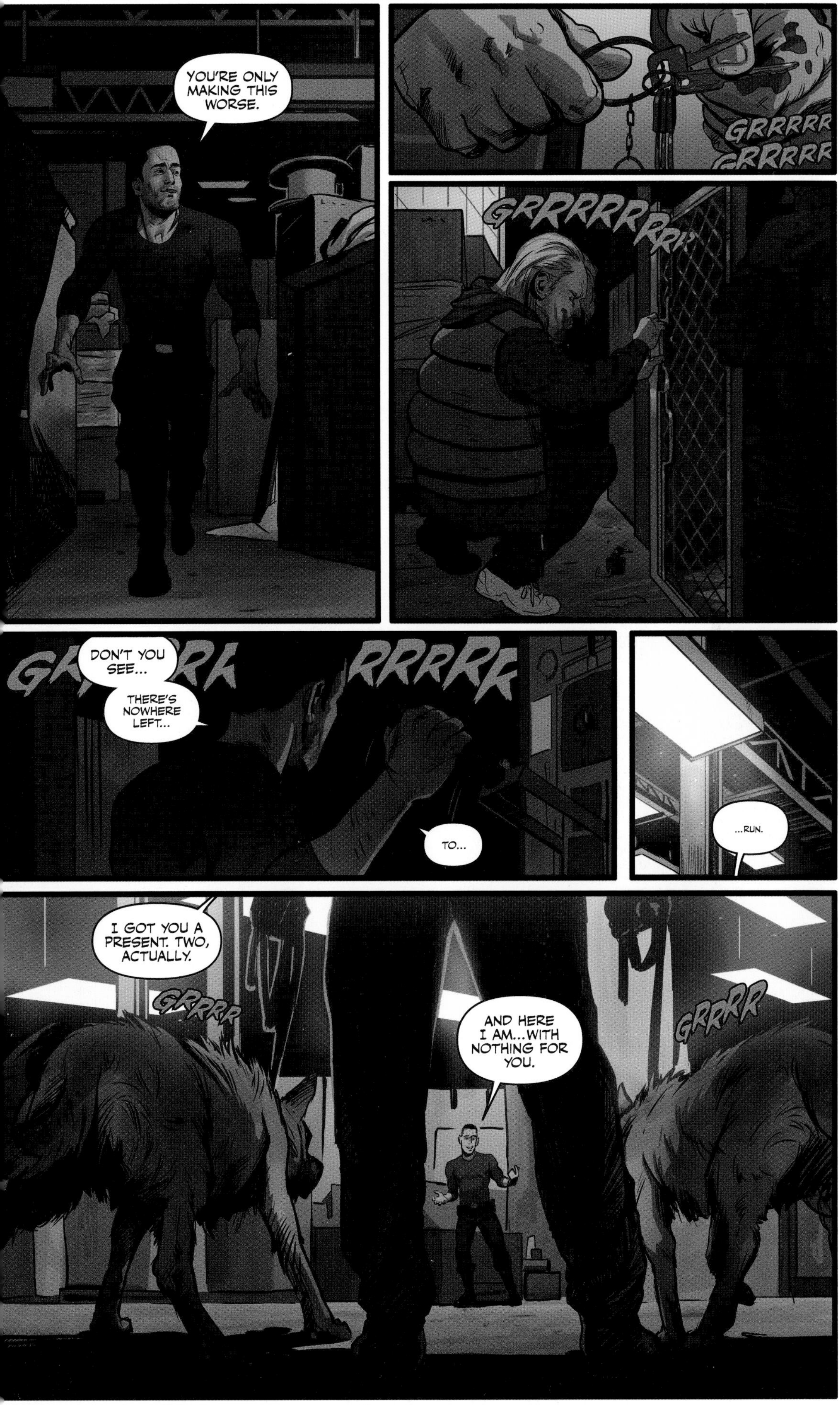
YOU'RE ONLY MAKING THIS WORSE.
GRRRRR GRRRRR
GRRRRRRRR!
DON'T YOU SEE...
THERE'S NOWHERE LEFT...
TO...
...RUN.
I GOT YOU A PRESENT. TWO, ACTUALLY.
GRRRR
AND HERE I AM...WITH NOTHING FOR YOU.
GRRRR

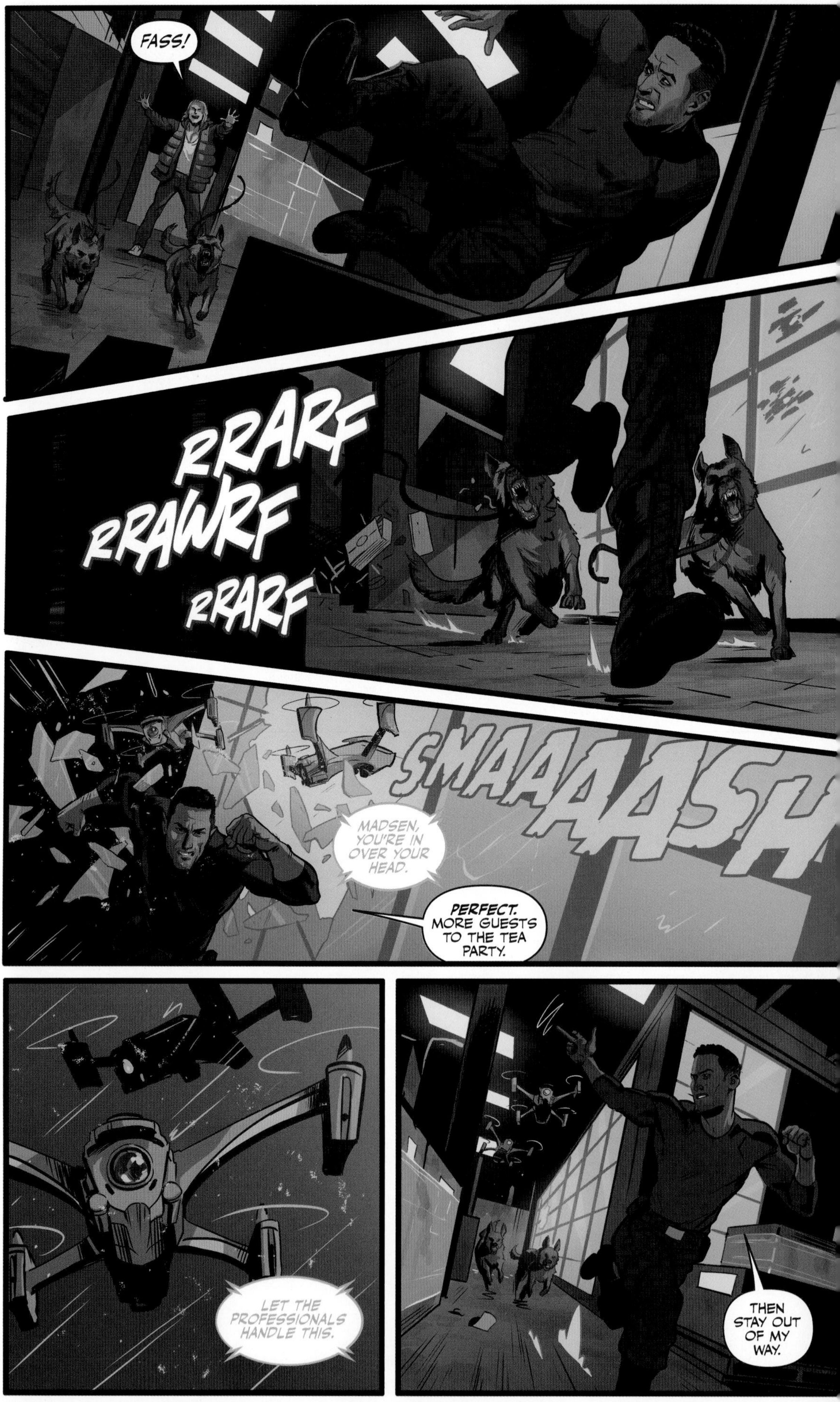
FASS!
RRARF
RRAWRF
RRARF
SMAAAASH
MADSEN, YOU'RE IN OVER YOUR HEAD.
PERFECT. MORE GUESTS TO THE TEA PARTY.
LET THE PROFESSIONALS HANDLE THIS.
THEN STAY OUT OF MY WAY.

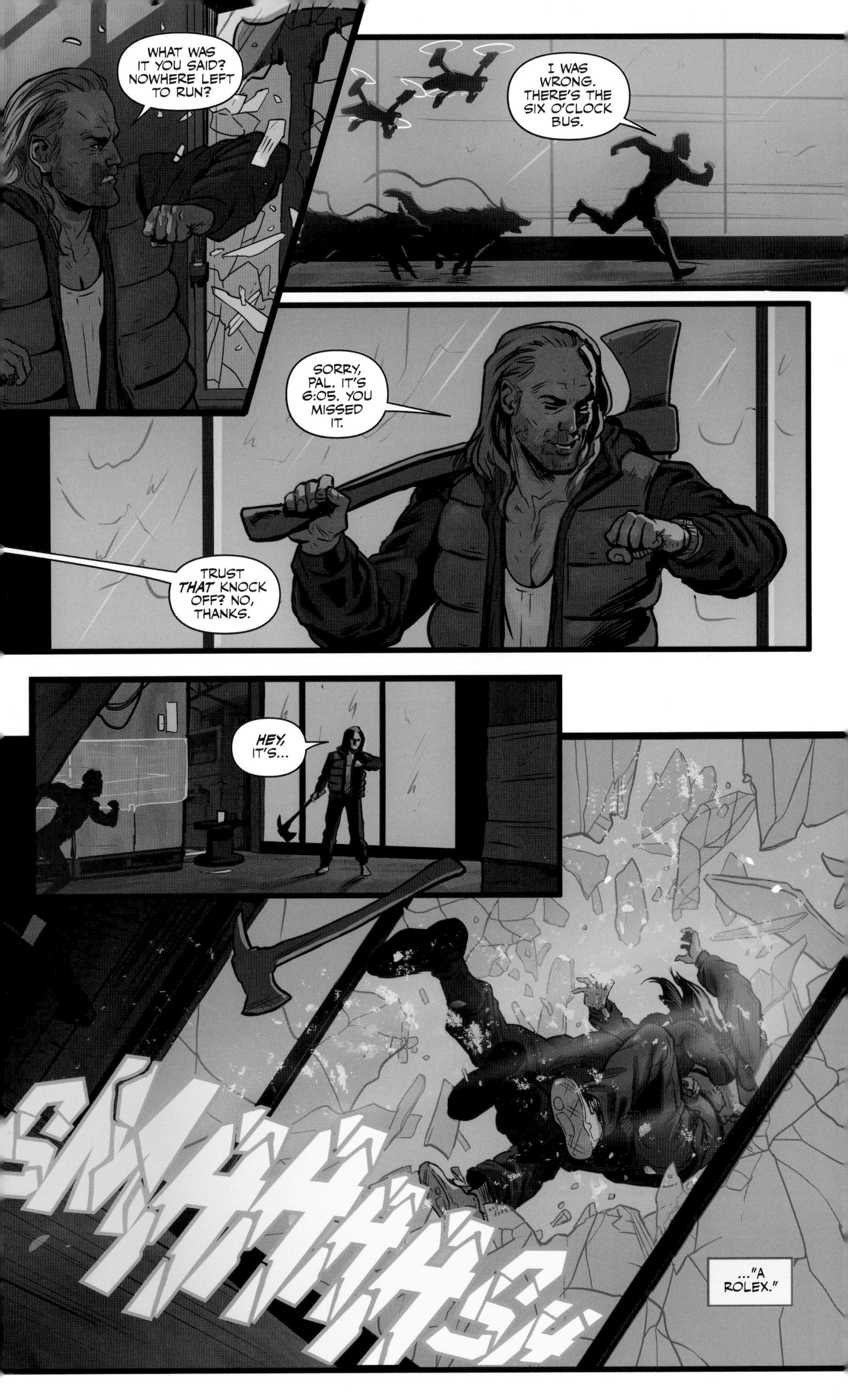
WHAT WAS IT YOU SAID? NOWHERE LEFT TO RUN?
I WAS WRONG. THERE'S THE SIX O'CLOCK BUS.
SORRY, PAL. IT'S 6:05. YOU MISSED IT.
TRUST *THAT* KNOCK OFF? NO, THANKS.
HEY, IT'S...
..."A ROLEX."

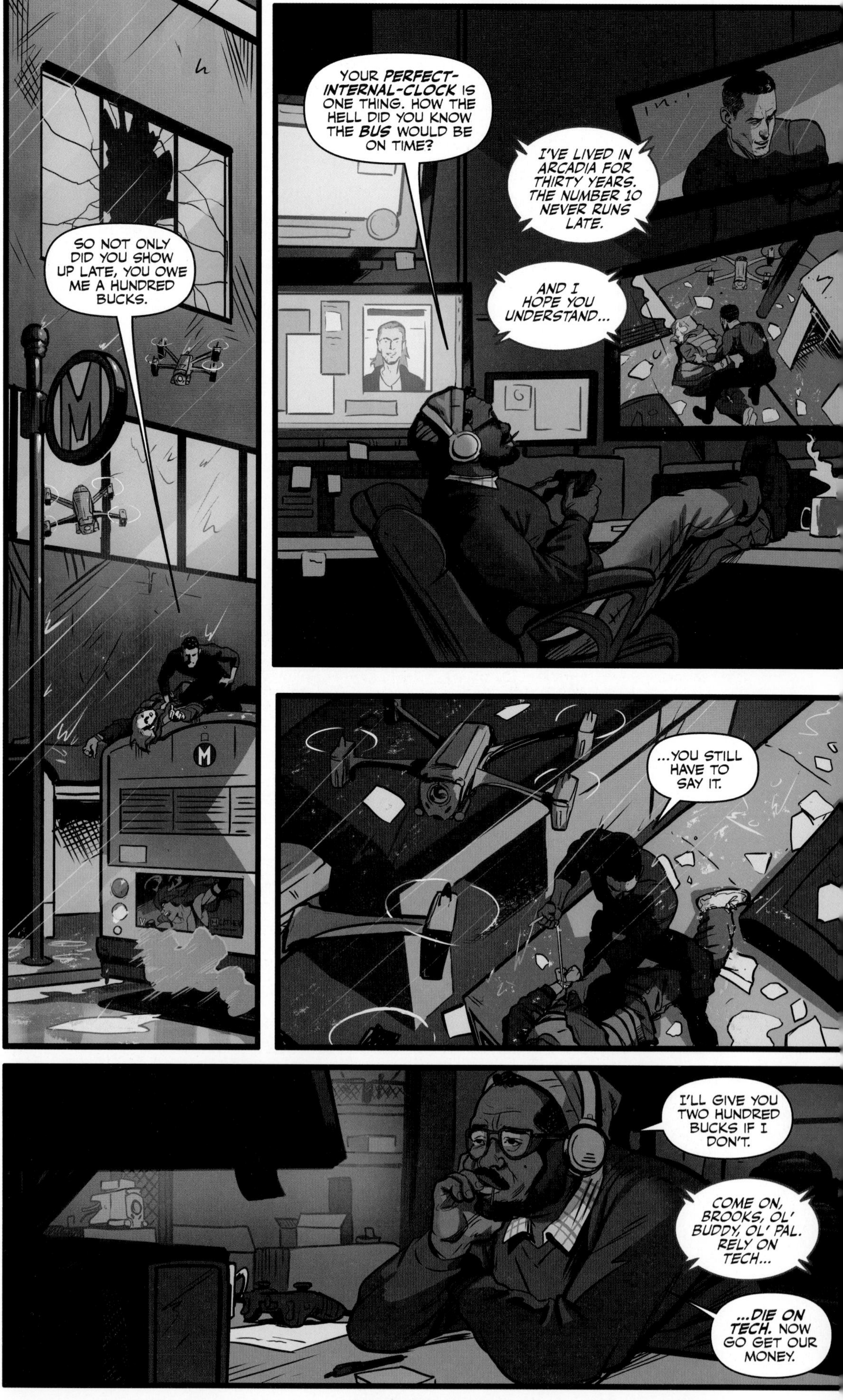
SO NOT ONLY DID YOU SHOW UP LATE, YOU OWE ME A HUNDRED BUCKS.
YOUR PERFECT-INTERNAL-CLOCK IS ONE THING. HOW THE HELL DID YOU KNOW THE BUS WOULD BE ON TIME?
I'VE LIVED IN ARCADIA FOR THIRTY YEARS. THE NUMBER 10 NEVER RUNS LATE.
AND I HOPE YOU UNDERSTAND...
...YOU STILL HAVE TO SAY IT.
I'LL GIVE YOU TWO HUNDRED BUCKS IF I DON'T.
COME ON, BROOKS, OL' BUDDY, OL' PAL. RELY ON TECH...
...DIE ON TECH. NOW GO GET OUR MONEY.

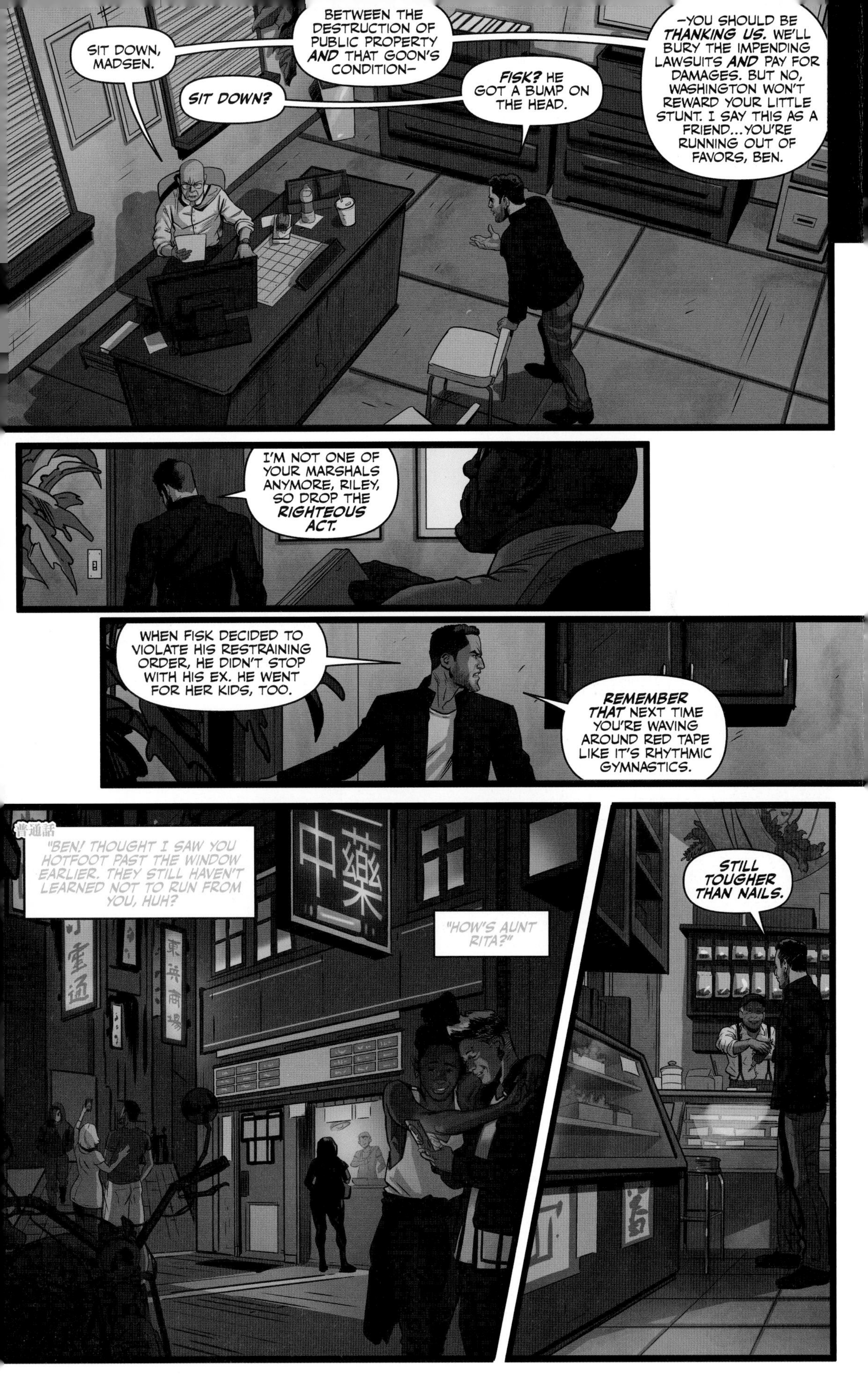
SIT DOWN, MADSEN.
BETWEEN THE DESTRUCTION OF PUBLIC PROPERTY AND THAT GOON'S CONDITION—
SIT DOWN?
FISK? HE GOT A BUMP ON THE HEAD.
—YOU SHOULD BE THANKING US. WE'LL BURY THE IMPENDING LAWSUITS AND PAY FOR DAMAGES. BUT NO, WASHINGTON WON'T REWARD YOUR LITTLE STUNT. I SAY THIS AS A FRIEND...YOU'RE RUNNING OUT OF FAVORS, BEN.
I'M NOT ONE OF YOUR MARSHALS ANYMORE, RILEY, SO DROP THE RIGHTEOUS ACT.
WHEN FISK DECIDED TO VIOLATE HIS RESTRAINING ORDER, HE DIDN'T STOP WITH HIS EX. HE WENT FOR HER KIDS, TOO.
REMEMBER THAT NEXT TIME YOU'RE WAVING AROUND RED TAPE LIKE IT'S RHYTHMIC GYMNASTICS.
普通話
"BEN! THOUGHT I SAW YOU HOTFOOT PAST THE WINDOW EARLIER. THEY STILL HAVEN'T LEARNED NOT TO RUN FROM YOU, HUH?
中藥
"HOW'S AUNT RITA?"
STILL TOUGHER THAN NAILS.

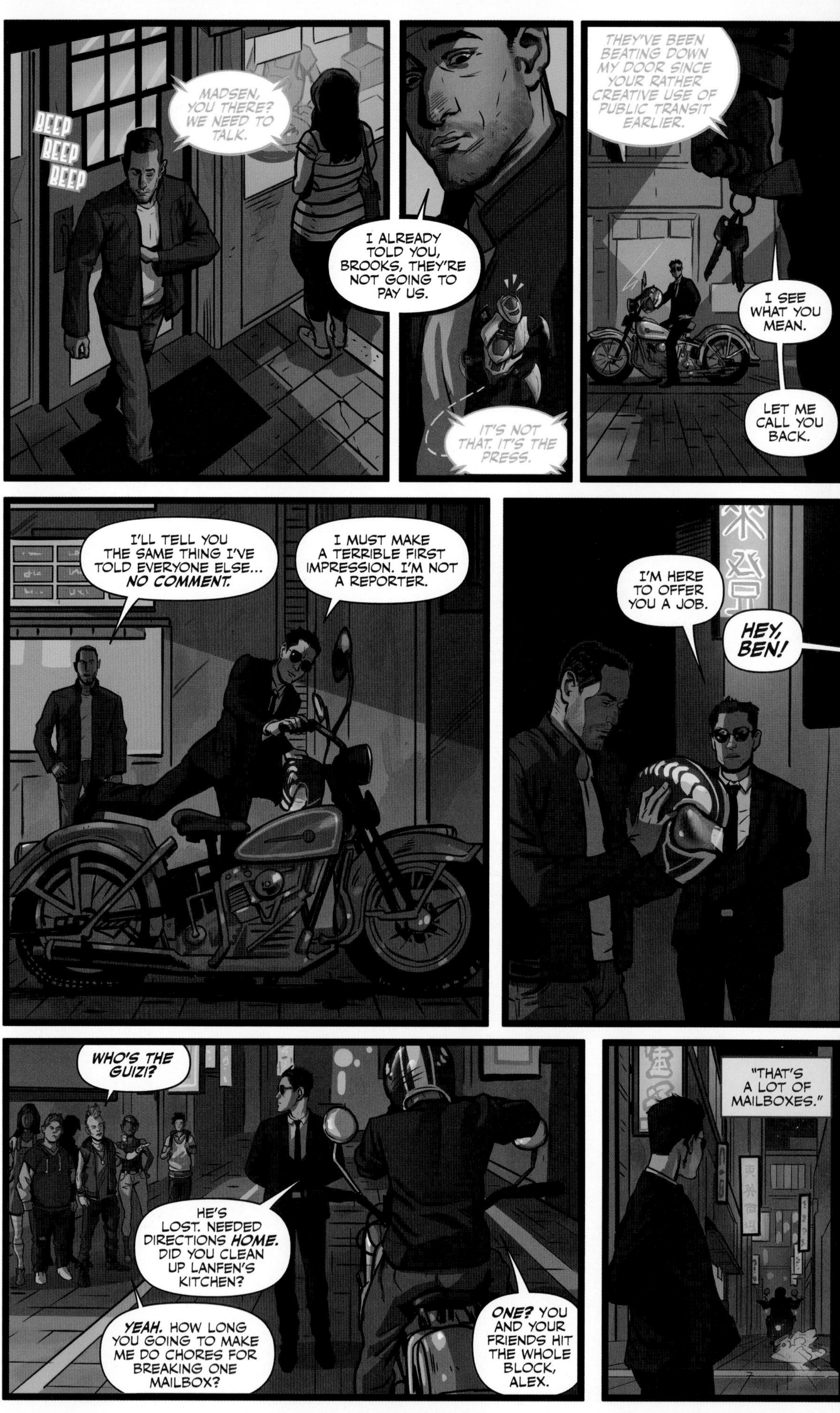
BEEP BEEP BEEP
MADSEN, YOU THERE? WE NEED TO TALK.
I ALREADY TOLD YOU, BROOKS, THEY'RE NOT GOING TO PAY US.
IT'S NOT THAT. IT'S THE PRESS.
THEY'VE BEEN BEATING DOWN MY DOOR SINCE YOUR RATHER CREATIVE USE OF PUBLIC TRANSIT EARLIER.
I SEE WHAT YOU MEAN.
LET ME CALL YOU BACK.
I'LL TELL YOU THE SAME THING I'VE TOLD EVERYONE ELSE... NO COMMENT.
I MUST MAKE A TERRIBLE FIRST IMPRESSION. I'M NOT A REPORTER.
I'M HERE TO OFFER YOU A JOB.
HEY, BEN!
WHO'S THE GUIZI?
HE'S LOST. NEEDED DIRECTIONS HOME. DID YOU CLEAN UP LANFEN'S KITCHEN?
YEAH. HOW LONG YOU GOING TO MAKE ME DO CHORES FOR BREAKING ONE MAILBOX?
ONE? YOU AND YOUR FRIENDS HIT THE WHOLE BLOCK, ALEX.
"THAT'S A LOT OF MAILBOXES."

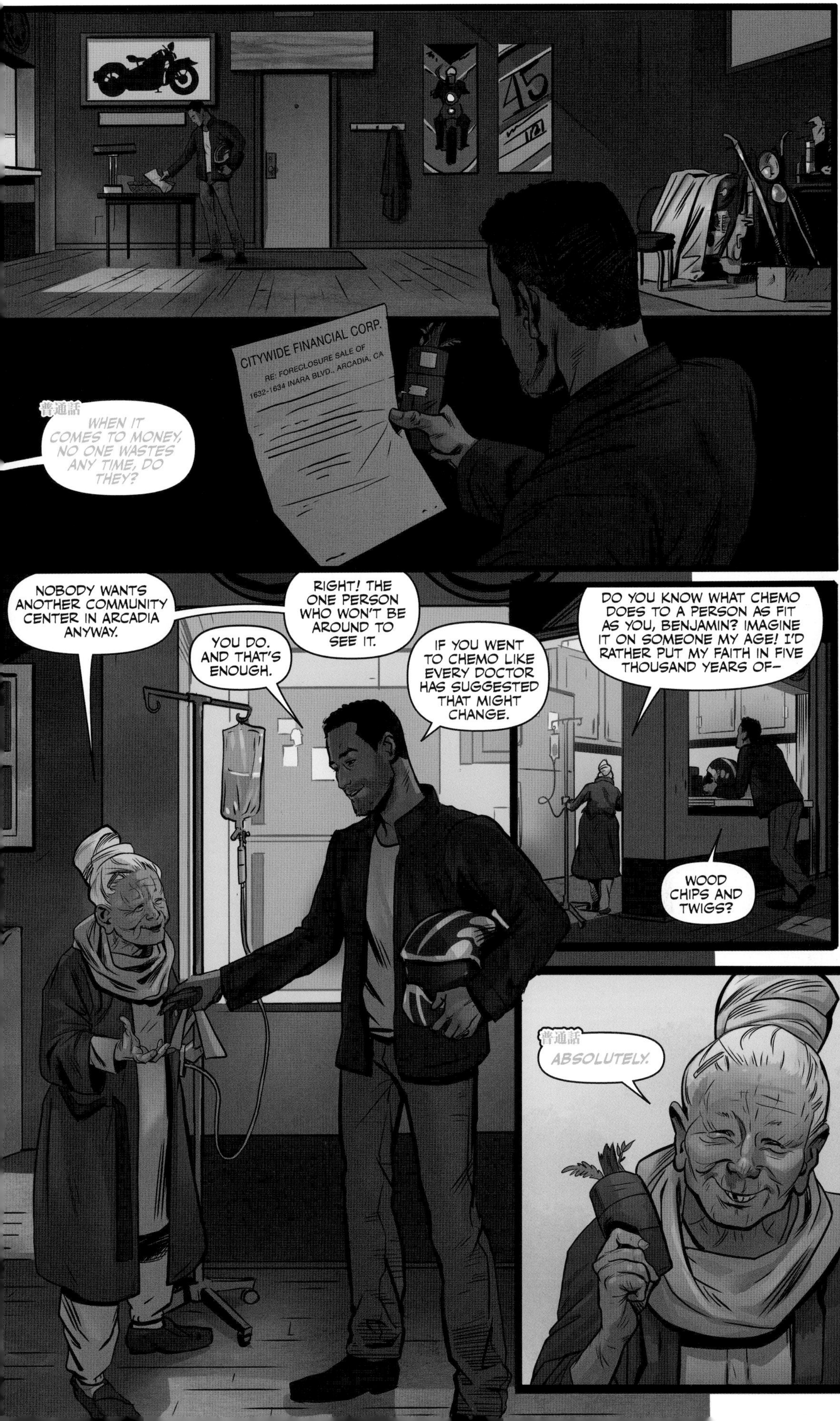

CITYWIDE FINANCIAL CORP.
RE: FORECLOSURE SALE OF
1632-1634 INARA BLVD., ARCADIA, CA
普通話
WHEN IT COMES TO MONEY, NO ONE WASTES ANY TIME, DO THEY?
NOBODY WANTS ANOTHER COMMUNITY CENTER IN ARCADIA ANYWAY.
YOU DO. AND THAT'S ENOUGH.
RIGHT! THE ONE PERSON WHO WON'T BE AROUND TO SEE IT.
IF YOU WENT TO CHEMO LIKE EVERY DOCTOR HAS SUGGESTED THAT MIGHT CHANGE.
DO YOU KNOW WHAT CHEMO DOES TO A PERSON AS FIT AS YOU, BENJAMIN? IMAGINE IT ON SOMEONE MY AGE! I'D RATHER PUT MY FAITH IN FIVE THOUSAND YEARS OF–
WOOD CHIPS AND TWIGS?
普通話
ABSOLUTELY.

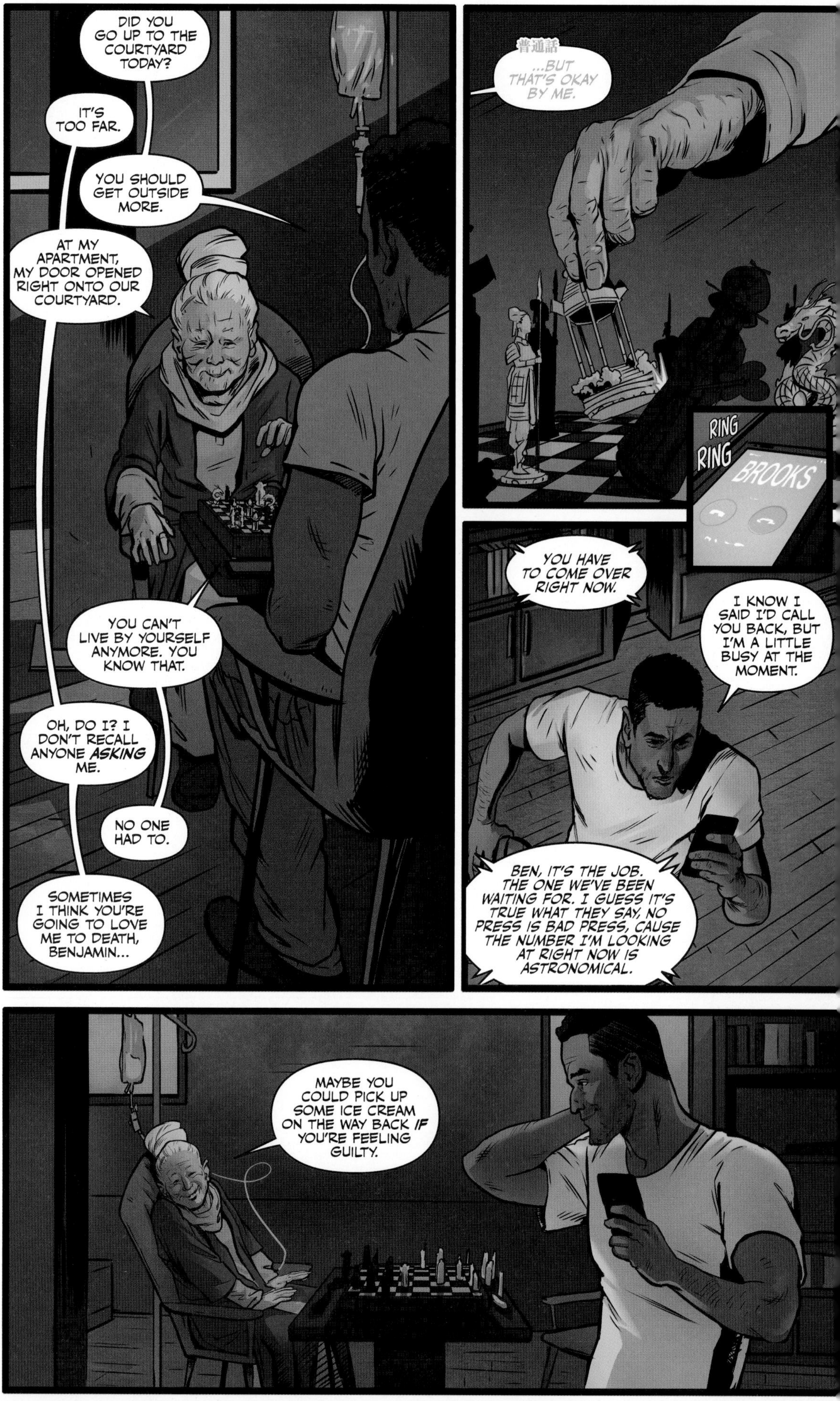

DID YOU GO UP TO THE COURTYARD TODAY?
IT'S TOO FAR.
YOU SHOULD GET OUTSIDE MORE.
AT MY APARTMENT, MY DOOR OPENED RIGHT ONTO OUR COURTYARD.
YOU CAN'T LIVE BY YOURSELF ANYMORE. YOU KNOW THAT.
OH, DO I? I DON'T RECALL ANYONE *ASKING* ME.
NO ONE HAD TO.
SOMETIMES I THINK YOU'RE GOING TO LOVE ME TO DEATH, BENJAMIN...
普通話
...BUT THAT'S OKAY BY ME.
RING
RING
BROOKS
YOU HAVE TO COME OVER RIGHT NOW.
I KNOW I SAID I'D CALL YOU BACK, BUT I'M A LITTLE BUSY AT THE MOMENT.
BEN, IT'S THE JOB. THE ONE WE'VE BEEN WAITING FOR. I GUESS IT'S TRUE WHAT THEY SAY, NO PRESS IS BAD PRESS, CAUSE THE NUMBER I'M LOOKING AT RIGHT NOW IS ASTRONOMICAL.
MAYBE YOU COULD PICK UP SOME ICE CREAM ON THE WAY BACK *IF* YOU'RE FEELING GUILTY.

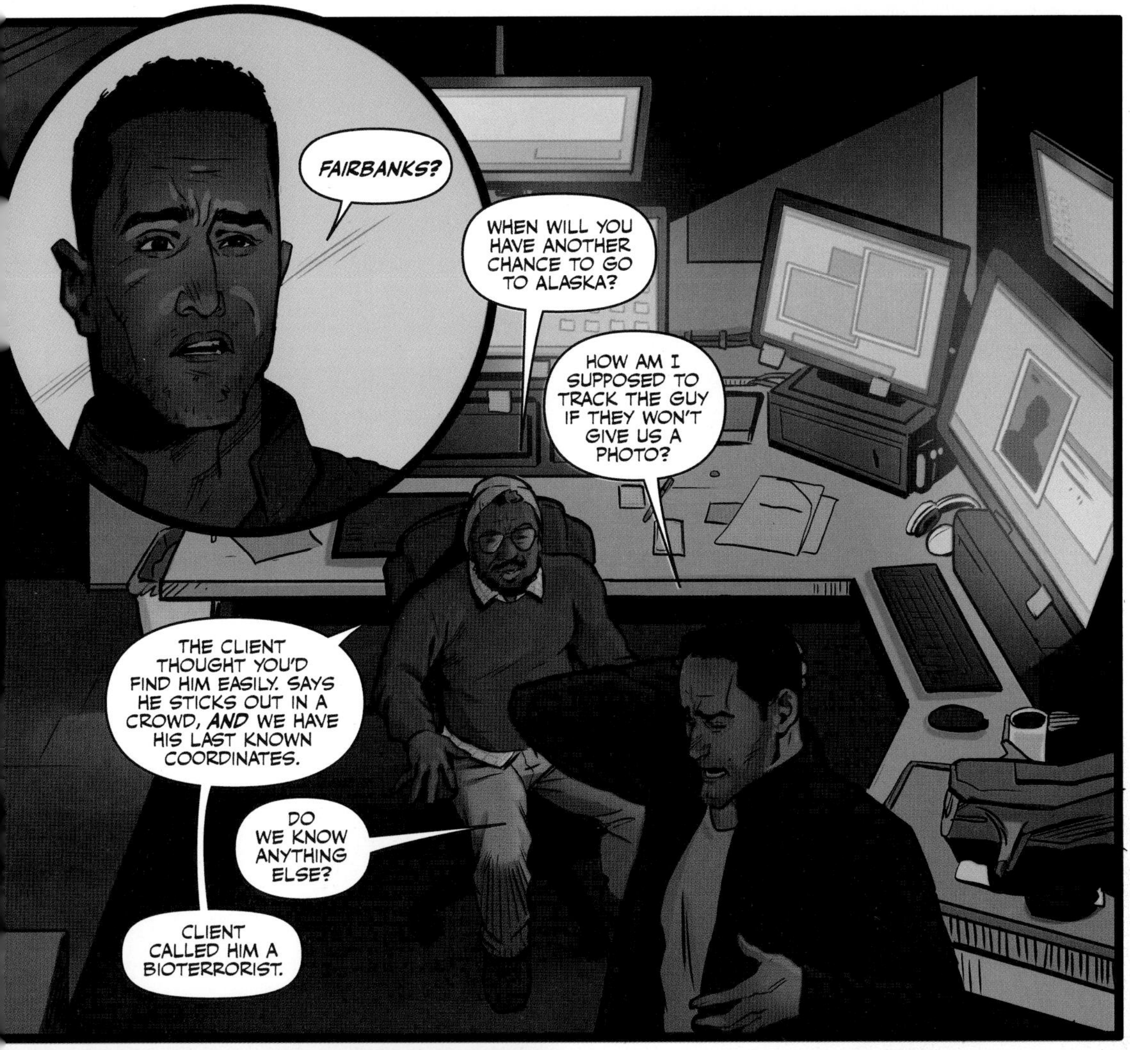
FAIRBANKS?
WHEN WILL YOU HAVE ANOTHER CHANCE TO GO TO ALASKA?
HOW AM I SUPPOSED TO TRACK THE GUY IF THEY WON'T GIVE US A PHOTO?
THE CLIENT THOUGHT YOU'D FIND HIM EASILY. SAYS HE STICKS OUT IN A CROWD, AND WE HAVE HIS LAST KNOWN COORDINATES.
DO WE KNOW ANYTHING ELSE?
CLIENT CALLED HIM A BIOTERRORIST.

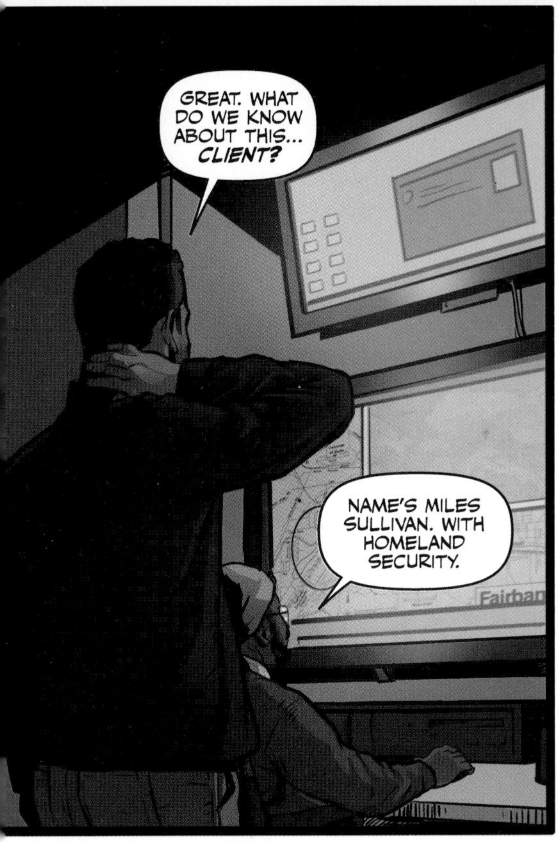
GREAT. WHAT DO WE KNOW ABOUT THIS... CLIENT?
NAME'S MILES SULLIVAN. WITH HOMELAND SECURITY.
Fairban

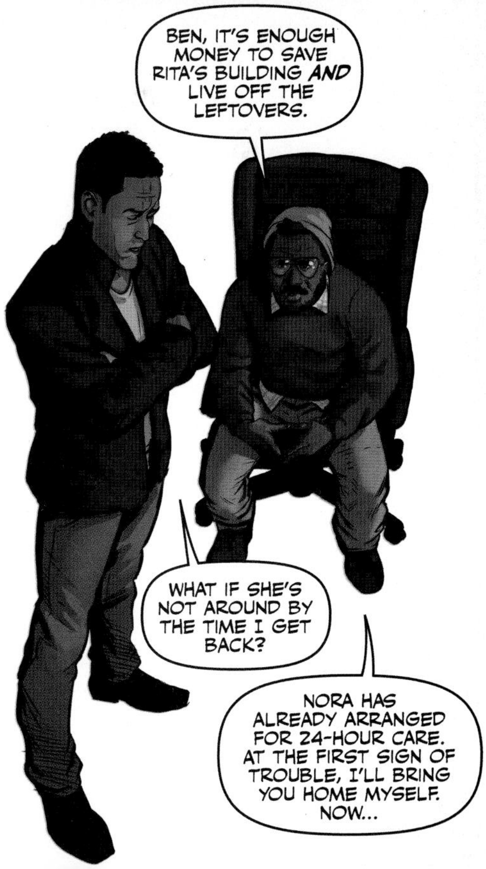
BEN, IT'S ENOUGH MONEY TO SAVE RITA'S BUILDING AND LIVE OFF THE LEFTOVERS.
WHAT IF SHE'S NOT AROUND BY THE TIME I GET BACK?
NORA HAS ALREADY ARRANGED FOR 24-HOUR CARE. AT THE FIRST SIGN OF TROUBLE, I'LL BRING YOU HOME MYSELF. NOW...

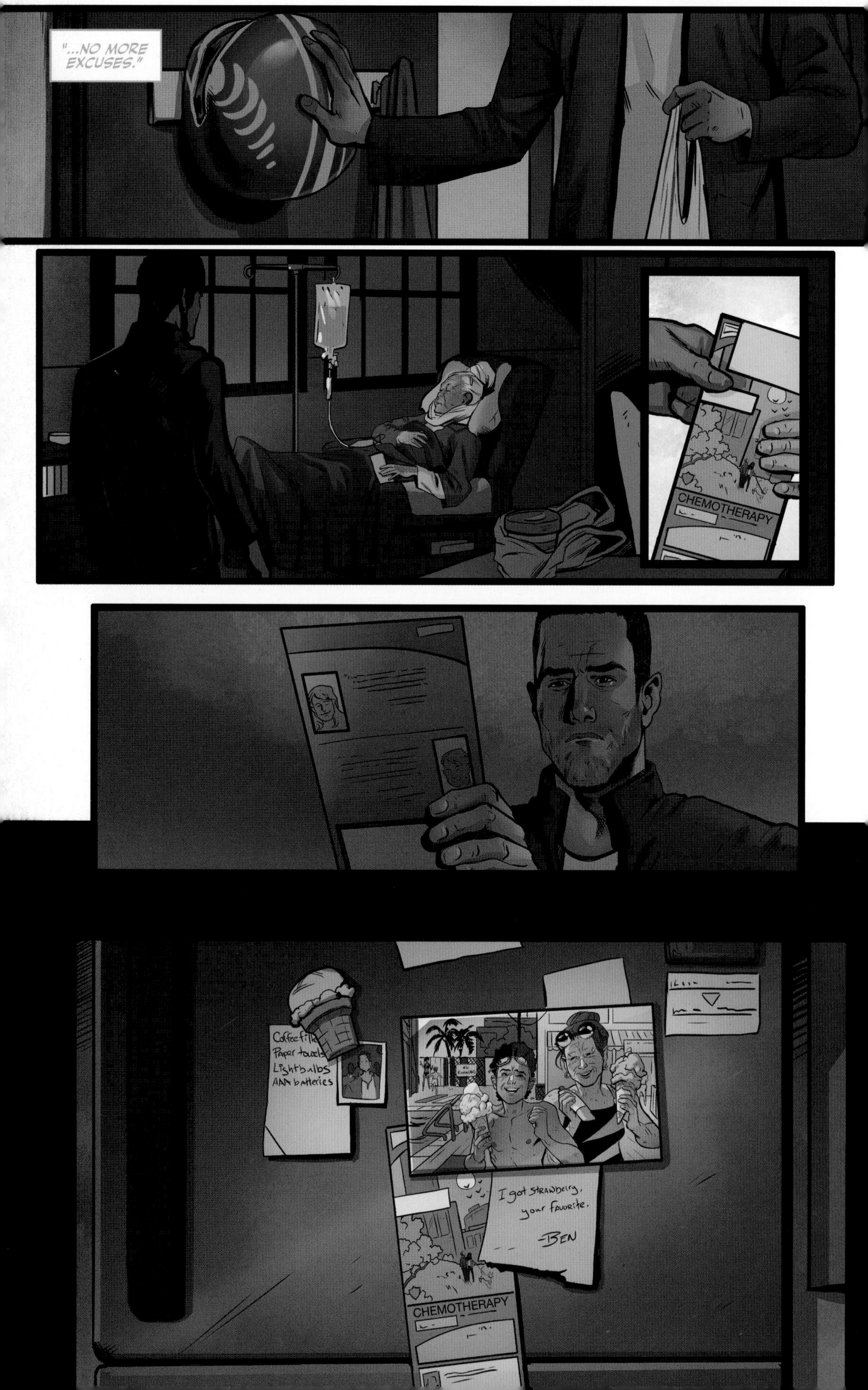
"...NO MORE EXCUSES."
CHEMOTHERAPY
Coffee filters
Paper towels
Lightbulbs
AA batteries
I got strawberry, your favorite.
-BEN
CHEMOTHERAPY

FUTURE SITE OF
THE LOEB ARCT
CONSERVATIO
CENTER

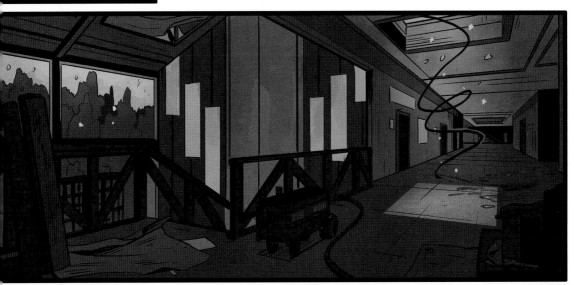

MORE OF THIS STUFF?

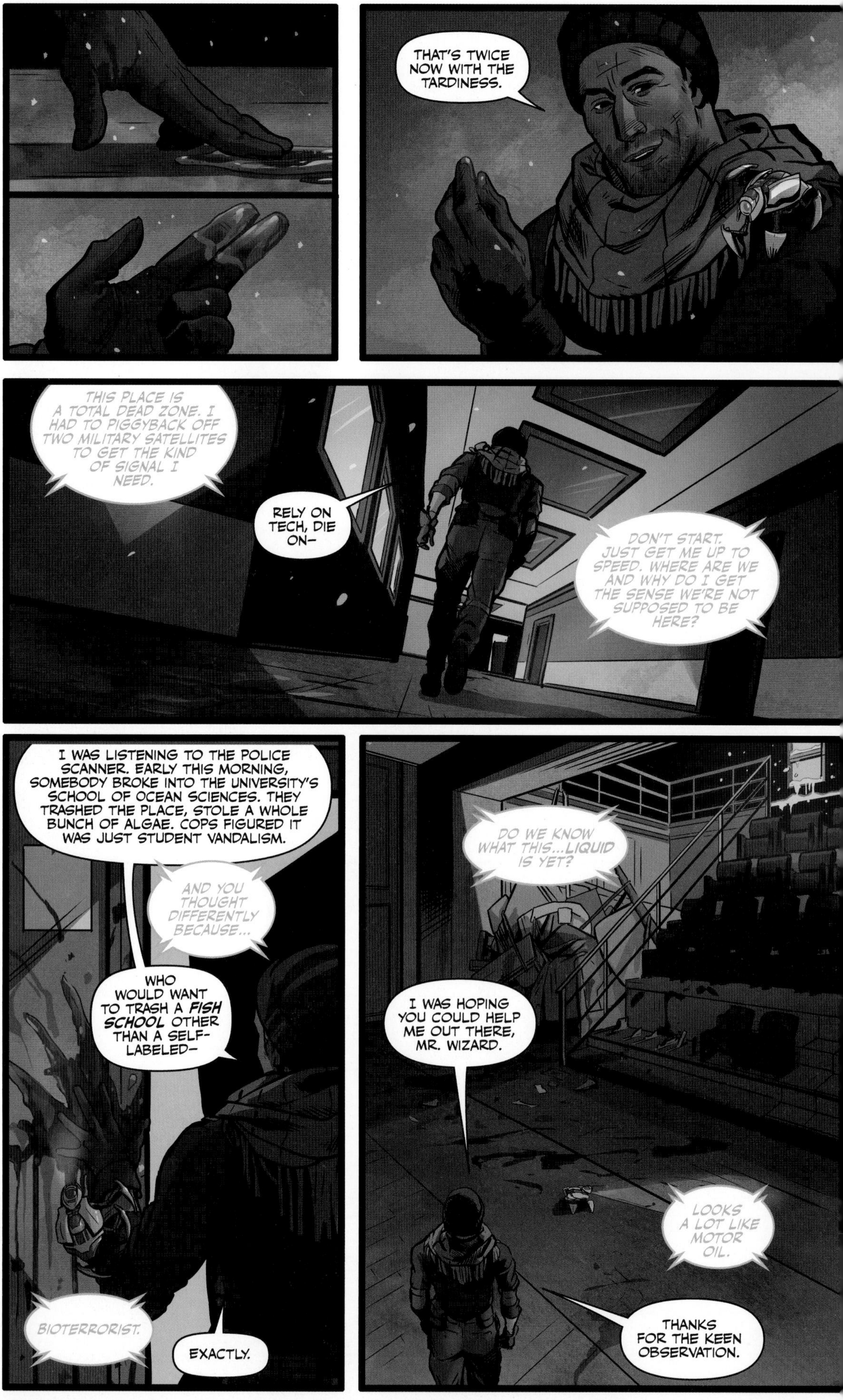
THAT'S TWICE NOW WITH THE TARDINESS.
THIS PLACE IS A TOTAL DEAD ZONE. I HAD TO PIGGYBACK OFF TWO MILITARY SATELLITES TO GET THE KIND OF SIGNAL I NEED.
RELY ON TECH, DIE ON–
DON'T START. JUST GET ME UP TO SPEED. WHERE ARE WE AND WHY DO I GET THE SENSE WE'RE NOT SUPPOSED TO BE HERE?
I WAS LISTENING TO THE POLICE SCANNER. EARLY THIS MORNING, SOMEBODY BROKE INTO THE UNIVERSITY'S SCHOOL OF OCEAN SCIENCES. THEY TRASHED THE PLACE, STOLE A WHOLE BUNCH OF ALGAE. COPS FIGURED IT WAS JUST STUDENT VANDALISM.
AND YOU THOUGHT DIFFERENTLY BECAUSE...
WHO WOULD WANT TO TRASH A ***FISH SCHOOL*** OTHER THAN A SELF-LABELED–
BIOTERRORIST.
EXACTLY.
DO WE KNOW WHAT THIS...***LIQUID*** IS YET?
I WAS HOPING YOU COULD HELP ME OUT THERE, MR. WIZARD.
LOOKS A LOT LIKE MOTOR OIL.
THANKS FOR THE KEEN OBSERVATION.

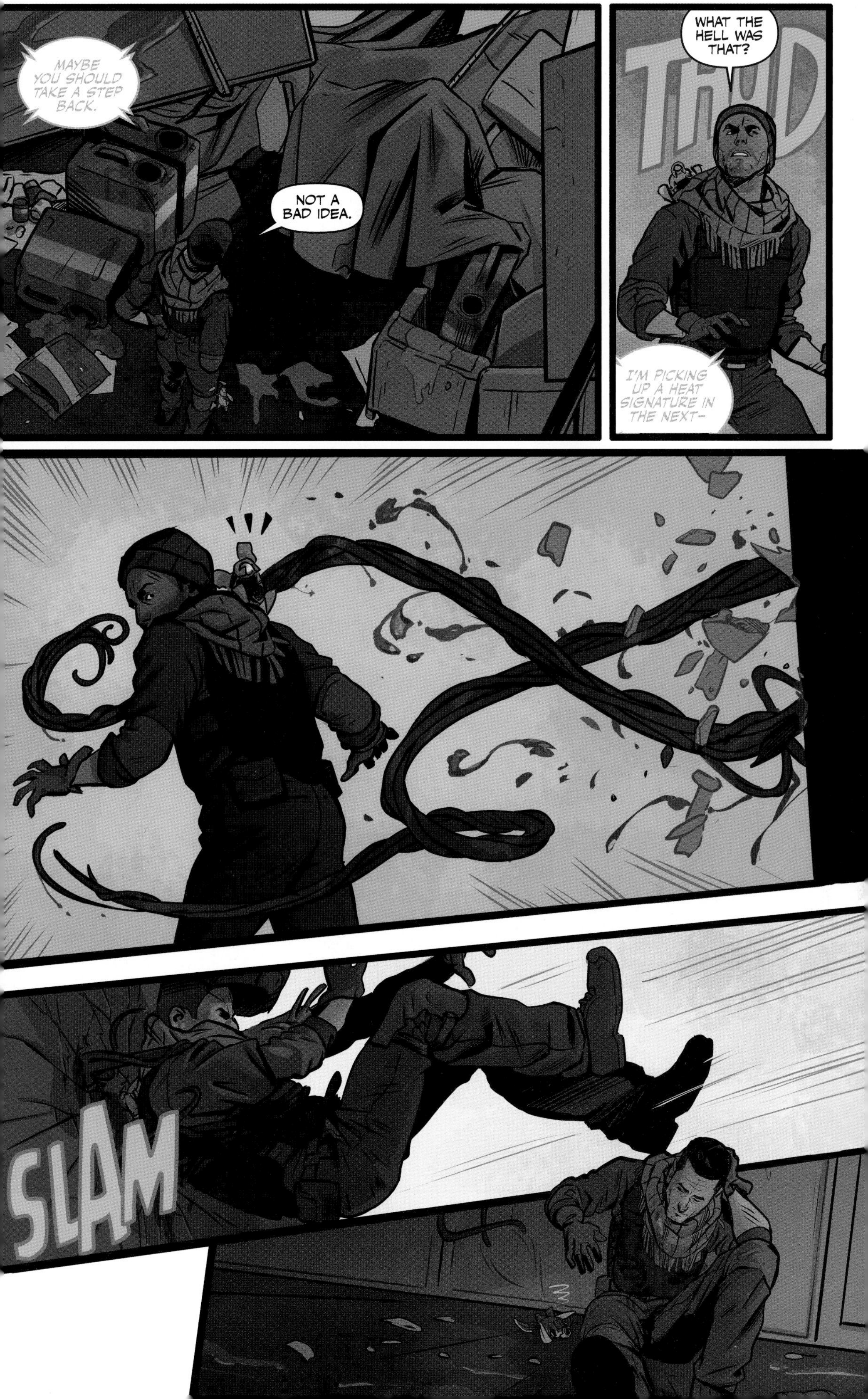
MAYBE YOU SHOULD TAKE A STEP BACK.
NOT A BAD IDEA.
WHAT THE HELL WAS THAT?
THUD
I'M PICKING UP A HEAT SIGNATURE IN THE NEXT—
SLAM

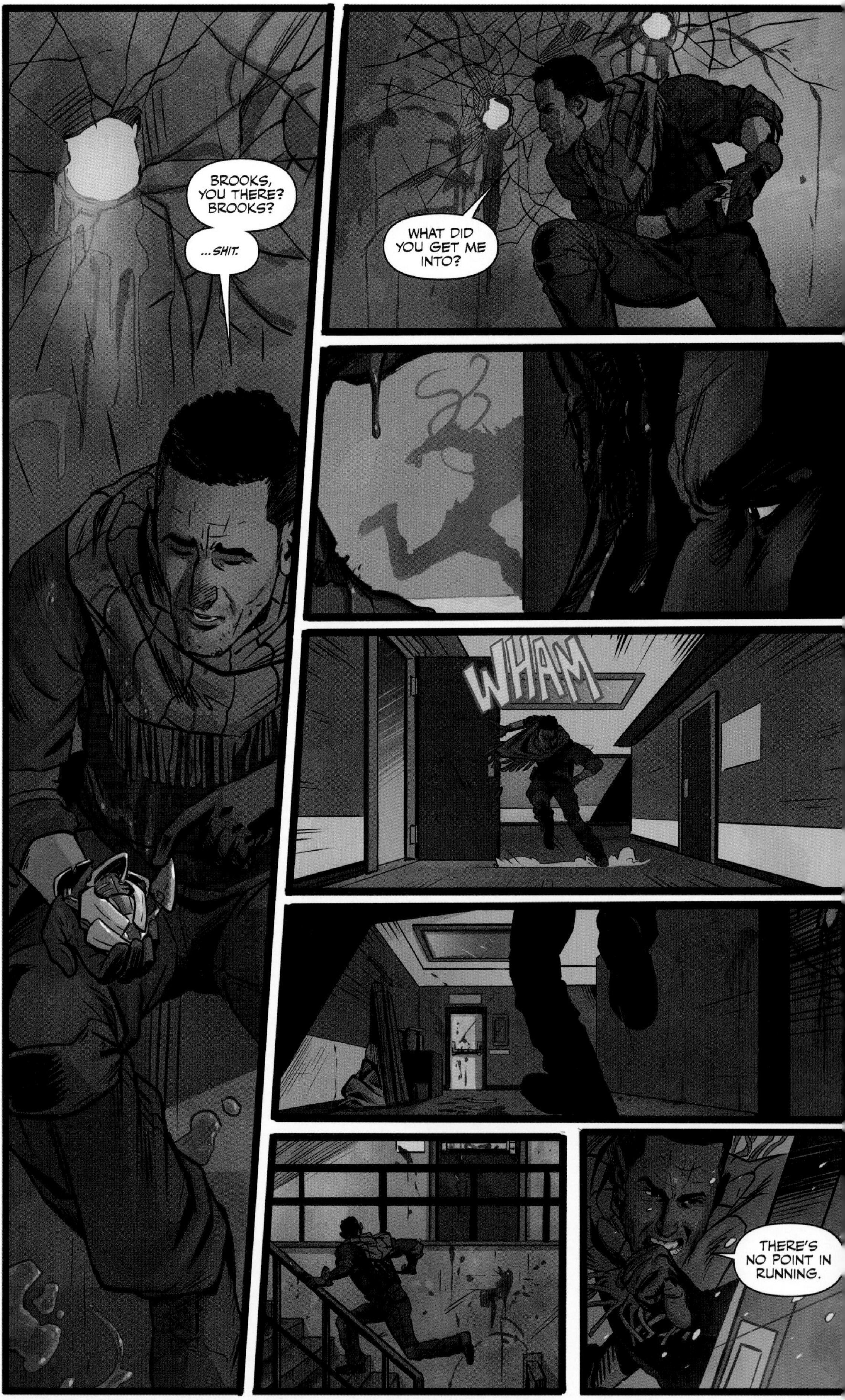
BROOKS, YOU THERE? BROOKS?
...SHIT.
WHAT DID YOU GET ME INTO?
WHAM
THERE'S NO POINT IN RUNNING.

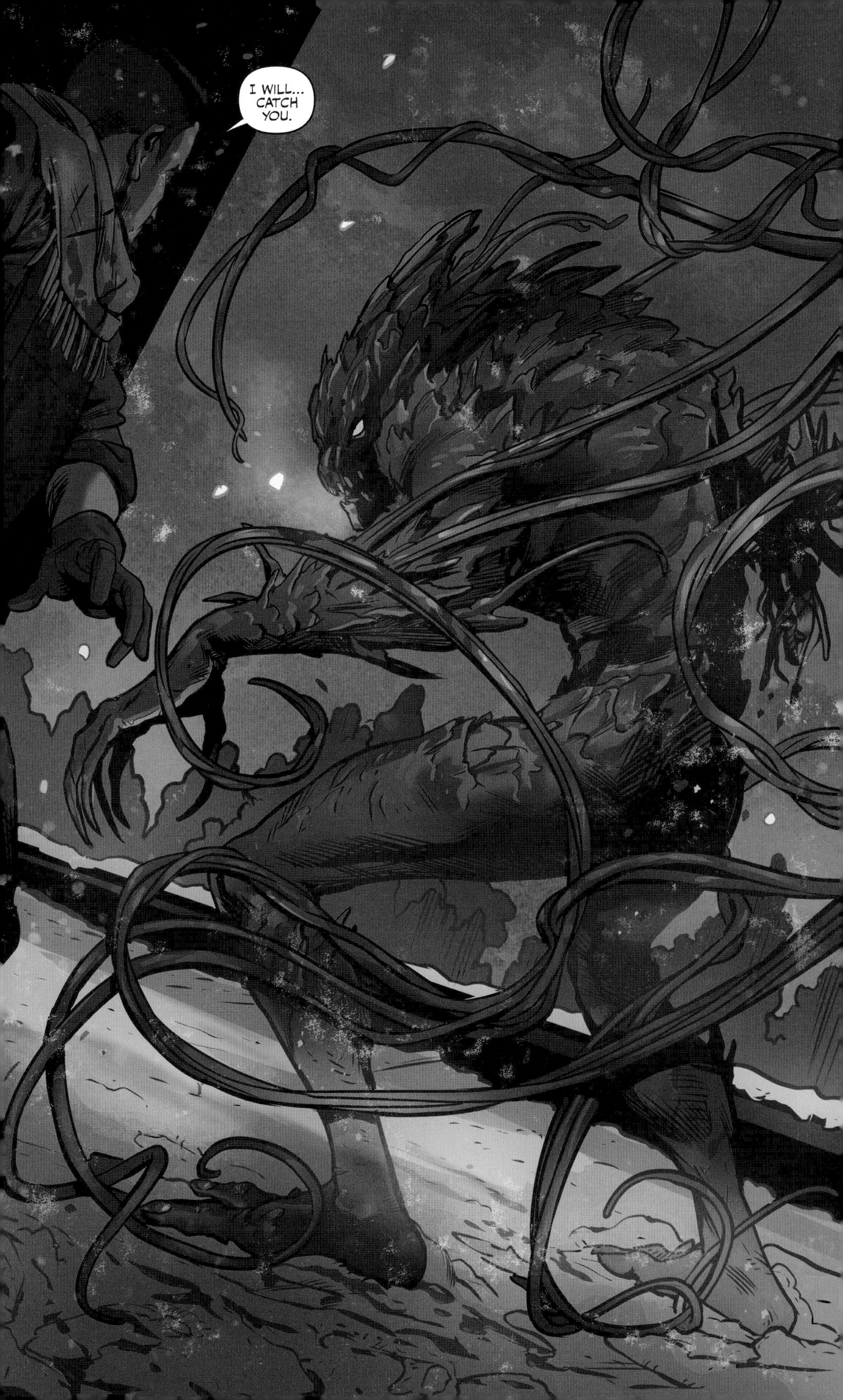
I WILL... CATCH YOU.

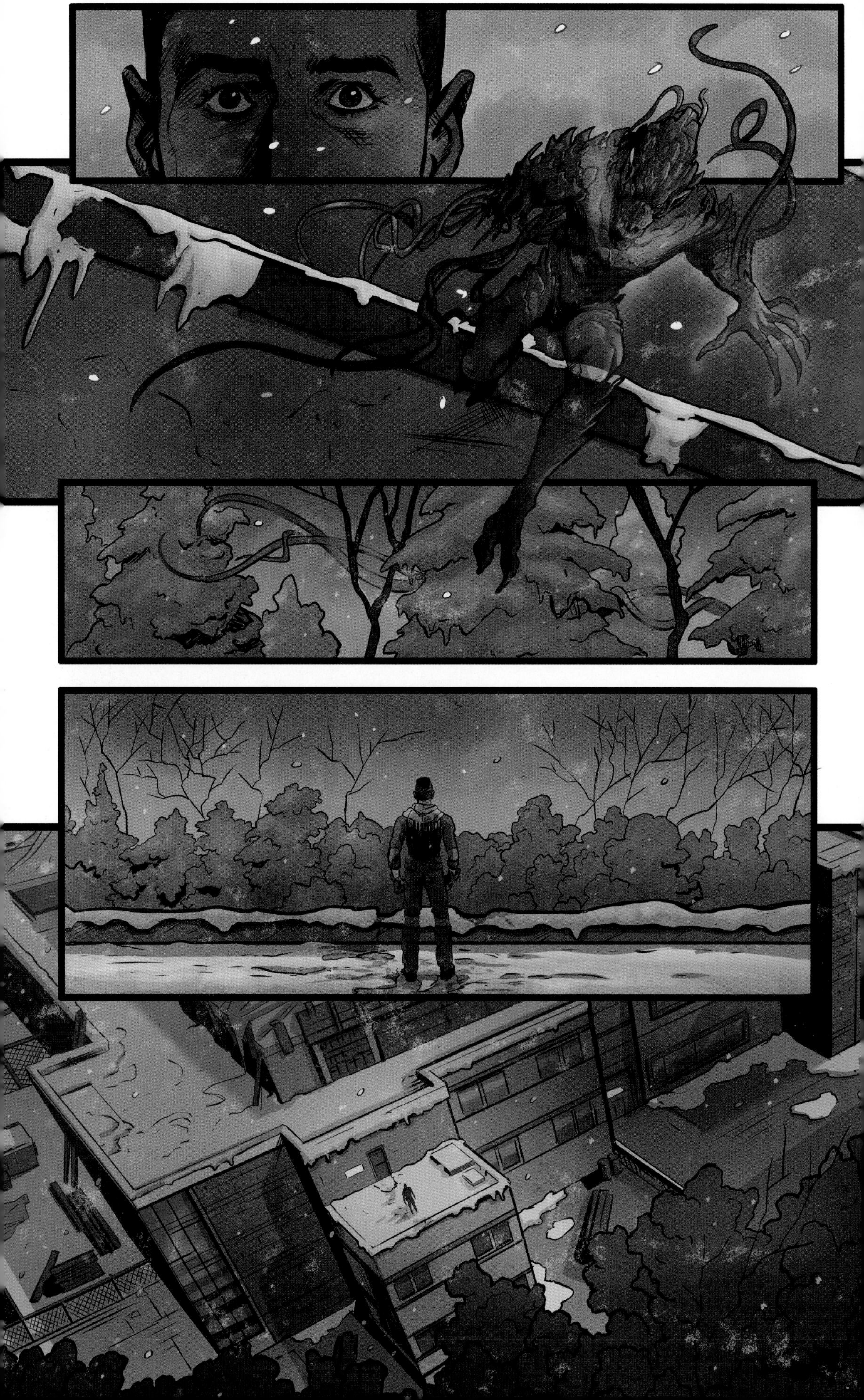

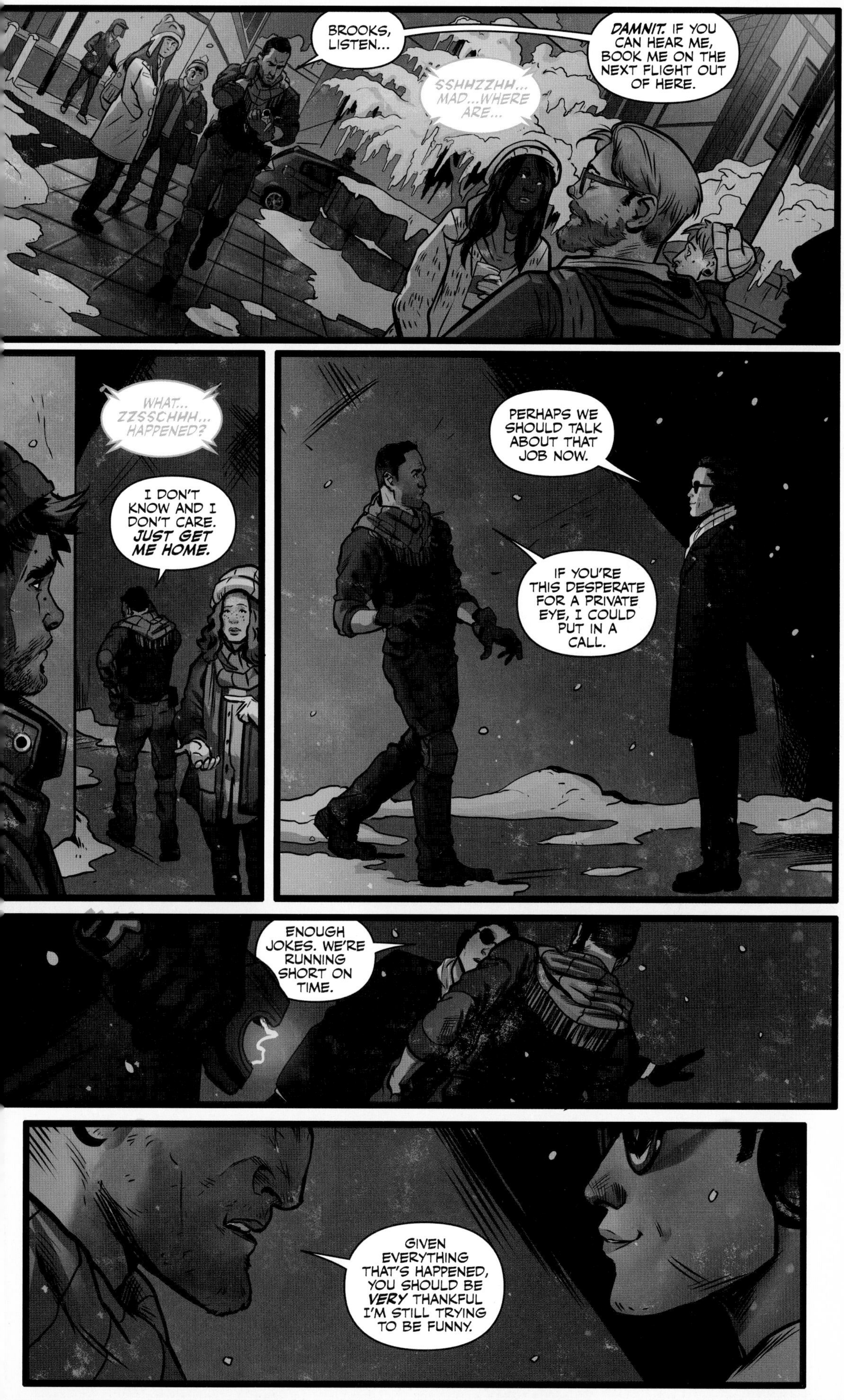
BROOKS, LISTEN...
DAMNIT. IF YOU CAN HEAR ME, BOOK ME ON THE NEXT FLIGHT OUT OF HERE.
SSHHZZHH... MAD...WHERE ARE...
WHAT... ZZSSCHHH... HAPPENED?
I DON'T KNOW AND I DON'T CARE. JUST GET ME HOME.
PERHAPS WE SHOULD TALK ABOUT THAT JOB NOW.
IF YOU'RE THIS DESPERATE FOR A PRIVATE EYE, I COULD PUT IN A CALL.
ENOUGH JOKES. WE'RE RUNNING SHORT ON TIME.
GIVEN EVERYTHING THAT'S HAPPENED, YOU SHOULD BE VERY THANKFUL I'M STILL TRYING TO BE FUNNY.

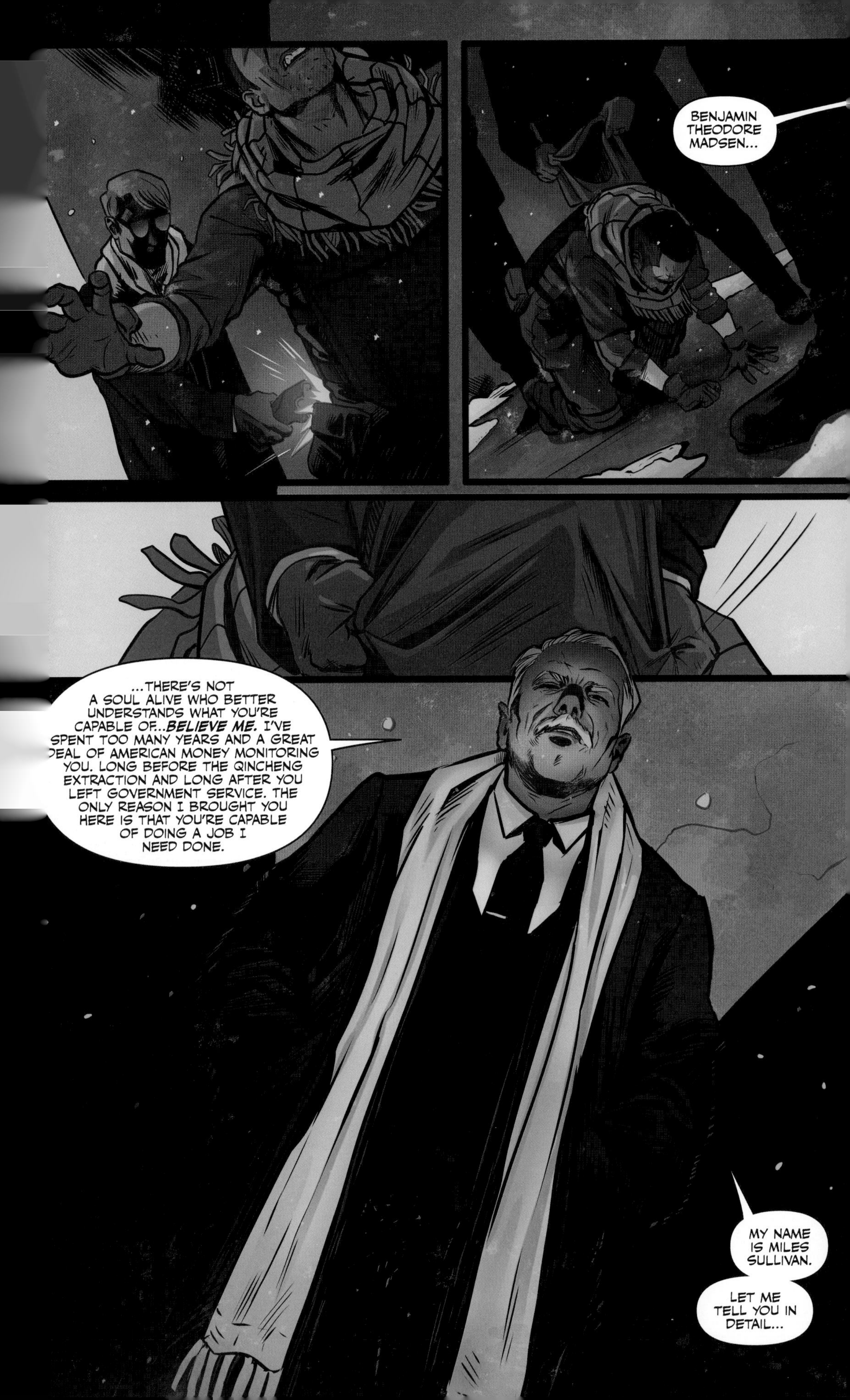
BENJAMIN THEODORE MADSEN...
...THERE'S NOT A SOUL ALIVE WHO BETTER UNDERSTANDS WHAT YOU'RE CAPABLE OF...*BELIEVE ME.* I'VE SPENT TOO MANY YEARS AND A GREAT DEAL OF AMERICAN MONEY MONITORING YOU. LONG BEFORE THE QINCHENG EXTRACTION AND LONG AFTER YOU LEFT GOVERNMENT SERVICE. THE ONLY REASON I BROUGHT YOU HERE IS THAT YOU'RE CAPABLE OF DOING A JOB I NEED DONE.
MY NAME IS MILES SULLIVAN.
LET ME TELL YOU IN DETAIL...

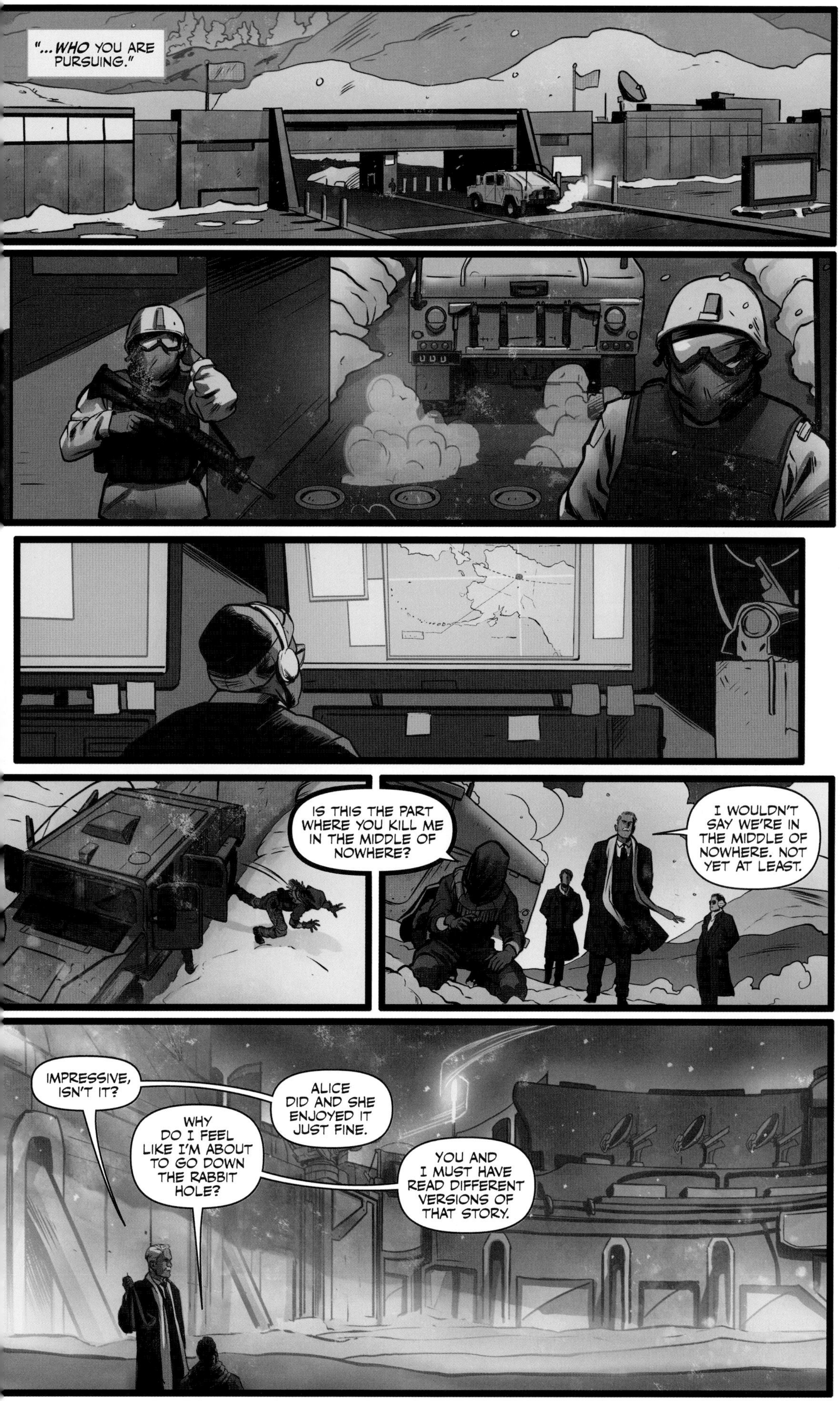
"...WHO YOU ARE PURSUING."
IS THIS THE PART WHERE YOU KILL ME IN THE MIDDLE OF NOWHERE?
I WOULDN'T SAY WE'RE IN THE MIDDLE OF NOWHERE. NOT YET AT LEAST.
IMPRESSIVE, ISN'T IT?
WHY DO I FEEL LIKE I'M ABOUT TO GO DOWN THE RABBIT HOLE?
ALICE DID AND SHE ENJOYED IT JUST FINE.
YOU AND I MUST HAVE READ DIFFERENT VERSIONS OF THAT STORY.

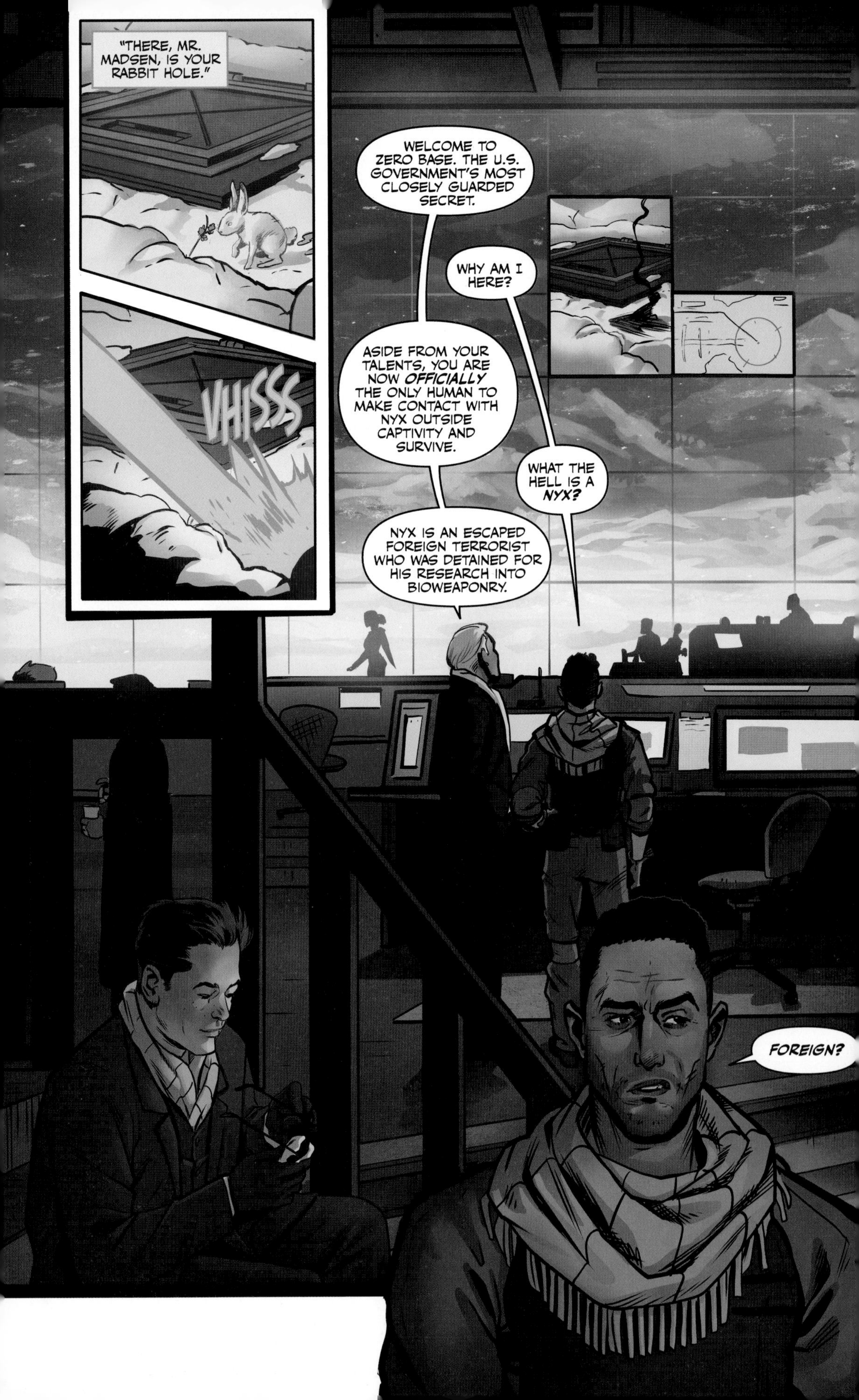
"THERE, MR. MADSEN, IS YOUR RABBIT HOLE."
VHISSS
WELCOME TO ZERO BASE. THE U.S. GOVERNMENT'S MOST CLOSELY GUARDED SECRET.
WHY AM I HERE?
ASIDE FROM YOUR TALENTS, YOU ARE NOW *OFFICIALLY* THE ONLY HUMAN TO MAKE CONTACT WITH NYX OUTSIDE CAPTIVITY AND SURVIVE.
WHAT THE HELL IS A *NYX?*
NYX IS AN ESCAPED FOREIGN TERRORIST WHO WAS DETAINED FOR HIS RESEARCH INTO BIOWEAPONRY.
FOREIGN?

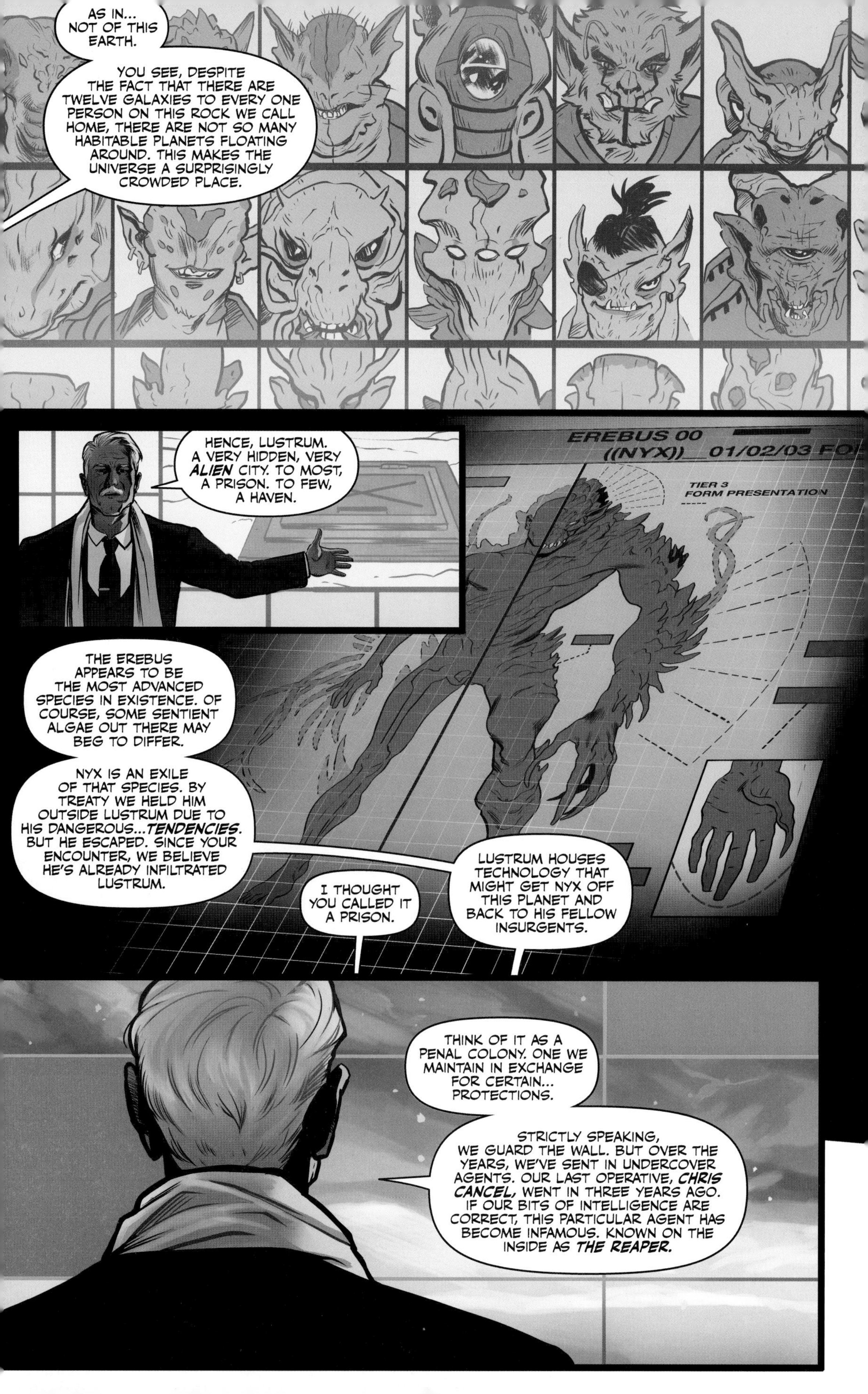
AS IN... NOT OF THIS EARTH.
YOU SEE, DESPITE THE FACT THAT THERE ARE TWELVE GALAXIES TO EVERY ONE PERSON ON THIS ROCK WE CALL HOME, THERE ARE NOT SO MANY HABITABLE PLANETS FLOATING AROUND. THIS MAKES THE UNIVERSE A SURPRISINGLY CROWDED PLACE.
HENCE, LUSTRUM. A VERY HIDDEN, VERY *ALIEN* CITY. TO MOST, A PRISON. TO FEW, A HAVEN.
EREBUS 00
((NYX)) 01/02/03 FO
TIER 3
FORM PRESENTATION
THE EREBUS APPEARS TO BE THE MOST ADVANCED SPECIES IN EXISTENCE. OF COURSE, SOME SENTIENT ALGAE OUT THERE MAY BEG TO DIFFER.
NYX IS AN EXILE OF THAT SPECIES. BY TREATY WE HELD HIM OUTSIDE LUSTRUM DUE TO HIS DANGEROUS...*TENDENCIES*. BUT HE ESCAPED. SINCE YOUR ENCOUNTER, WE BELIEVE HE'S ALREADY INFILTRATED LUSTRUM.
I THOUGHT YOU CALLED IT A PRISON.
LUSTRUM HOUSES TECHNOLOGY THAT MIGHT GET NYX OFF THIS PLANET AND BACK TO HIS FELLOW INSURGENTS.
THINK OF IT AS A PENAL COLONY. ONE WE MAINTAIN IN EXCHANGE FOR CERTAIN... PROTECTIONS.
STRICTLY SPEAKING, WE GUARD THE WALL. BUT OVER THE YEARS, WE'VE SENT IN UNDERCOVER AGENTS. OUR LAST OPERATIVE, *CHRIS CANCEL,* WENT IN THREE YEARS AGO. IF OUR BITS OF INTELLIGENCE ARE CORRECT, THIS PARTICULAR AGENT HAS BECOME INFAMOUS. KNOWN ON THE INSIDE AS *THE REAPER.*

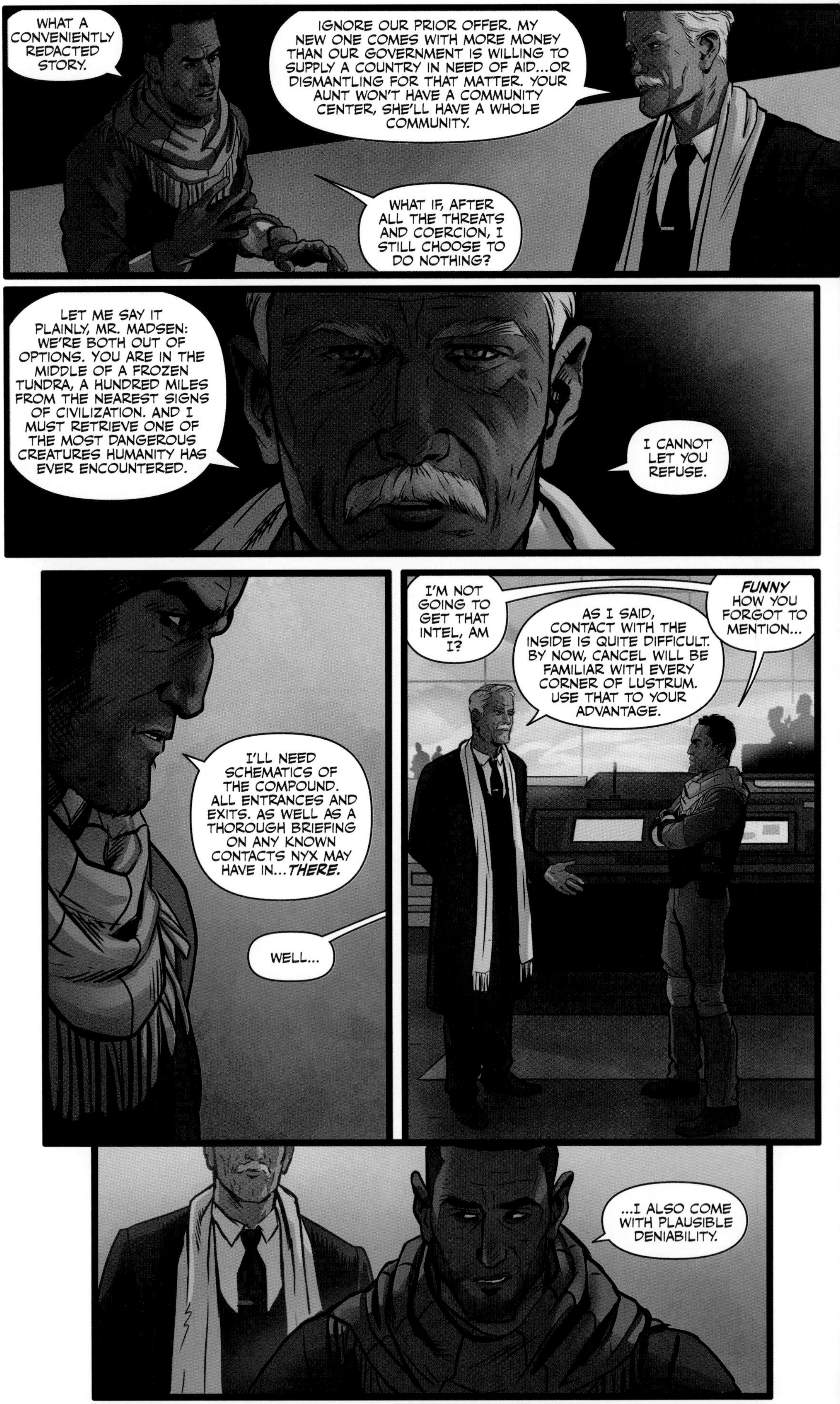
WHAT A CONVENIENTLY REDACTED STORY.
IGNORE OUR PRIOR OFFER. MY NEW ONE COMES WITH MORE MONEY THAN OUR GOVERNMENT IS WILLING TO SUPPLY A COUNTRY IN NEED OF AID...OR DISMANTLING FOR THAT MATTER. YOUR AUNT WON'T HAVE A COMMUNITY CENTER, SHE'LL HAVE A WHOLE COMMUNITY.
WHAT IF, AFTER ALL THE THREATS AND COERCION, I STILL CHOOSE TO DO NOTHING?
LET ME SAY IT PLAINLY, MR. MADSEN: WE'RE BOTH OUT OF OPTIONS. YOU ARE IN THE MIDDLE OF A FROZEN TUNDRA, A HUNDRED MILES FROM THE NEAREST SIGNS OF CIVILIZATION. AND I MUST RETRIEVE ONE OF THE MOST DANGEROUS CREATURES HUMANITY HAS EVER ENCOUNTERED.
I CANNOT LET YOU REFUSE.
I'LL NEED SCHEMATICS OF THE COMPOUND. ALL ENTRANCES AND EXITS. AS WELL AS A THOROUGH BRIEFING ON ANY KNOWN CONTACTS NYX MAY HAVE IN...*THERE.*
WELL...
AS I SAID, CONTACT WITH THE INSIDE IS QUITE DIFFICULT. BY NOW, CANCEL WILL BE FAMILIAR WITH EVERY CORNER OF LUSTRUM. USE THAT TO YOUR ADVANTAGE.
I'M NOT GOING TO GET THAT INTEL, AM I?
FUNNY HOW YOU FORGOT TO MENTION...
...I ALSO COME WITH PLAUSIBLE DENIABILITY.

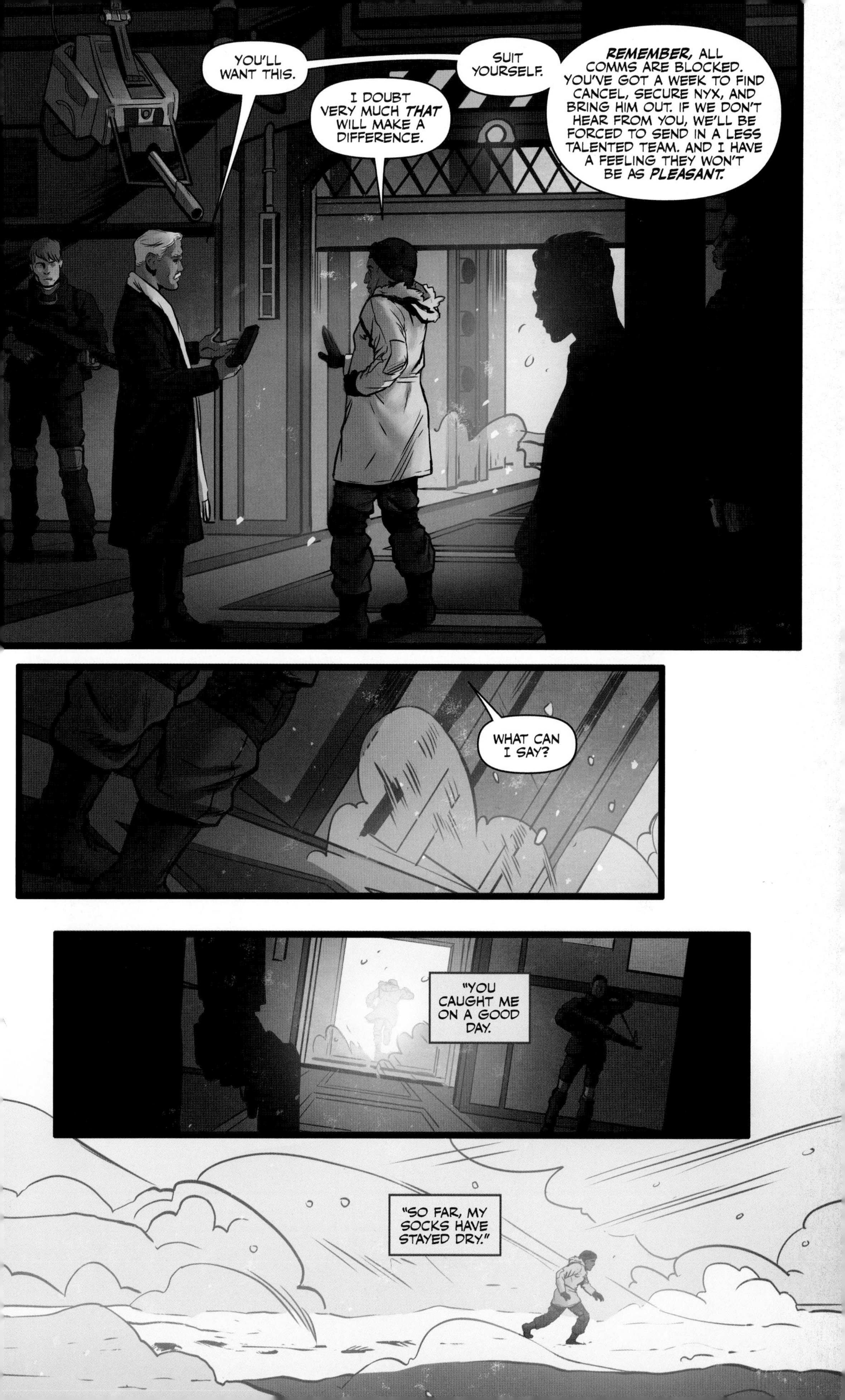
YOU'LL WANT THIS.
SUIT YOURSELF.
I DOUBT VERY MUCH THAT WILL MAKE A DIFFERENCE.
REMEMBER, ALL COMMS ARE BLOCKED. YOU'VE GOT A WEEK TO FIND CANCEL, SECURE NYX, AND BRING HIM OUT. IF WE DON'T HEAR FROM YOU, WE'LL BE FORCED TO SEND IN A LESS TALENTED TEAM. AND I HAVE A FEELING THEY WON'T BE AS PLEASANT.
WHAT CAN I SAY?
"YOU CAUGHT ME ON A GOOD DAY.
"SO FAR, MY SOCKS HAVE STAYED DRY."

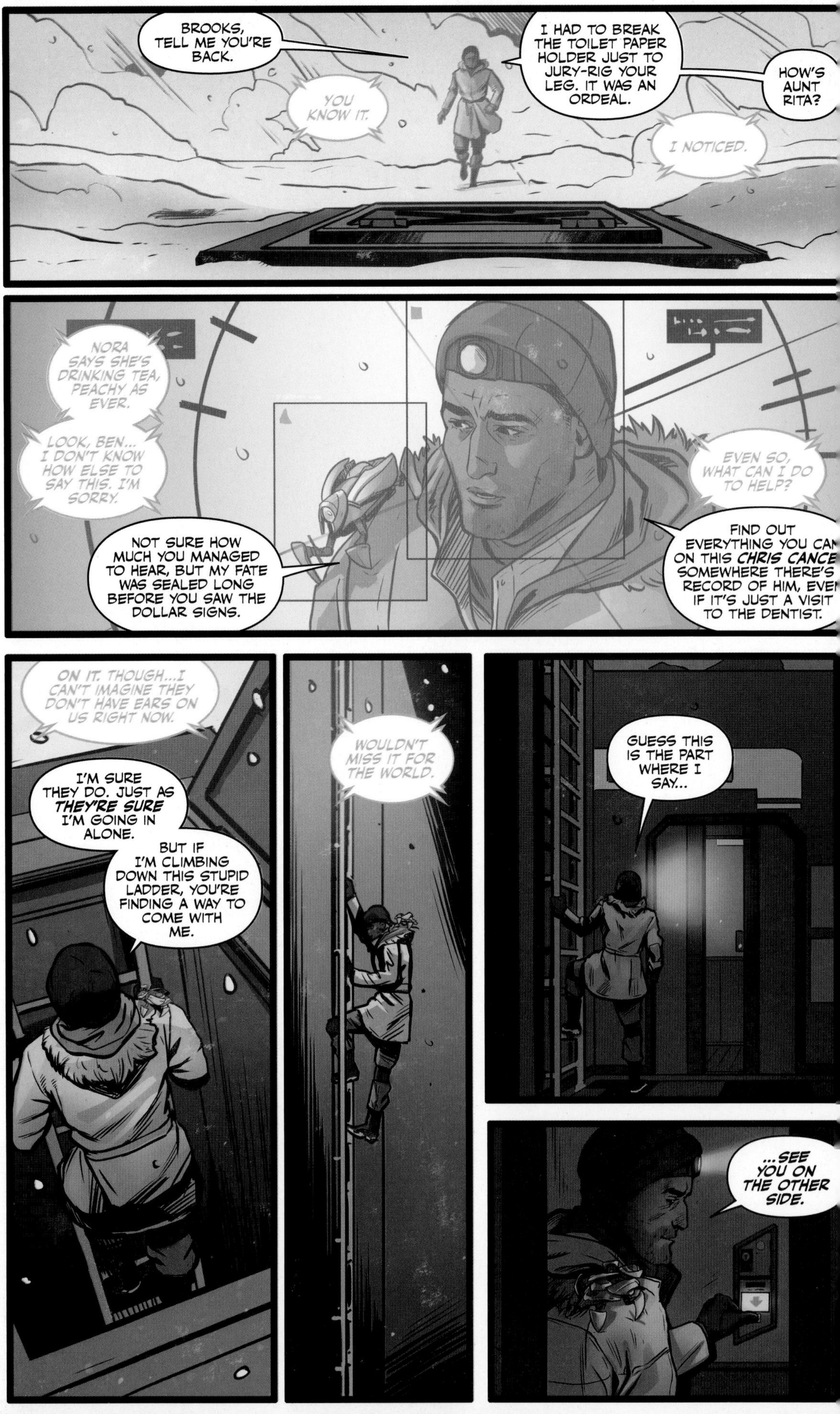
BROOKS, TELL ME YOU'RE BACK.
YOU KNOW IT.
I HAD TO BREAK THE TOILET PAPER HOLDER JUST TO JURY-RIG YOUR LEG. IT WAS AN ORDEAL.
I NOTICED.
HOW'S AUNT RITA?
NORA SAYS SHE'S DRINKING TEA, PEACHY AS EVER.
LOOK, BEN... I DON'T KNOW HOW ELSE TO SAY THIS. I'M SORRY.
NOT SURE HOW MUCH YOU MANAGED TO HEAR, BUT MY FATE WAS SEALED LONG BEFORE YOU SAW THE DOLLAR SIGNS.
EVEN SO, WHAT CAN I DO TO HELP?
FIND OUT EVERYTHING YOU CAN ON THIS *CHRIS CANCE* SOMEWHERE THERE'S RECORD OF HIM, EVEN IF IT'S JUST A VISIT TO THE DENTIST.
ON IT. THOUGH...I CAN'T IMAGINE THEY DON'T HAVE EARS ON US RIGHT NOW.
I'M SURE THEY DO. JUST AS *THEY'RE SURE* I'M GOING IN ALONE.
BUT IF I'M CLIMBING DOWN THIS STUPID LADDER, YOU'RE FINDING A WAY TO COME WITH ME.
WOULDN'T MISS IT FOR THE WORLD.
GUESS THIS IS THE PART WHERE I SAY...
...SEE YOU ON THE OTHER SIDE.

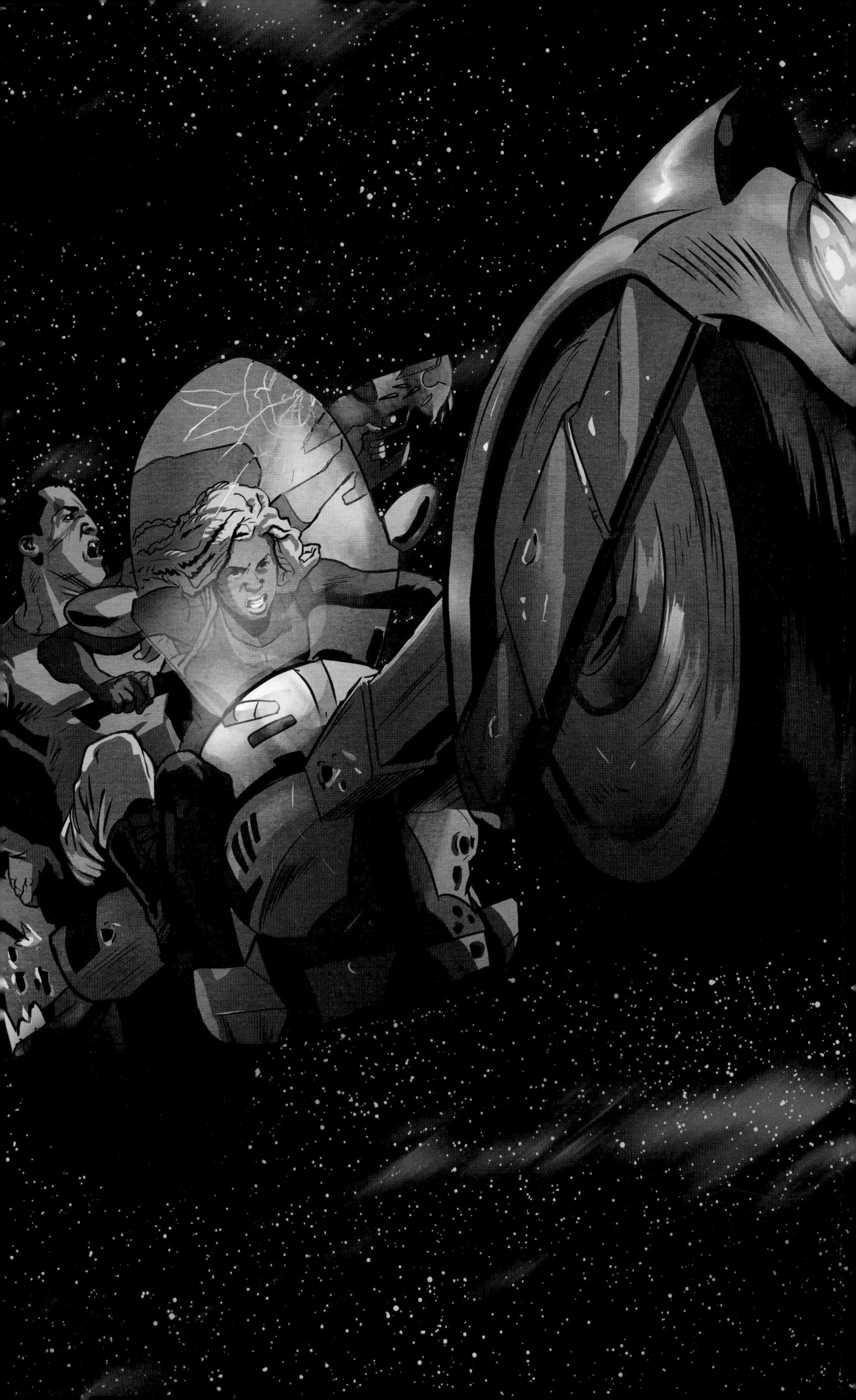

CHAPTER 2

DAVNO
SPECIES: KAKORI PUNCTATUS
PLANET OF ORIGIN: TUATAA

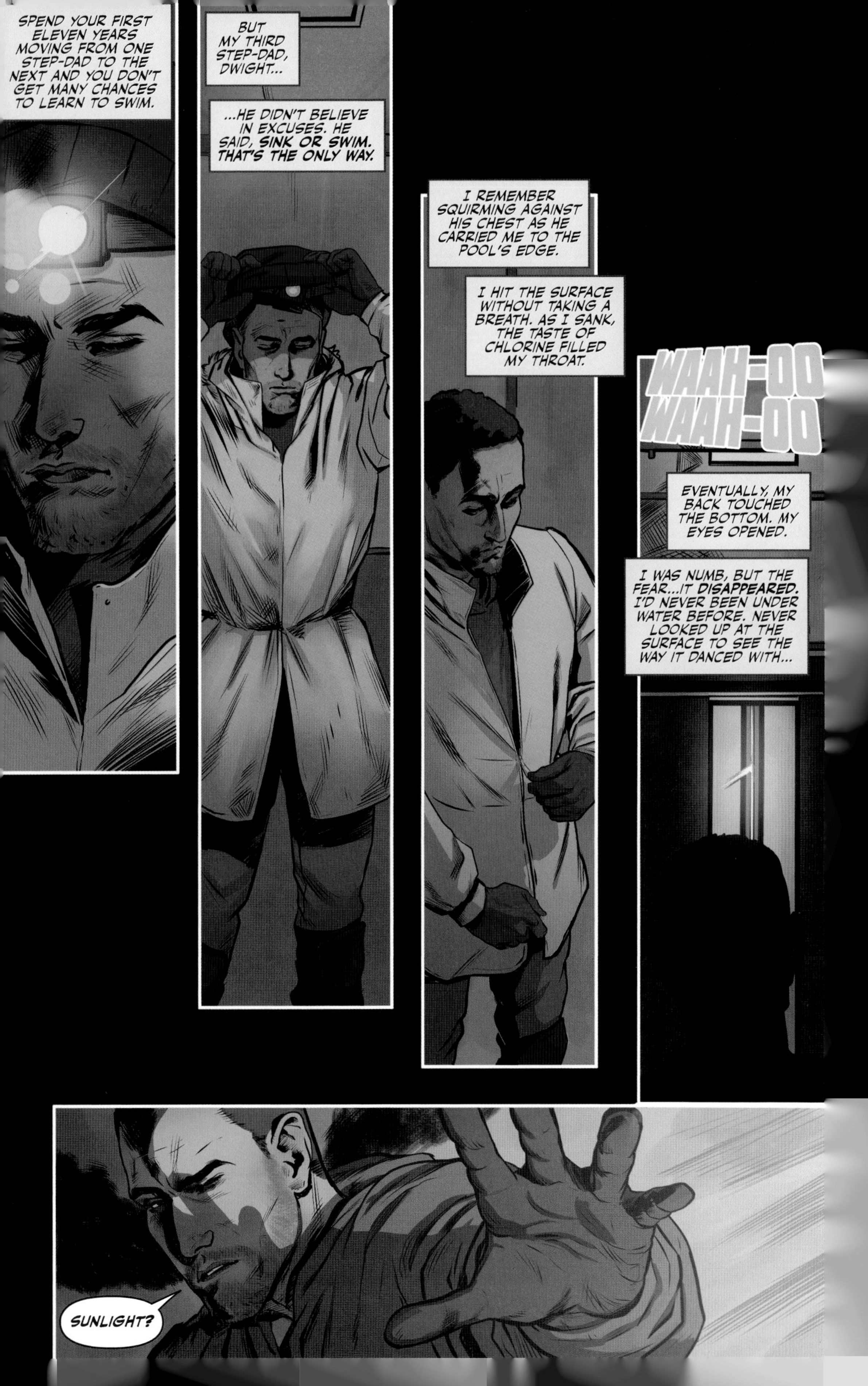
SPEND YOUR FIRST ELEVEN YEARS MOVING FROM ONE STEP-DAD TO THE NEXT AND YOU DON'T GET MANY CHANCES TO LEARN TO SWIM.
BUT MY THIRD STEP-DAD, DWIGHT...
...HE DIDN'T BELIEVE IN EXCUSES. HE SAID, SINK OR SWIM. THAT'S THE ONLY WAY.
I REMEMBER SQUIRMING AGAINST HIS CHEST AS HE CARRIED ME TO THE POOL'S EDGE.
I HIT THE SURFACE WITHOUT TAKING A BREATH. AS I SANK, THE TASTE OF CHLORINE FILLED MY THROAT.
WAAH-OO WAAH-OO
EVENTUALLY, MY BACK TOUCHED THE BOTTOM. MY EYES OPENED.
I WAS NUMB, BUT THE FEAR...IT DISAPPEARED. I'D NEVER BEEN UNDER WATER BEFORE. NEVER LOOKED UP AT THE SURFACE TO SEE THE WAY IT DANCED WITH...
SUNLIGHT?

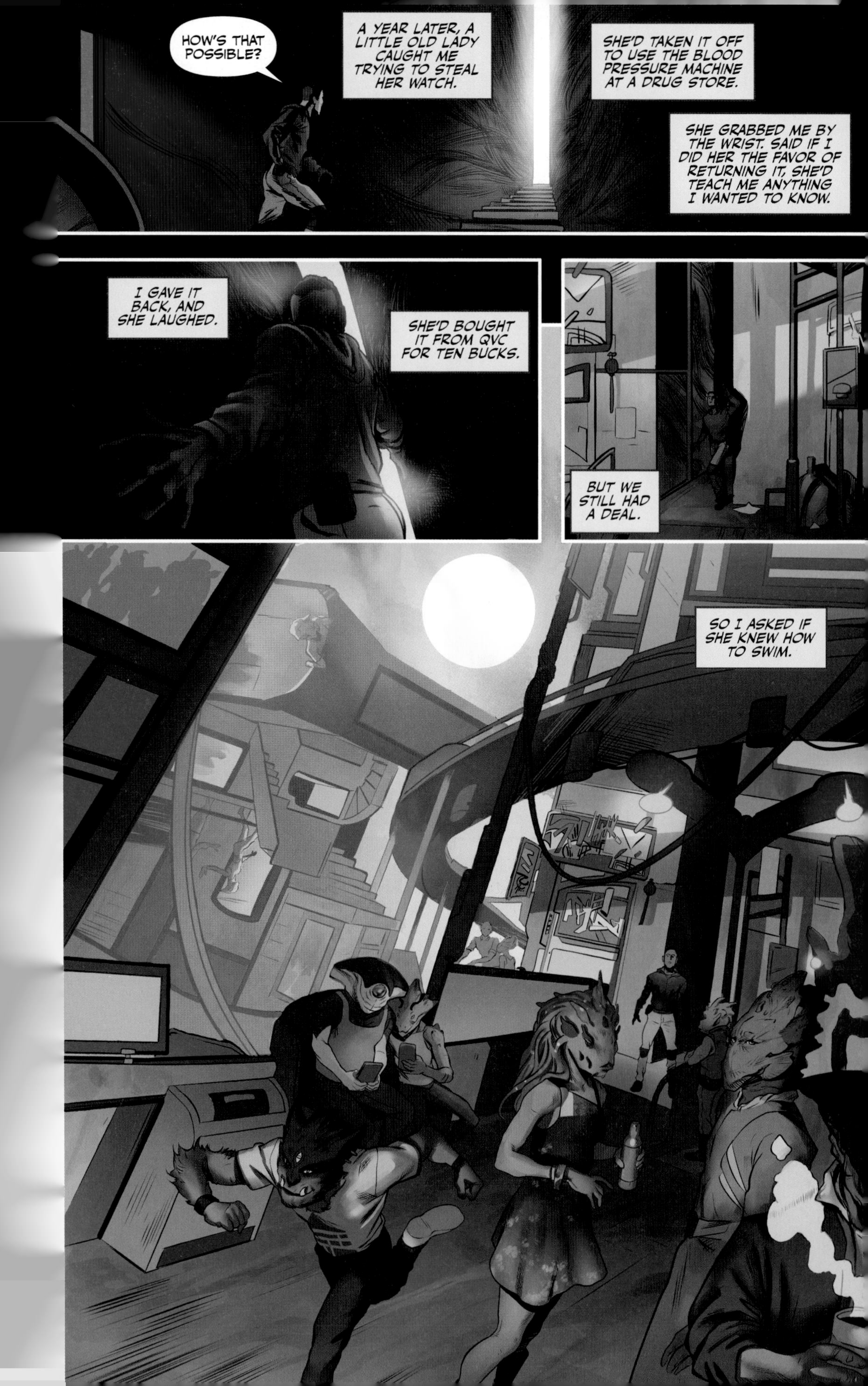
HOW'S THAT POSSIBLE?
A YEAR LATER, A LITTLE OLD LADY CAUGHT ME TRYING TO STEAL HER WATCH.
SHE'D TAKEN IT OFF TO USE THE BLOOD PRESSURE MACHINE AT A DRUG STORE.
SHE GRABBED ME BY THE WRIST. SAID IF I DID HER THE FAVOR OF RETURNING IT, SHE'D TEACH ME ANYTHING I WANTED TO KNOW.
I GAVE IT BACK, AND SHE LAUGHED.
SHE'D BOUGHT IT FROM QVC FOR TEN BUCKS.
BUT WE STILL HAD A DEAL.
SO I ASKED IF SHE KNEW HOW TO SWIM.

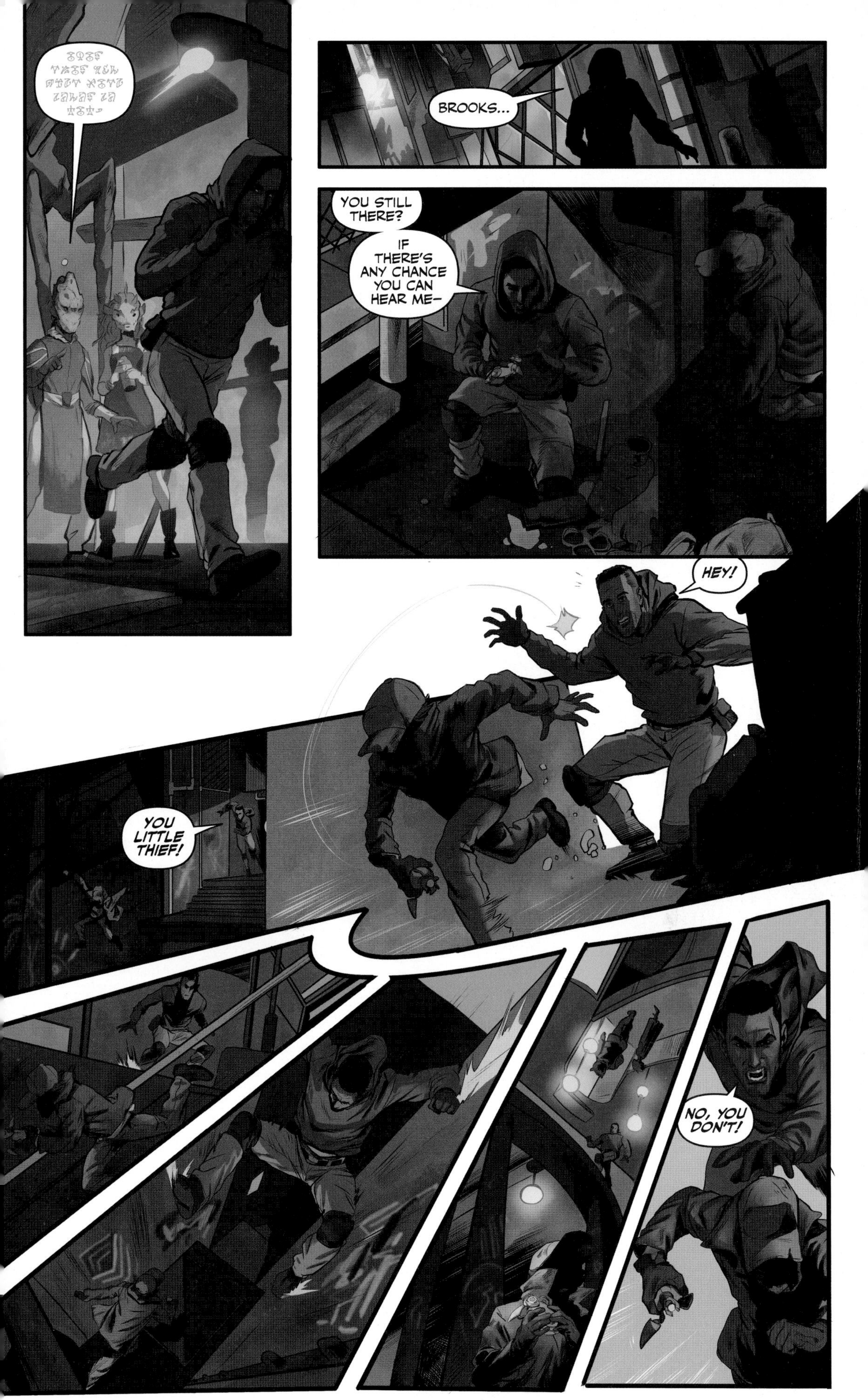
BROOKS...
YOU STILL THERE?
IF THERE'S ANY CHANCE YOU CAN HEAR ME–
HEY!
YOU LITTLE THIEF!
NO, YOU DON'T!

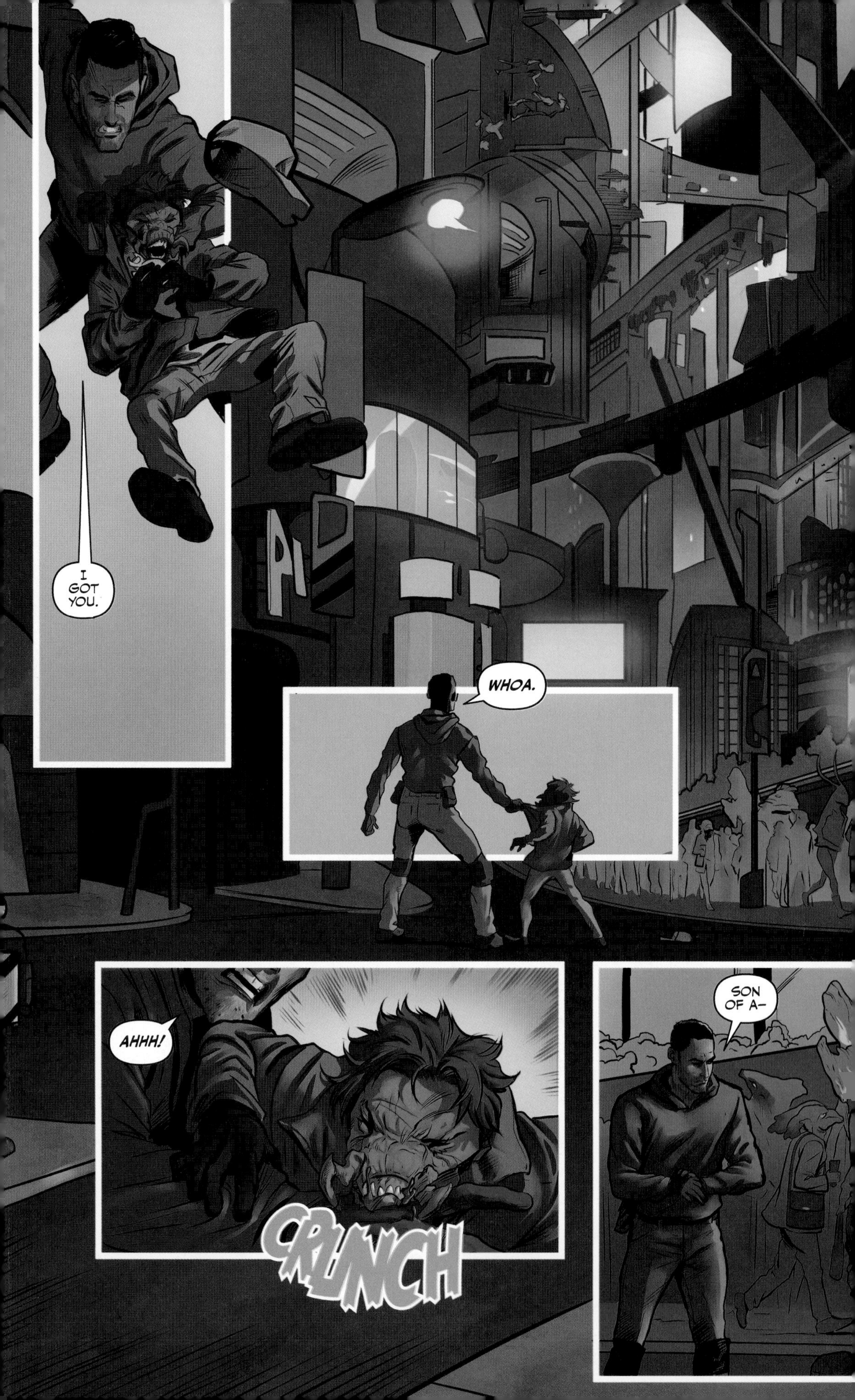
I GOT YOU.
WHOA.
AHHH!
CRUNCH
SON OF A–

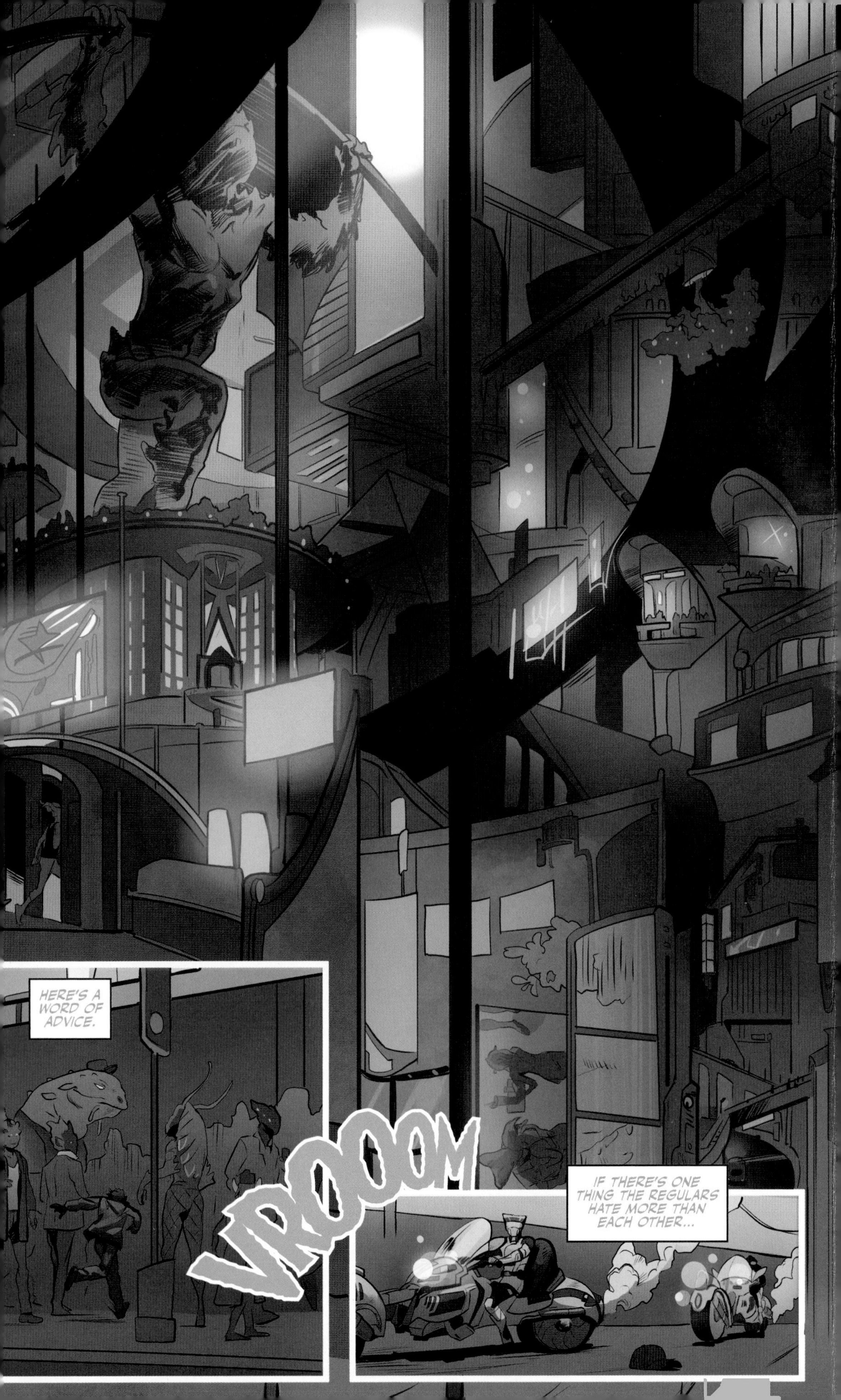
HERE'S A WORD OF ADVICE.
VROOOOM
IF THERE'S ONE THING THE REGULARS HATE MORE THAN EACH OTHER...

...IT'S HUMANS.

SO WHAT HAPPENED TO YOUR HAND?

THE WELCOMING COMMITTEE.

NEW TO THIS WARD?

YOU COULD SAY THAT. HOW'D YOU KNOW I SPEAK ENGLISH?

CAN'T RUN MUCH OF A BAR WITHOUT TRANSLATORS TURNED ON. WHAT WARD YOU COME FROM?

ONE WHERE THEY SERVE BEER.

REGULARS MAY NOT LIKE HUMANS, BUT I NEVER SAID THEY DON'T LIKE YOUR REFRESHMENTS.

SEEMS YOU'RE MAKING NEW FRIENDS.

I'VE GOT ONE OF THOSE FACES. EVERYONE THINKS THEY KNOW ME.

HE CERTAINLY DOES.

ᐱᐱᓂᐟ ᐃᐱᑕᒪ ᑐᓯᐟ ᐃᓐ ᑕᐱ ᑐ ᓂᑐᐱᑐᓇᒧ ᐸᑲ ᐱᑌᑯ ᓇᑐᓄ

WHY AREN'T THE TRANSLATORS WORKING ON HIM?

HE MUST HAVE A JAMMER.

WHY WOULD HE NEED A JAMMER?

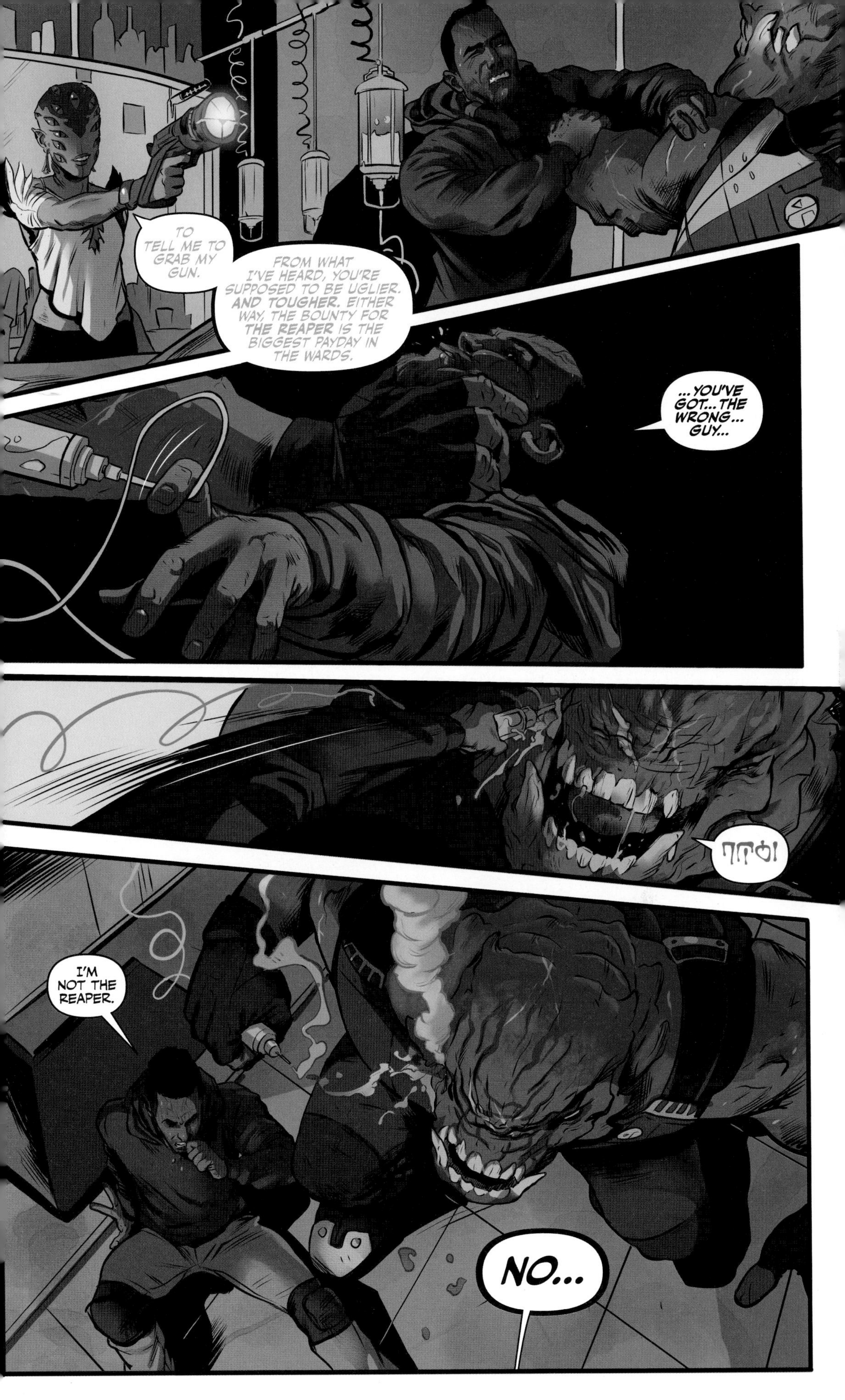
TO TELL ME TO GRAB MY GUN.
FROM WHAT I'VE HEARD, YOU'RE SUPPOSED TO BE UGLIER. AND TOUGHER. EITHER WAY, THE BOUNTY FOR THE REAPER IS THE BIGGEST PAYDAY IN THE WARDS.
...YOU'VE GOT...THE WRONG... GUY...
I'M NOT THE REAPER.
NO...

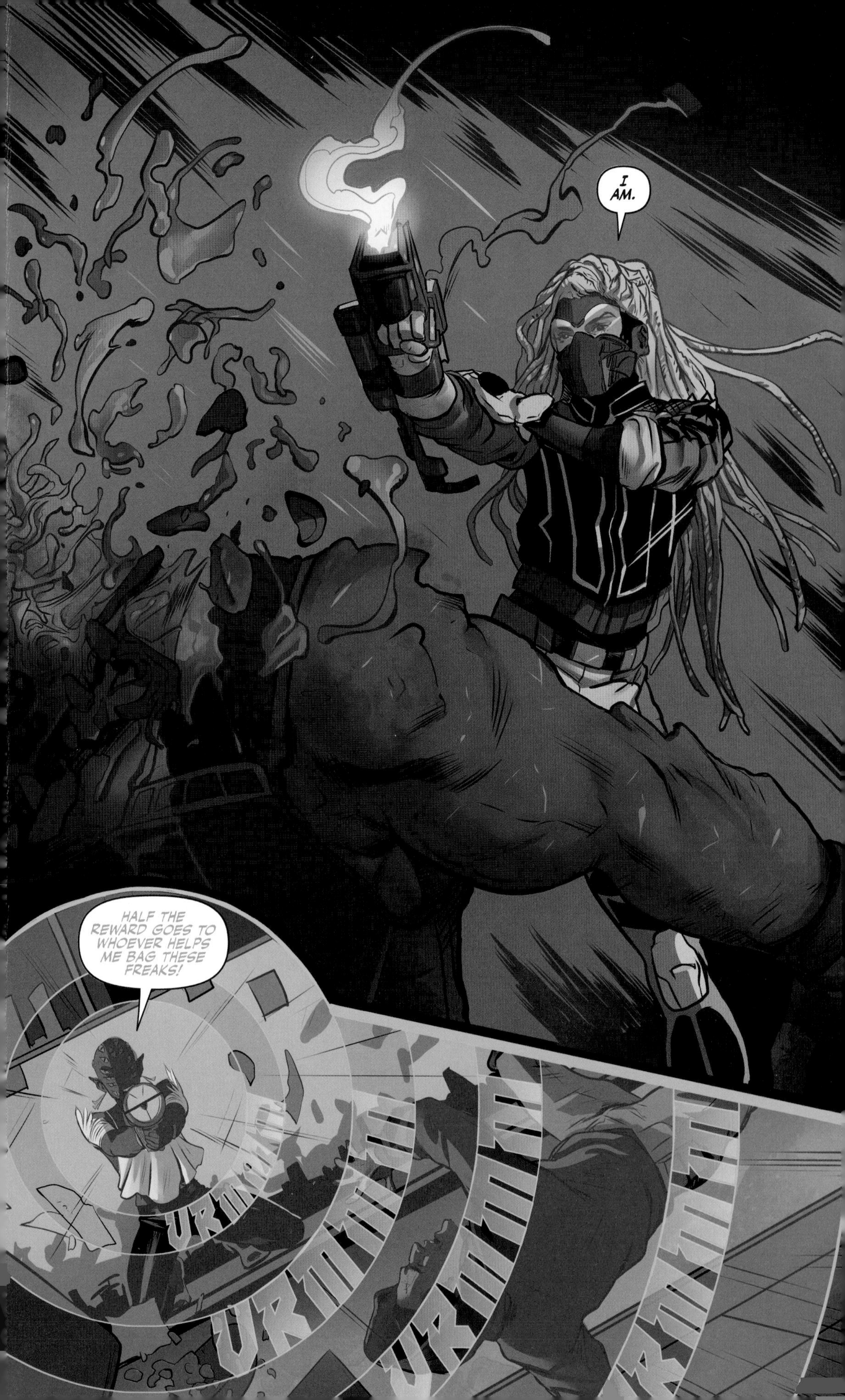
I AM.
HALF THE REWARD GOES TO WHOEVER HELPS ME BAG THESE FREAKS!
URRRR
URRRR
URRRR
URRRR

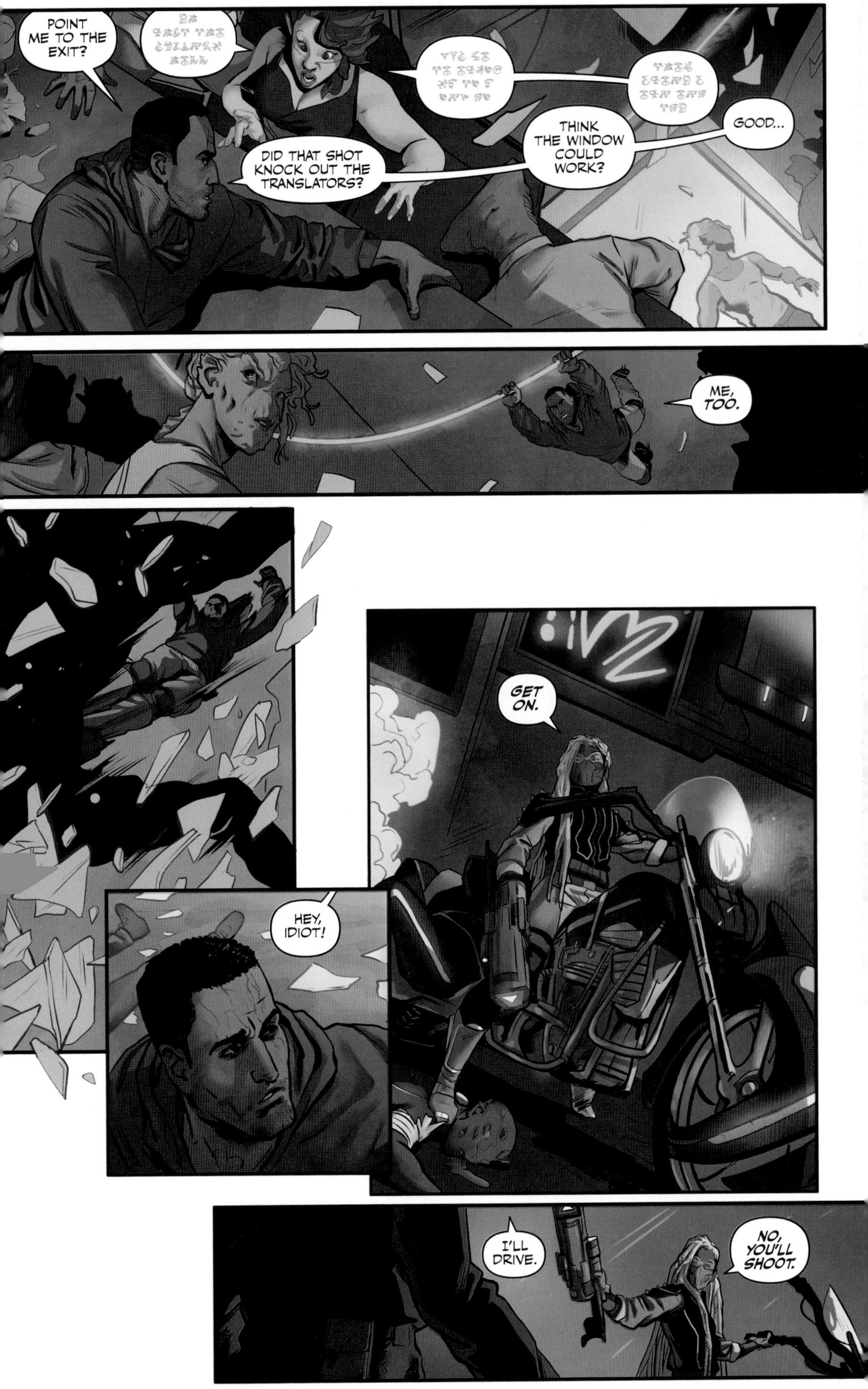
POINT ME TO THE EXIT?
DID THAT SHOT KNOCK OUT THE TRANSLATORS?
THINK THE WINDOW COULD WORK?
GOOD...
ME, TOO.
GET ON.
HEY, IDIOT!
I'LL DRIVE.
NO, YOU'LL SHOOT.

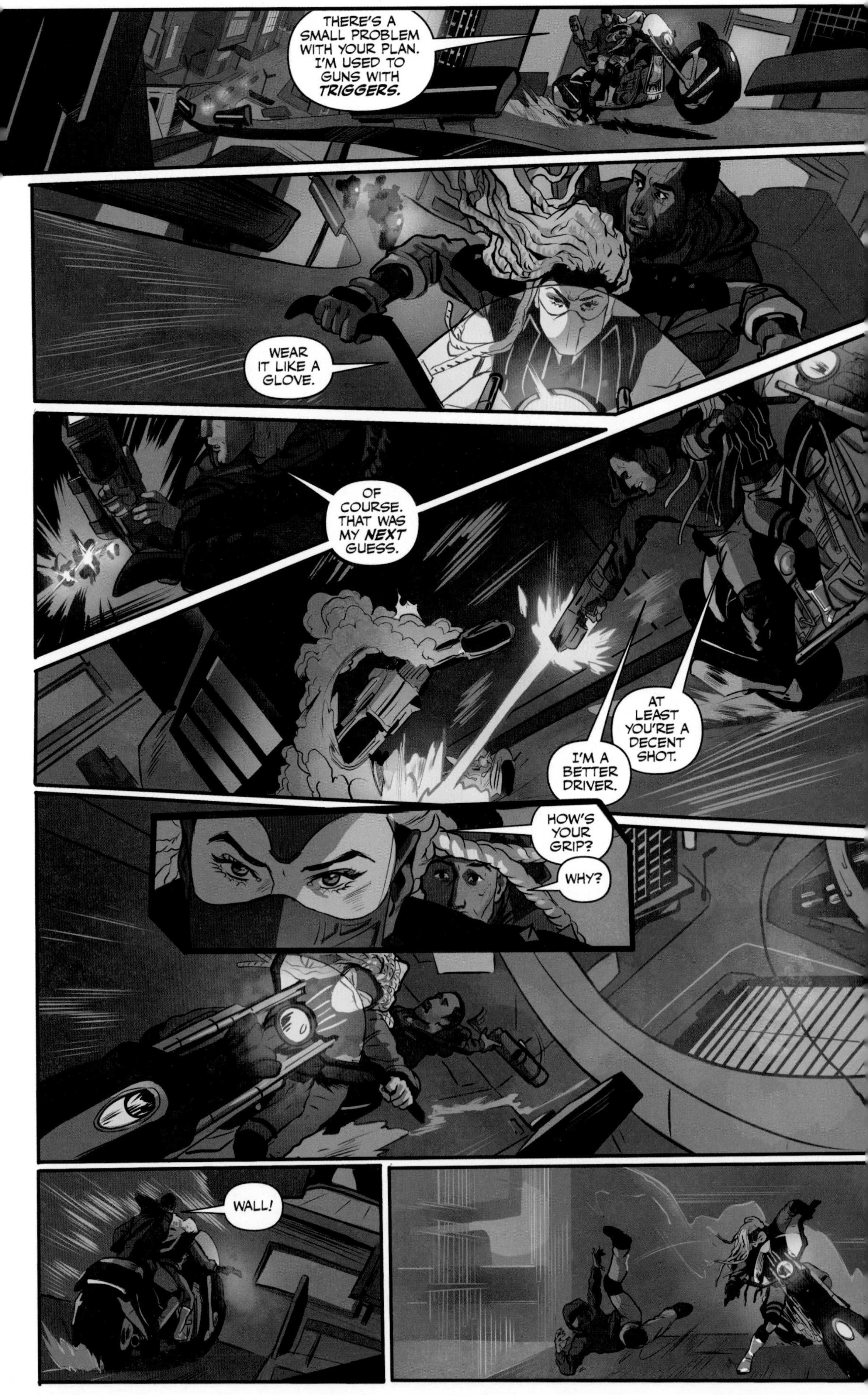
THERE'S A SMALL PROBLEM WITH YOUR PLAN. I'M USED TO GUNS WITH TRIGGERS.
WEAR IT LIKE A GLOVE.
OF COURSE. THAT WAS MY NEXT GUESS.
AT LEAST YOU'RE A DECENT SHOT.
I'M A BETTER DRIVER.
HOW'S YOUR GRIP?
WHY?
WALL!

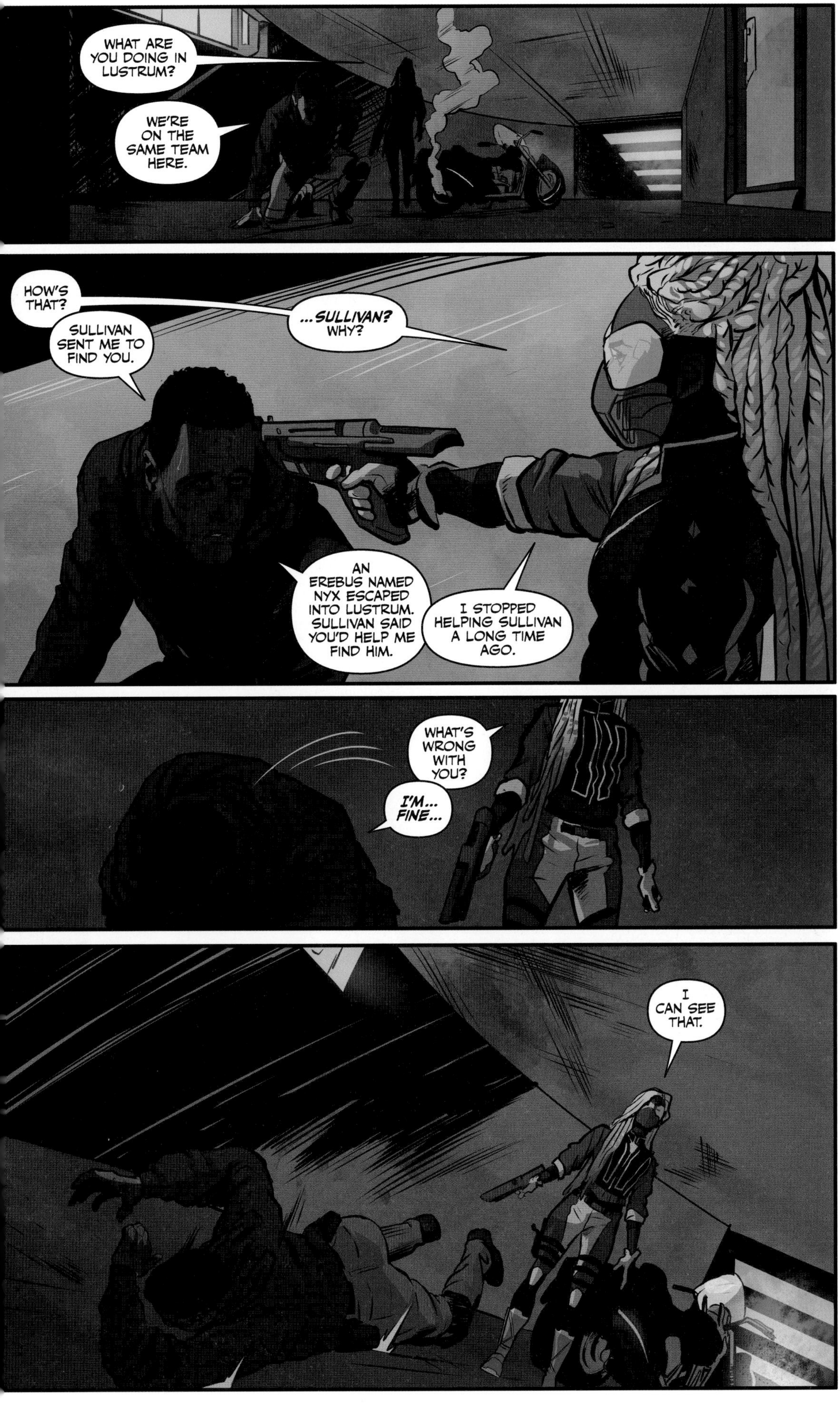
WHAT ARE YOU DOING IN LUSTRUM?
WE'RE ON THE SAME TEAM HERE.
HOW'S THAT?
SULLIVAN SENT ME TO FIND YOU.
...SULLIVAN? WHY?
AN EREBUS NAMED NYX ESCAPED INTO LUSTRUM. SULLIVAN SAID YOU'D HELP ME FIND HIM.
I STOPPED HELPING SULLIVAN A LONG TIME AGO.
WHAT'S WRONG WITH YOU?
I'M... FINE...
I CAN SEE THAT.

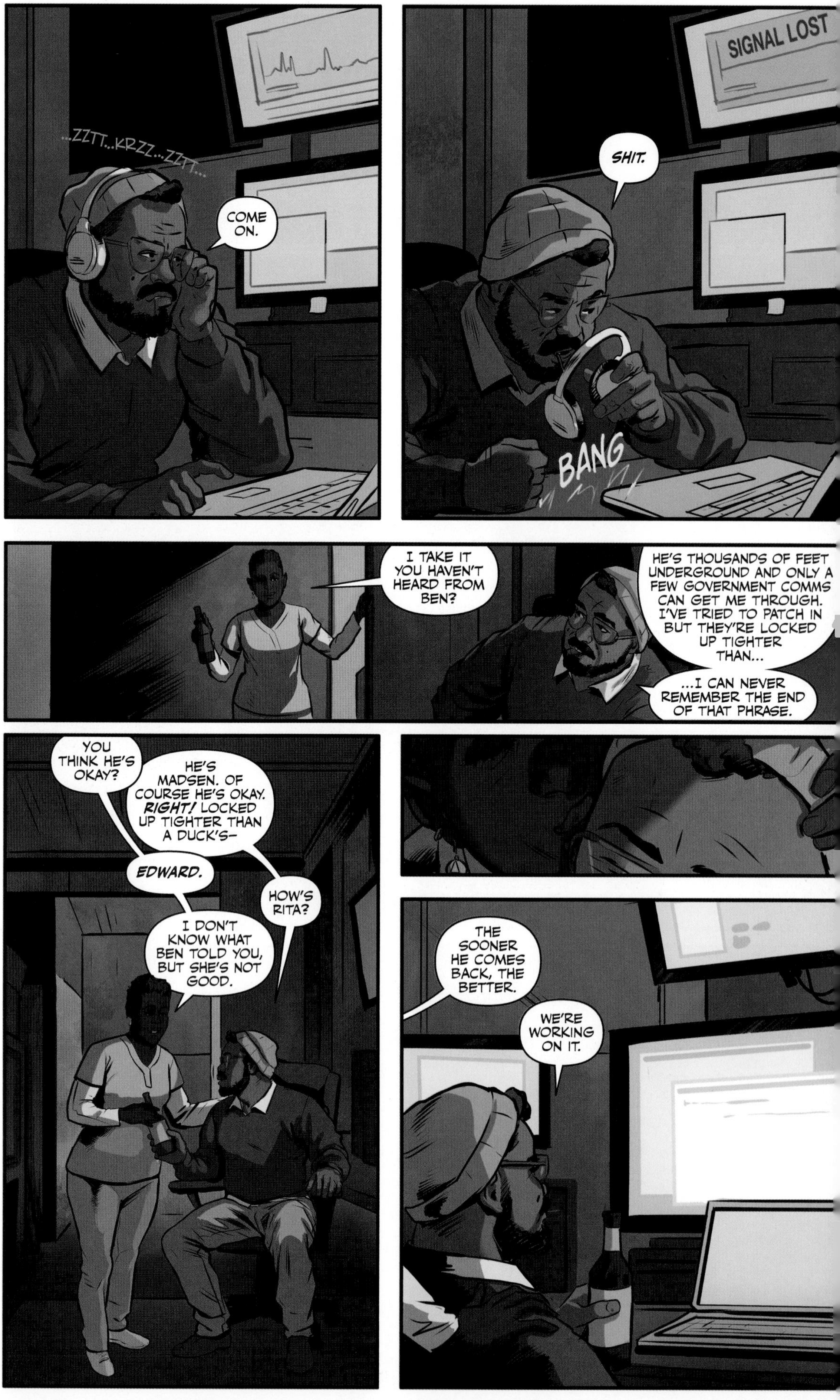
...ZZTT...KRZZ...ZZTT...
COME ON.
SIGNAL LOST
SHIT.
BANG
I TAKE IT YOU HAVEN'T HEARD FROM BEN?
HE'S THOUSANDS OF FEET UNDERGROUND AND ONLY A FEW GOVERNMENT COMMS CAN GET ME THROUGH. I'VE TRIED TO PATCH IN BUT THEY'RE LOCKED UP TIGHTER THAN...
...I CAN NEVER REMEMBER THE END OF THAT PHRASE.
YOU THINK HE'S OKAY?
HE'S MADSEN. OF COURSE HE'S OKAY. RIGHT! LOCKED UP TIGHTER THAN A DUCK'S–
EDWARD.
HOW'S RITA?
I DON'T KNOW WHAT BEN TOLD YOU, BUT SHE'S NOT GOOD.
THE SOONER HE COMES BACK, THE BETTER.
WE'RE WORKING ON IT.

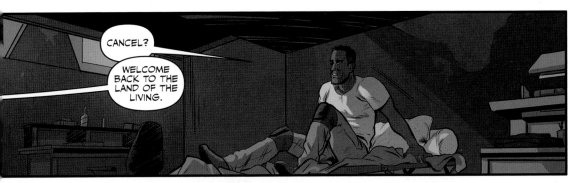

CANCEL?

WELCOME BACK TO THE LAND OF THE LIVING.

SORT OF.

WHO'S AUNT RITA? FEVER DREAMS HAD YOU TALKING.

...WHERE AM I?

TWENTY-FIVE FEET BELOW THE WHITE SUN WARD. DRINK THIS.

SMELLS LIKE *POISON.*

FIRE WITH FIRE, RIGHT? YOU WERE BITTEN BY A CAERELIAN. A YOUNG ONE, THOUGH, SO YOU'LL LIVE.

YEAH, THAT BRAT STOLE SOMETHING FROM ME.

THAT *BRAT* HAS NO PARENTS, NO HOME, AND HASN'T EATEN IN THREE DAYS. SHE DOES FAVORS FOR ME. FOR WHAT I PAID TO GET YOUR TOY BACK, SHE'LL EAT FOR A WEEK.

PROBABLY THE BEST THING TO SAY NOW IS...*THANK YOU.*

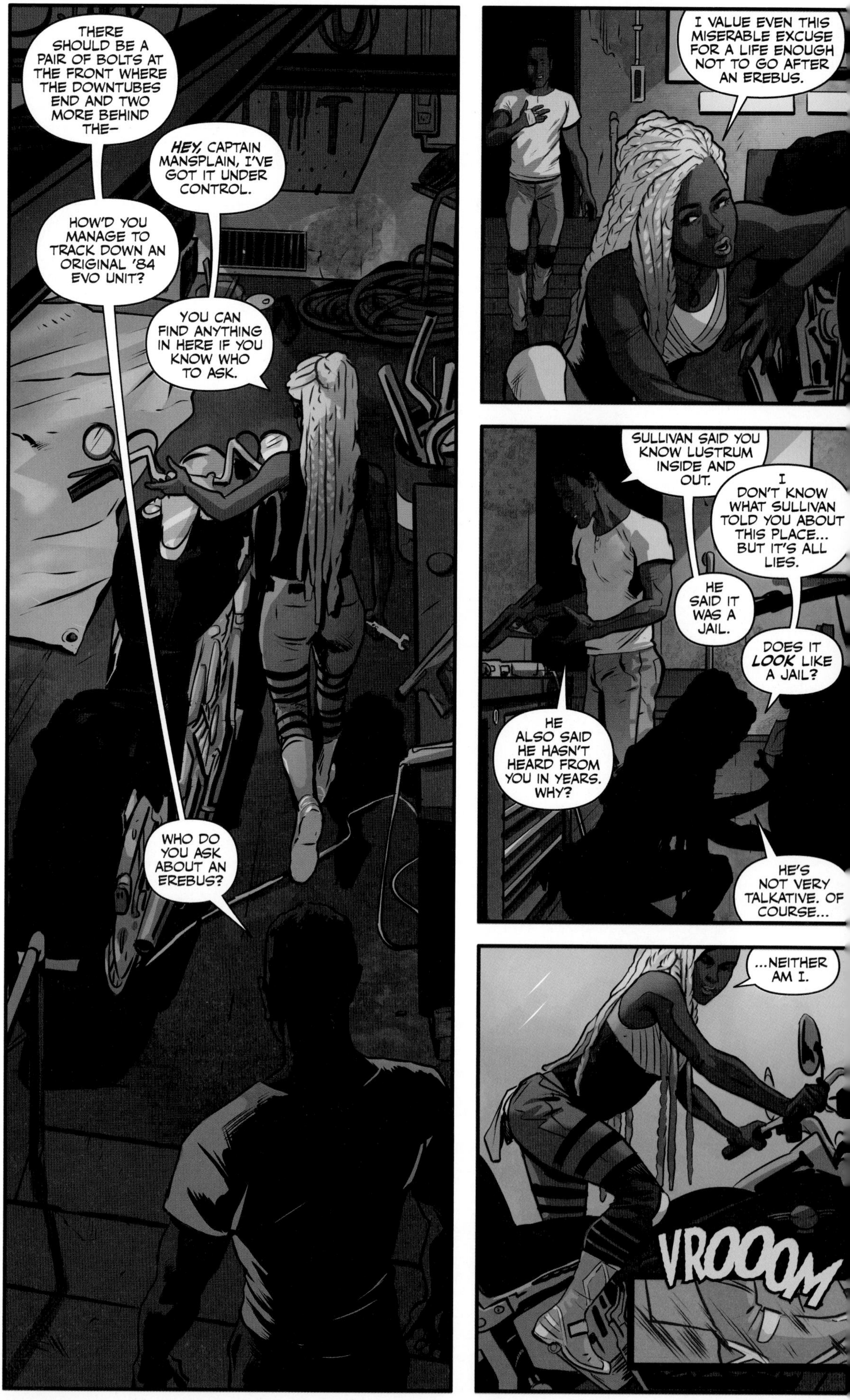
THERE SHOULD BE A PAIR OF BOLTS AT THE FRONT WHERE THE DOWNTUBES END AND TWO MORE BEHIND THE–
HEY, CAPTAIN MANSPLAIN, I'VE GOT IT UNDER CONTROL.
HOW'D YOU MANAGE TO TRACK DOWN AN ORIGINAL '84 EVO UNIT?
YOU CAN FIND ANYTHING IN HERE IF YOU KNOW WHO TO ASK.
WHO DO YOU ASK ABOUT AN EREBUS?
I VALUE EVEN THIS MISERABLE EXCUSE FOR A LIFE ENOUGH NOT TO GO AFTER AN EREBUS.
SULLIVAN SAID YOU KNOW LUSTRUM INSIDE AND OUT.
I DON'T KNOW WHAT SULLIVAN TOLD YOU ABOUT THIS PLACE... BUT IT'S ALL LIES.
HE SAID IT WAS A JAIL.
DOES IT LOOK LIKE A JAIL?
HE ALSO SAID HE HASN'T HEARD FROM YOU IN YEARS. WHY?
HE'S NOT VERY TALKATIVE. OF COURSE...
...NEITHER AM I.
VROOOM

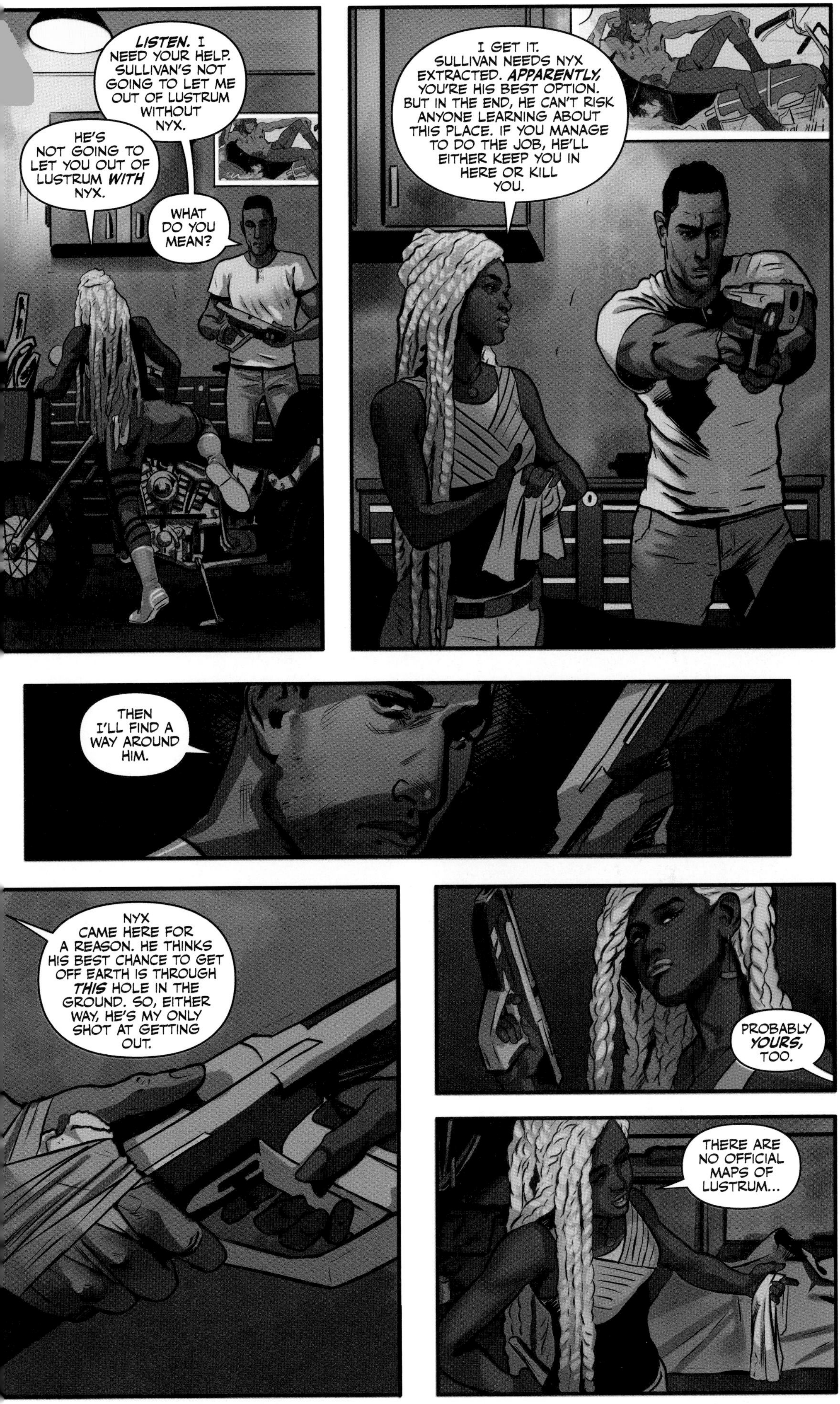
LISTEN. I NEED YOUR HELP. SULLIVAN'S NOT GOING TO LET ME OUT OF LUSTRUM WITHOUT NYX.
HE'S NOT GOING TO LET YOU OUT OF LUSTRUM WITH NYX.
WHAT DO YOU MEAN?
I GET IT. SULLIVAN NEEDS NYX EXTRACTED. APPARENTLY, YOU'RE HIS BEST OPTION. BUT IN THE END, HE CAN'T RISK ANYONE LEARNING ABOUT THIS PLACE. IF YOU MANAGE TO DO THE JOB, HE'LL EITHER KEEP YOU IN HERE OR KILL YOU.
THEN I'LL FIND A WAY AROUND HIM.
NYX CAME HERE FOR A REASON. HE THINKS HIS BEST CHANCE TO GET OFF EARTH IS THROUGH THIS HOLE IN THE GROUND. SO, EITHER WAY, HE'S MY ONLY SHOT AT GETTING OUT.
PROBABLY YOURS, TOO.
THERE ARE NO OFFICIAL MAPS OF LUSTRUM...

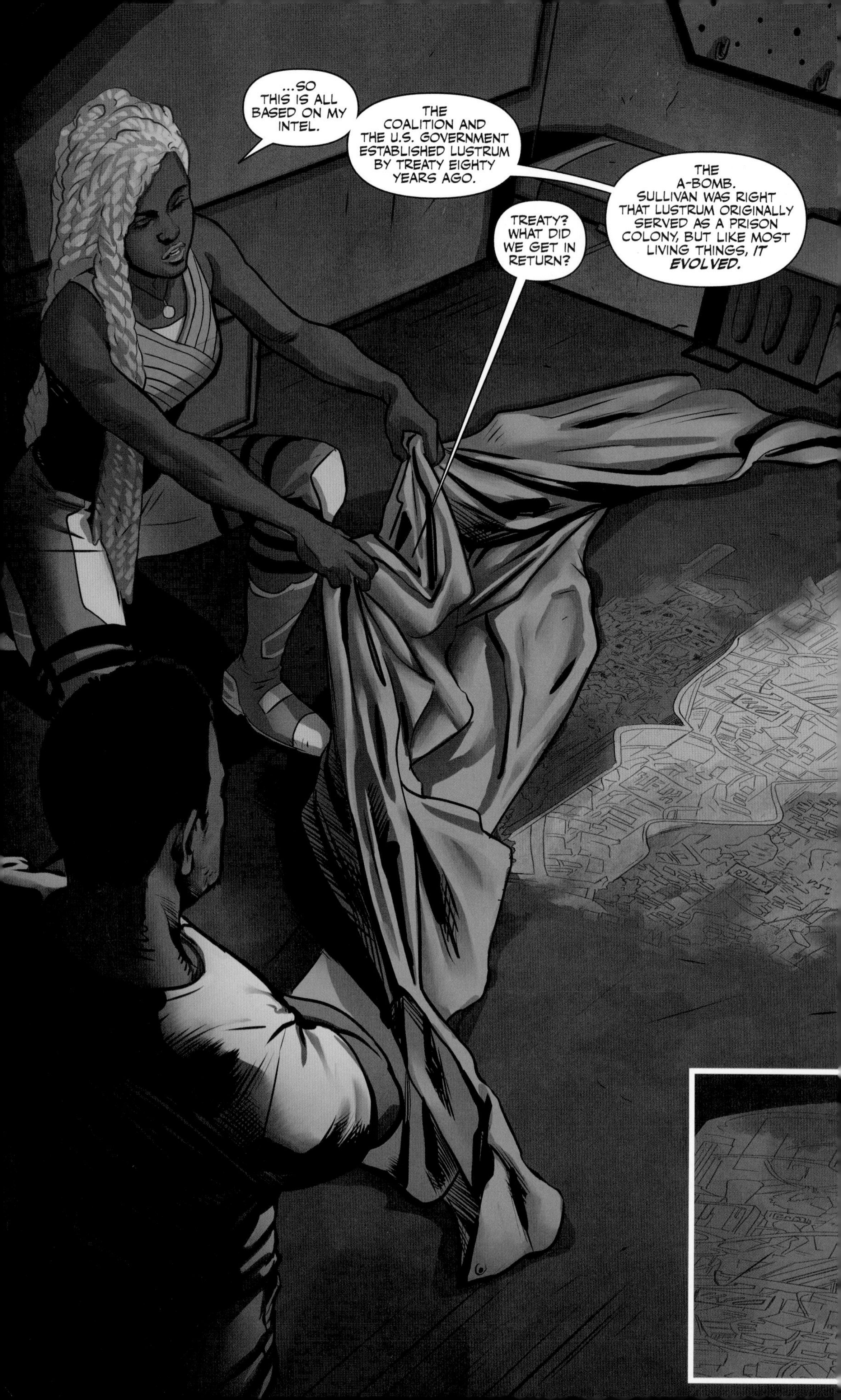
...SO THIS IS ALL BASED ON MY INTEL.
THE COALITION AND THE U.S. GOVERNMENT ESTABLISHED LUSTRUM BY TREATY EIGHTY YEARS AGO.
THE A-BOMB. SULLIVAN WAS RIGHT THAT LUSTRUM ORIGINALLY SERVED AS A PRISON COLONY, BUT LIKE MOST LIVING THINGS, *IT* ***EVOLVED.***
TREATY? WHAT DID WE GET IN RETURN?

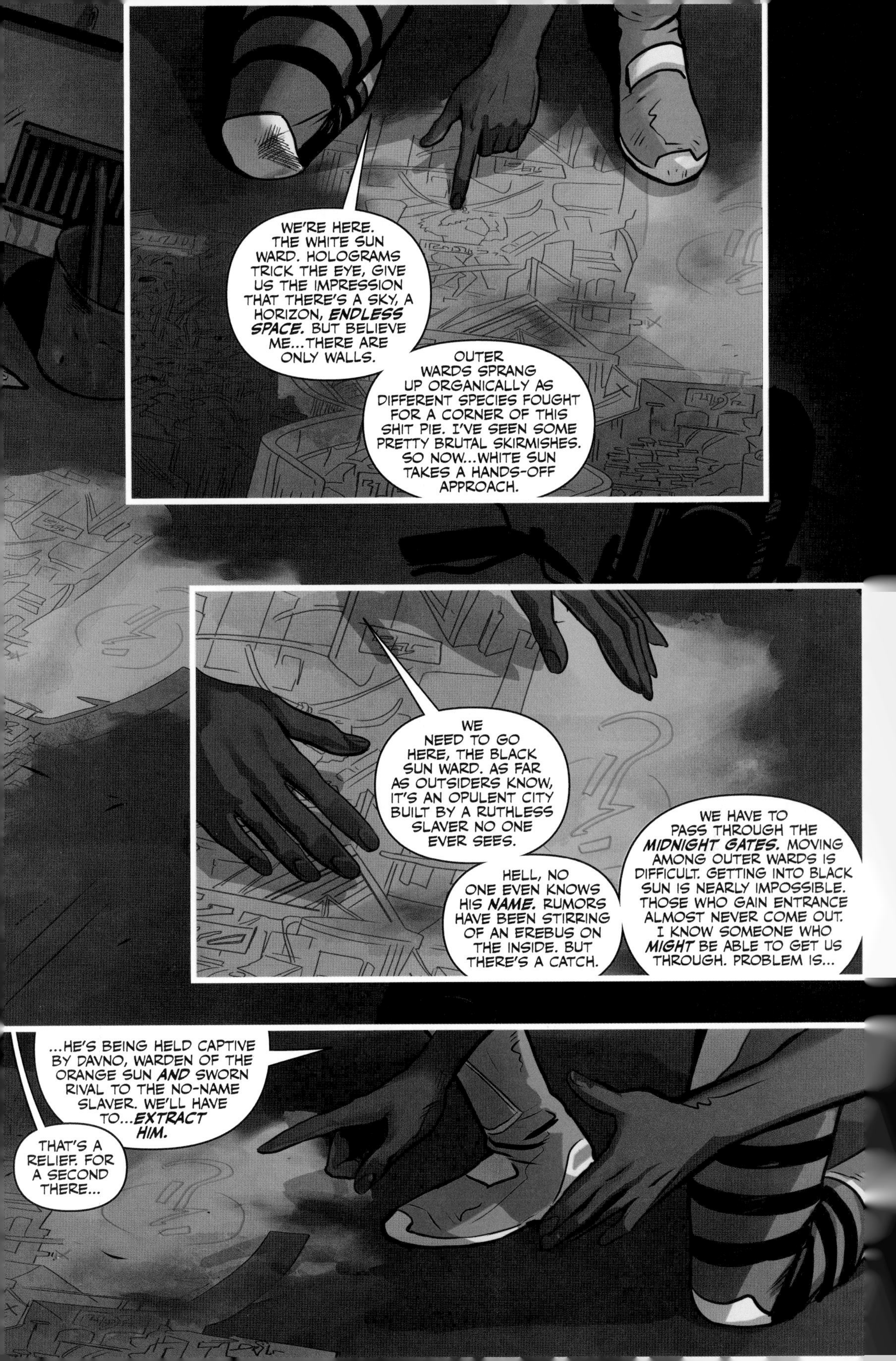
WE'RE HERE. THE WHITE SUN WARD. HOLOGRAMS TRICK THE EYE, GIVE US THE IMPRESSION THAT THERE'S A SKY, A HORIZON, ENDLESS SPACE. BUT BELIEVE ME...THERE ARE ONLY WALLS.
OUTER WARDS SPRANG UP ORGANICALLY AS DIFFERENT SPECIES FOUGHT FOR A CORNER OF THIS SHIT PIE. I'VE SEEN SOME PRETTY BRUTAL SKIRMISHES. SO NOW...WHITE SUN TAKES A HANDS-OFF APPROACH.
WE NEED TO GO HERE, THE BLACK SUN WARD. AS FAR AS OUTSIDERS KNOW, IT'S AN OPULENT CITY BUILT BY A RUTHLESS SLAVER NO ONE EVER SEES.
HELL, NO ONE EVEN KNOWS HIS NAME. RUMORS HAVE BEEN STIRRING OF AN EREBUS ON THE INSIDE. BUT THERE'S A CATCH.
WE HAVE TO PASS THROUGH THE MIDNIGHT GATES. MOVING AMONG OUTER WARDS IS DIFFICULT. GETTING INTO BLACK SUN IS NEARLY IMPOSSIBLE. THOSE WHO GAIN ENTRANCE ALMOST NEVER COME OUT. I KNOW SOMEONE WHO MIGHT BE ABLE TO GET US THROUGH. PROBLEM IS...
...HE'S BEING HELD CAPTIVE BY DAVNO, WARDEN OF THE ORANGE SUN AND SWORN RIVAL TO THE NO-NAME SLAVER. WE'LL HAVE TO...EXTRACT HIM.
THAT'S A RELIEF. FOR A SECOND THERE...

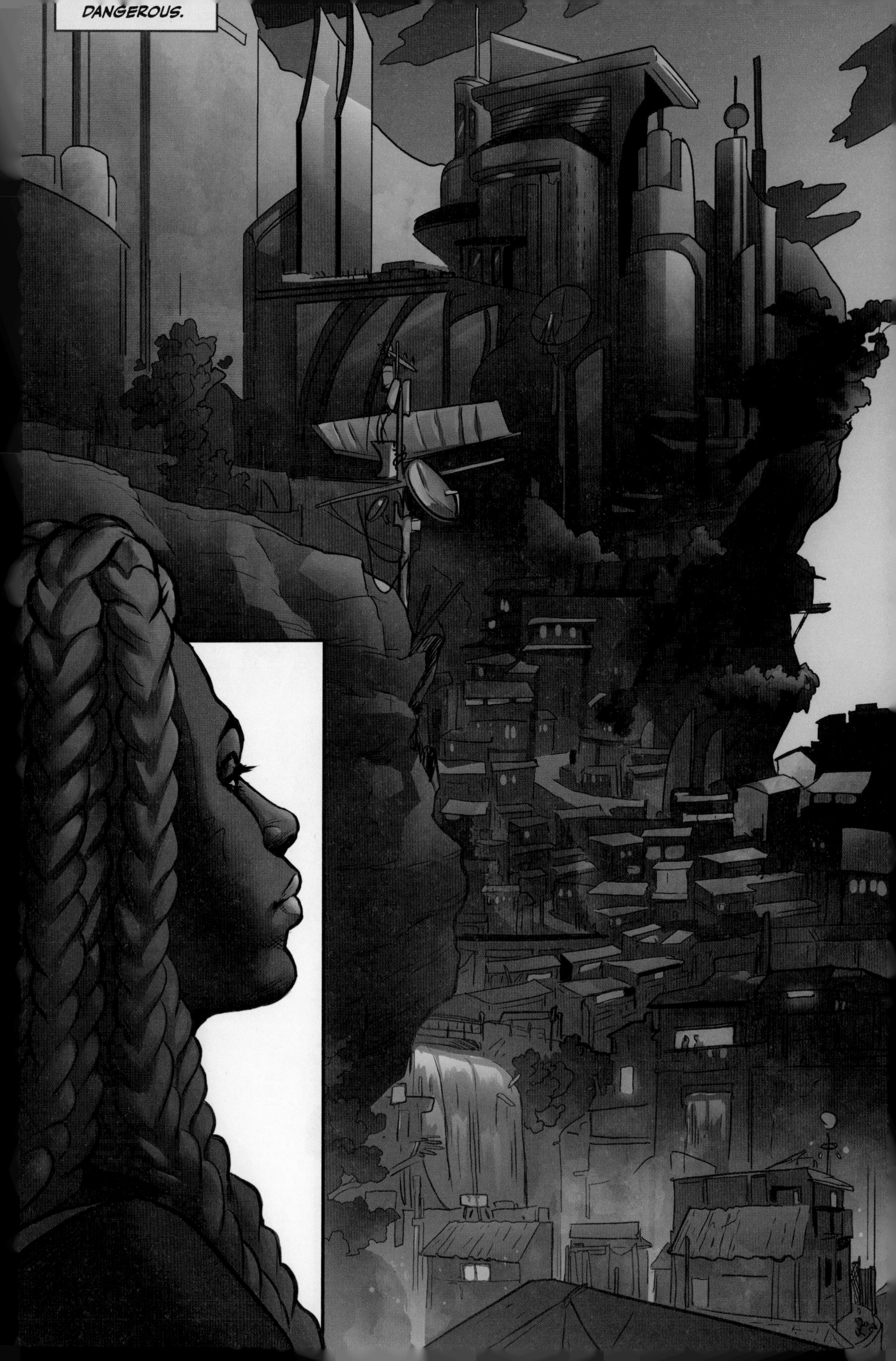
DANGEROUS.

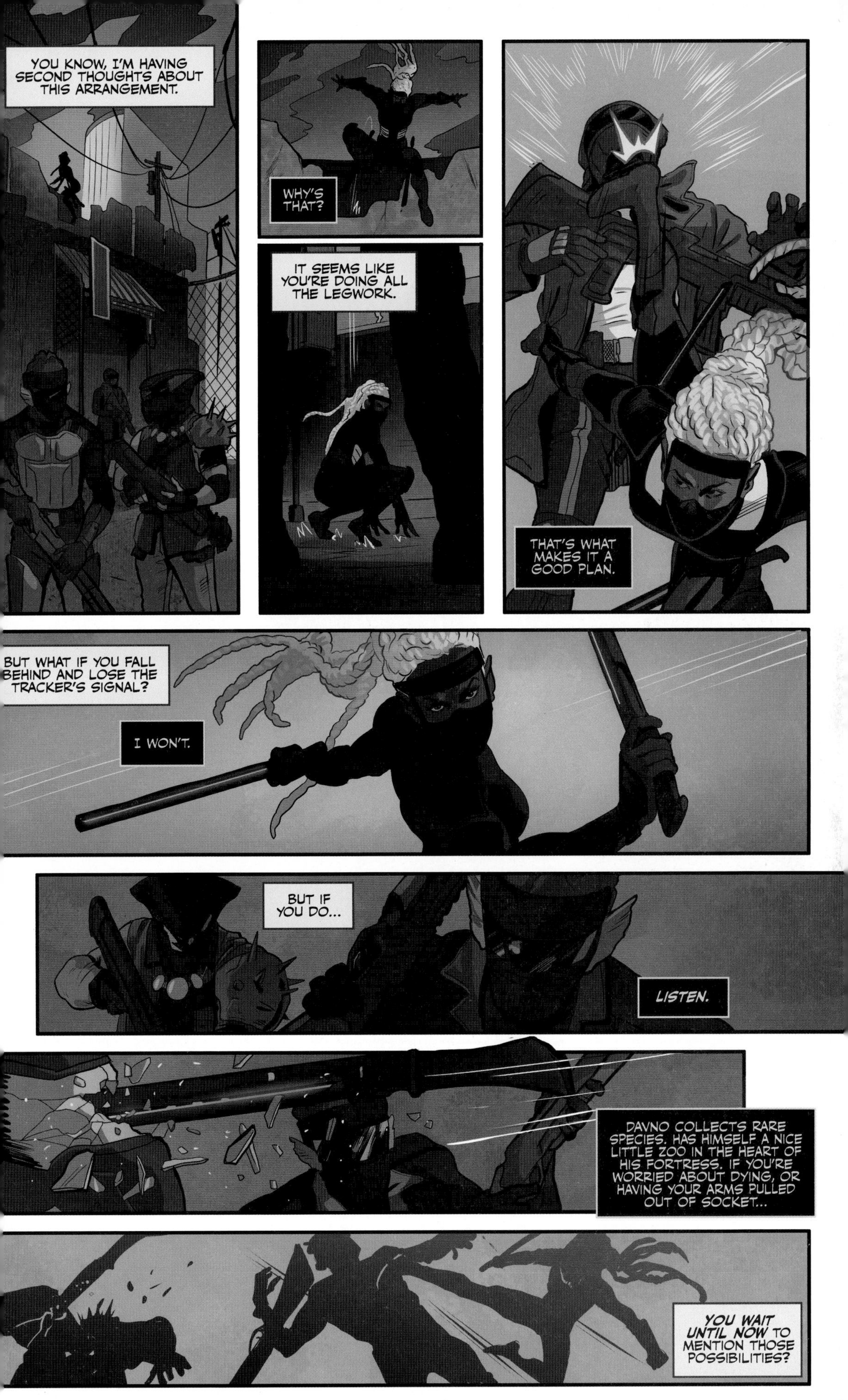

YOU KNOW, I'M HAVING SECOND THOUGHTS ABOUT THIS ARRANGEMENT.
WHY'S THAT?
IT SEEMS LIKE YOU'RE DOING ALL THE LEGWORK.
THAT'S WHAT MAKES IT A GOOD PLAN.
BUT WHAT IF YOU FALL BEHIND AND LOSE THE TRACKER'S SIGNAL?
I WON'T.
BUT IF YOU DO...
LISTEN.
DAVNO COLLECTS RARE SPECIES. HAS HIMSELF A NICE LITTLE ZOO IN THE HEART OF HIS FORTRESS. IF YOU'RE WORRIED ABOUT DYING, OR HAVING YOUR ARMS PULLED OUT OF SOCKET...
YOU WAIT UNTIL NOW TO MENTION THOSE POSSIBILITIES?

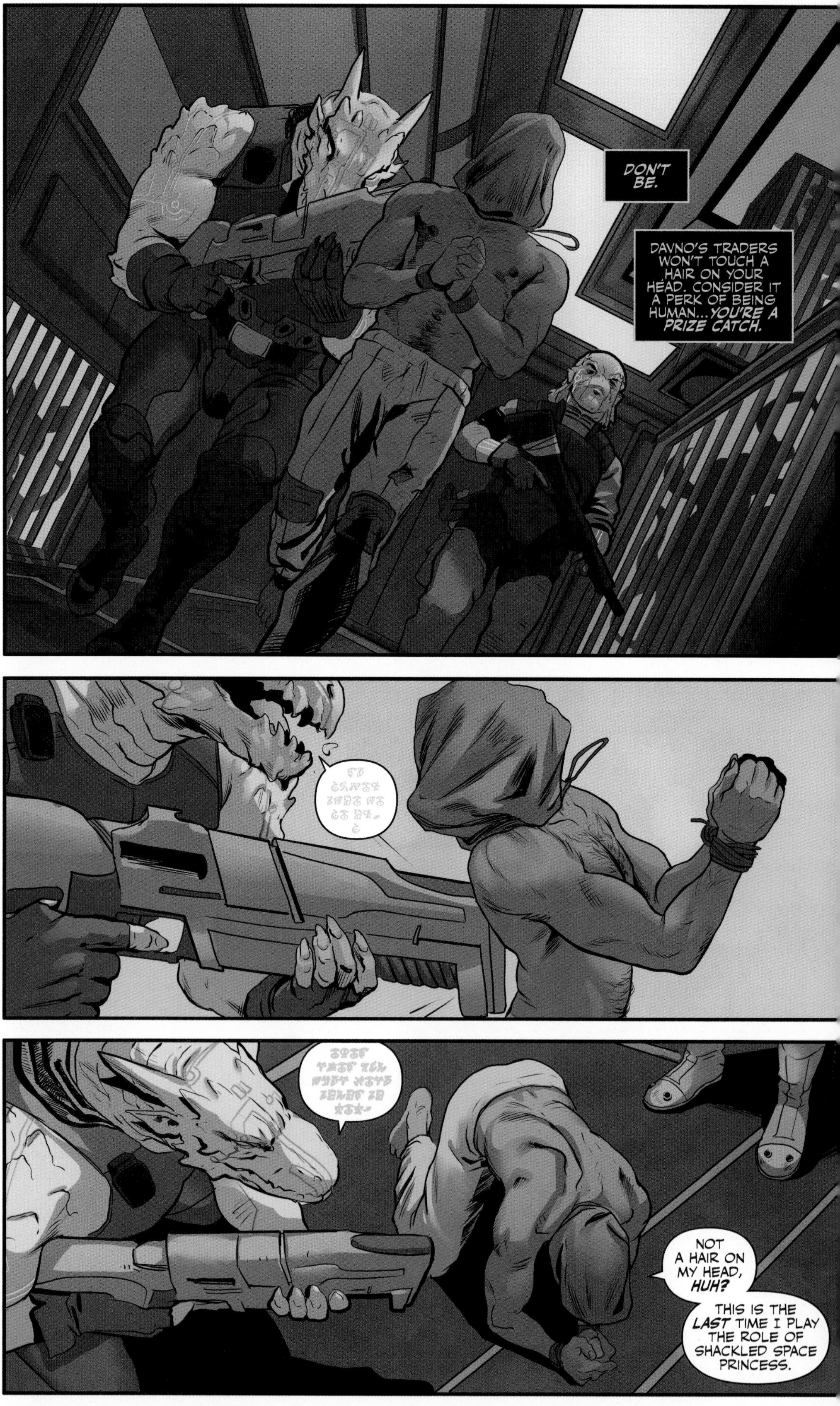
DON'T BE.
DAVNO'S TRADERS WON'T TOUCH A HAIR ON YOUR HEAD. CONSIDER IT A PERK OF BEING HUMAN...*YOU'RE A PRIZE CATCH.*
NOT A HAIR ON MY HEAD, *HUH?*
THIS IS THE *LAST* TIME I PLAY THE ROLE OF SHACKLED SPACE PRINCESS.

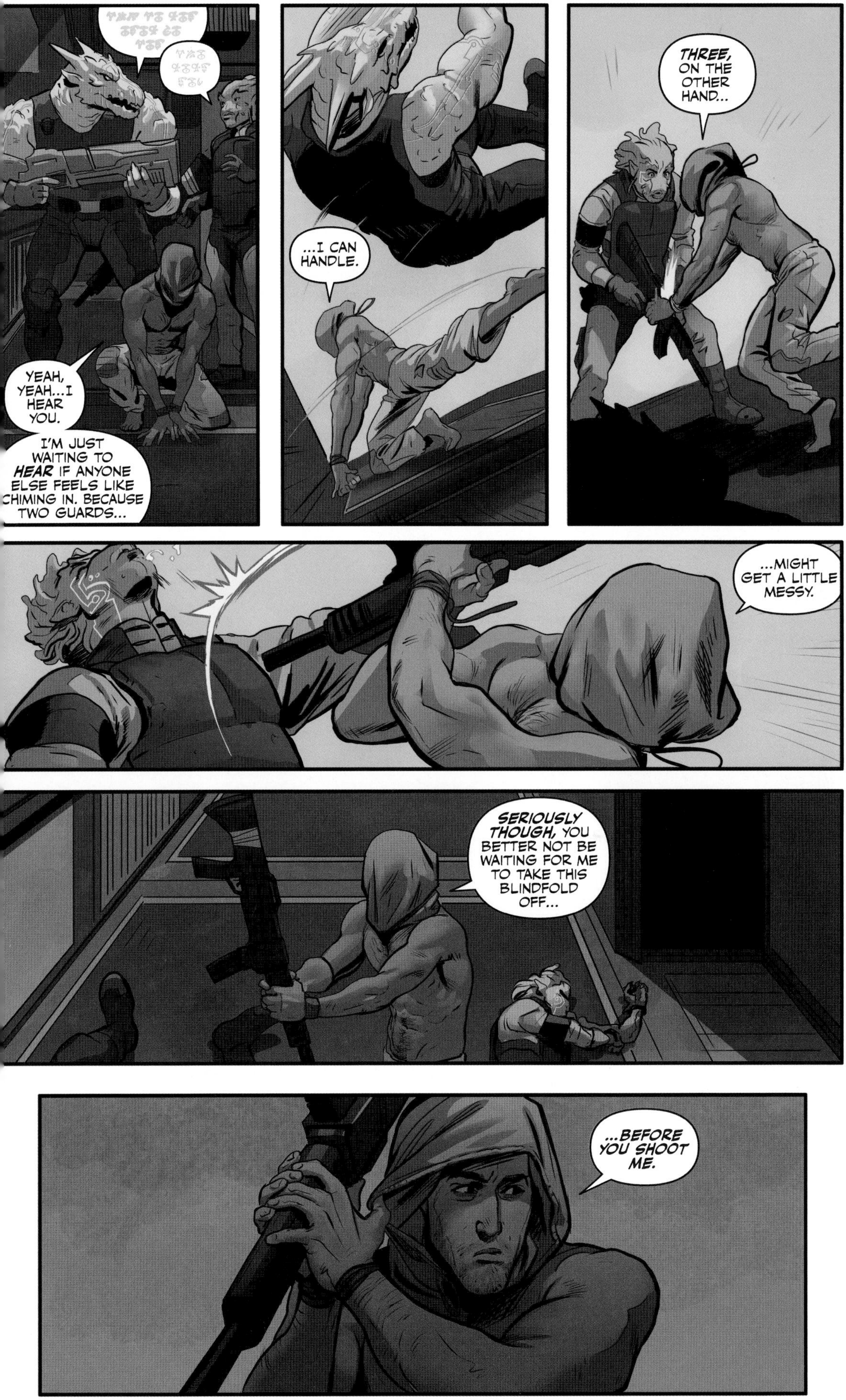
YEAH, YEAH...I HEAR YOU.
I'M JUST WAITING TO HEAR IF ANYONE ELSE FEELS LIKE CHIMING IN. BECAUSE TWO GUARDS...
...I CAN HANDLE.
THREE, ON THE OTHER HAND...
...MIGHT GET A LITTLE MESSY.
SERIOUSLY THOUGH, YOU BETTER NOT BE WAITING FOR ME TO TAKE THIS BLINDFOLD OFF...
...BEFORE YOU SHOOT ME.

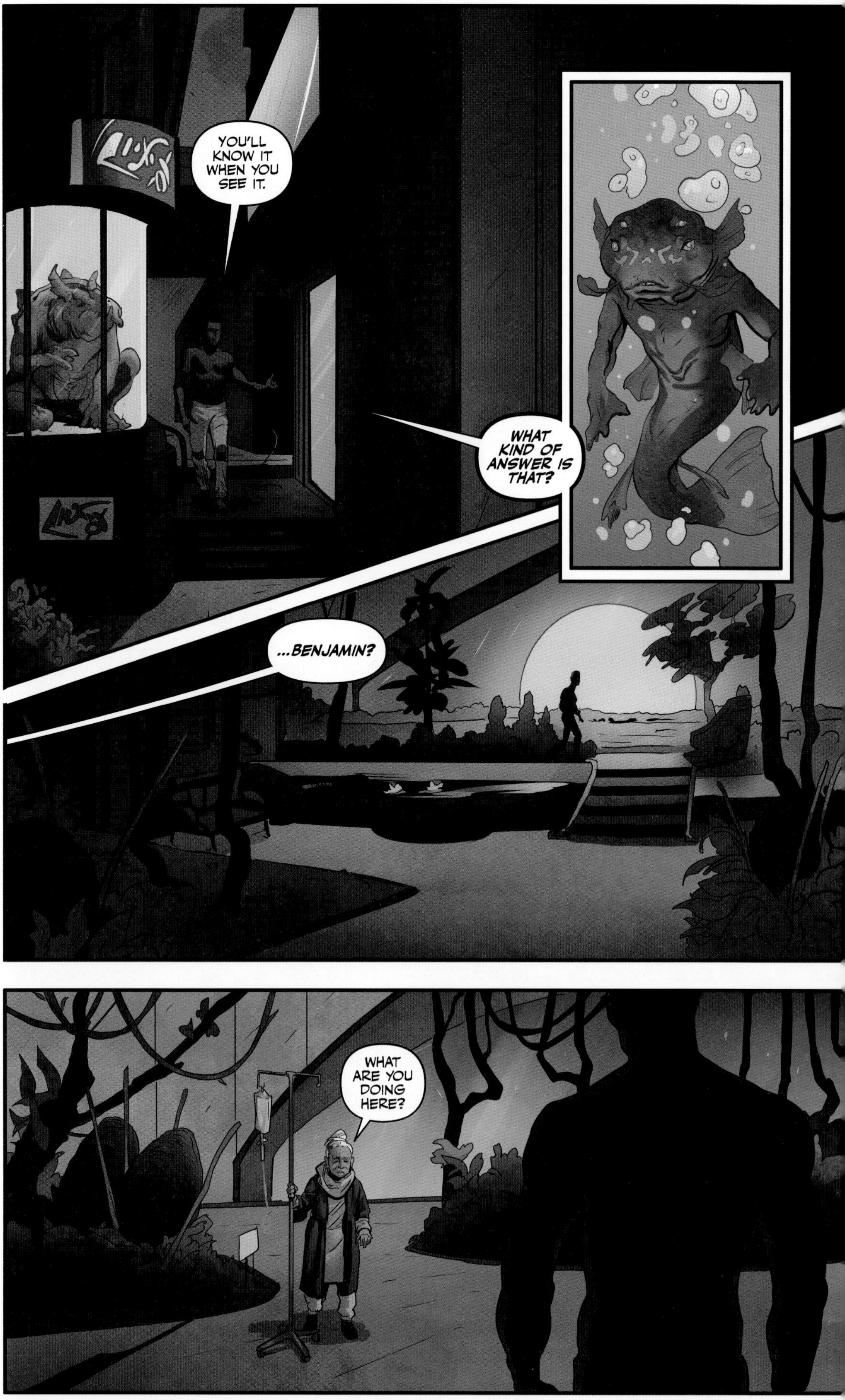
YOU'LL KNOW IT WHEN YOU SEE IT.
WHAT KIND OF ANSWER IS THAT?
...BENJAMIN?
WHAT ARE YOU DOING HERE?

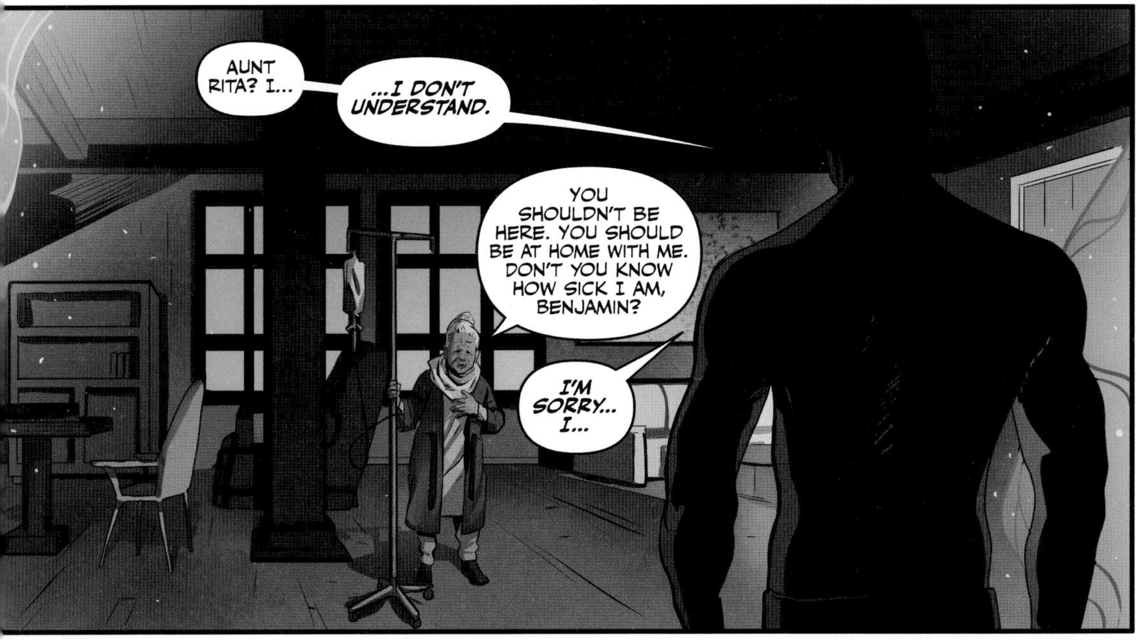
AUNT RITA? I...
...I DON'T UNDERSTAND.
YOU SHOULDN'T BE HERE. YOU SHOULD BE AT HOME WITH ME. DON'T YOU KNOW HOW SICK I AM, BENJAMIN?
I'M SORRY... I...

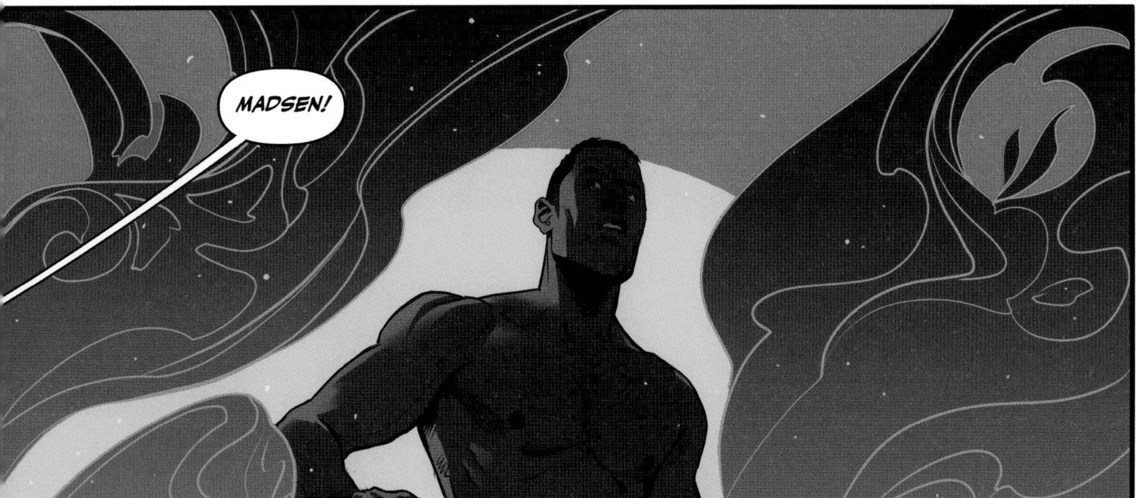
MADSEN!

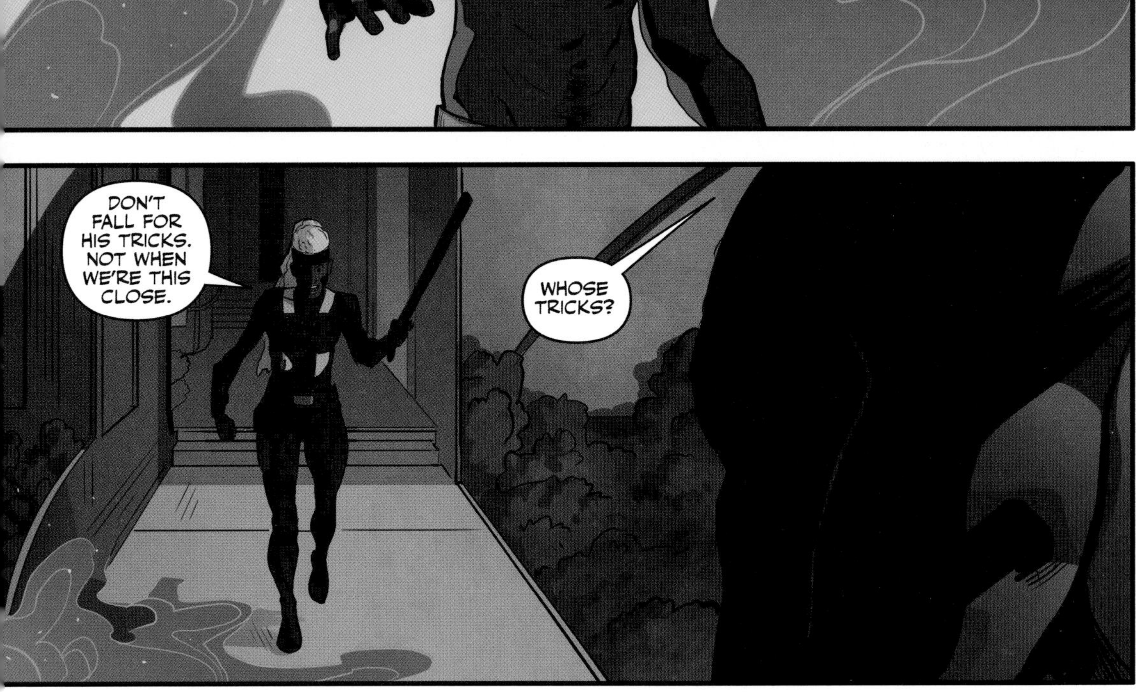
DON'T FALL FOR HIS TRICKS. NOT WHEN WE'RE THIS CLOSE.
WHOSE TRICKS?

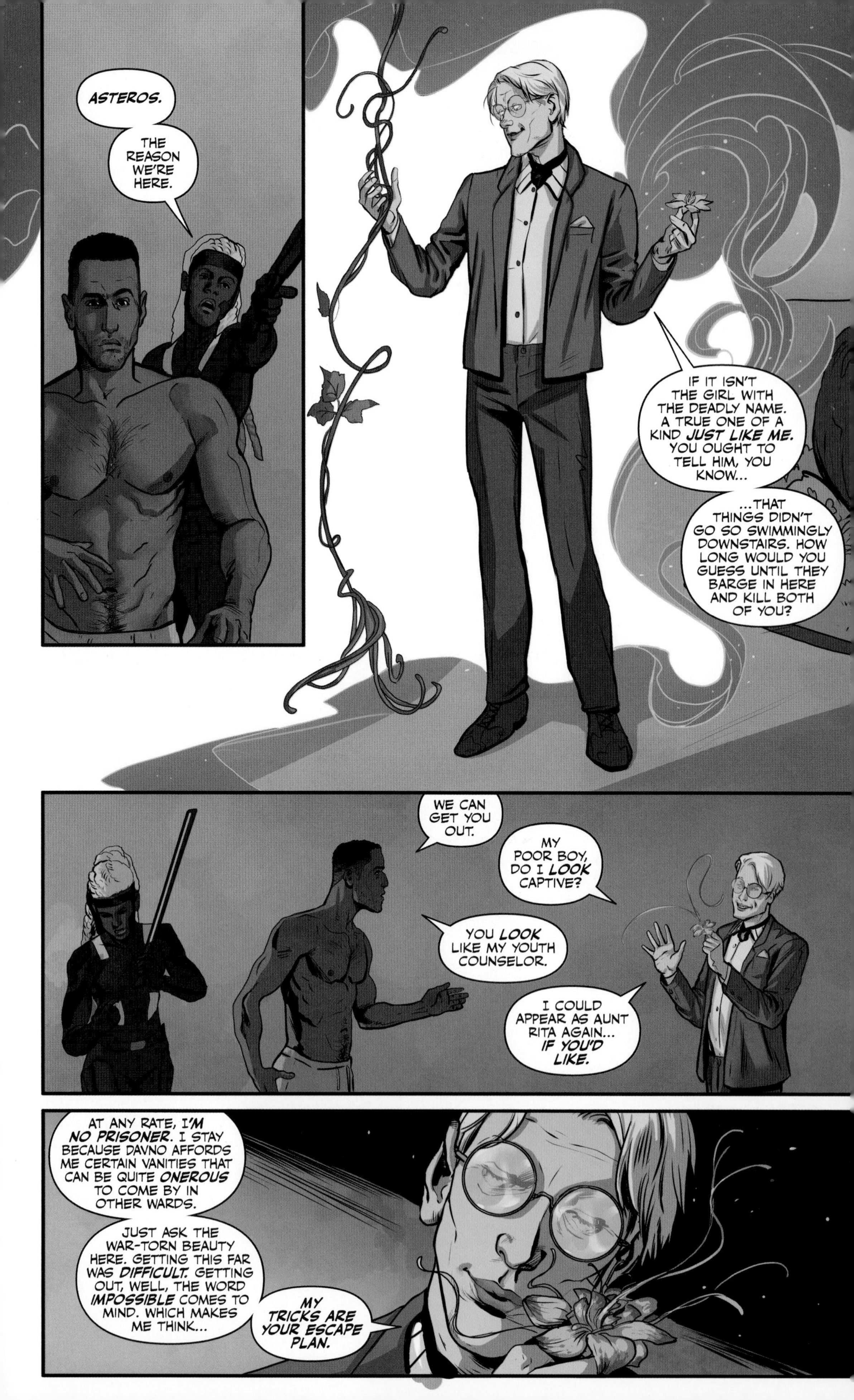
ASTEROS.
THE REASON WE'RE HERE.
IF IT ISN'T THE GIRL WITH THE DEADLY NAME. A TRUE ONE OF A KIND JUST LIKE ME. YOU OUGHT TO TELL HIM, YOU KNOW...
...THAT THINGS DIDN'T GO SO SWIMMINGLY DOWNSTAIRS. HOW LONG WOULD YOU GUESS UNTIL THEY BARGE IN HERE AND KILL BOTH OF YOU?
WE CAN GET YOU OUT.
MY POOR BOY, DO I LOOK CAPTIVE?
YOU LOOK LIKE MY YOUTH COUNSELOR.
I COULD APPEAR AS AUNT RITA AGAIN... IF YOU'D LIKE.
AT ANY RATE, I'M NO PRISONER. I STAY BECAUSE DAVNO AFFORDS ME CERTAIN VANITIES THAT CAN BE QUITE ONEROUS TO COME BY IN OTHER WARDS.
JUST ASK THE WAR-TORN BEAUTY HERE. GETTING THIS FAR WAS DIFFICULT. GETTING OUT, WELL, THE WORD IMPOSSIBLE COMES TO MIND. WHICH MAKES ME THINK...
MY TRICKS ARE YOUR ESCAPE PLAN.

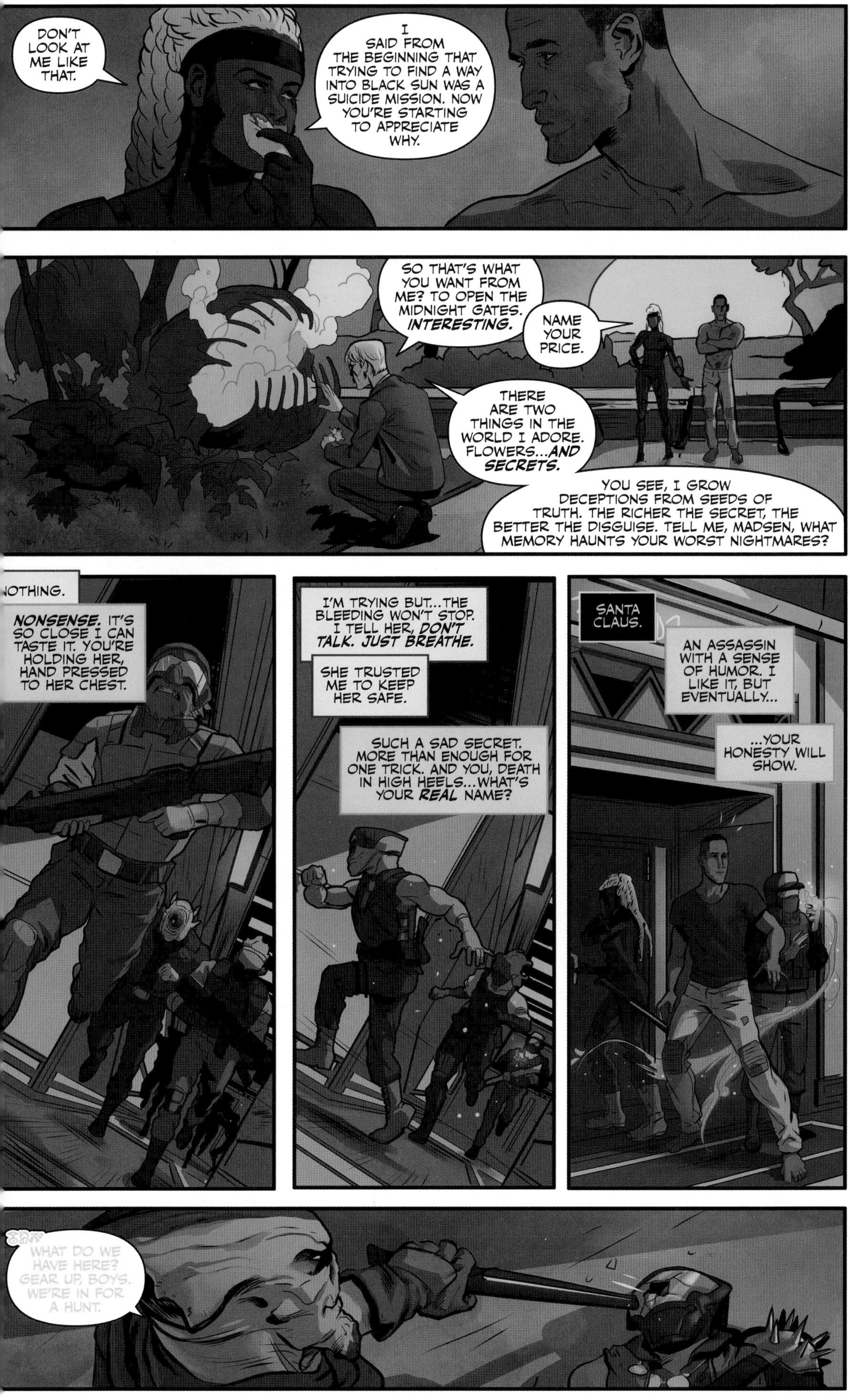
DON'T LOOK AT ME LIKE THAT.
I SAID FROM THE BEGINNING THAT TRYING TO FIND A WAY INTO BLACK SUN WAS A SUICIDE MISSION. NOW YOU'RE STARTING TO APPRECIATE WHY.
SO THAT'S WHAT YOU WANT FROM ME? TO OPEN THE MIDNIGHT GATES. *INTERESTING.*
NAME YOUR PRICE.
THERE ARE TWO THINGS IN THE WORLD I ADORE. FLOWERS...*AND SECRETS.*
YOU SEE, I GROW DECEPTIONS FROM SEEDS OF TRUTH. THE RICHER THE SECRET, THE BETTER THE DISGUISE. TELL ME, MADSEN, WHAT MEMORY HAUNTS YOUR WORST NIGHTMARES?
NOTHING.
NONSENSE. IT'S SO CLOSE I CAN TASTE IT. YOU'RE HOLDING HER, HAND PRESSED TO HER CHEST.
I'M TRYING BUT...THE BLEEDING WON'T STOP. I TELL HER, *DON'T TALK. JUST BREATHE.*
SHE TRUSTED ME TO KEEP HER SAFE.
SUCH A SAD SECRET. MORE THAN ENOUGH FOR ONE TRICK. AND YOU, DEATH IN HIGH HEELS...WHAT'S YOUR *REAL* NAME?
SANTA CLAUS.
AN ASSASSIN WITH A SENSE OF HUMOR. I LIKE IT, BUT EVENTUALLY...
...YOUR HONESTY WILL SHOW.
WHAT DO WE HAVE HERE? GEAR UP, BOYS. WE'RE IN FOR A HUNT.

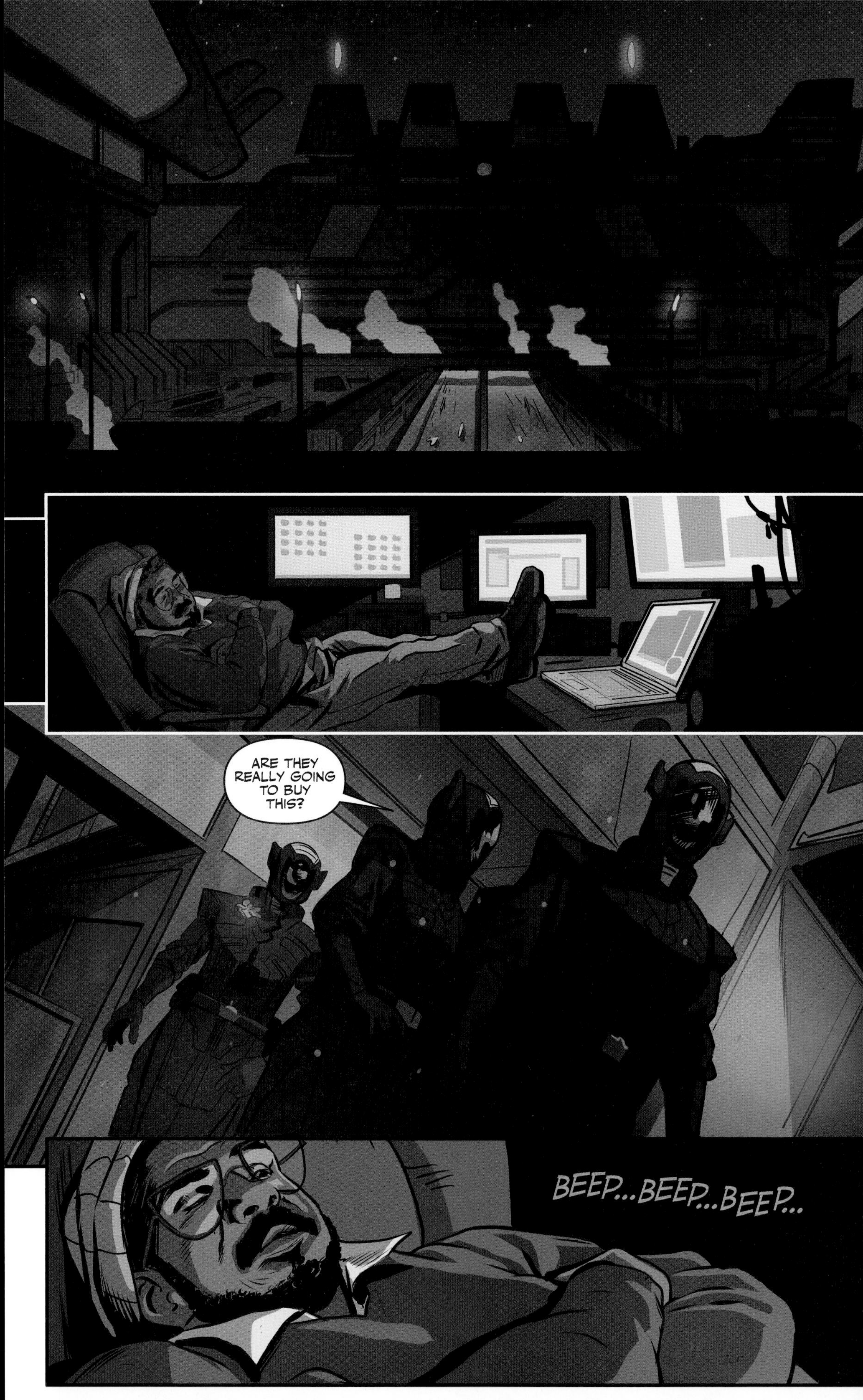
ARE THEY REALLY GOING TO BUY THIS?
BEEP...BEEP...BEEP...

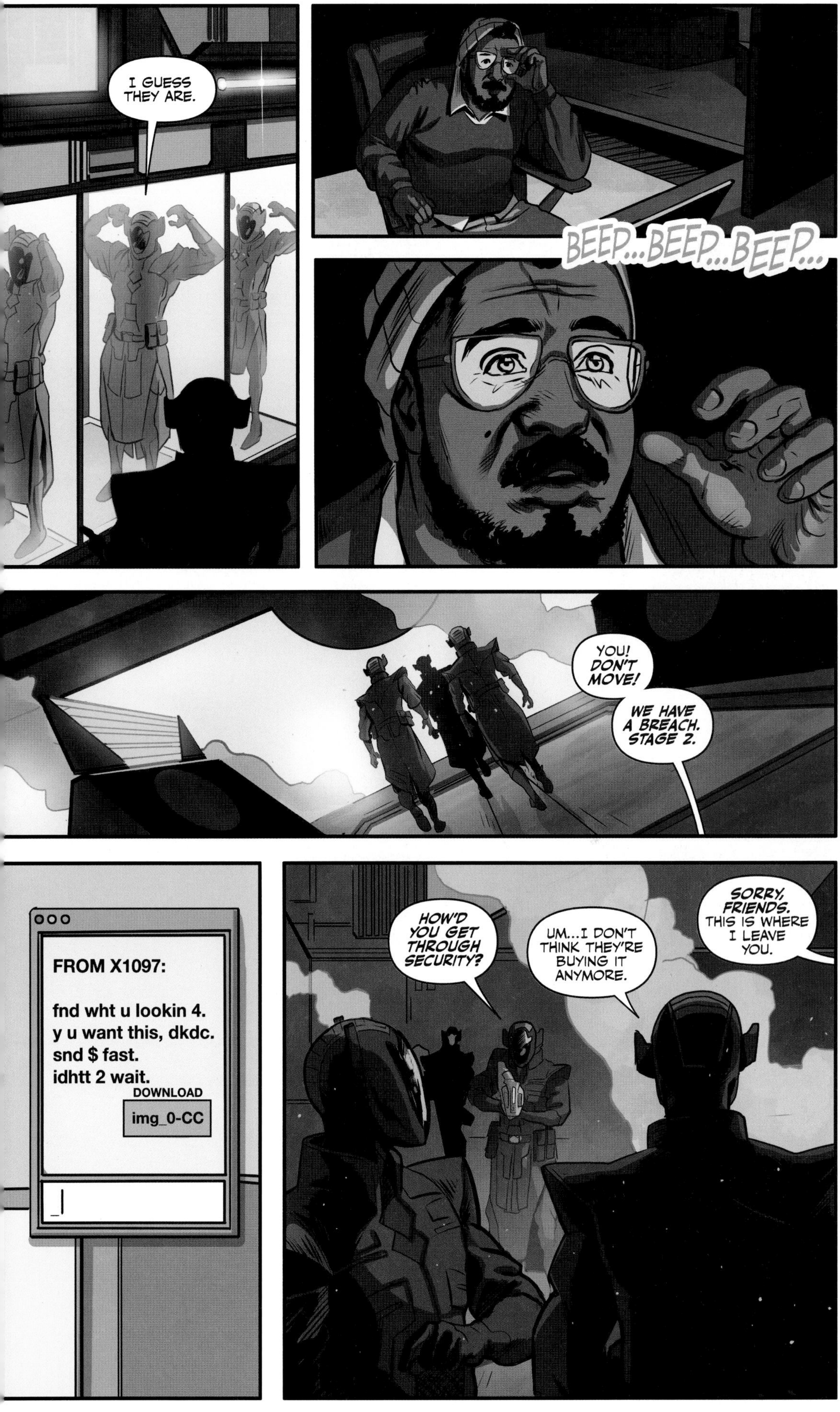
I GUESS THEY ARE.
BEEP...BEEP...BEEP...
YOU! DON'T MOVE!
WE HAVE A BREACH. STAGE 2.
FROM X1097:
fnd wht u lookin 4.
y u want this, dkdc.
snd $ fast.
idhtt 2 wait.
DOWNLOAD
img_0-CC
HOW'D YOU GET THROUGH SECURITY?
UM...I DON'T THINK THEY'RE BUYING IT ANYMORE.
SORRY, FRIENDS. THIS IS WHERE I LEAVE YOU.

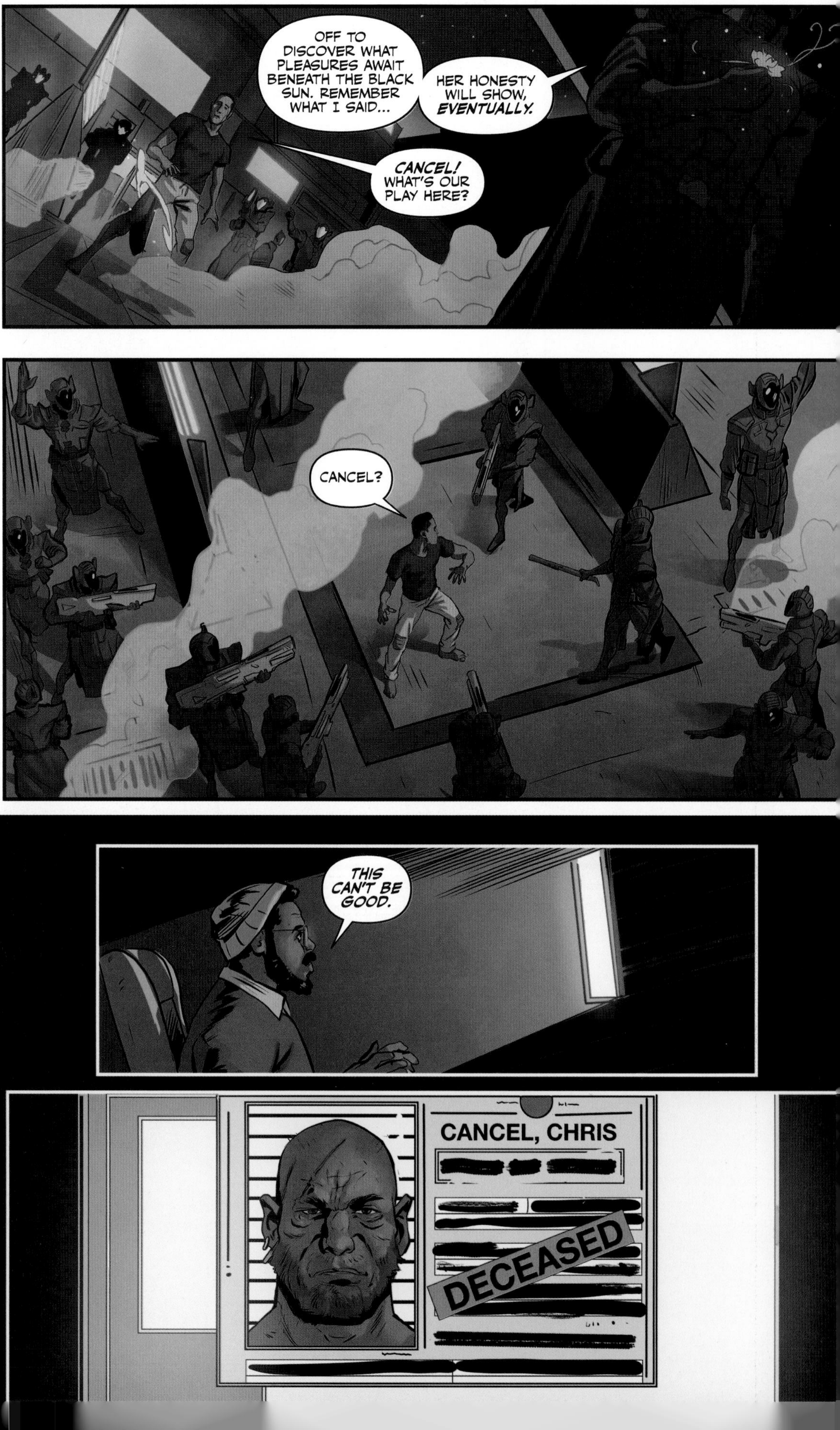
OFF TO DISCOVER WHAT PLEASURES AWAIT BENEATH THE BLACK SUN. REMEMBER WHAT I SAID...
HER HONESTY WILL SHOW, *EVENTUALLY.*
CANCEL! WHAT'S OUR PLAY HERE?
CANCEL?
THIS CAN'T BE GOOD.
CANCEL, CHRIS
[redacted]
DECEASED
[redacted]

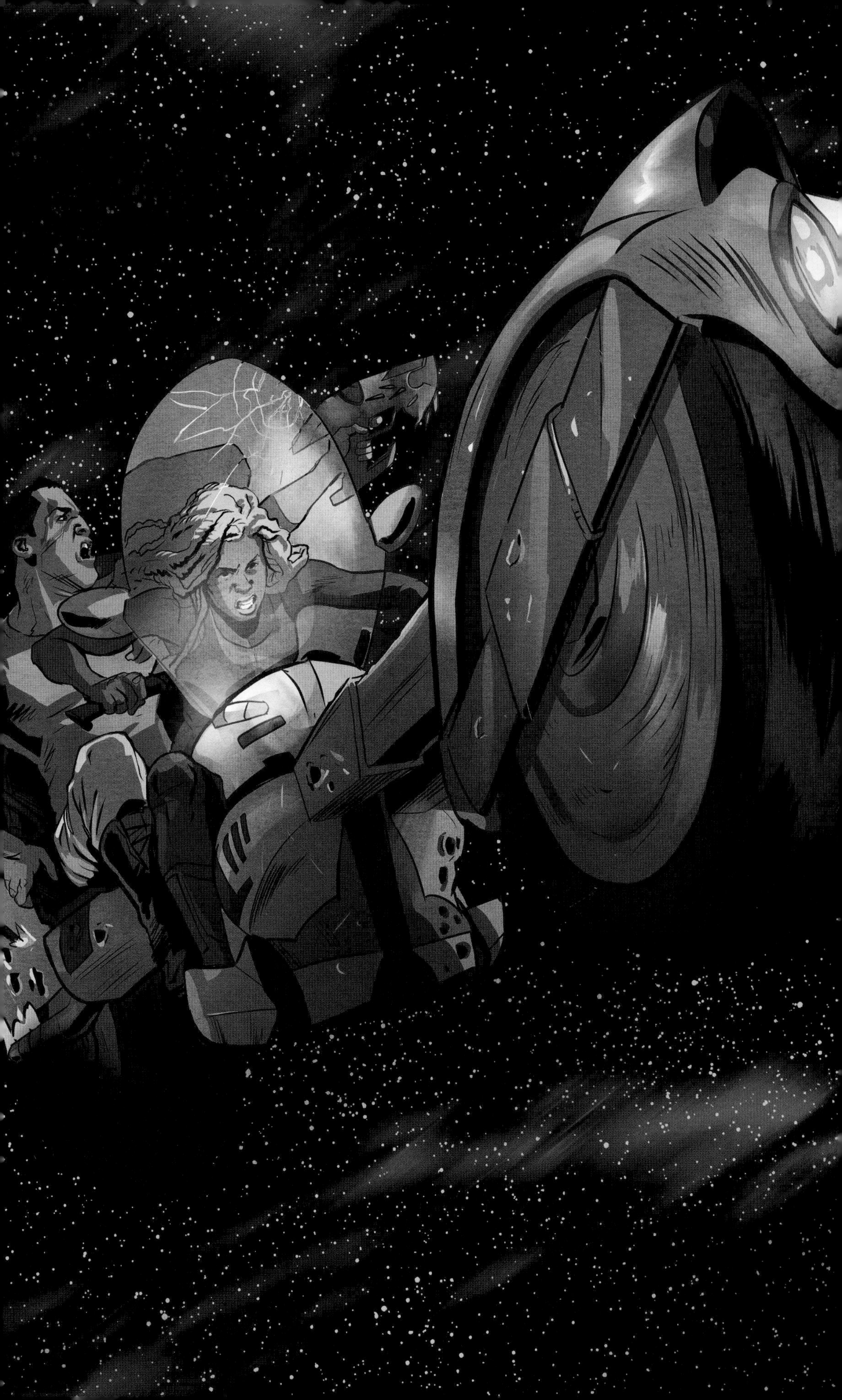

CHAPTER **3**

MALADY
SPECIES: MIZAR
PLANET OF ORIGIN: IZARINE

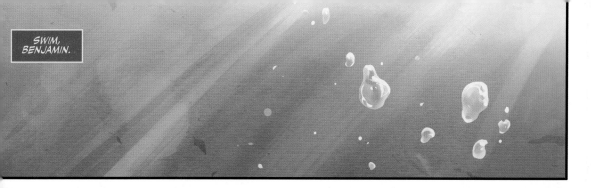

SWIM, BENJAMIN.

AUNT RITA WAS PUSHING SIXTY THE FIRST TIME SHE TOOK ME TO THE POOL.

MUST HAVE BEEN AN ODD THING TO WITNESS. ME...SHIVERING AT ITS EDGE WHILE AN OLD LADY WHO DIDN'T LOOK A THING LIKE ME SAID AGAIN AND AGAIN IN THE CALMEST VOICE...

SWIM, BENJAMIN.

I SPENT HOURS ON THAT CONCRETE, FEET TURNED TO PRUNES, WATCHING HER WRINKLED SKIN SWEEP THROUGH THE WATER.

ANGRY BECAUSE I WAS EMBARRASSED, BECAUSE SHE WAS PATIENT, BECAUSE SHE WOULDN'T GIVE UP.

JUST SWIM.

WHEN I FINALLY LEAPT INTO THE POOL, I WAS TERRIFIED.

NOT ABOUT DROWNING. NOT THAT TIME.

NO, I WAS TERRIFIED...

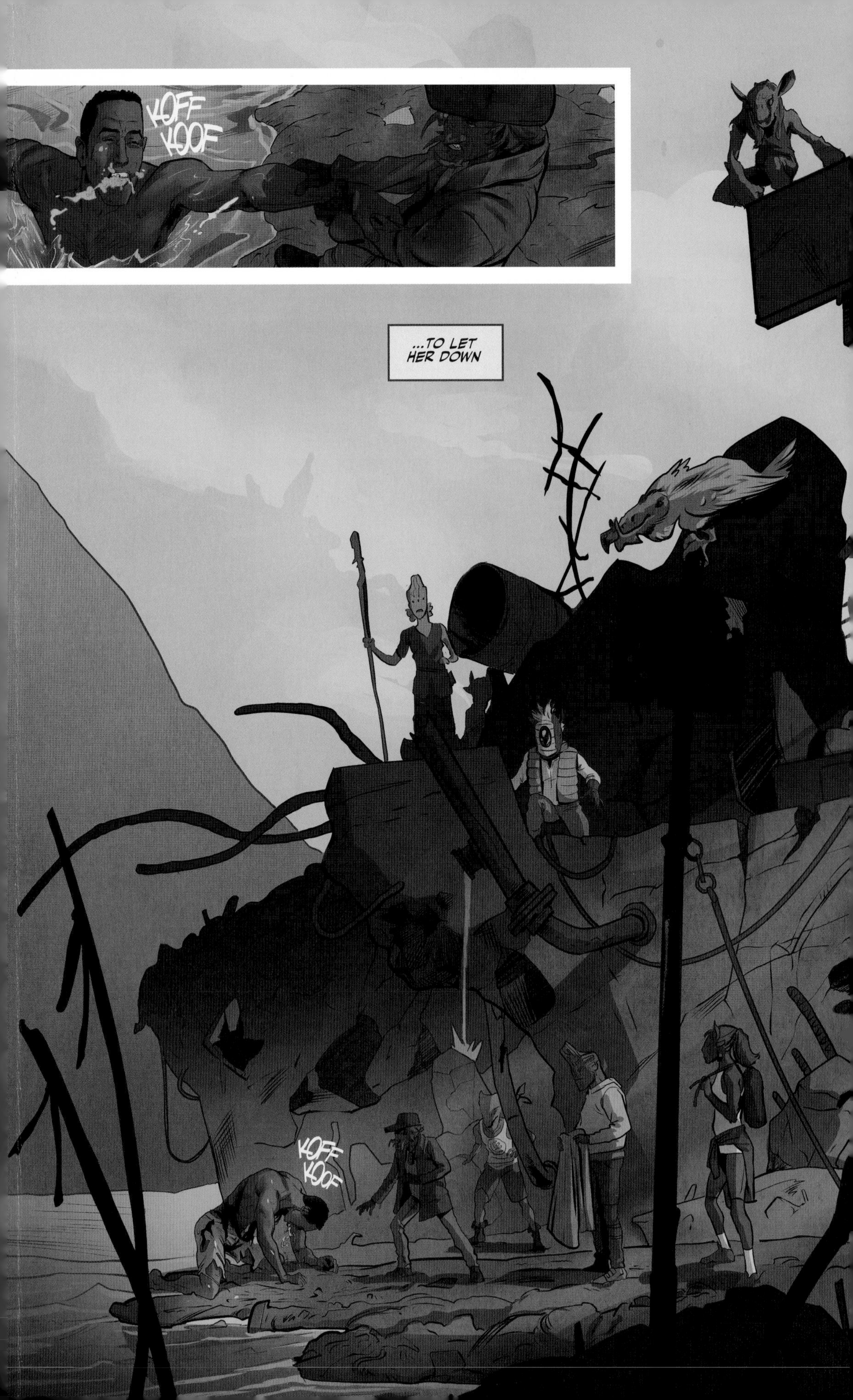
KOFF KOOF
...TO LET HER DOWN
KOFF KOOF

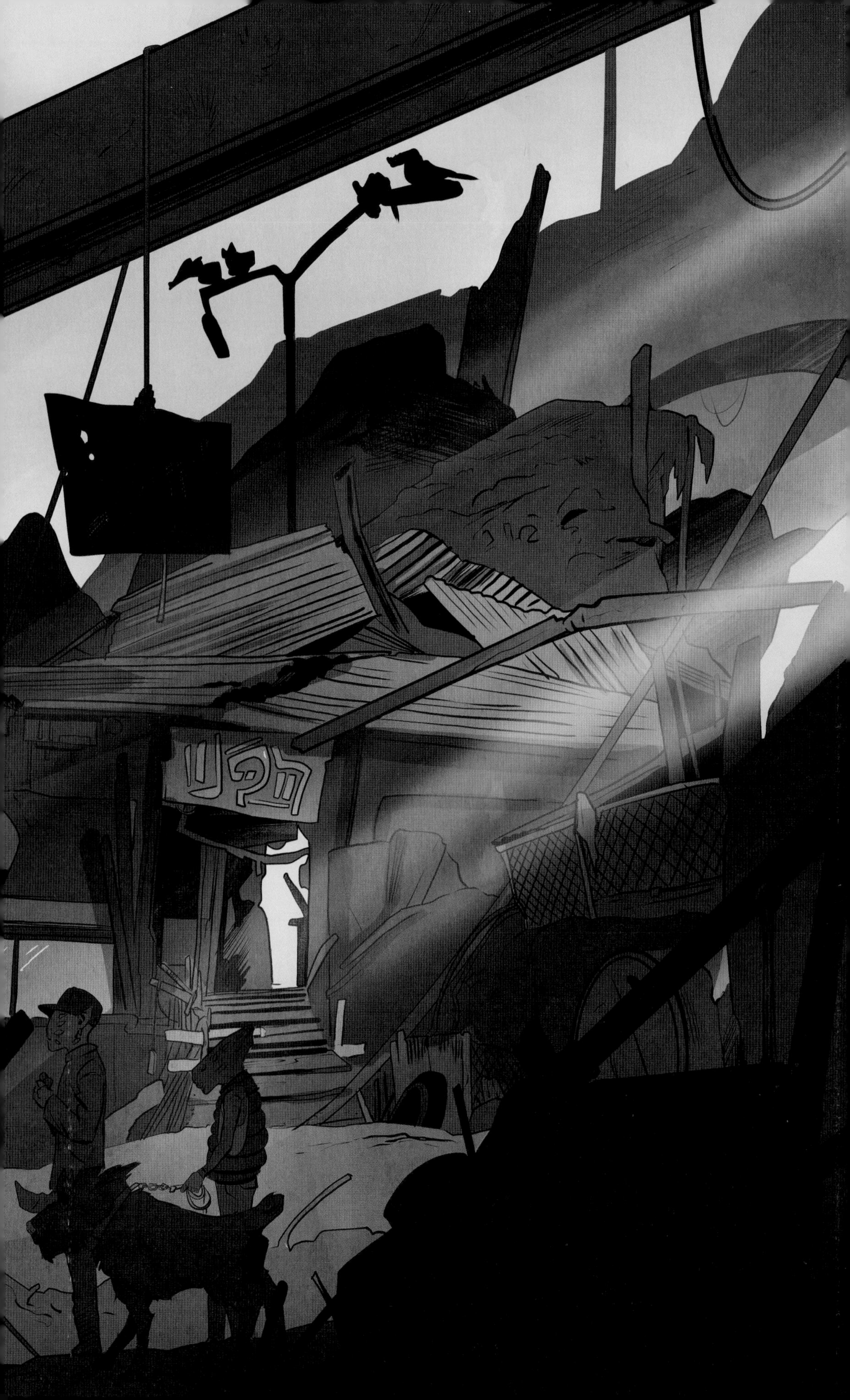

MOMENTS EARLIER...

DO NOT MOVE!

WE HAVE THE INFILTRATOR SURROUN—

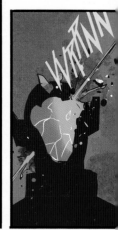

WRRNN

SEND THE BLACK-HEARTED BASTARDS TO HELL!

CAPTURE THE HUMAN! DON'T LET HIM GET AWAY!

NO, NO.

LET THE HUMAN GET AWAY.

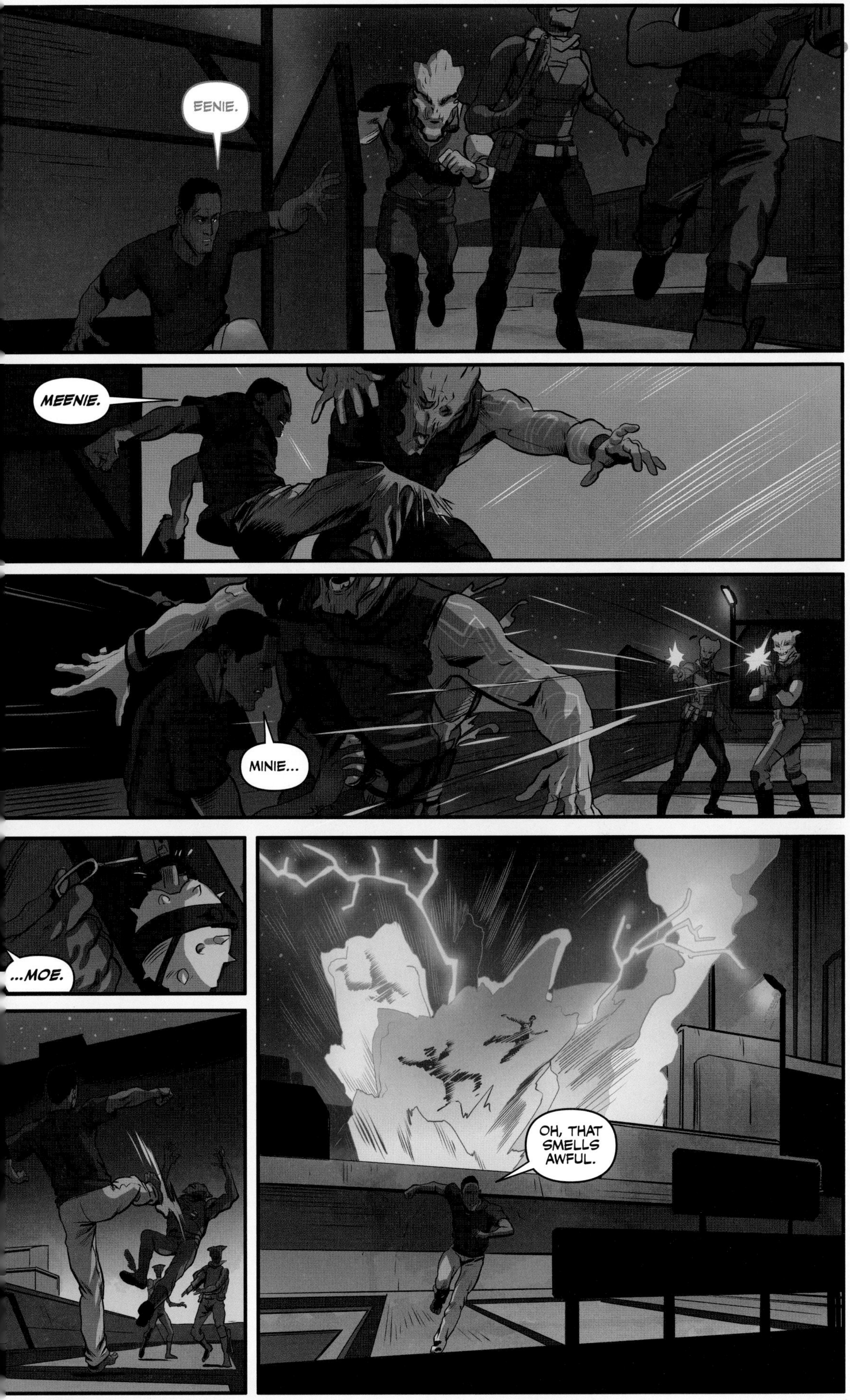
EENIE.
MEENIE.
MINIE...
...MOE.
OH, THAT SMELLS AWFUL.

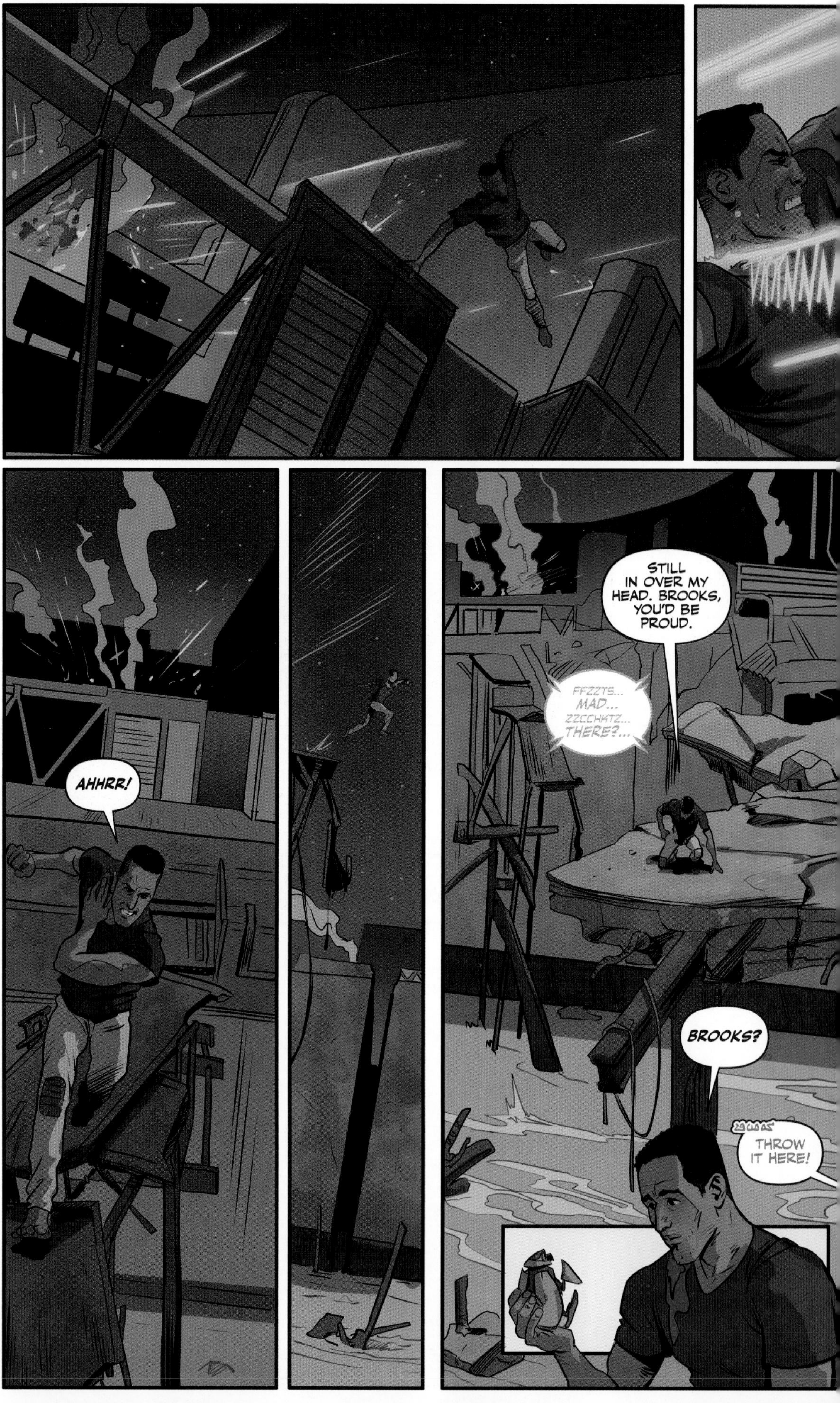
AHHRR!
STILL IN OVER MY HEAD. BROOKS, YOU'D BE PROUD.
FFZZTS... MAD... ZZCCHKTZ... THERE?...
BROOKS?
THROW IT HERE!

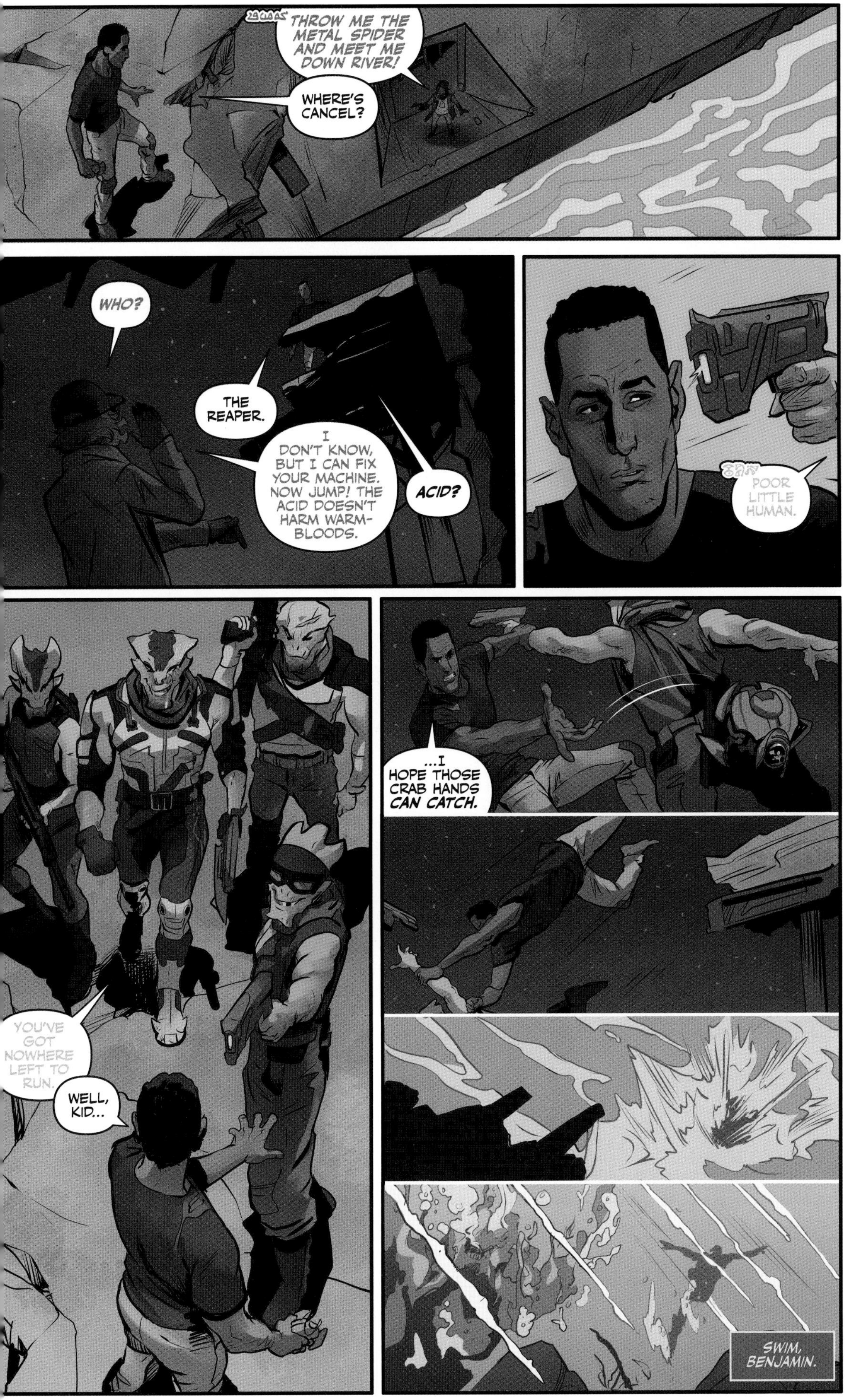
THROW ME THE METAL SPIDER AND MEET ME DOWN RIVER!
WHERE'S CANCEL?
WHO?
THE REAPER.
I DON'T KNOW, BUT I CAN FIX YOUR MACHINE. NOW JUMP! THE ACID DOESN'T HARM WARM-BLOODS.
ACID?
POOR LITTLE HUMAN.
YOU'VE GOT NOWHERE LEFT TO RUN.
WELL, KID...
...I HOPE THOSE CRAB HANDS CAN CATCH.
SWIM, BENJAMIN.

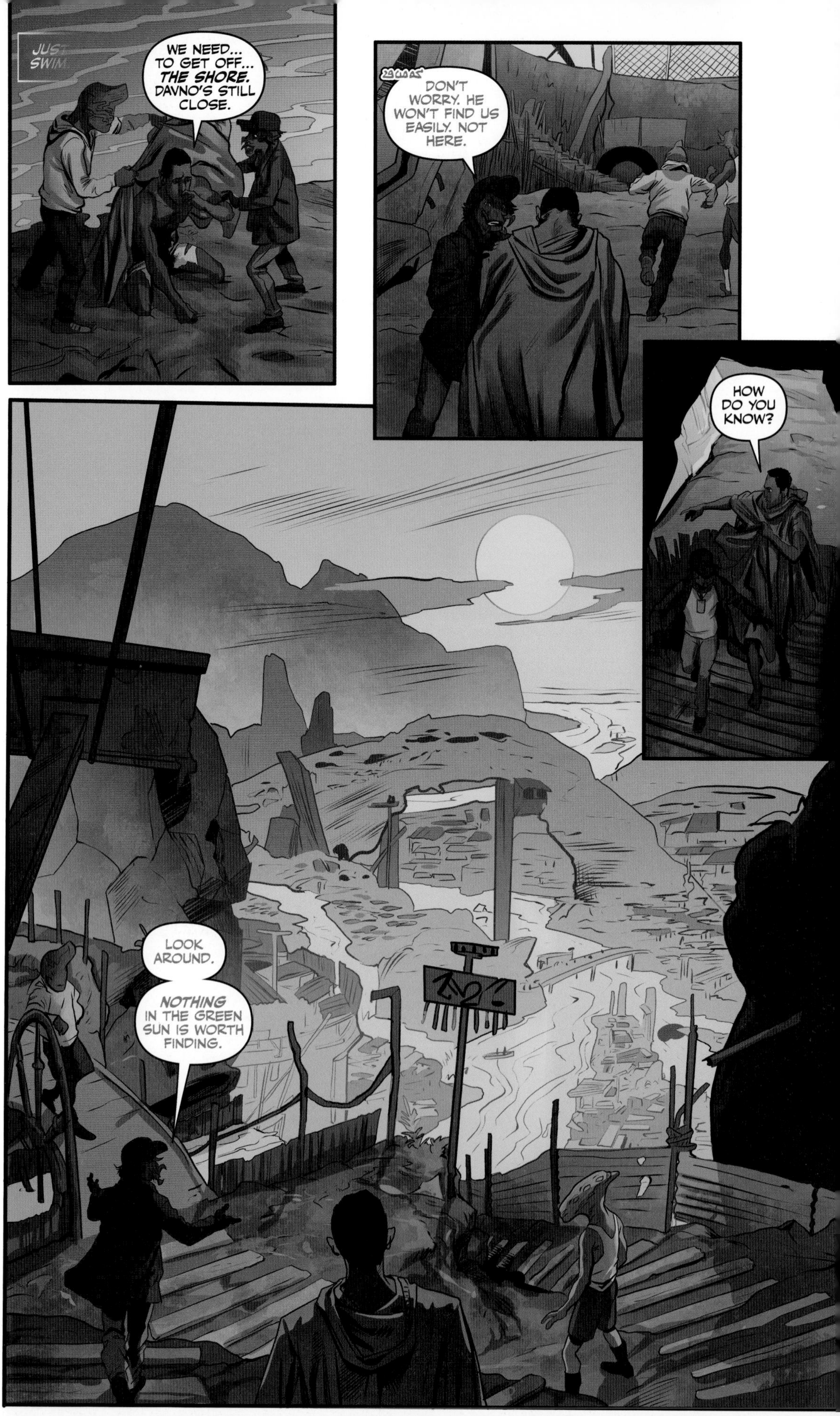
WE NEED... TO GET OFF... THE SHORE. DAVNO'S STILL CLOSE.
DON'T WORRY. HE WON'T FIND US EASILY. NOT HERE.
HOW DO YOU KNOW?
LOOK AROUND.
NOTHING IN THE GREEN SUN IS WORTH FINDING.

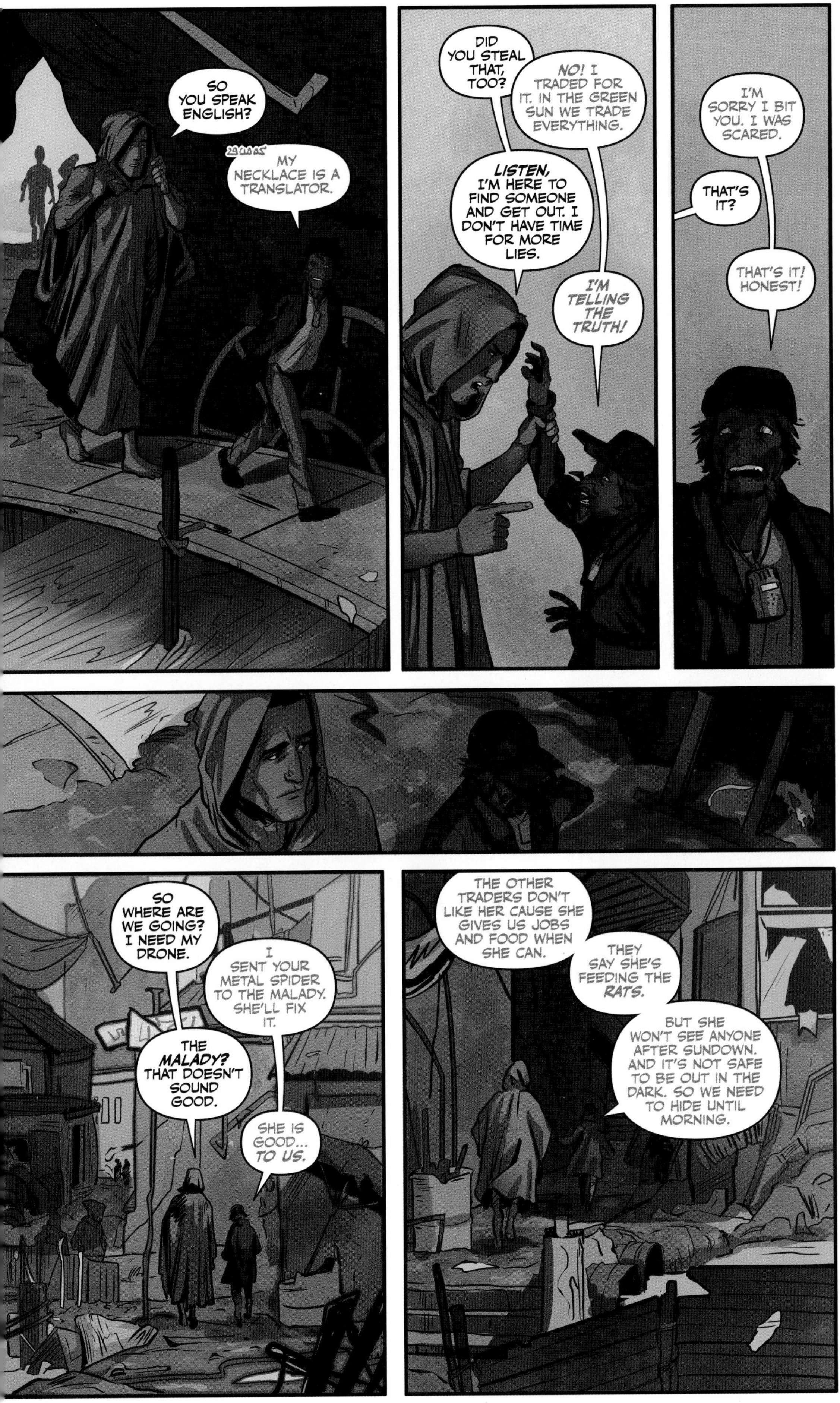

SO YOU SPEAK ENGLISH?
MY NECKLACE IS A TRANSLATOR.
DID YOU STEAL THAT, TOO?
NO! I TRADED FOR IT. IN THE GREEN SUN WE TRADE EVERYTHING.
LISTEN, I'M HERE TO FIND SOMEONE AND GET OUT. I DON'T HAVE TIME FOR MORE LIES.
I'M TELLING THE TRUTH!
I'M SORRY I BIT YOU. I WAS SCARED.
THAT'S IT?
THAT'S IT! HONEST!
SO WHERE ARE WE GOING? I NEED MY DRONE.
I SENT YOUR METAL SPIDER TO THE MALADY. SHE'LL FIX IT.
THE MALADY? THAT DOESN'T SOUND GOOD.
SHE IS GOOD... TO US.
THE OTHER TRADERS DON'T LIKE HER CAUSE SHE GIVES US JOBS AND FOOD WHEN SHE CAN.
THEY SAY SHE'S FEEDING THE RATS.
BUT SHE WON'T SEE ANYONE AFTER SUNDOWN. AND IT'S NOT SAFE TO BE OUT IN THE DARK. SO WE NEED TO HIDE UNTIL MORNING.

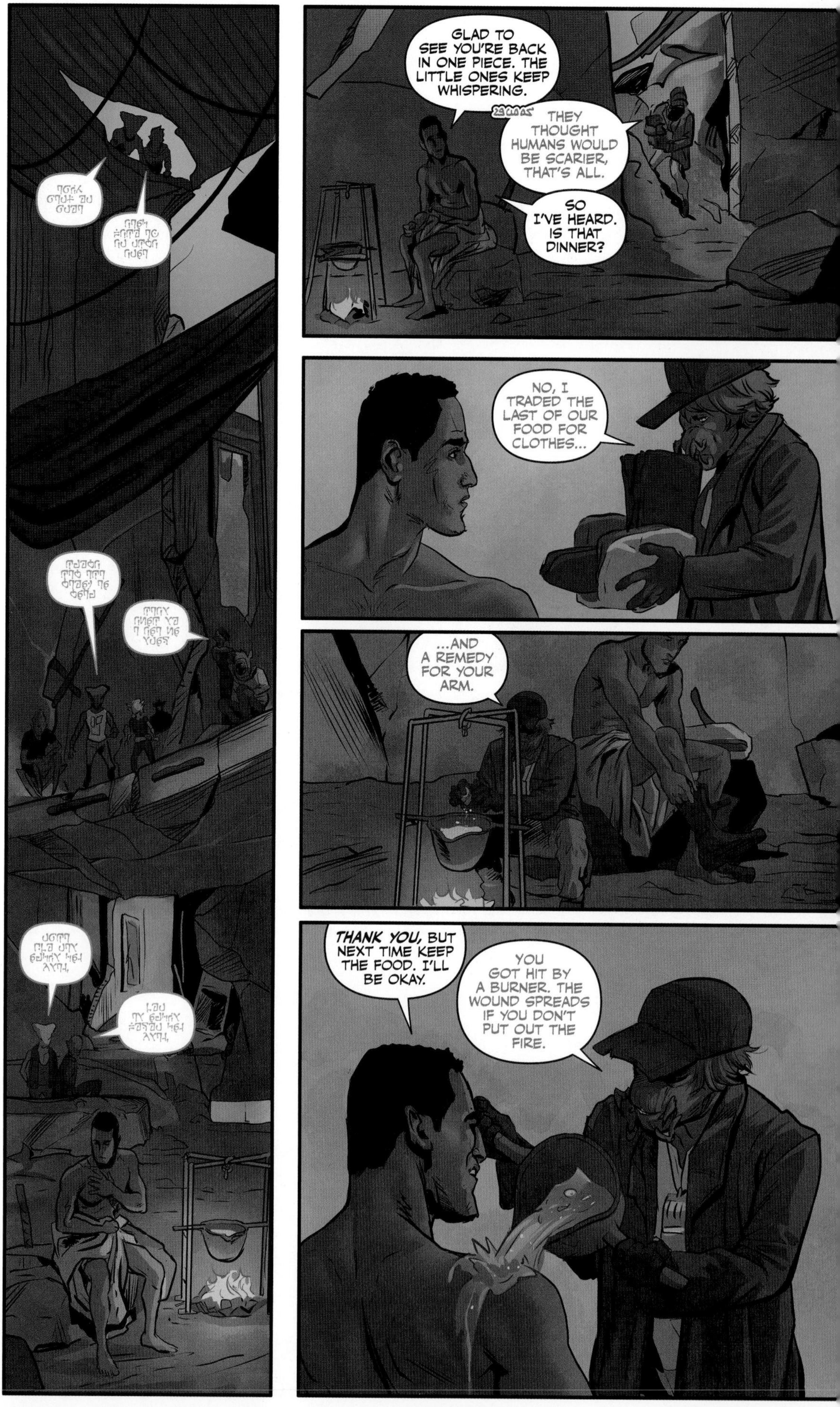
GLAD TO SEE YOU'RE BACK IN ONE PIECE. THE LITTLE ONES KEEP WHISPERING.
THEY THOUGHT HUMANS WOULD BE SCARIER, THAT'S ALL.
SO I'VE HEARD. IS THAT DINNER?
NO, I TRADED THE LAST OF OUR FOOD FOR CLOTHES...
...AND A REMEDY FOR YOUR ARM.
THANK YOU, BUT NEXT TIME KEEP THE FOOD. I'LL BE OKAY.
YOU GOT HIT BY A BURNER. THE WOUND SPREADS IF YOU DON'T PUT OUT THE FIRE.

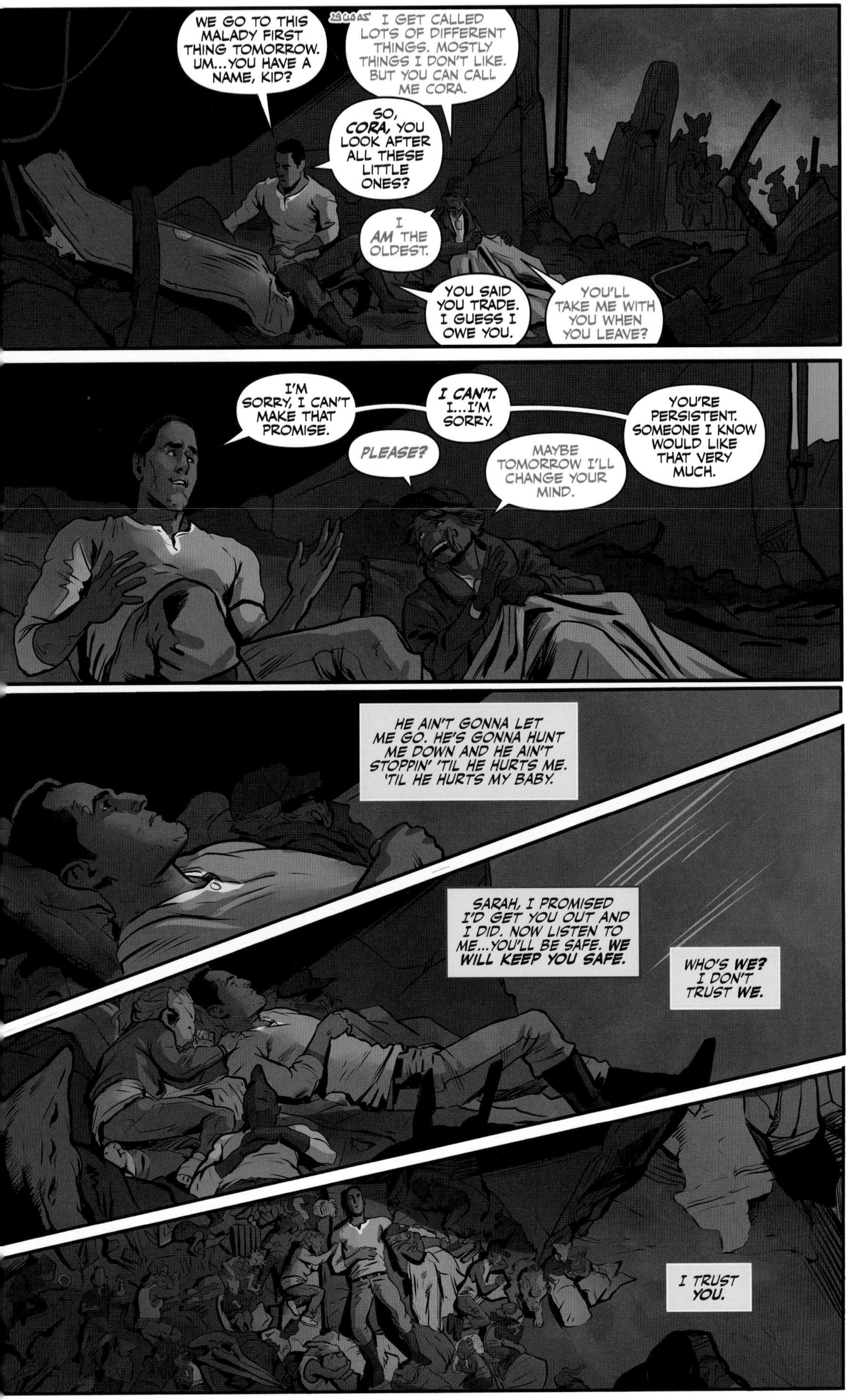
WE GO TO THIS MALADY FIRST THING TOMORROW. UM...YOU HAVE A NAME, KID?
I GET CALLED LOTS OF DIFFERENT THINGS. MOSTLY THINGS I DON'T LIKE. BUT YOU CAN CALL ME CORA.
SO, CORA, YOU LOOK AFTER ALL THESE LITTLE ONES?
I AM THE OLDEST.
YOU SAID YOU TRADE. I GUESS I OWE YOU.
YOU'LL TAKE ME WITH YOU WHEN YOU LEAVE?
I'M SORRY, I CAN'T MAKE THAT PROMISE.
PLEASE?
I CAN'T. I...I'M SORRY.
MAYBE TOMORROW I'LL CHANGE YOUR MIND.
YOU'RE PERSISTENT. SOMEONE I KNOW WOULD LIKE THAT VERY MUCH.
HE AIN'T GONNA LET ME GO. HE'S GONNA HUNT ME DOWN AND HE AIN'T STOPPIN' 'TIL HE HURTS ME. 'TIL HE HURTS MY BABY.
SARAH, I PROMISED I'D GET YOU OUT AND I DID. NOW LISTEN TO ME...YOU'LL BE SAFE. WE WILL KEEP YOU SAFE.
WHO'S WE? I DON'T TRUST WE.
I TRUST YOU.

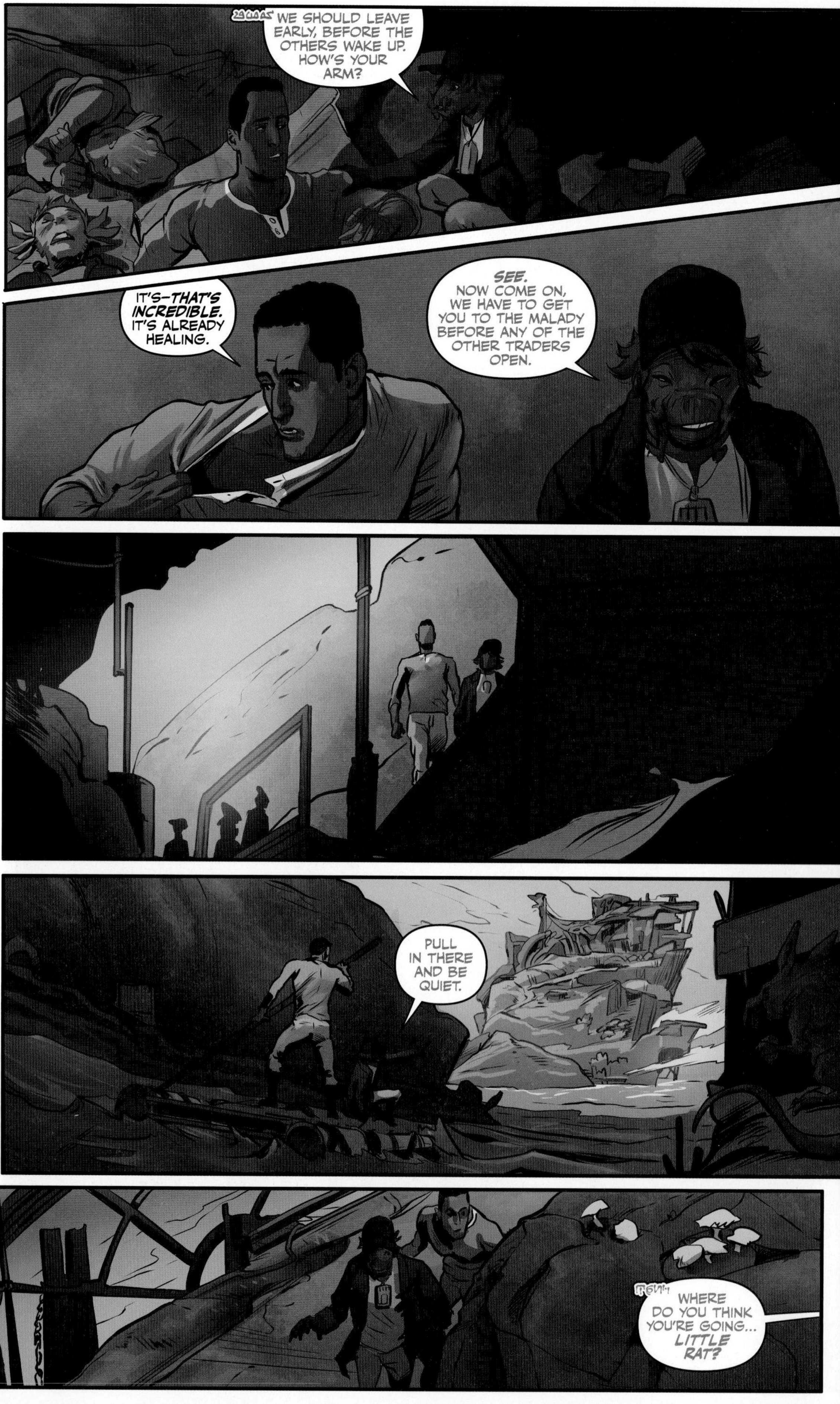
WE SHOULD LEAVE EARLY, BEFORE THE OTHERS WAKE UP. HOW'S YOUR ARM?
IT'S—*THAT'S* *INCREDIBLE.* IT'S ALREADY HEALING.
SEE. NOW COME ON, WE HAVE TO GET YOU TO THE MALADY BEFORE ANY OF THE OTHER TRADERS OPEN.
PULL IN THERE AND BE QUIET.
WHERE DO YOU THINK YOU'RE GOING... *LITTLE RAT?*

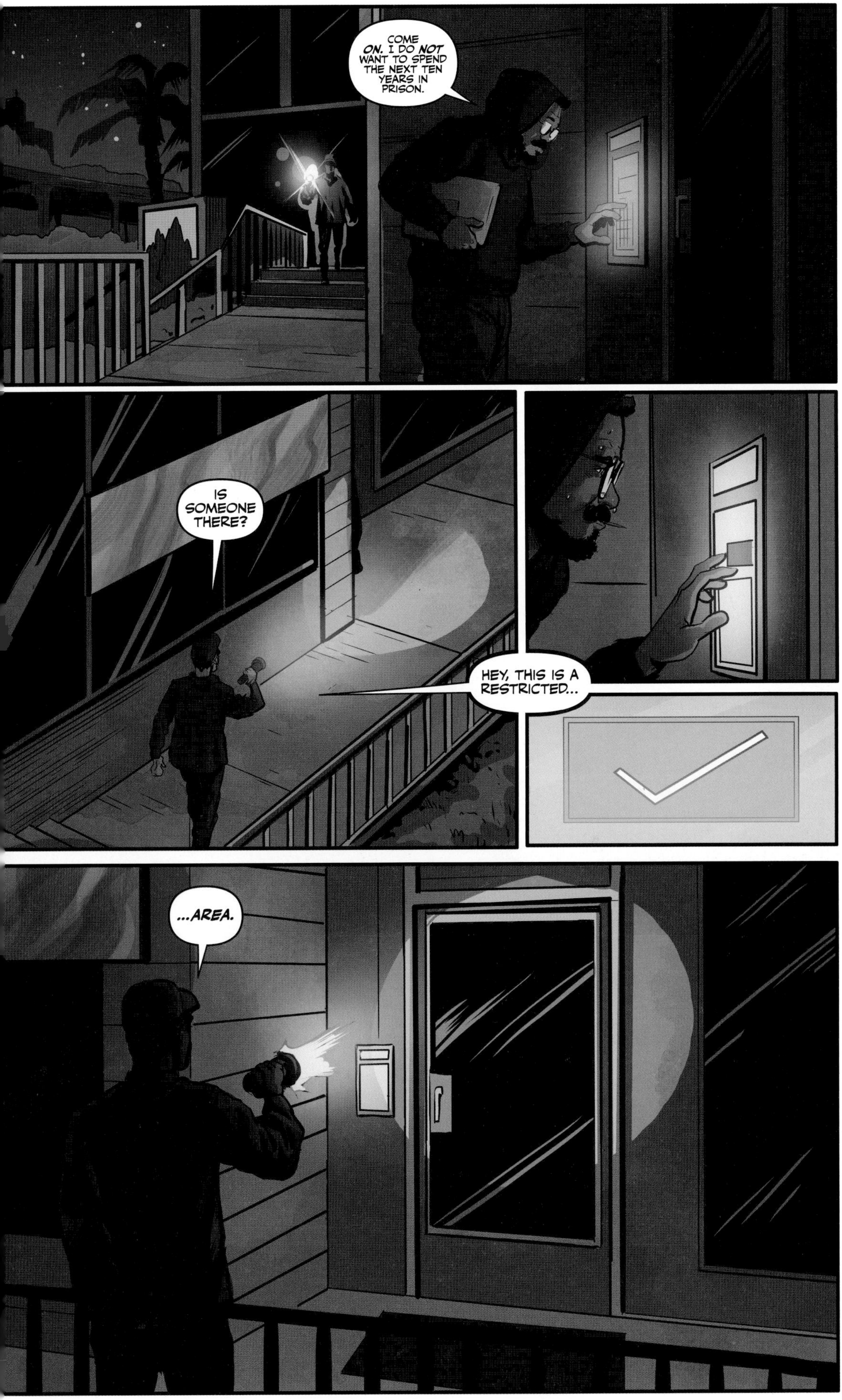
COME ON. I DO NOT WANT TO SPEND THE NEXT TEN YEARS IN PRISON.
IS SOMEONE THERE?
HEY, THIS IS A RESTRICTED...
...AREA.

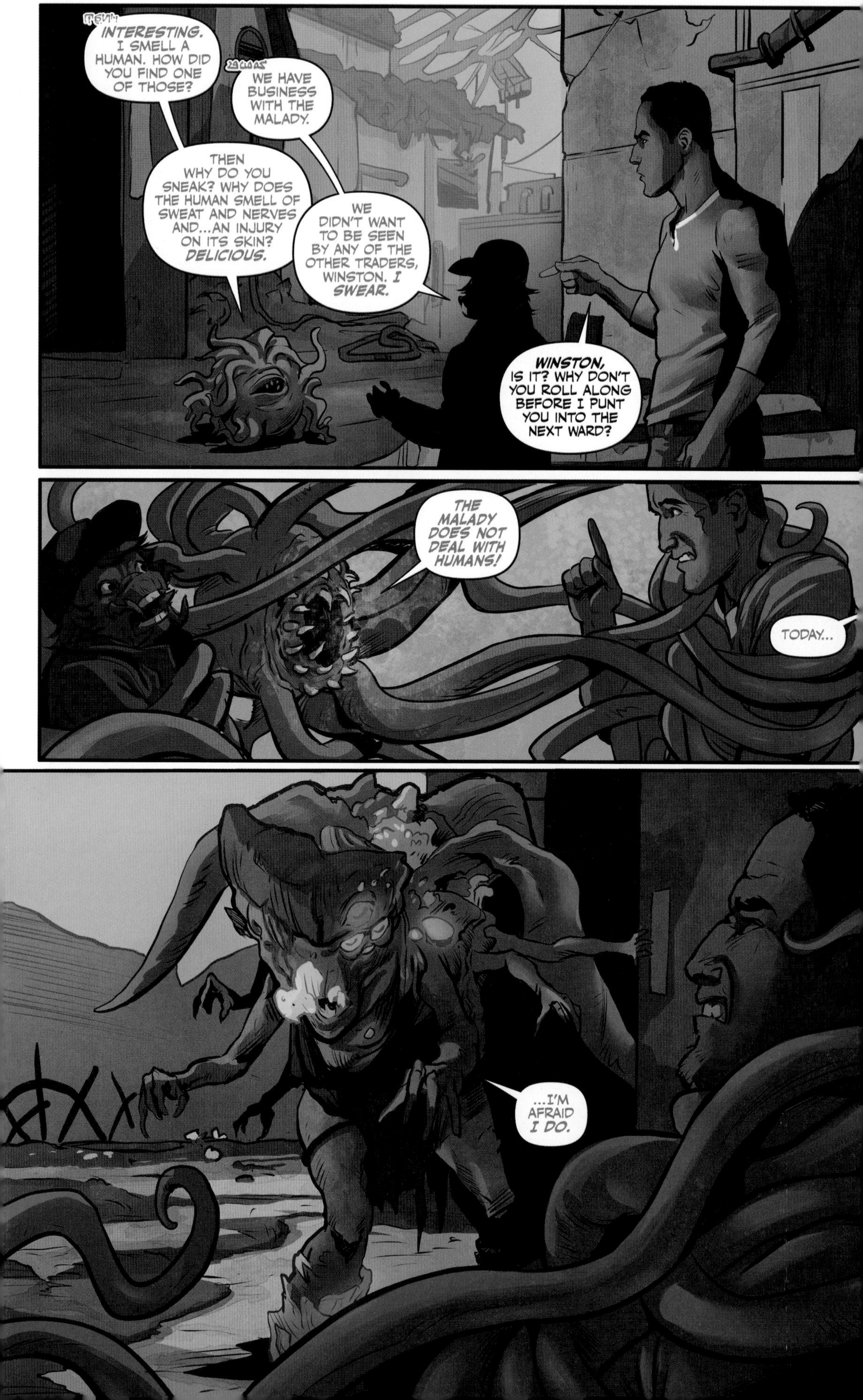
INTERESTING. I SMELL A HUMAN. HOW DID YOU FIND ONE OF THOSE?
WE HAVE BUSINESS WITH THE MALADY.
THEN WHY DO YOU SNEAK? WHY DOES THE HUMAN SMELL OF SWEAT AND NERVES AND...AN INJURY ON ITS SKIN? DELICIOUS.
WE DIDN'T WANT TO BE SEEN BY ANY OF THE OTHER TRADERS, WINSTON. I SWEAR.
WINSTON, IS IT? WHY DON'T YOU ROLL ALONG BEFORE I PUNT YOU INTO THE NEXT WARD?
THE MALADY DOES NOT DEAL WITH HUMANS!
TODAY...
...I'M AFRAID I DO.

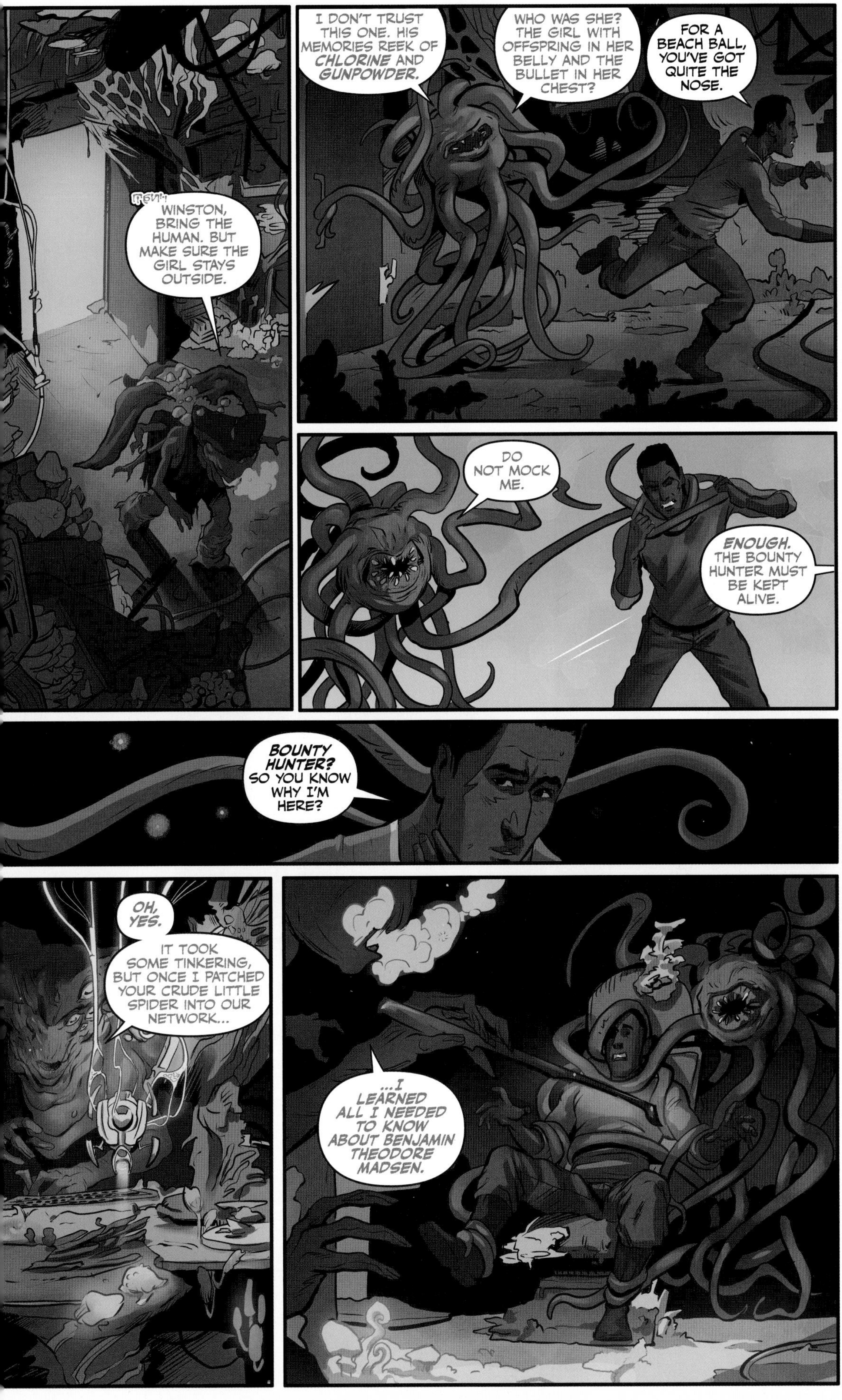
WINSTON, BRING THE HUMAN. BUT MAKE SURE THE GIRL STAYS OUTSIDE.
I DON'T TRUST THIS ONE. HIS MEMORIES REEK OF CHLORINE AND GUNPOWDER.
WHO WAS SHE? THE GIRL WITH OFFSPRING IN HER BELLY AND THE BULLET IN HER CHEST?
FOR A BEACH BALL, YOU'VE GOT QUITE THE NOSE.
DO NOT MOCK ME.
ENOUGH. THE BOUNTY HUNTER MUST BE KEPT ALIVE.
BOUNTY HUNTER? SO YOU KNOW WHY I'M HERE?
OH, YES.
IT TOOK SOME TINKERING, BUT ONCE I PATCHED YOUR CRUDE LITTLE SPIDER INTO OUR NETWORK...
...I LEARNED ALL I NEEDED TO KNOW ABOUT BENJAMIN THEODORE MADSEN.

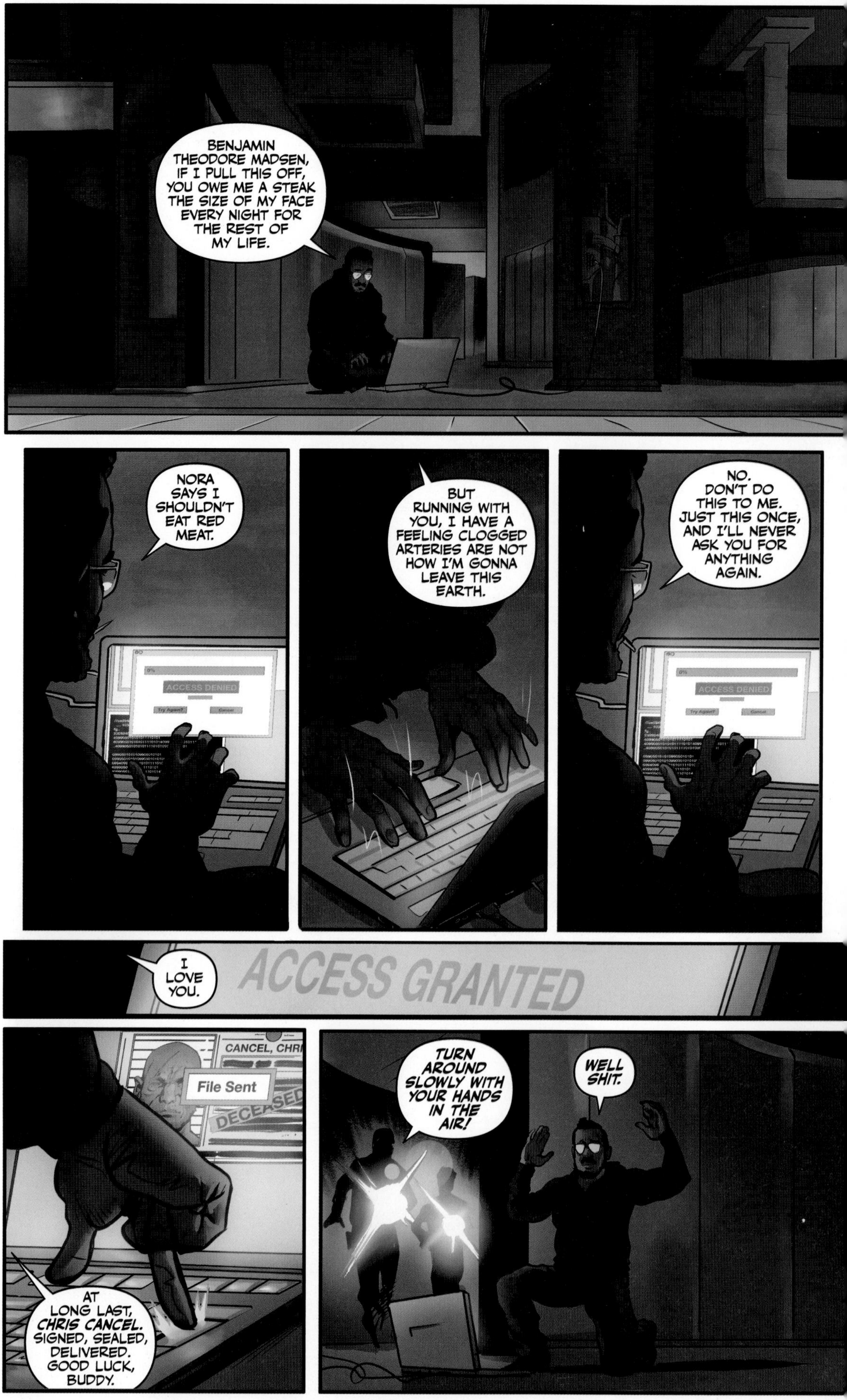
BENJAMIN THEODORE MADSEN, IF I PULL THIS OFF, YOU OWE ME A STEAK THE SIZE OF MY FACE EVERY NIGHT FOR THE REST OF MY LIFE.
NORA SAYS I SHOULDN'T EAT RED MEAT.
ACCESS DENIED
Try Again?
Cancel
BUT RUNNING WITH YOU, I HAVE A FEELING CLOGGED ARTERIES ARE NOT HOW I'M GONNA LEAVE THIS EARTH.
NO. DON'T DO THIS TO ME. JUST THIS ONCE, AND I'LL NEVER ASK YOU FOR ANYTHING AGAIN.
ACCESS DENIED
Try Again?
Cancel
I LOVE YOU.
ACCESS GRANTED
CANCEL, CHRI
File Sent
DECEASED
AT LONG LAST, CHRIS CANCEL. SIGNED, SEALED, DELIVERED. GOOD LUCK, BUDDY.
TURN AROUND SLOWLY WITH YOUR HANDS IN THE AIR!
WELL SHIT.

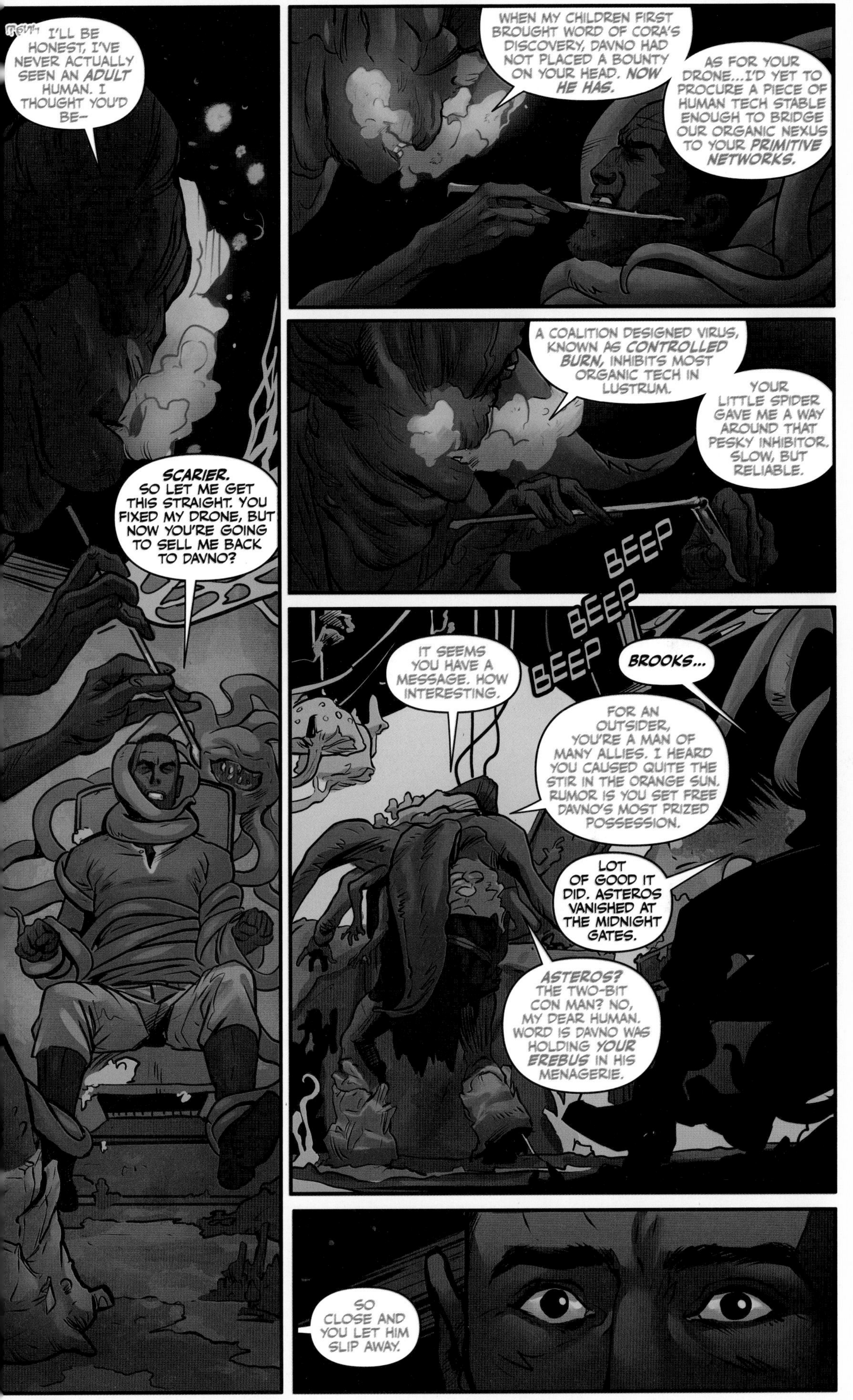

I'LL BE HONEST, I'VE NEVER ACTUALLY SEEN AN *ADULT* HUMAN. I THOUGHT YOU'D BE-
SCARIER. SO LET ME GET THIS STRAIGHT. YOU FIXED MY DRONE, BUT NOW YOU'RE GOING TO SELL ME BACK TO DAVNO?
WHEN MY CHILDREN FIRST BROUGHT WORD OF CORA'S DISCOVERY, DAVNO HAD NOT PLACED A BOUNTY ON YOUR HEAD. *NOW HE HAS.*
AS FOR YOUR DRONE...I'D YET TO PROCURE A PIECE OF HUMAN TECH STABLE ENOUGH TO BRIDGE OUR ORGANIC NEXUS TO YOUR *PRIMITIVE NETWORKS.*
A COALITION DESIGNED VIRUS, KNOWN AS *CONTROLLED BURN,* INHIBITS MOST ORGANIC TECH IN LUSTRUM.
YOUR LITTLE SPIDER GAVE ME A WAY AROUND THAT PESKY INHIBITOR. SLOW, BUT RELIABLE.
BEEP
BEEP
BEEP
IT SEEMS YOU HAVE A MESSAGE. HOW INTERESTING.
BROOKS...
FOR AN OUTSIDER, YOU'RE A MAN OF MANY ALLIES. I HEARD YOU CAUSED QUITE THE STIR IN THE ORANGE SUN. RUMOR IS YOU SET FREE DAVNO'S MOST PRIZED POSSESSION.
LOT OF GOOD IT DID. ASTEROS VANISHED AT THE MIDNIGHT GATES.
ASTEROS? THE TWO-BIT CON MAN? NO, MY DEAR HUMAN. WORD IS DAVNO WAS HOLDING *YOUR EREBUS* IN HIS MENAGERIE.
SO CLOSE AND YOU LET HIM SLIP AWAY.

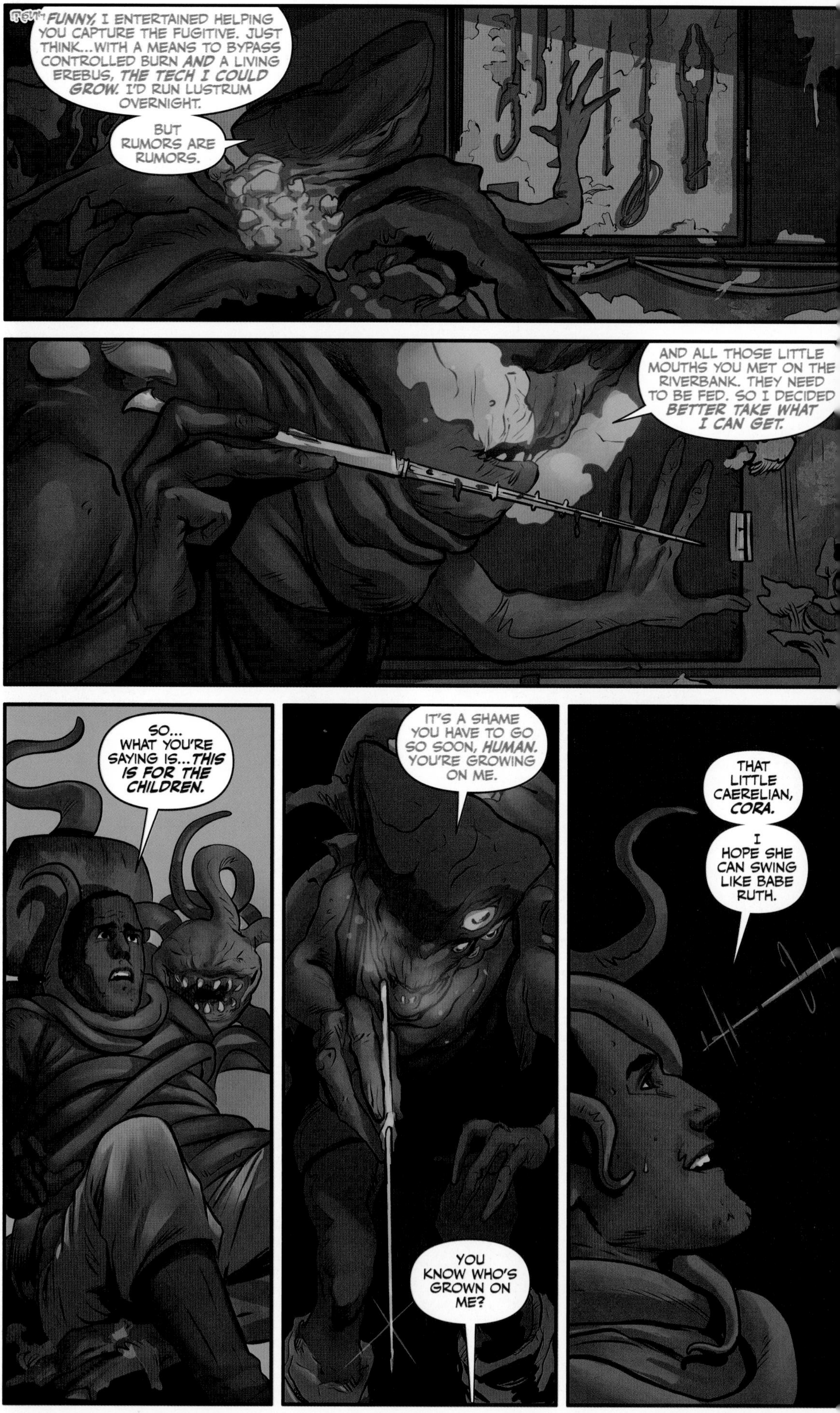
FUNNY, I ENTERTAINED HELPING YOU CAPTURE THE FUGITIVE. JUST THINK...WITH A MEANS TO BYPASS CONTROLLED BURN AND A LIVING EREBUS, THE TECH I COULD GROW. I'D RUN LUSTRUM OVERNIGHT.
BUT RUMORS ARE RUMORS.
AND ALL THOSE LITTLE MOUTHS YOU MET ON THE RIVERBANK. THEY NEED TO BE FED. SO I DECIDED BETTER TAKE WHAT I CAN GET.
SO... WHAT YOU'RE SAYING IS...THIS IS FOR THE CHILDREN.
IT'S A SHAME YOU HAVE TO GO SO SOON, HUMAN. YOU'RE GROWING ON ME.
YOU KNOW WHO'S GROWN ON ME?
THAT LITTLE CAERELIAN, CORA.
I HOPE SHE CAN SWING LIKE BABE RUTH.

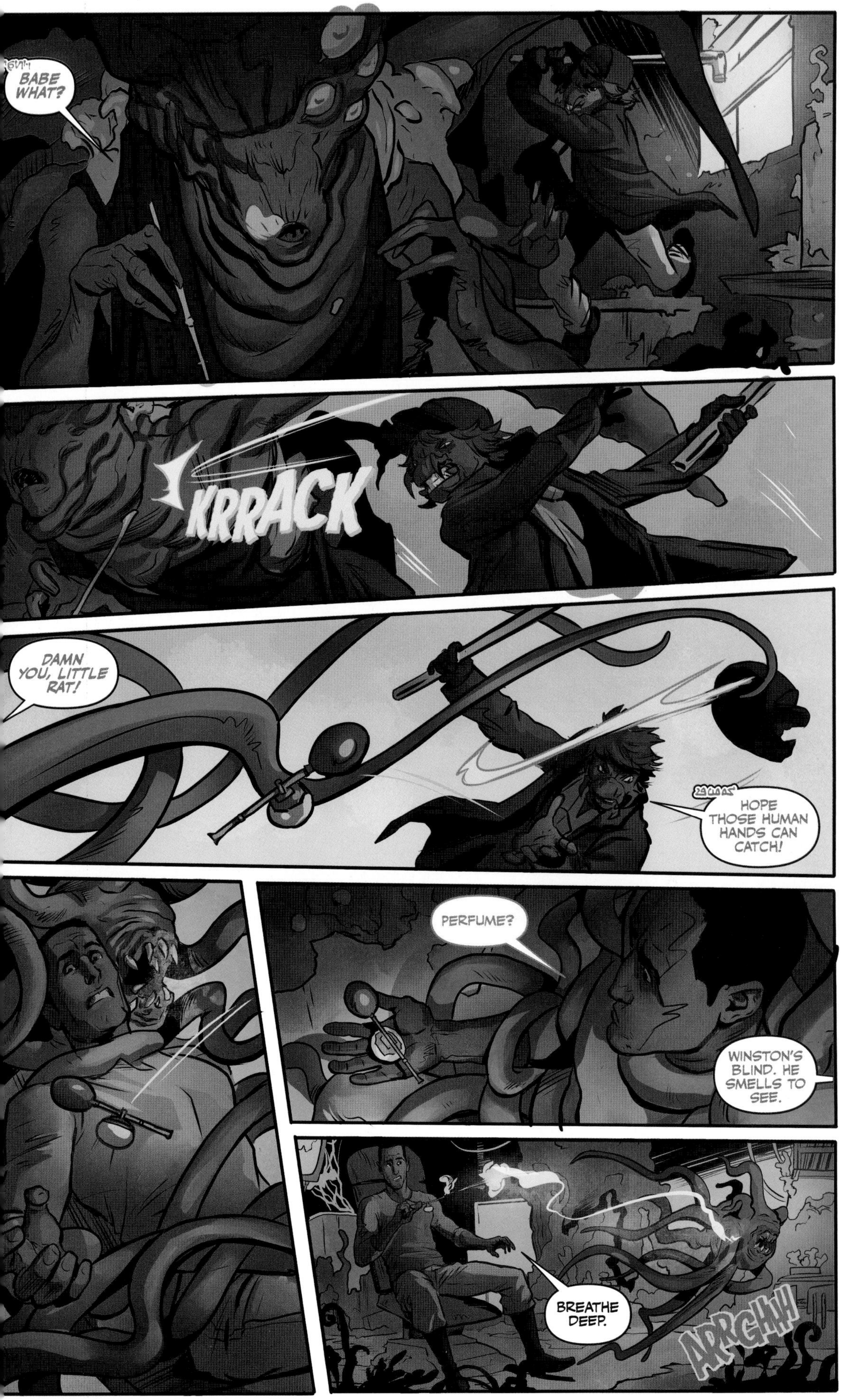
BABE
WHAT?
KRRACK
DAMN YOU, LITTLE RAT!
HOPE THOSE HUMAN HANDS CAN CATCH!
PERFUME?
WINSTON'S BLIND. HE SMELLS TO SEE.
BREATHE DEEP.
ARRGHHH

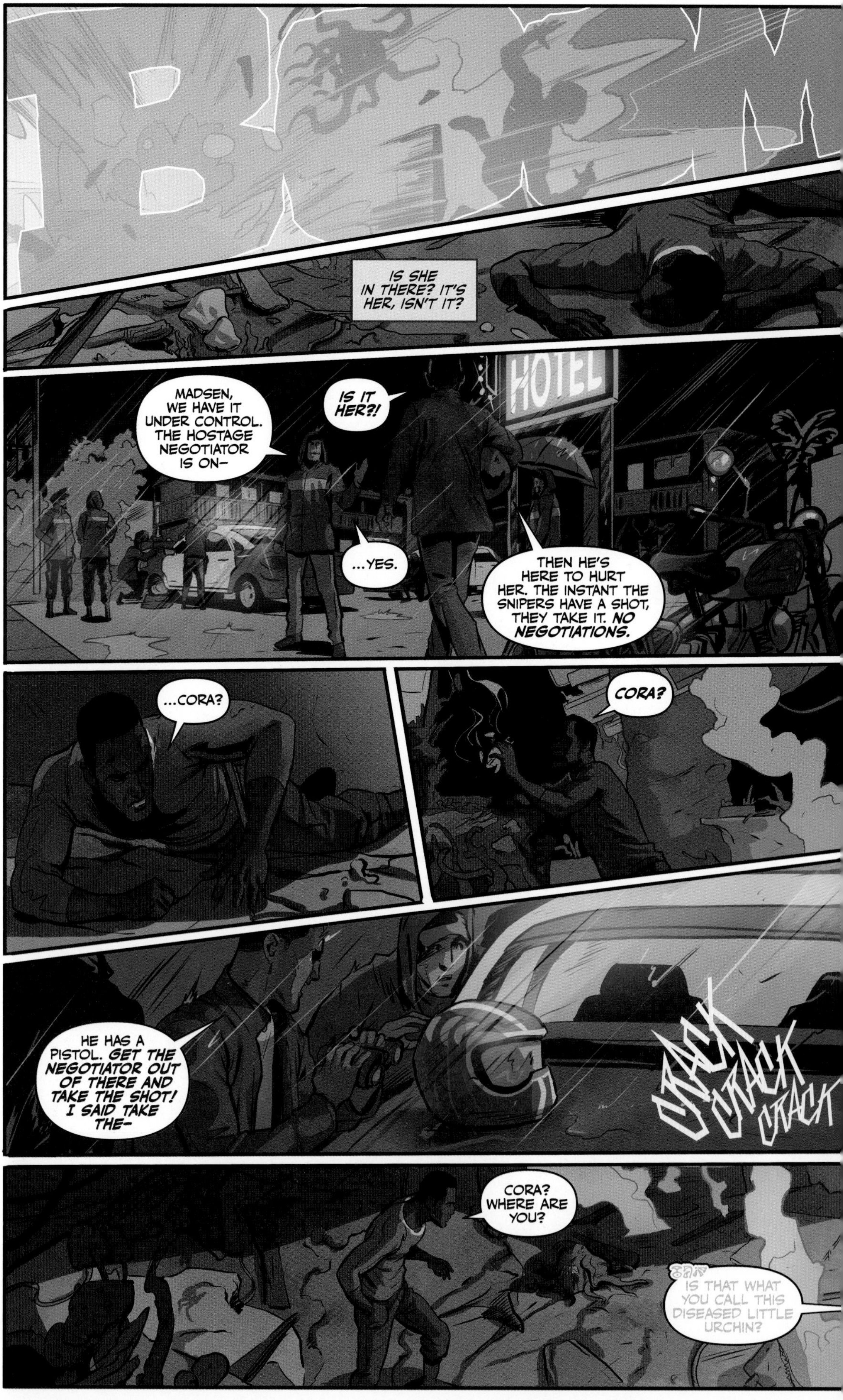

IS SHE IN THERE? IT'S HER, ISN'T IT?
MADSEN, WE HAVE IT UNDER CONTROL. THE HOSTAGE NEGOTIATOR IS ON–
IS IT HER?!
HOTEL
...YES.
THEN HE'S HERE TO HURT HER. THE INSTANT THE SNIPERS HAVE A SHOT, THEY TAKE IT. NO NEGOTIATIONS.
...CORA?
CORA?
HE HAS A PISTOL. GET THE NEGOTIATOR OUT OF THERE AND TAKE THE SHOT! I SAID TAKE THE–
CRACK CRACK CRACK
CORA? WHERE ARE YOU?
IS THAT WHAT YOU CALL THIS DISEASED LITTLE URCHIN?

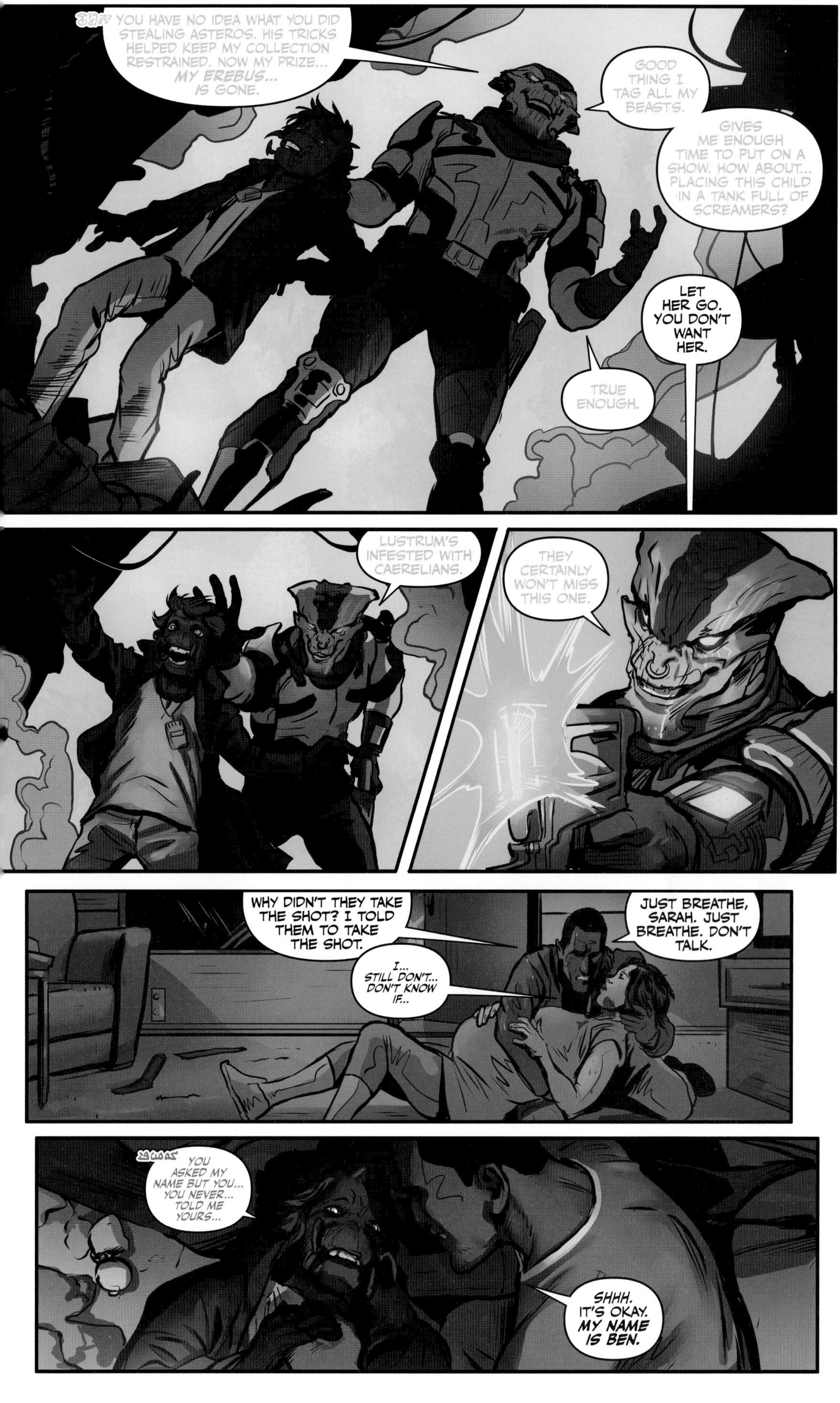
YOU HAVE NO IDEA WHAT YOU DID STEALING ASTEROS. HIS TRICKS HELPED KEEP MY COLLECTION RESTRAINED. NOW MY PRIZE... MY EREBUS... IS GONE.
GOOD THING I TAG ALL MY BEASTS.
GIVES ME ENOUGH TIME TO PUT ON A SHOW. HOW ABOUT... PLACING THIS CHILD IN A TANK FULL OF SCREAMERS?
LET HER GO. YOU DON'T WANT HER.
TRUE ENOUGH.
LUSTRUM'S INFESTED WITH CAERELIANS.
THEY CERTAINLY WON'T MISS THIS ONE.
WHY DIDN'T THEY TAKE THE SHOT? I TOLD THEM TO TAKE THE SHOT.
JUST BREATHE, SARAH. JUST BREATHE. DON'T TALK.
I... STILL DON'T... DON'T KNOW IF...
YOU ASKED MY NAME BUT YOU... YOU NEVER... TOLD ME YOURS...
SHHH. IT'S OKAY. MY NAME IS BEN.

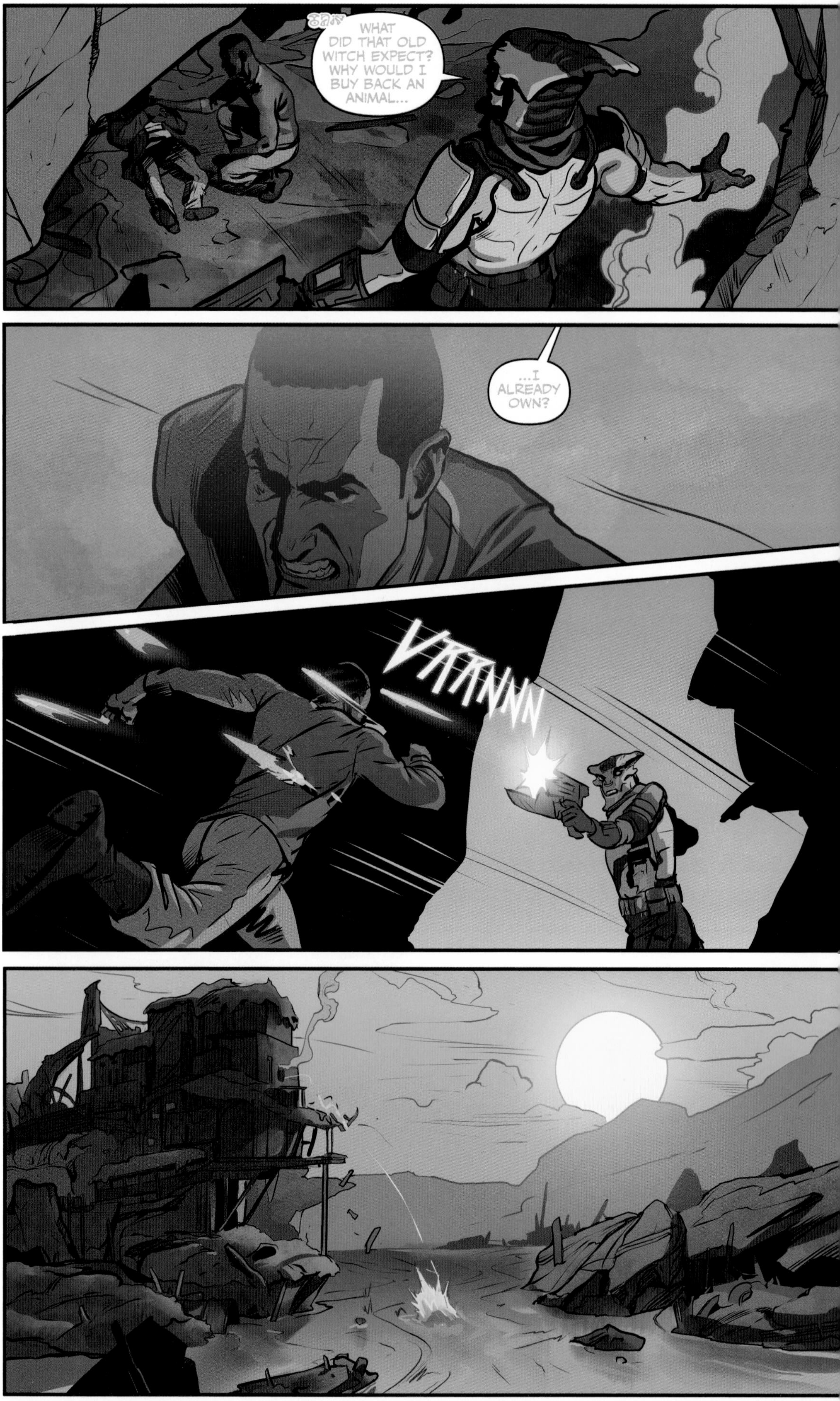
WHAT DID THAT OLD WITCH EXPECT? WHY WOULD I BUY BACK AN ANIMAL...
...I ALREADY OWN?
VRRNNN

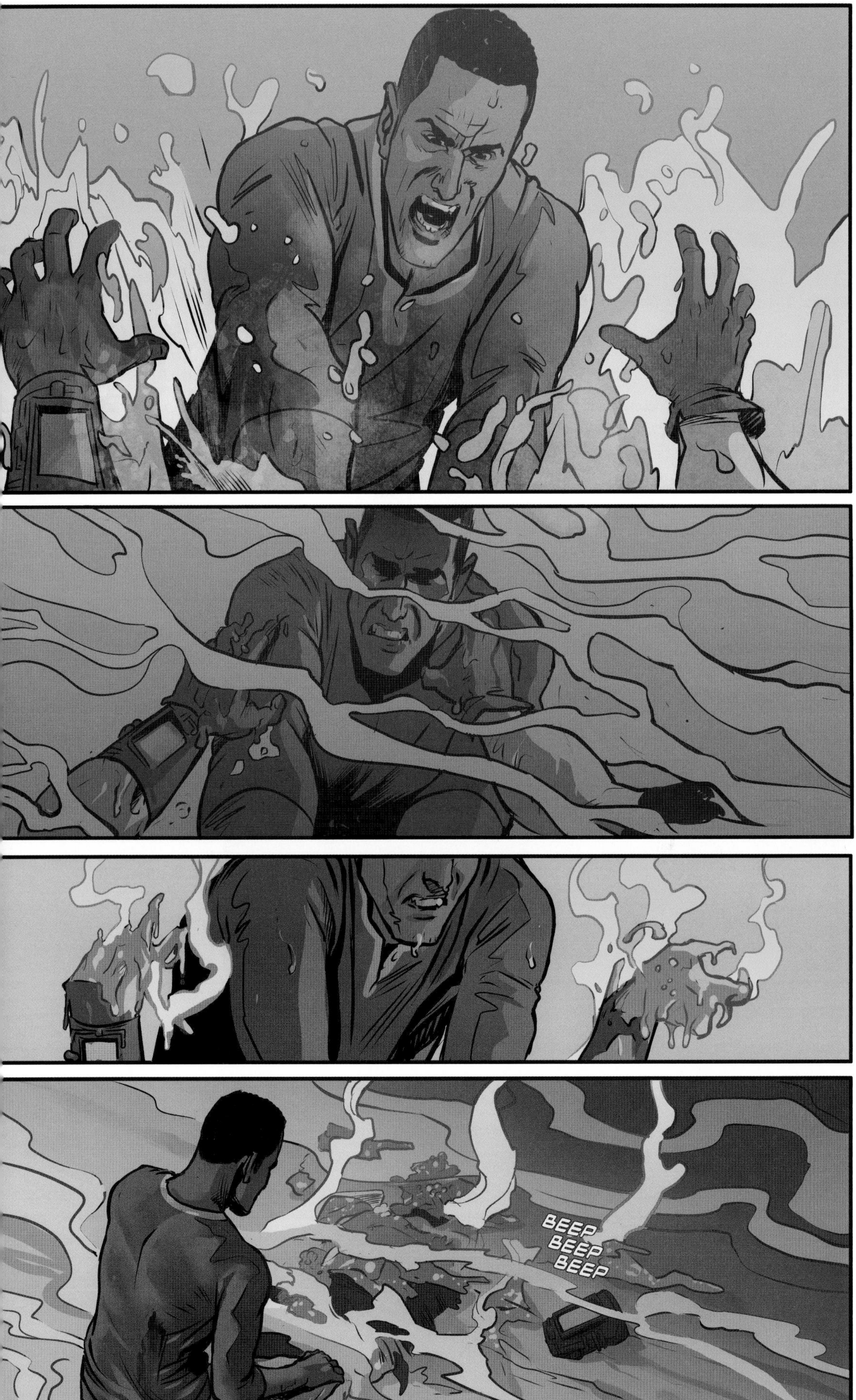
BEEP
BEEP
BEEP

BEEP
BEEP
BEEP

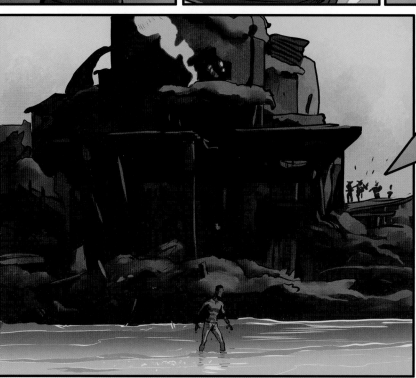

TUK TUK TUK TUK TUK TUK TUK TUK TUK TUK TUK TUK TUK TUK

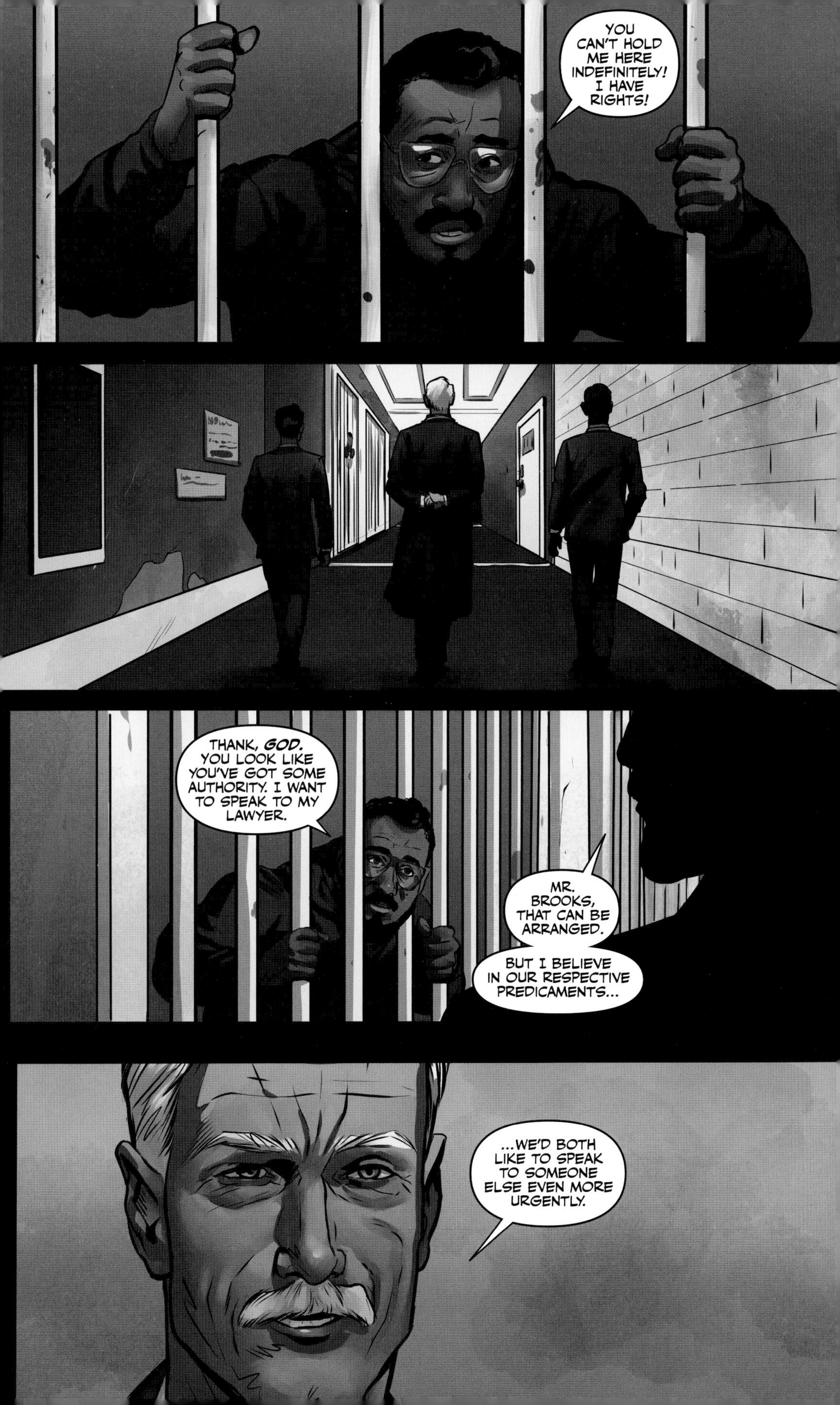
YOU CAN'T HOLD ME HERE INDEFINITELY! I HAVE RIGHTS!
THANK, *GOD.* YOU LOOK LIKE YOU'VE GOT SOME AUTHORITY. I WANT TO SPEAK TO MY LAWYER.
MR. BROOKS, THAT CAN BE ARRANGED.
BUT I BELIEVE IN OUR RESPECTIVE PREDICAMENTS...
...WE'D BOTH LIKE TO SPEAK TO SOMEONE ELSE EVEN MORE URGENTLY.

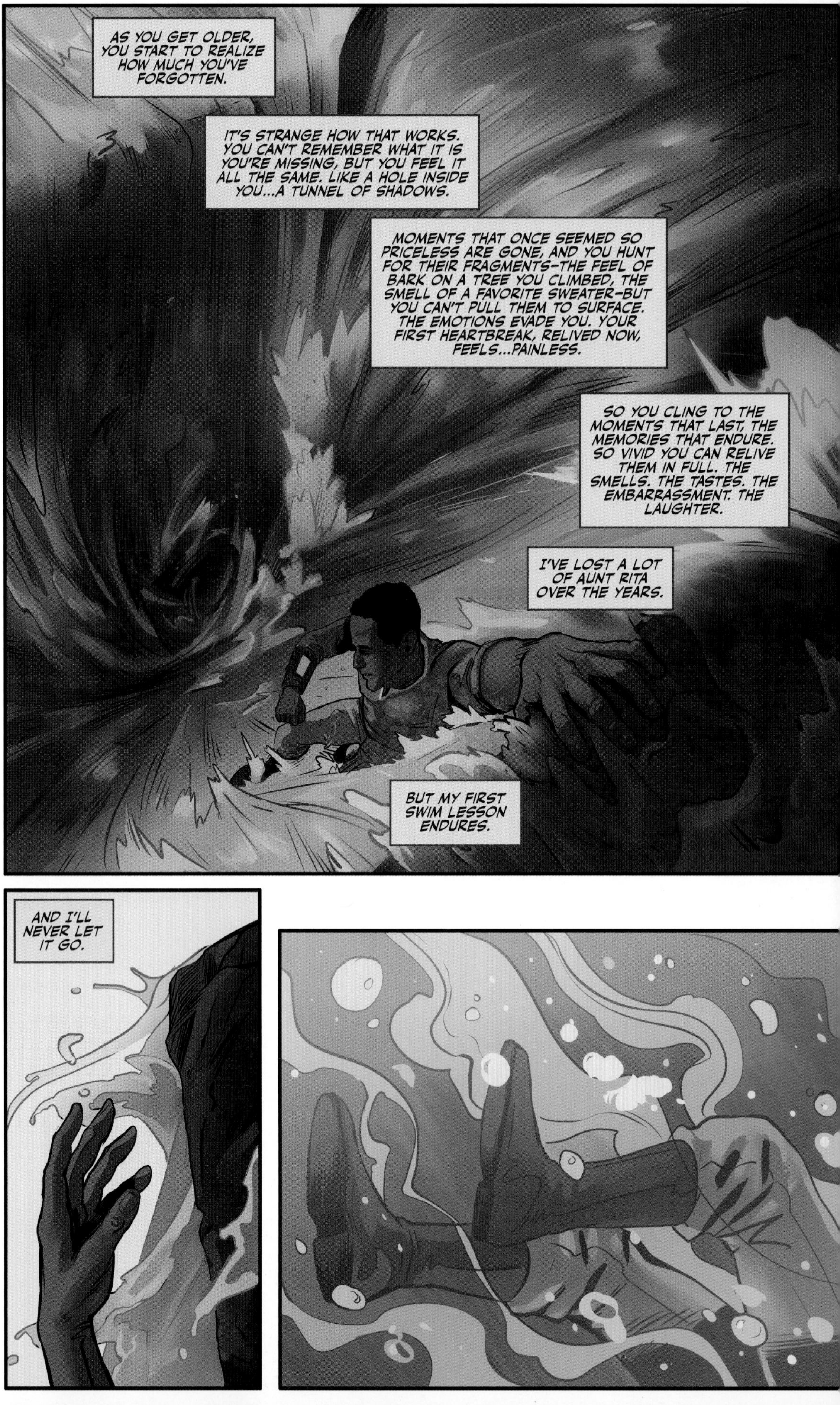
AS YOU GET OLDER, YOU START TO REALIZE HOW MUCH YOU'VE FORGOTTEN.
IT'S STRANGE HOW THAT WORKS. YOU CAN'T REMEMBER WHAT IT IS YOU'RE MISSING, BUT YOU FEEL IT ALL THE SAME. LIKE A HOLE INSIDE YOU...A TUNNEL OF SHADOWS.
MOMENTS THAT ONCE SEEMED SO PRICELESS ARE GONE, AND YOU HUNT FOR THEIR FRAGMENTS–THE FEEL OF BARK ON A TREE YOU CLIMBED, THE SMELL OF A FAVORITE SWEATER–BUT YOU CAN'T PULL THEM TO SURFACE. THE EMOTIONS EVADE YOU. YOUR FIRST HEARTBREAK, RELIVED NOW, FEELS...PAINLESS.
SO YOU CLING TO THE MOMENTS THAT LAST, THE MEMORIES THAT ENDURE. SO VIVID YOU CAN RELIVE THEM IN FULL. THE SMELLS. THE TASTES. THE EMBARRASSMENT. THE LAUGHTER.
I'VE LOST A LOT OF AUNT RITA OVER THE YEARS.
BUT MY FIRST SWIM LESSON ENDURES.
AND I'LL NEVER LET IT GO.

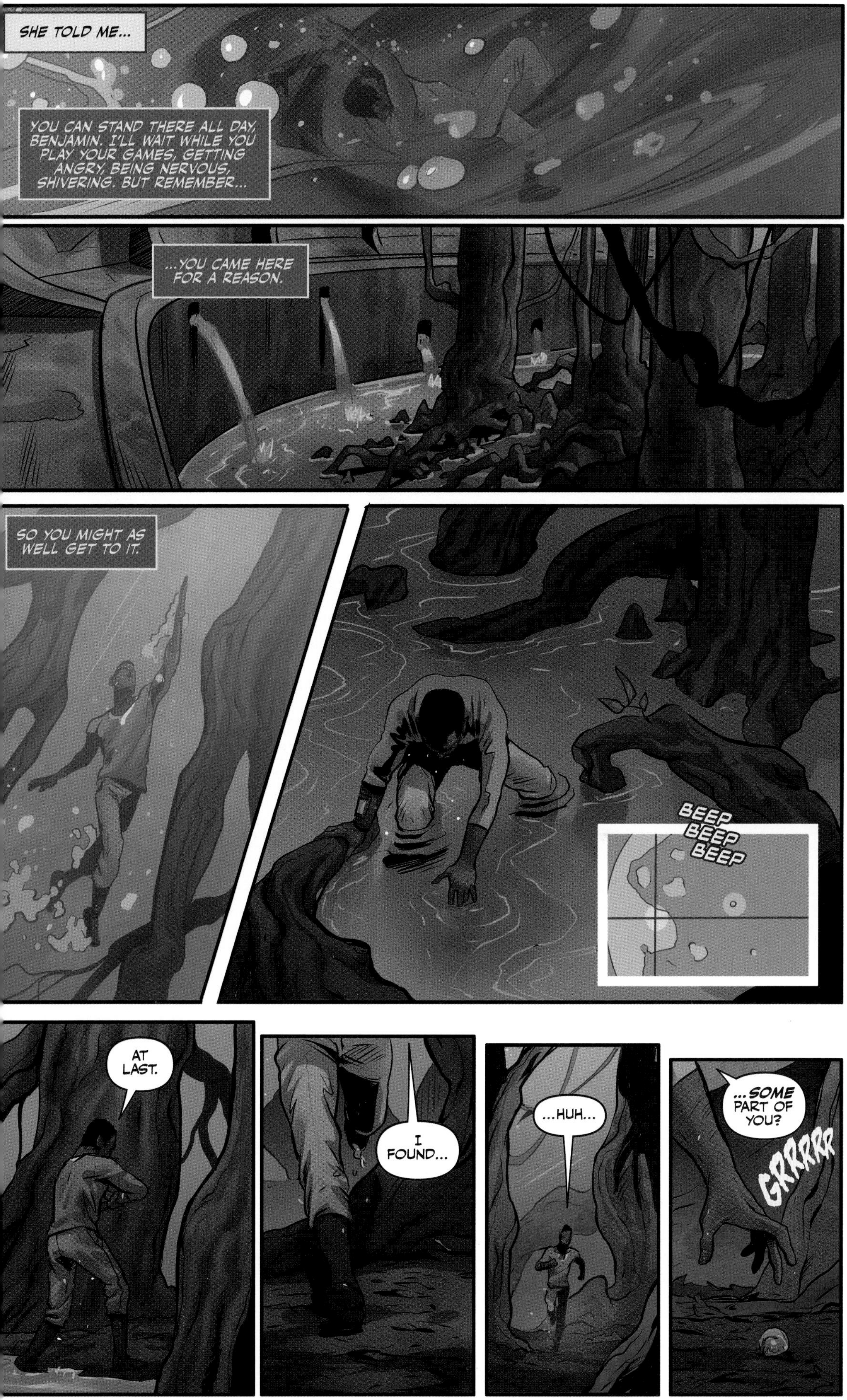
SHE TOLD ME...
YOU CAN STAND THERE ALL DAY, BENJAMIN. I'LL WAIT WHILE YOU PLAY YOUR GAMES, GETTING ANGRY, BEING NERVOUS, SHIVERING. BUT REMEMBER...
...YOU CAME HERE FOR A REASON.
SO YOU MIGHT AS WELL GET TO IT.
BEEP BEEP BEEP
AT LAST.
I FOUND...
...HUH...
...SOME PART OF YOU?
GRRRRR

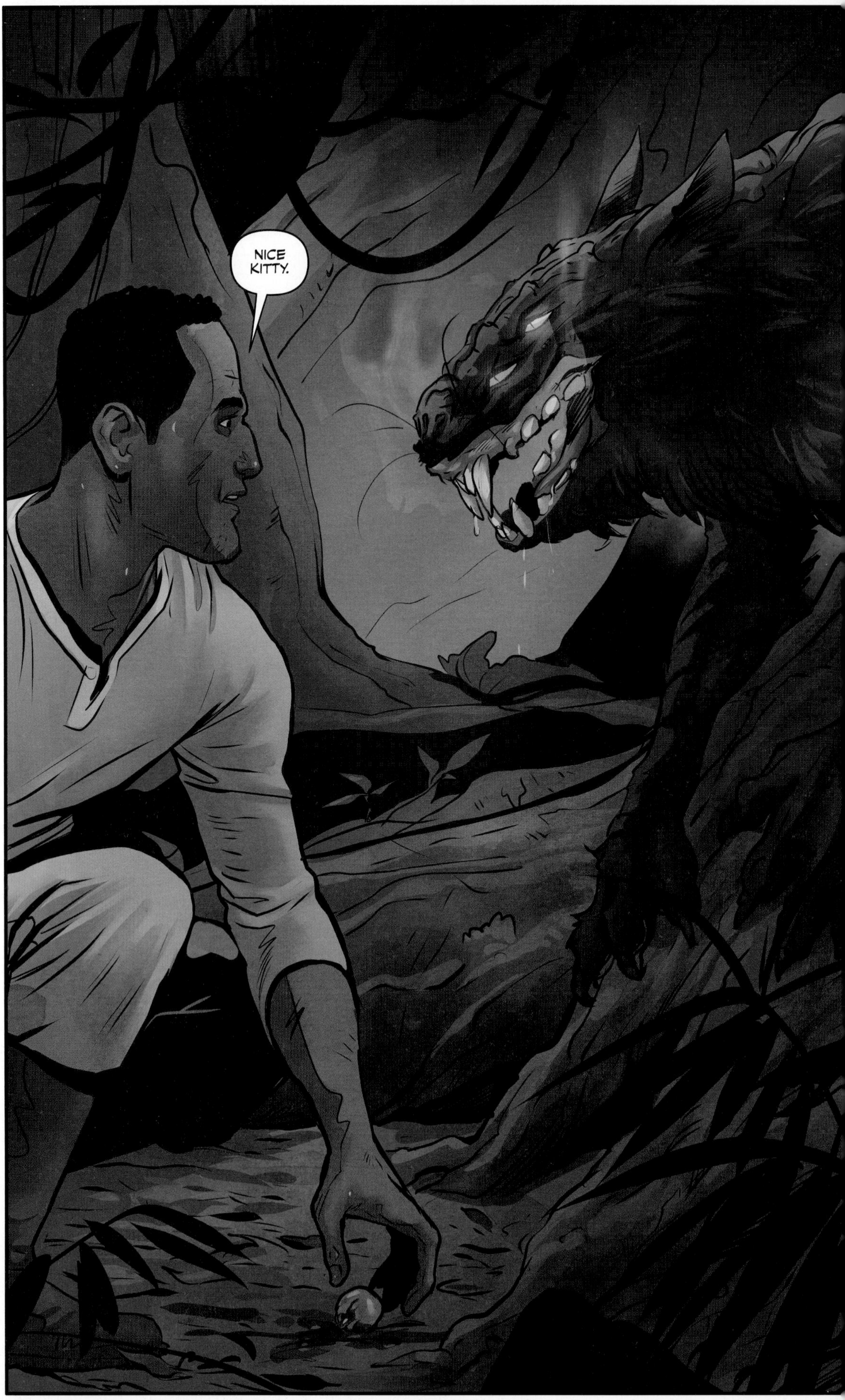
NICE KITTY.

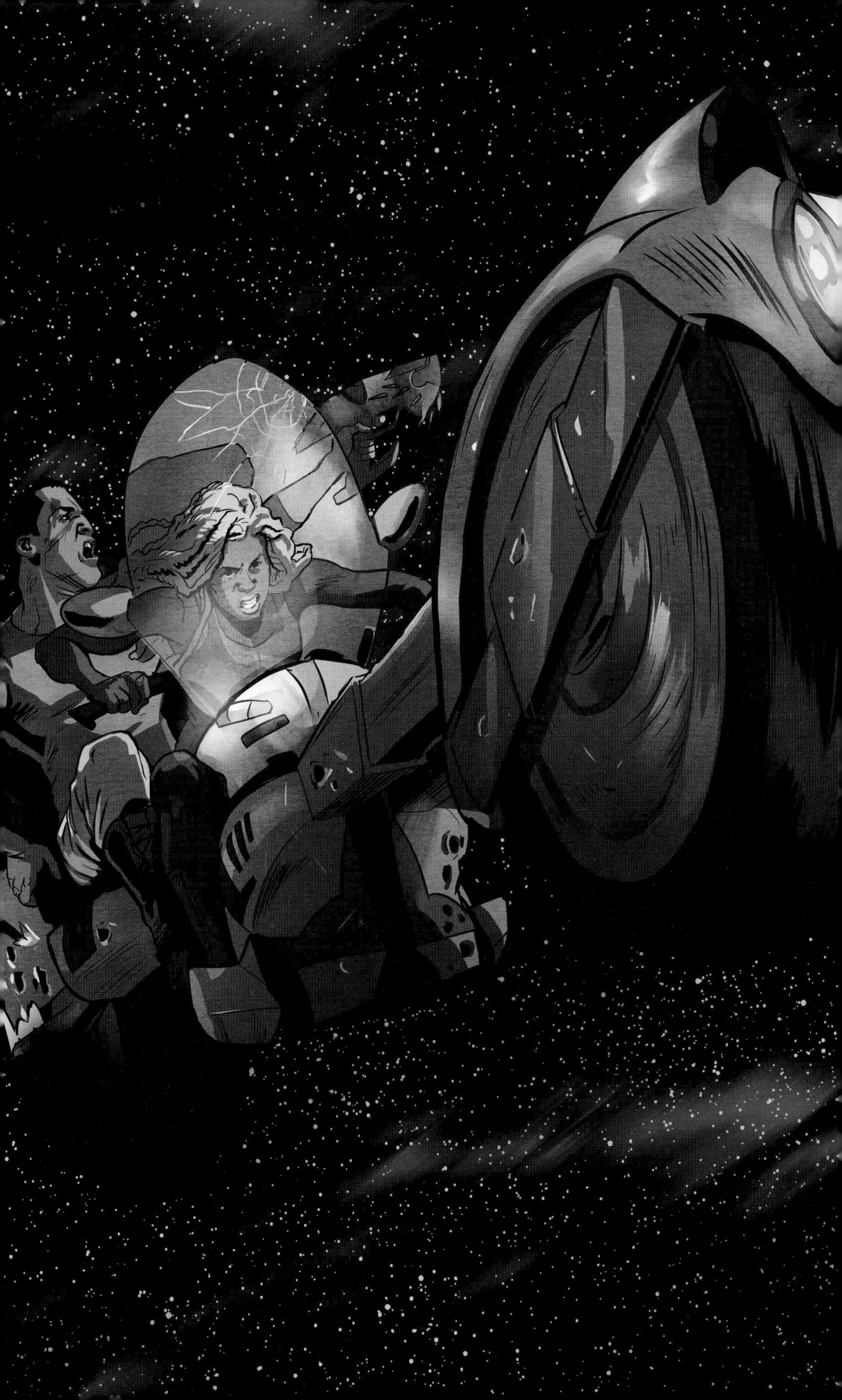

CHAPTER 4

NYX
SPECIES: EREBUS
PLANET OF ORIGIN: IMERA

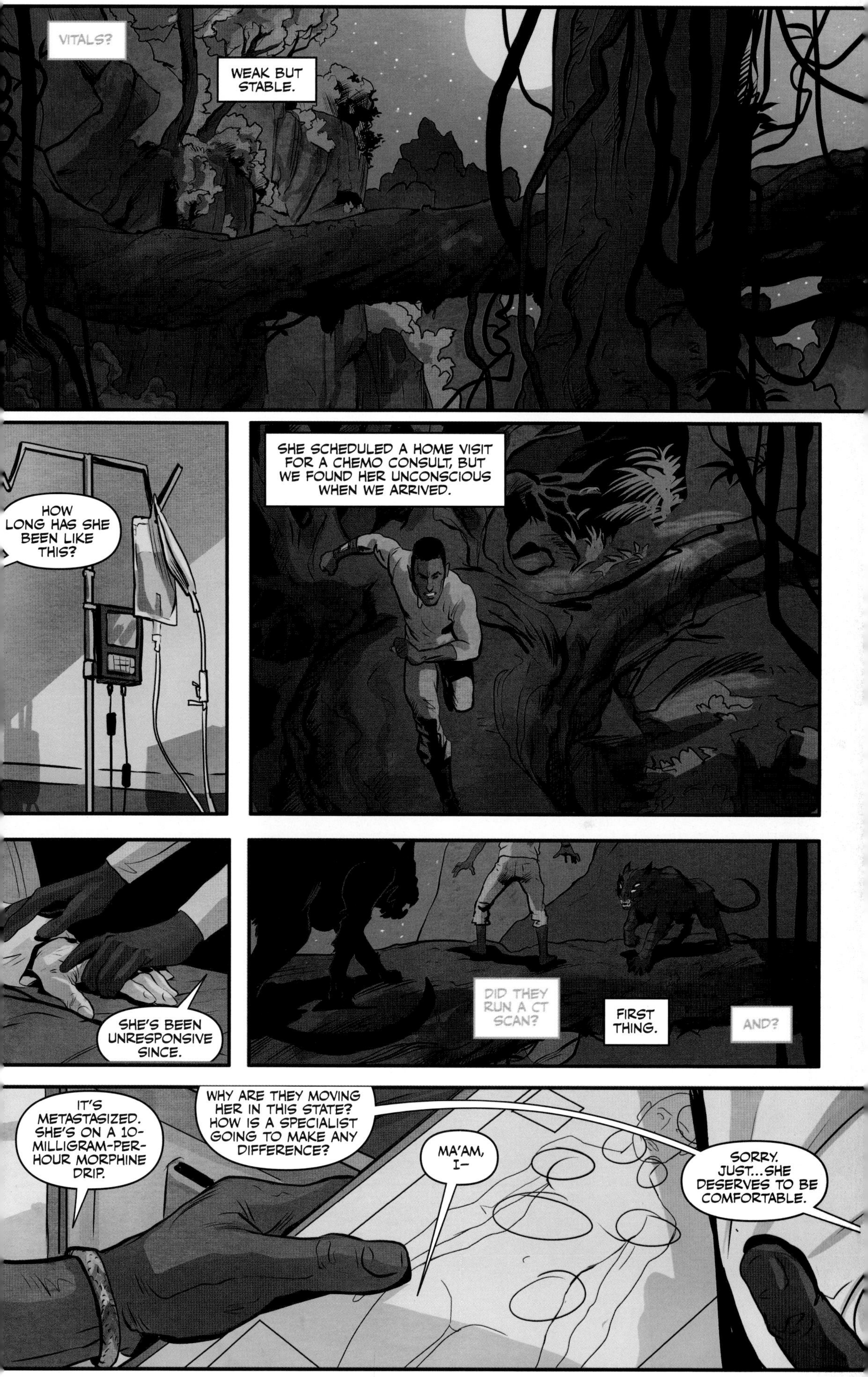
VITALS?
WEAK BUT STABLE.
HOW LONG HAS SHE BEEN LIKE THIS?
SHE SCHEDULED A HOME VISIT FOR A CHEMO CONSULT, BUT WE FOUND HER UNCONSCIOUS WHEN WE ARRIVED.
SHE'S BEEN UNRESPONSIVE SINCE.
DID THEY RUN A CT SCAN?
FIRST THING.
AND?
IT'S METASTASIZED. SHE'S ON A 10-MILLIGRAM-PER-HOUR MORPHINE DRIP.
WHY ARE THEY MOVING HER IN THIS STATE? HOW IS A SPECIALIST GOING TO MAKE ANY DIFFERENCE?
MA'AM, I–
SORRY. JUST...SHE DESERVES TO BE COMFORTABLE.

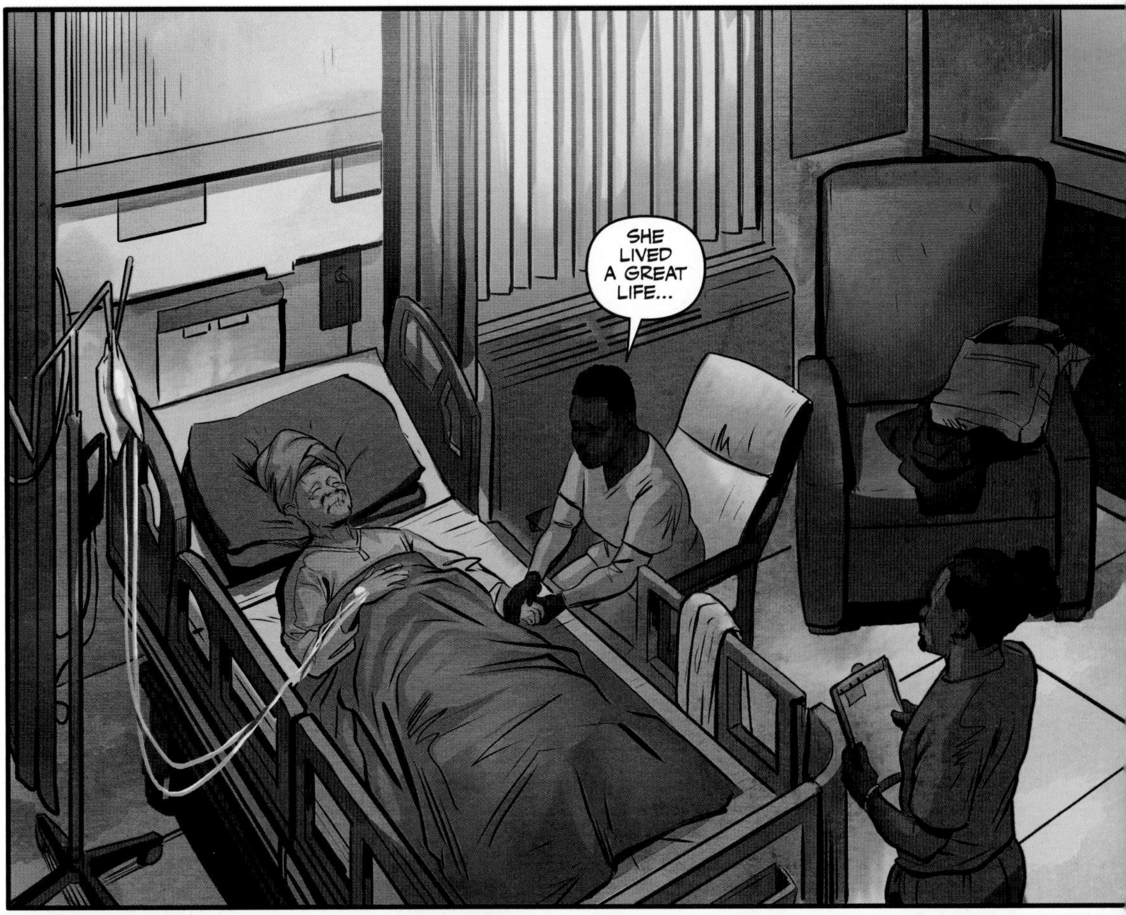
SHE LIVED A GREAT LIFE...

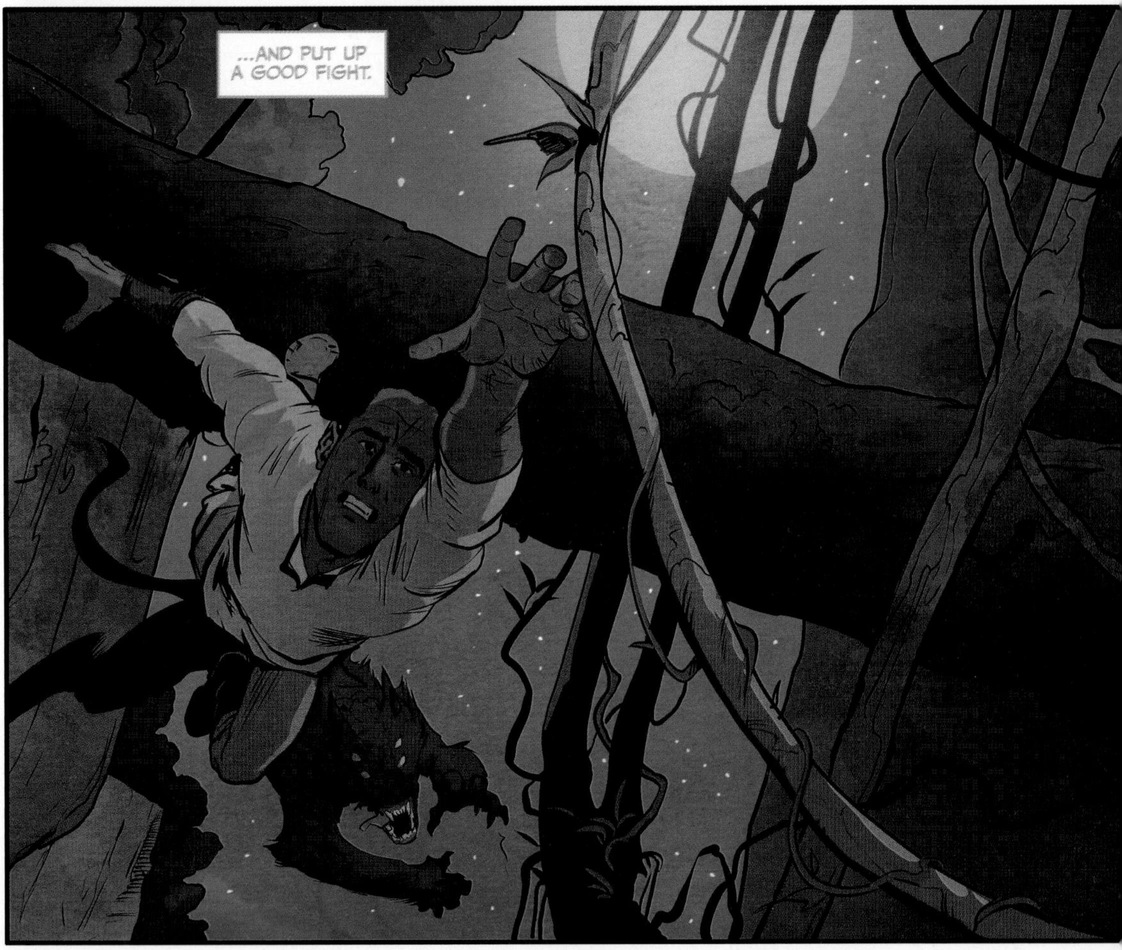
...AND PUT UP A GOOD FIGHT.

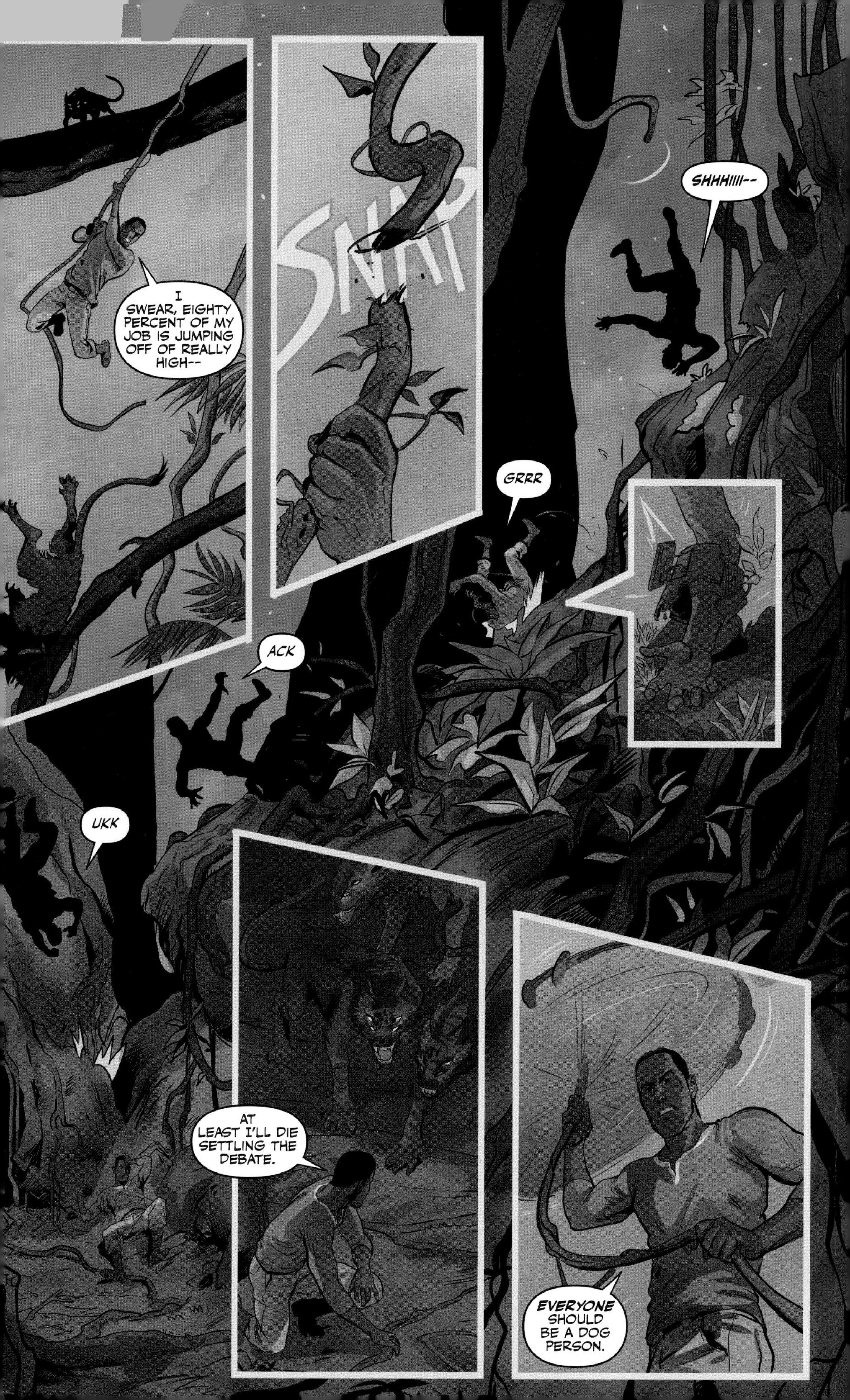
I SWEAR, EIGHTY PERCENT OF MY JOB IS JUMPING OFF OF REALLY HIGH--
SNAP
SHHHIIII--
GRRR
ACK
UKK
AT LEAST I'LL DIE SETTLING THE DEBATE.
EVERYONE SHOULD BE A DOG PERSON.

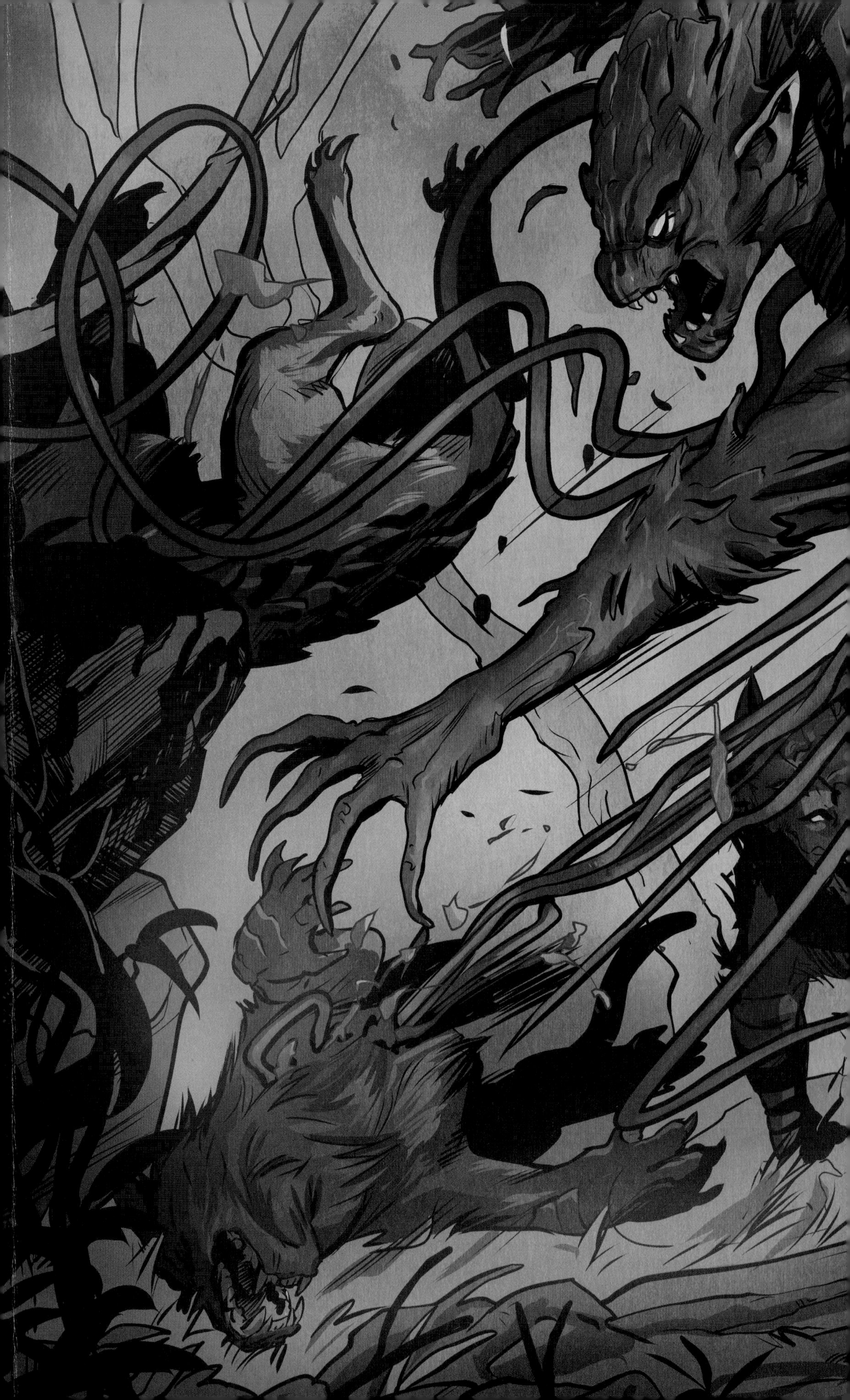

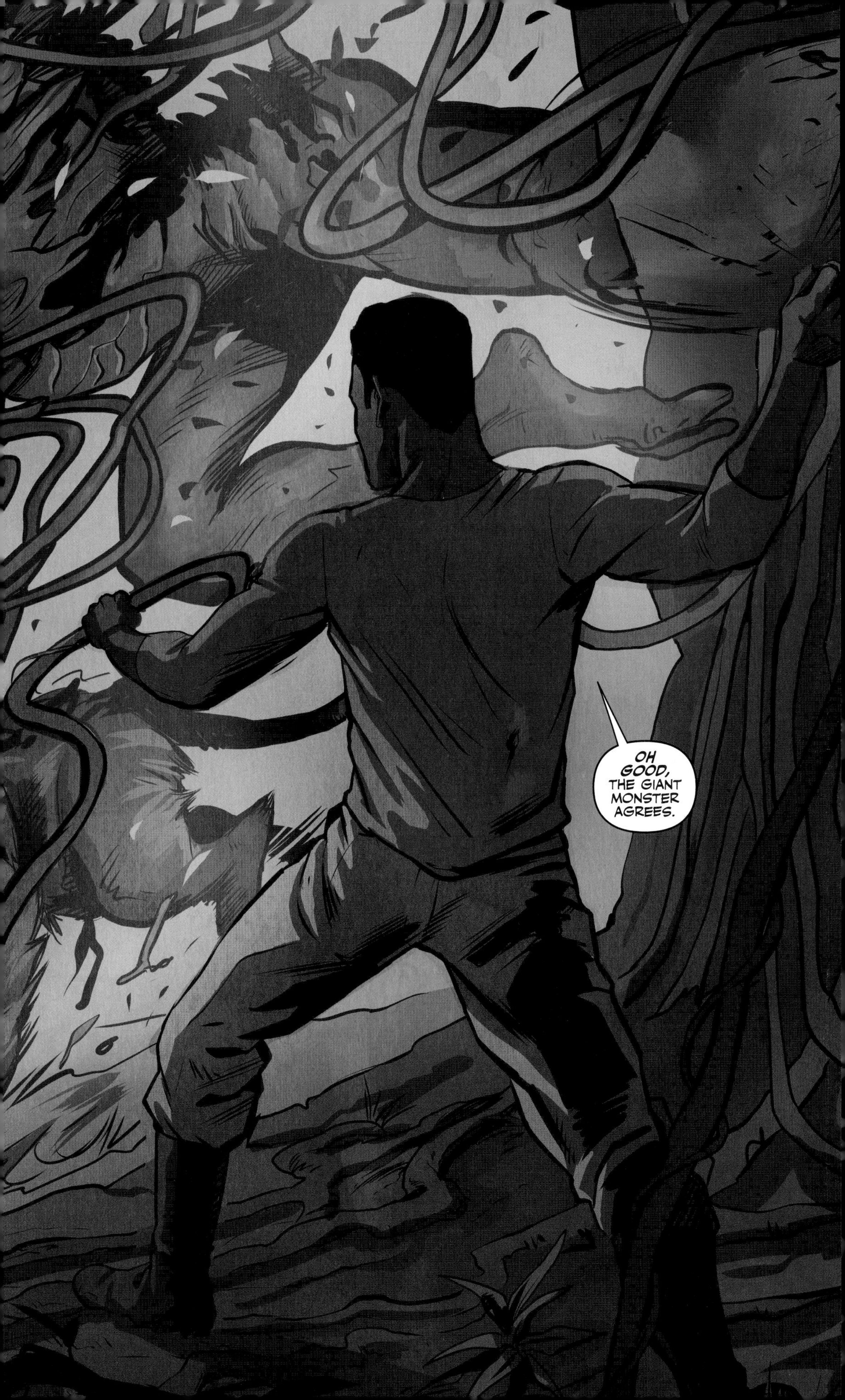
OH GOOD, THE GIANT MONSTER AGREES.

I'M GOING TO TELL YOU A STORY. THE KIND, I BELIEVE, YOU WOULD CALL A FAIRYTALE.

SOME SAY IT IS A STORY SO OLD IT DATES BACK TO OUR HOME PLANET.

IF THERE EVER WAS SUCH A PLACE.

A LITTLE GIRL HAD MANY BROTHERS AND SISTERS, BUT NO HOME. THE RAIN HAD STOPPED AND EVERYONE THIRSTED. THEIR BELLIES WERE EMPTY.

THE SUN WAS HOT AND ALL THE CHILDREN WANTED SHADE.

EVERY DAY THE GIRL TOLD HER BROTHERS AND SISTERS, "I DO NOT THIRST. I DO NOT HUNGER. *I AM A TREE.*"

EVERY DAY SHE TOLD THIS LIE.

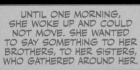

UNTIL ONE MORNING, SHE WOKE UP AND COULD NOT MOVE. SHE WANTED TO SAY SOMETHING TO HER BROTHERS, TO HER SISTERS, WHO GATHERED AROUND HER.

BUT SHE WAS A TREE. AND TREES DO NOT SPEAK.

SO THEY CUT HER DOWN AND BUILT A HOME.

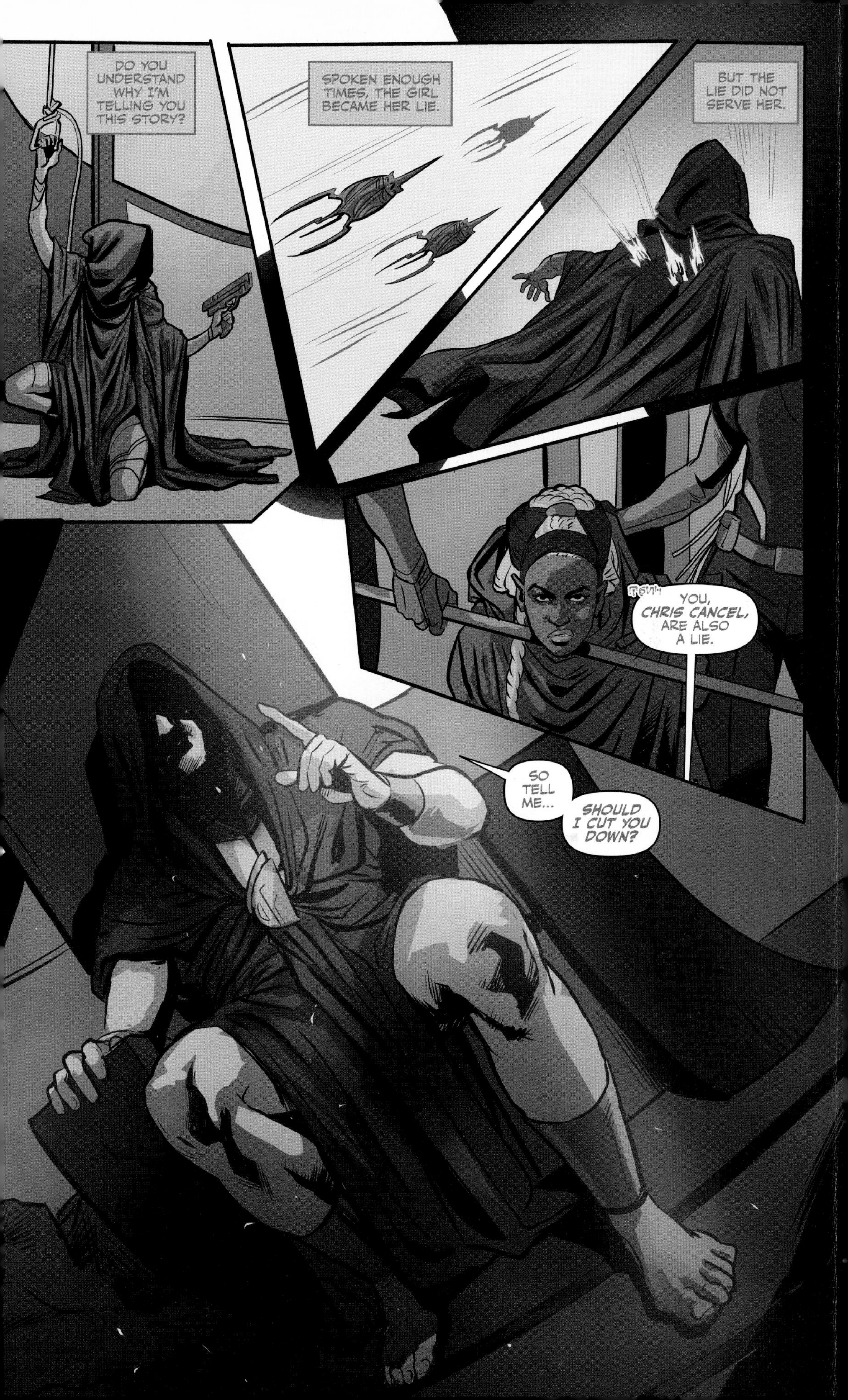
DO YOU UNDERSTAND WHY I'M TELLING YOU THIS STORY?
SPOKEN ENOUGH TIMES, THE GIRL BECAME HER LIE.
BUT THE LIE DID NOT SERVE HER.
YOU, CHRIS CANCEL, ARE ALSO A LIE.
SO TELL ME...
SHOULD I CUT YOU DOWN?

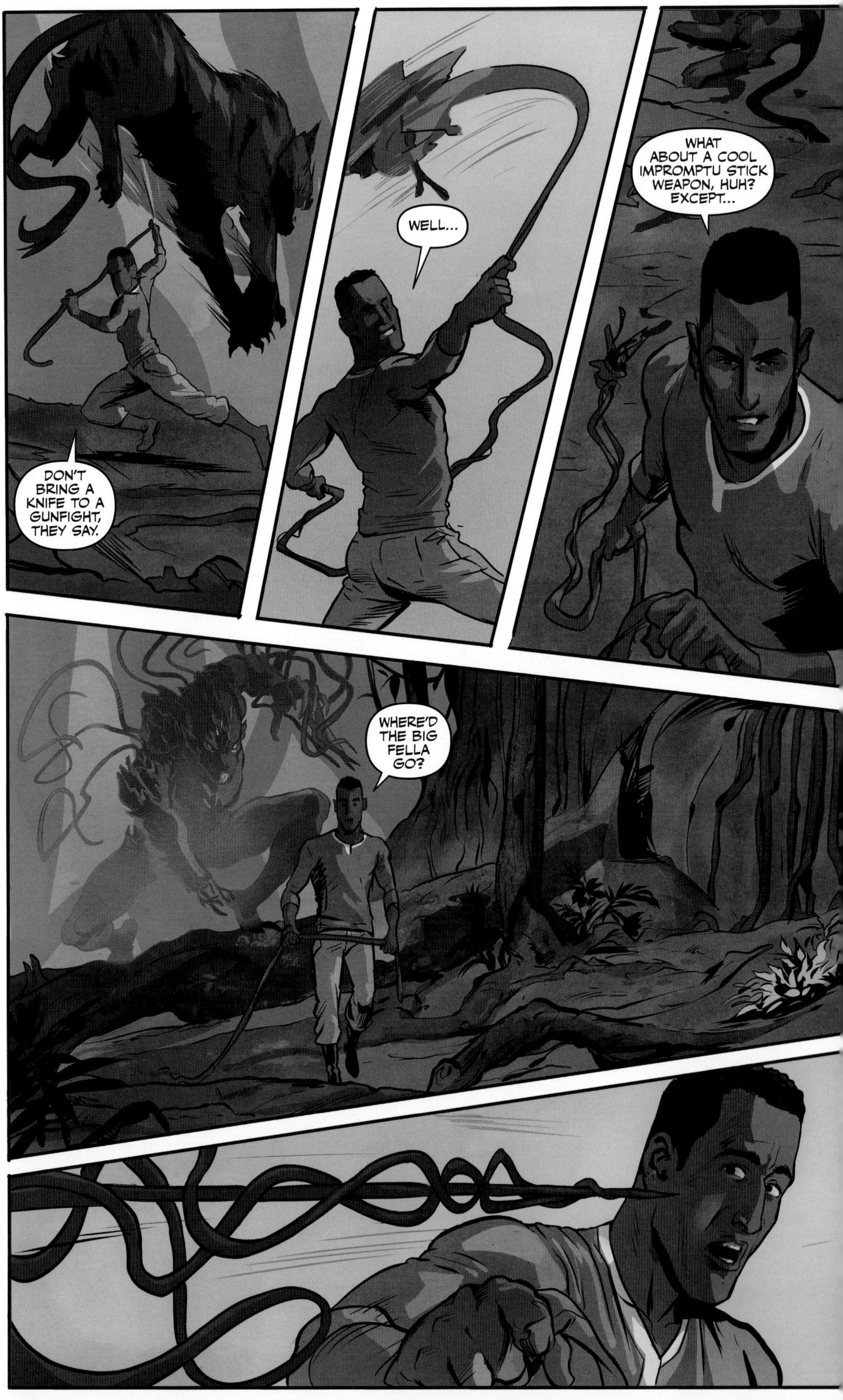
DON'T BRING A KNIFE TO A GUNFIGHT, THEY SAY.
WELL...
WHAT ABOUT A COOL IMPROMPTU STICK WEAPON, HUH? EXCEPT...
WHERE'D THE BIG FELLA GO?

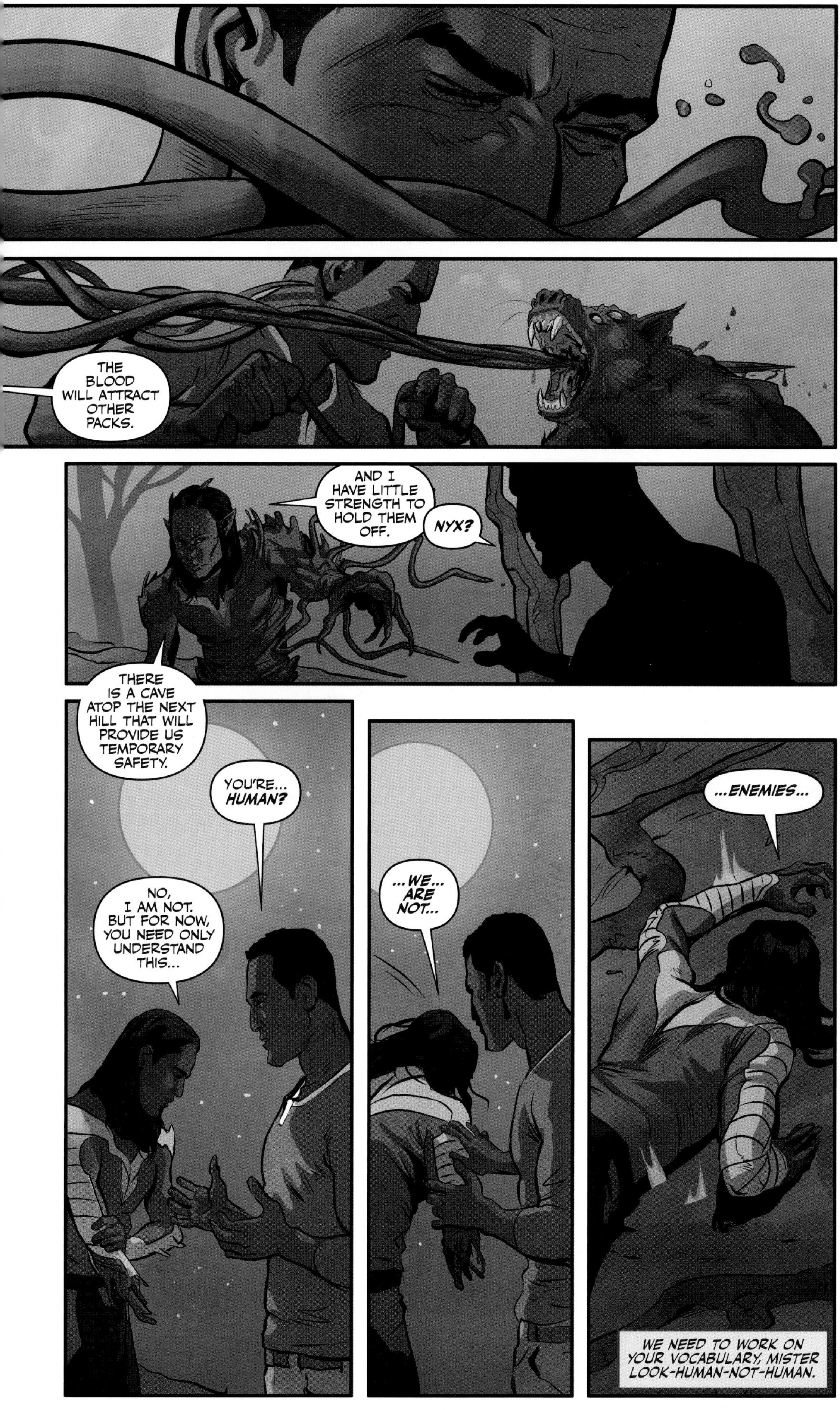
THE BLOOD WILL ATTRACT OTHER PACKS.
AND I HAVE LITTLE STRENGTH TO HOLD THEM OFF.
NYX?
THERE IS A CAVE ATOP THE NEXT HILL THAT WILL PROVIDE US TEMPORARY SAFETY.
YOU'RE... HUMAN?
NO, I AM NOT. BUT FOR NOW, YOU NEED ONLY UNDERSTAND THIS...
...WE... ARE NOT...
...ENEMIES...
WE NEED TO WORK ON YOUR VOCABULARY, MISTER LOOK-HUMAN-NOT-HUMAN.

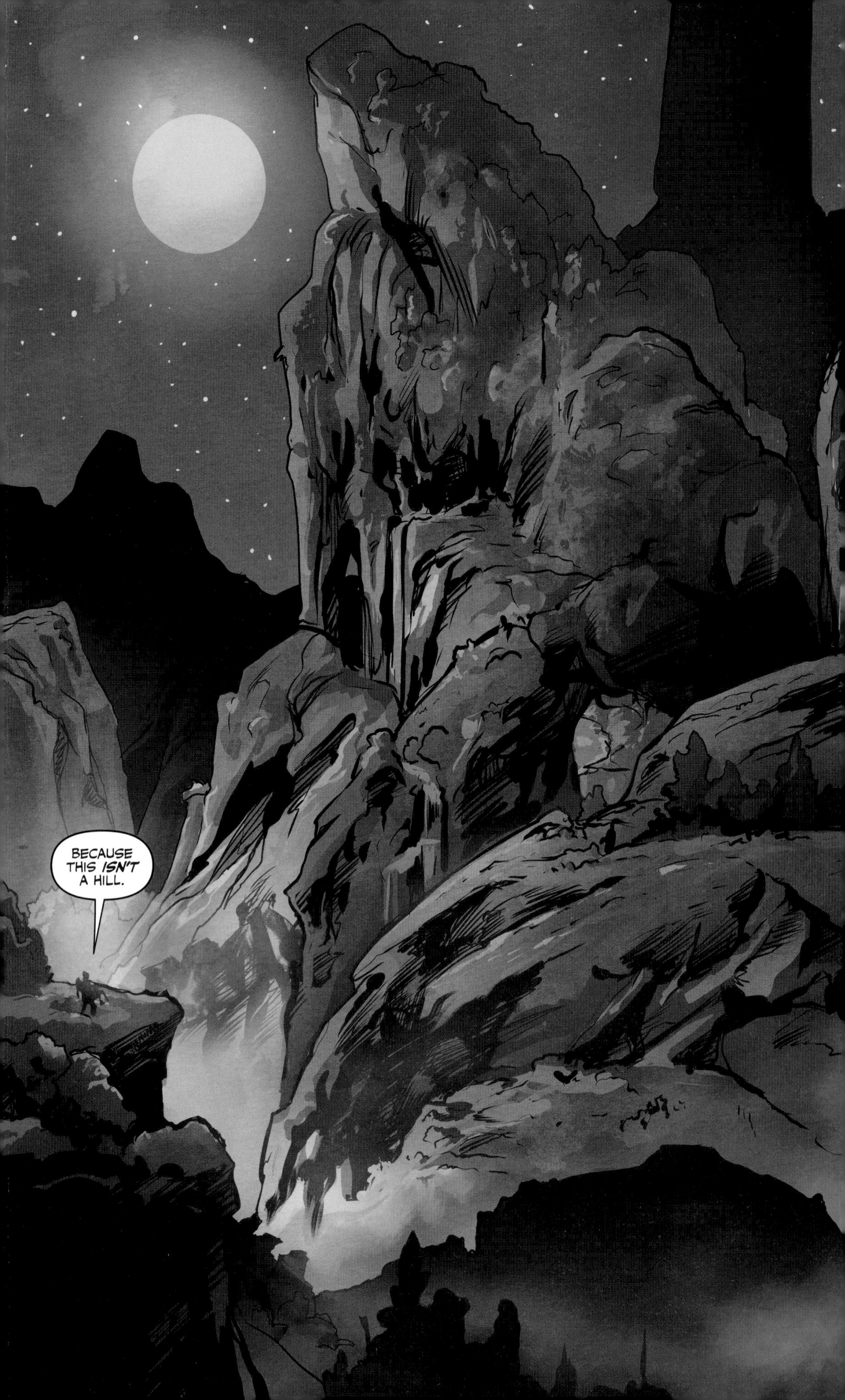
BECAUSE THIS *ISN'T* A HILL.

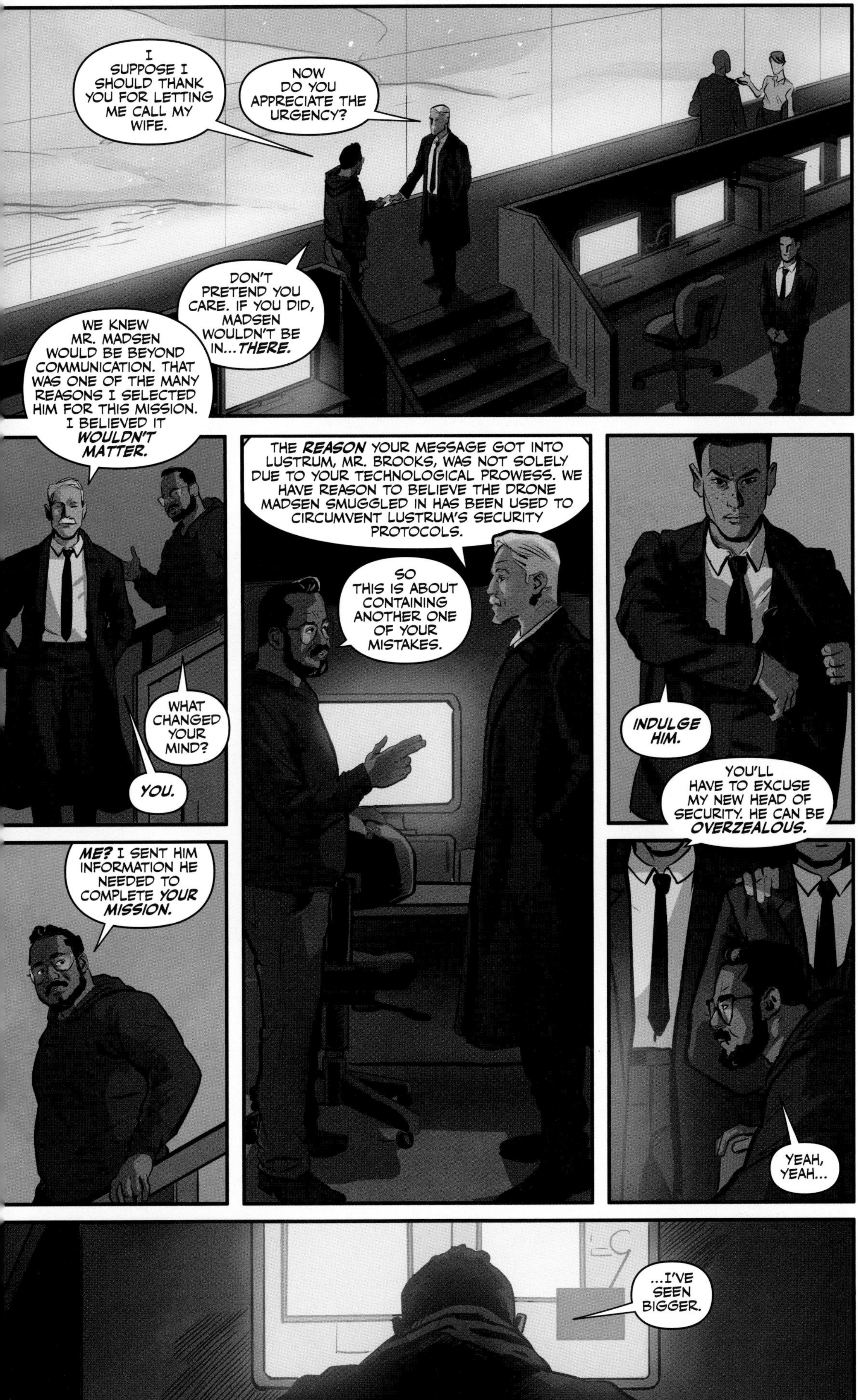
I SUPPOSE I SHOULD THANK YOU FOR LETTING ME CALL MY WIFE.
NOW DO YOU APPRECIATE THE URGENCY?
DON'T PRETEND YOU CARE. IF YOU DID, MADSEN WOULDN'T BE IN... THERE.
WE KNEW MR. MADSEN WOULD BE BEYOND COMMUNICATION. THAT WAS ONE OF THE MANY REASONS I SELECTED HIM FOR THIS MISSION. I BELIEVED IT WOULDN'T MATTER.
WHAT CHANGED YOUR MIND?
YOU.
ME? I SENT HIM INFORMATION HE NEEDED TO COMPLETE YOUR MISSION.
THE REASON YOUR MESSAGE GOT INTO LUSTRUM, MR. BROOKS, WAS NOT SOLELY DUE TO YOUR TECHNOLOGICAL PROWESS. WE HAVE REASON TO BELIEVE THE DRONE MADSEN SMUGGLED IN HAS BEEN USED TO CIRCUMVENT LUSTRUM'S SECURITY PROTOCOLS.
SO THIS IS ABOUT CONTAINING ANOTHER ONE OF YOUR MISTAKES.
INDULGE HIM.
YOU'LL HAVE TO EXCUSE MY NEW HEAD OF SECURITY. HE CAN BE OVERZEALOUS.
YEAH, YEAH...
...I'VE SEEN BIGGER.

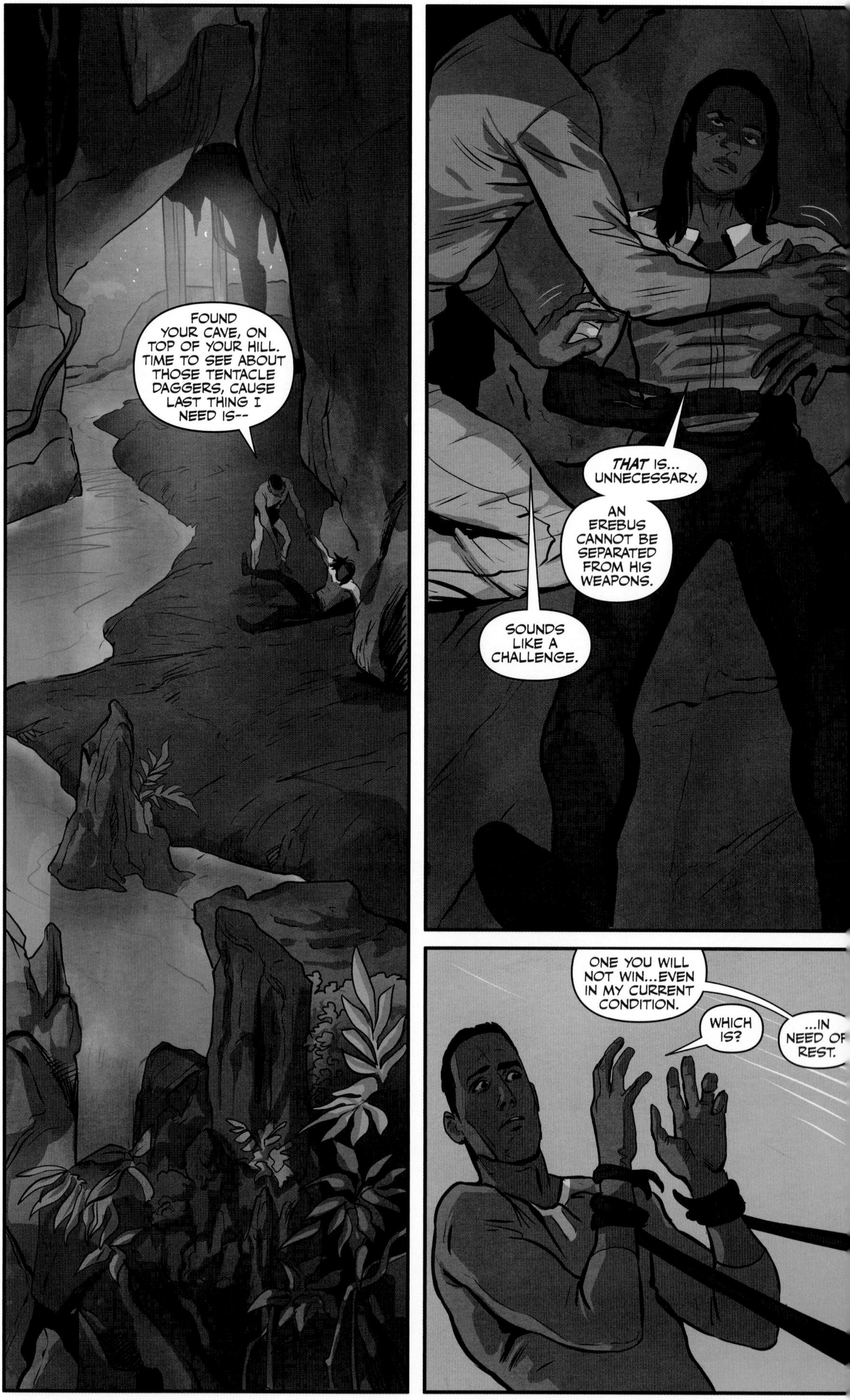
FOUND YOUR CAVE, ON TOP OF YOUR HILL. TIME TO SEE ABOUT THOSE TENTACLE DAGGERS, CAUSE LAST THING I NEED IS--
THAT IS... UNNECESSARY.
AN EREBUS CANNOT BE SEPARATED FROM HIS WEAPONS.
SOUNDS LIKE A CHALLENGE.
ONE YOU WILL NOT WIN...EVEN IN MY CURRENT CONDITION.
WHICH IS?
...IN NEED OF REST.

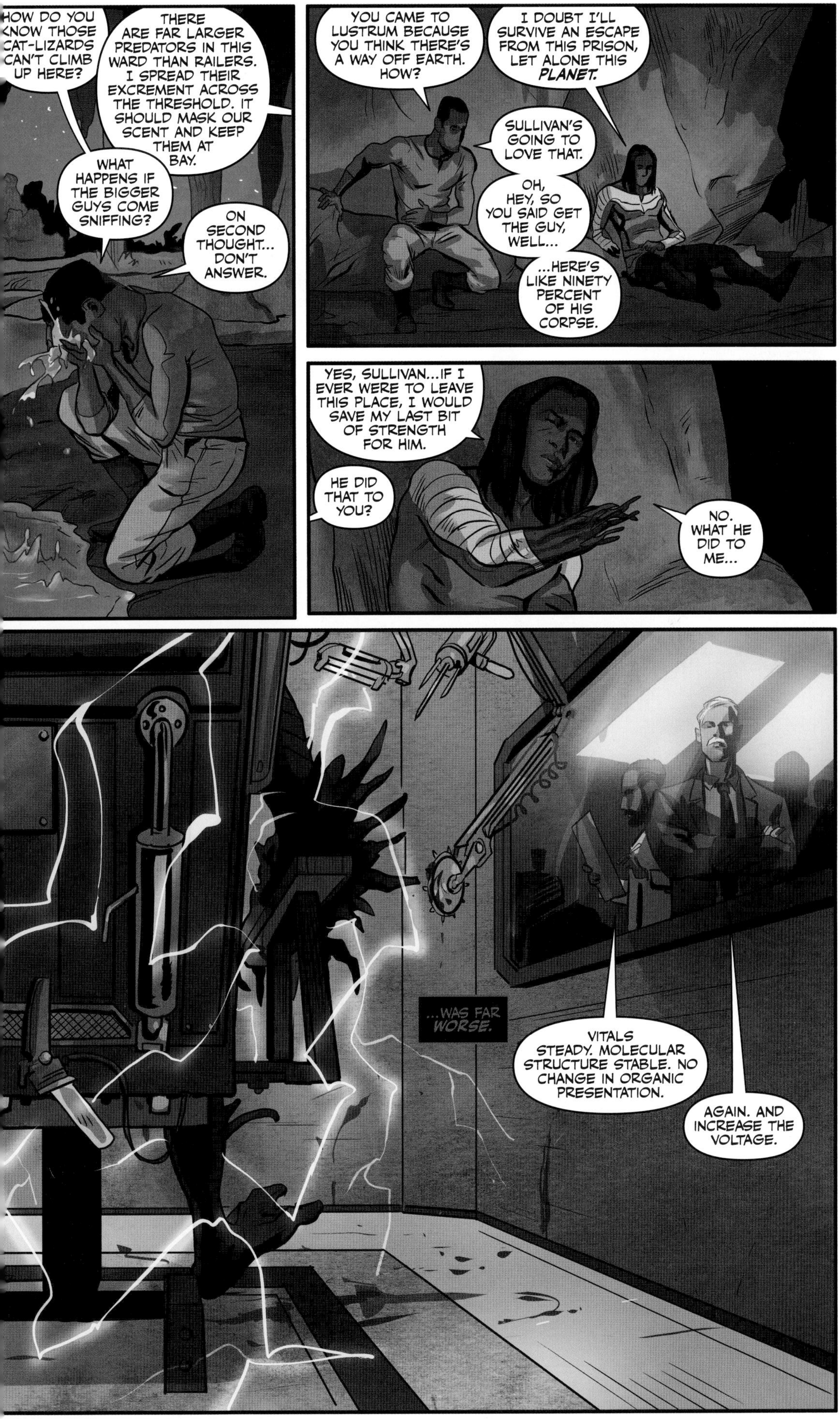
HOW DO YOU KNOW THOSE CAT-LIZARDS CAN'T CLIMB UP HERE?
THERE ARE FAR LARGER PREDATORS IN THIS WARD THAN RAILERS. I SPREAD THEIR EXCREMENT ACROSS THE THRESHOLD. IT SHOULD MASK OUR SCENT AND KEEP THEM AT BAY.
WHAT HAPPENS IF THE BIGGER GUYS COME SNIFFING?
ON SECOND THOUGHT... DON'T ANSWER.
YOU CAME TO LUSTRUM BECAUSE YOU THINK THERE'S A WAY OFF EARTH. HOW?
I DOUBT I'LL SURVIVE AN ESCAPE FROM THIS PRISON, LET ALONE THIS PLANET.
SULLIVAN'S GOING TO LOVE THAT.
OH, HEY, SO YOU SAID GET THE GUY, WELL...
...HERE'S LIKE NINETY PERCENT OF HIS CORPSE.
YES, SULLIVAN...IF I EVER WERE TO LEAVE THIS PLACE, I WOULD SAVE MY LAST BIT OF STRENGTH FOR HIM.
HE DID THAT TO YOU?
NO. WHAT HE DID TO ME...
...WAS FAR WORSE.
VITALS STEADY. MOLECULAR STRUCTURE STABLE. NO CHANGE IN ORGANIC PRESENTATION.
AGAIN. AND INCREASE THE VOLTAGE.

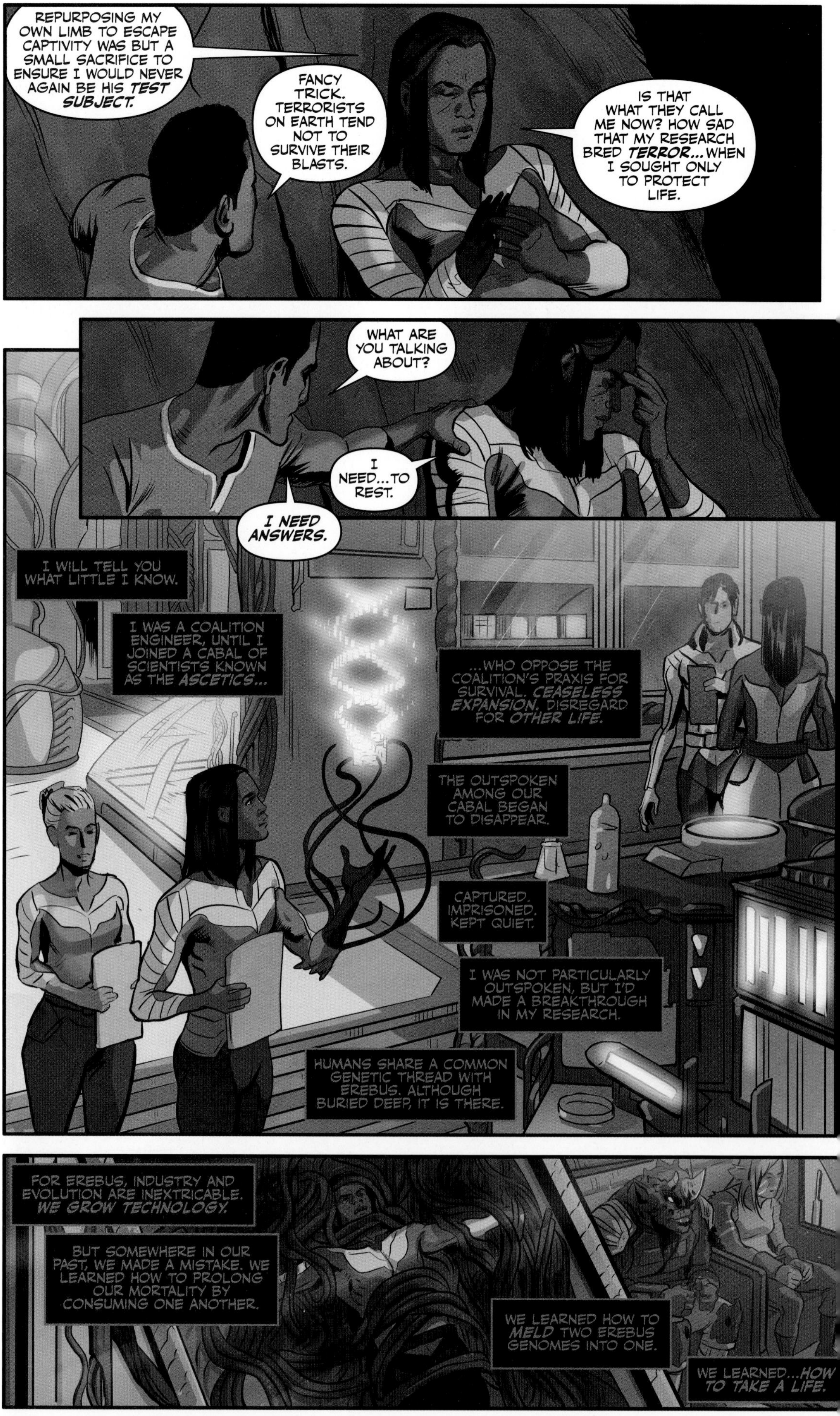

REPURPOSING MY OWN LIMB TO ESCAPE CAPTIVITY WAS BUT A SMALL SACRIFICE TO ENSURE I WOULD NEVER AGAIN BE HIS *TEST SUBJECT.*
FANCY TRICK. TERRORISTS ON EARTH TEND NOT TO SURVIVE THEIR BLASTS.
IS THAT WHAT THEY CALL ME NOW? HOW SAD THAT MY RESEARCH BRED *TERROR...* WHEN I SOUGHT ONLY TO PROTECT LIFE.
WHAT ARE YOU TALKING ABOUT?
I NEED...TO REST.
I NEED ANSWERS.
I WILL TELL YOU WHAT LITTLE I KNOW.
I WAS A COALITION ENGINEER, UNTIL I JOINED A CABAL OF SCIENTISTS KNOWN AS THE *ASCETICS...*
...WHO OPPOSE THE COALITION'S PRAXIS FOR SURVIVAL. *CEASELESS EXPANSION.* DISREGARD FOR *OTHER LIFE.*
THE OUTSPOKEN AMONG OUR CABAL BEGAN TO DISAPPEAR.
CAPTURED. IMPRISONED. KEPT QUIET.
I WAS NOT PARTICULARLY OUTSPOKEN, BUT I'D MADE A BREAKTHROUGH IN MY RESEARCH.
HUMANS SHARE A COMMON GENETIC THREAD WITH EREBUS. ALTHOUGH BURIED DEEP, IT IS THERE.
FOR EREBUS, INDUSTRY AND EVOLUTION ARE INEXTRICABLE. *WE GROW TECHNOLOGY.*
BUT SOMEWHERE IN OUR PAST, WE MADE A MISTAKE. WE LEARNED HOW TO PROLONG OUR MORTALITY BY CONSUMING ONE ANOTHER.
WE LEARNED HOW TO *MELD* TWO EREBUS GENOMES INTO ONE.
WE LEARNED...*HOW TO TAKE A LIFE.*

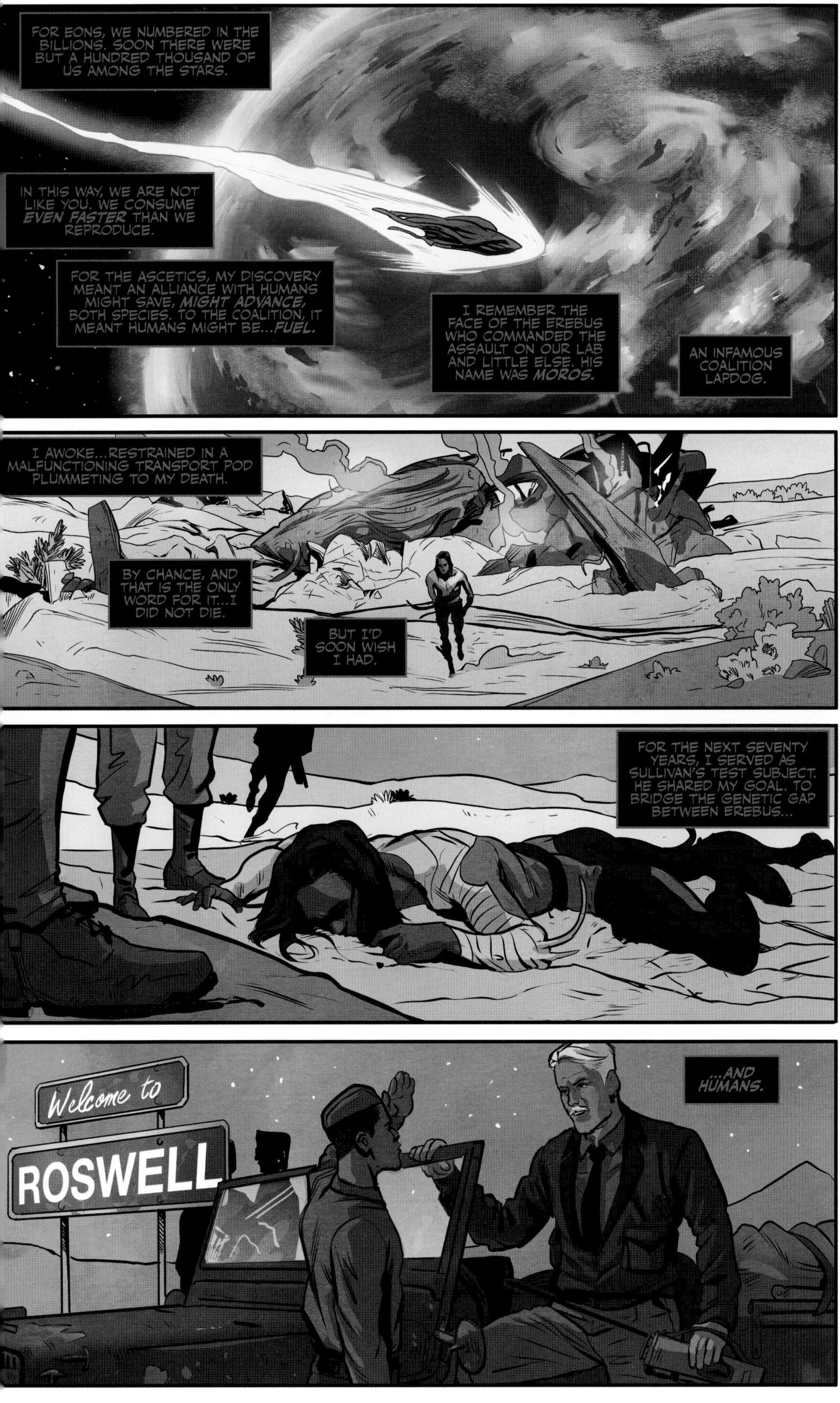
FOR EONS, WE NUMBERED IN THE BILLIONS. SOON THERE WERE BUT A HUNDRED THOUSAND OF US AMONG THE STARS.
IN THIS WAY, WE ARE NOT LIKE YOU. WE CONSUME *EVEN FASTER* THAN WE REPRODUCE.
FOR THE ASCETICS, MY DISCOVERY MEANT AN ALLIANCE WITH HUMANS MIGHT SAVE, *MIGHT ADVANCE,* BOTH SPECIES. TO THE COALITION, IT MEANT HUMANS MIGHT BE...*FUEL.*
I REMEMBER THE FACE OF THE EREBUS WHO COMMANDED THE ASSAULT ON OUR LAB AND LITTLE ELSE. HIS NAME WAS *MOROS.*
AN INFAMOUS COALITION LAPDOG.
I AWOKE...RESTRAINED IN A MALFUNCTIONING TRANSPORT POD PLUMMETING TO MY DEATH.
BY CHANCE, AND THAT IS THE ONLY WORD FOR IT...I DID NOT DIE.
BUT I'D SOON WISH I HAD.
FOR THE NEXT SEVENTY YEARS, I SERVED AS SULLIVAN'S TEST SUBJECT. HE SHARED MY GOAL. TO BRIDGE THE GENETIC GAP BETWEEN EREBUS...
Welcome to
ROSWELL
...AND HUMANS.

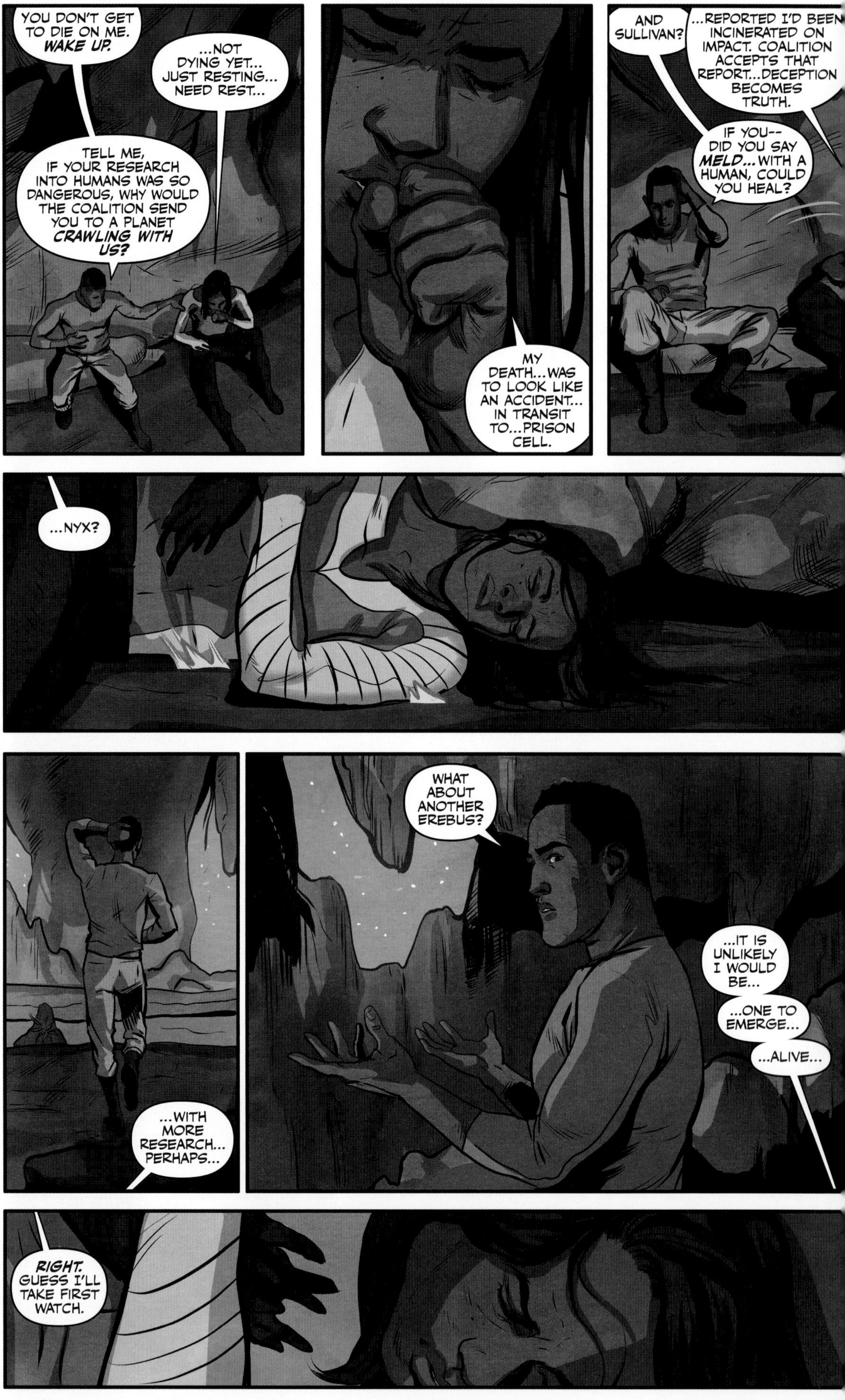

YOU DON'T GET TO DIE ON ME. WAKE UP.
...NOT DYING YET... JUST RESTING... NEED REST...
TELL ME, IF YOUR RESEARCH INTO HUMANS WAS SO DANGEROUS, WHY WOULD THE COALITION SEND YOU TO A PLANET CRAWLING WITH US?
MY DEATH...WAS TO LOOK LIKE AN ACCIDENT... IN TRANSIT TO...PRISON CELL.
AND SULLIVAN?
...REPORTED I'D BEEN INCINERATED ON IMPACT. COALITION ACCEPTS THAT REPORT...DECEPTION BECOMES TRUTH.
IF YOU-- DID YOU SAY MELD...WITH A HUMAN, COULD YOU HEAL?
...NYX?
...WITH MORE RESEARCH... PERHAPS...
WHAT ABOUT ANOTHER EREBUS?
...IT IS UNLIKELY I WOULD BE...
...ONE TO EMERGE...
...ALIVE...
RIGHT. GUESS I'LL TAKE FIRST WATCH.

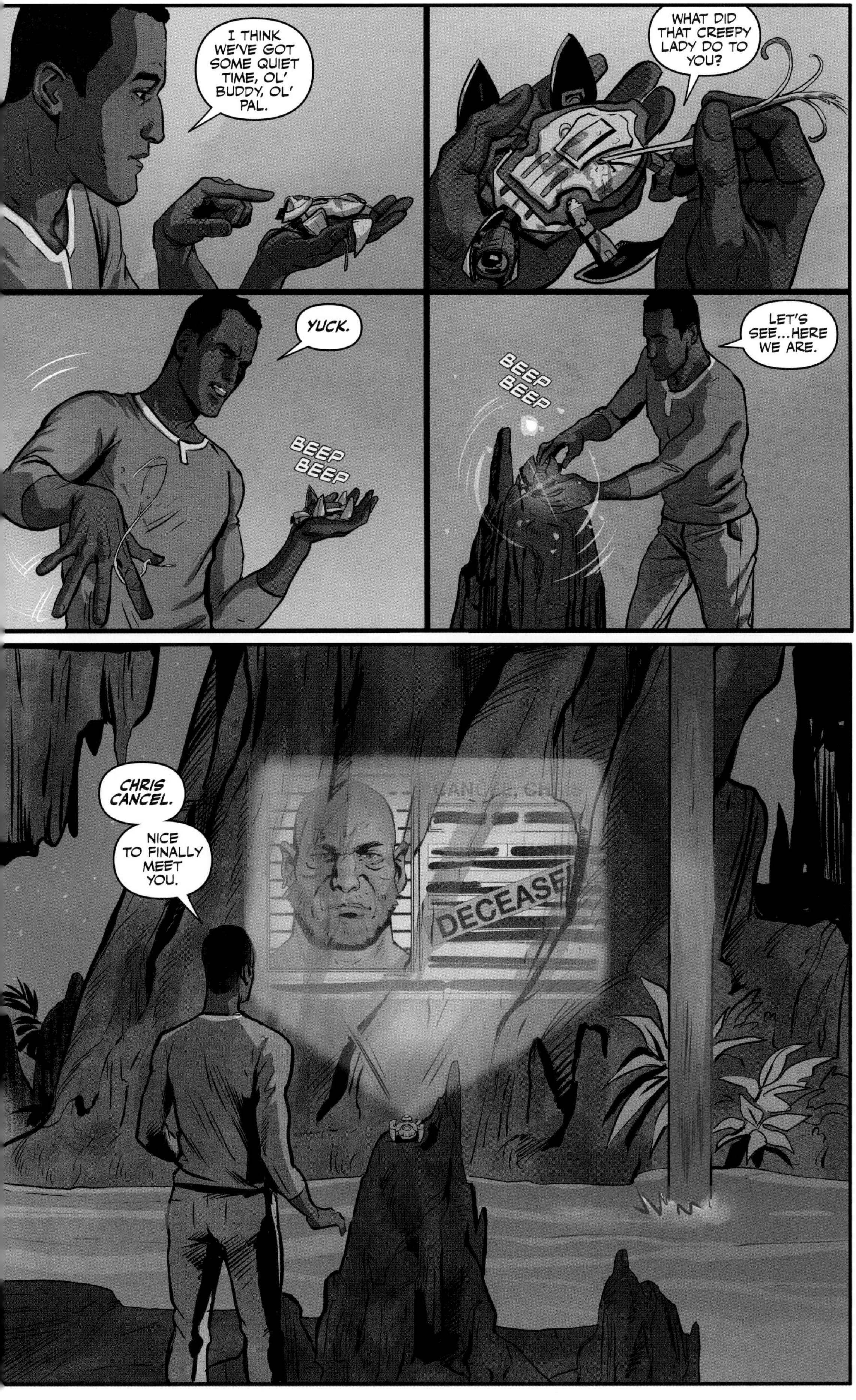
I THINK WE'VE GOT SOME QUIET TIME, OL' BUDDY, OL' PAL.
WHAT DID THAT CREEPY LADY DO TO YOU?
YUCK.
BEEP BEEP
LET'S SEE...HERE WE ARE.
BEEP BEEP
CHRIS CANCEL.
NICE TO FINALLY MEET YOU.
CANCEL, CHRIS
DECEASE

YOU.

I'D SAY THE PLEASURE'S ALL MINE...BUT OBVIOUSLY IT'S NOT.

EASY.

WHO ARE YOU?

I'M NO ONE.

THAT'S NOT AN ANSWER.

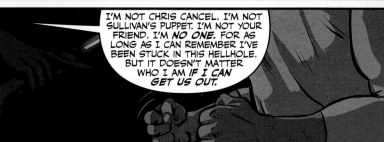

I'M NOT CHRIS CANCEL. I'M NOT SULLIVAN'S PUPPET. I'M NOT YOUR FRIEND. I'M *NO ONE*. FOR AS LONG AS I CAN REMEMBER I'VE BEEN STUCK IN THIS HELLHOLE. BUT IT DOESN'T MATTER WHO I AM *IF I CAN GET US OUT*.

US?

YOU PROVED USEFUL. I BUGGED YOUR DRONE, FOUND THE WARDEN OF THE BLACK SUN, AND NEGOTIATED OUR PASSAGE THROUGH THE MIDNIGHT GATES. WE BRING HIM WHAT HE WANTS, HE GETS US OUT.

YOU DON'T EXPECT ME TO BELIEVE ANY OF THIS, DO YOU?

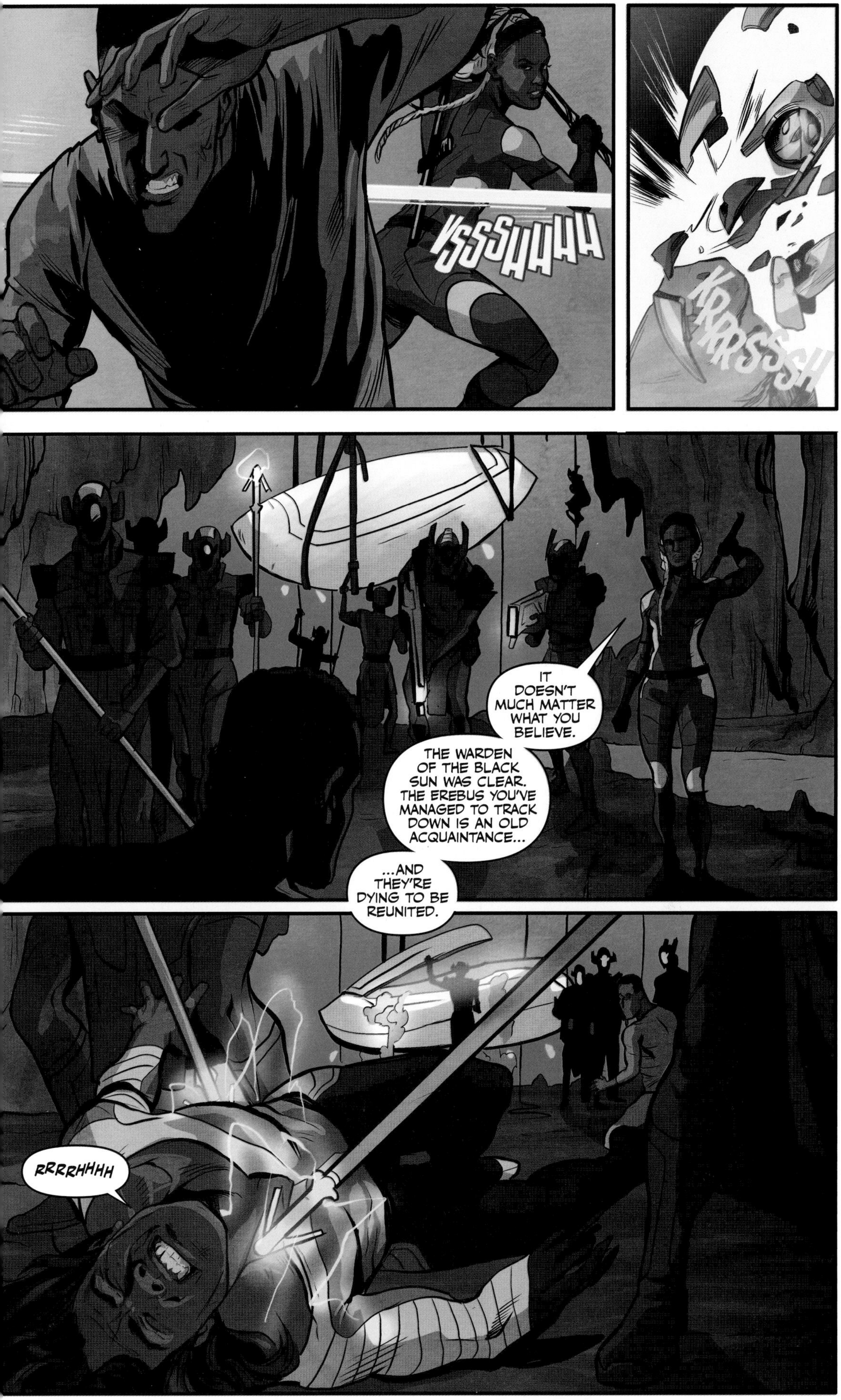
VSSSHHHH
KRRRSSSSH
IT DOESN'T MUCH MATTER WHAT YOU BELIEVE.
THE WARDEN OF THE BLACK SUN WAS CLEAR. THE EREBUS YOU'VE MANAGED TO TRACK DOWN IS AN OLD ACQUAINTANCE...
...AND THEY'RE DYING TO BE REUNITED.
RRRRHHHH

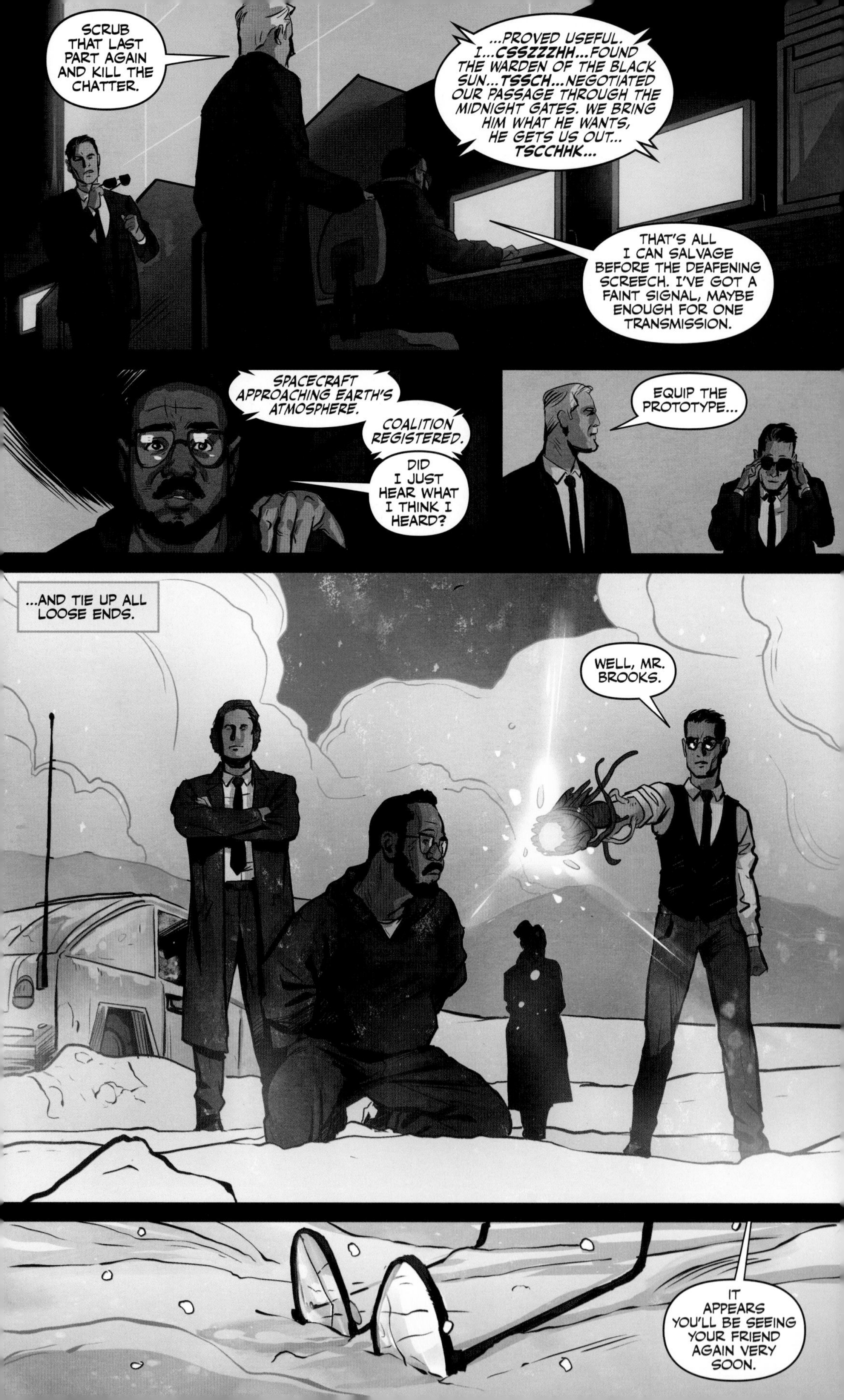
SCRUB THAT LAST PART AGAIN AND KILL THE CHATTER.
...PROVED USEFUL. I...CSSZZZHH...FOUND THE WARDEN OF THE BLACK SUN...TSSCH...NEGOTIATED OUR PASSAGE THROUGH THE MIDNIGHT GATES. WE BRING HIM WHAT HE WANTS, HE GETS US OUT... TSCCHHK...
THAT'S ALL I CAN SALVAGE BEFORE THE DEAFENING SCREECH. I'VE GOT A FAINT SIGNAL, MAYBE ENOUGH FOR ONE TRANSMISSION.
SPACECRAFT APPROACHING EARTH'S ATMOSPHERE.
COALITION REGISTERED.
DID I JUST HEAR WHAT I THINK I HEARD?
EQUIP THE PROTOTYPE...
...AND TIE UP ALL LOOSE ENDS.
WELL, MR. BROOKS.
IT APPEARS YOU'LL BE SEEING YOUR FRIEND AGAIN VERY SOON.

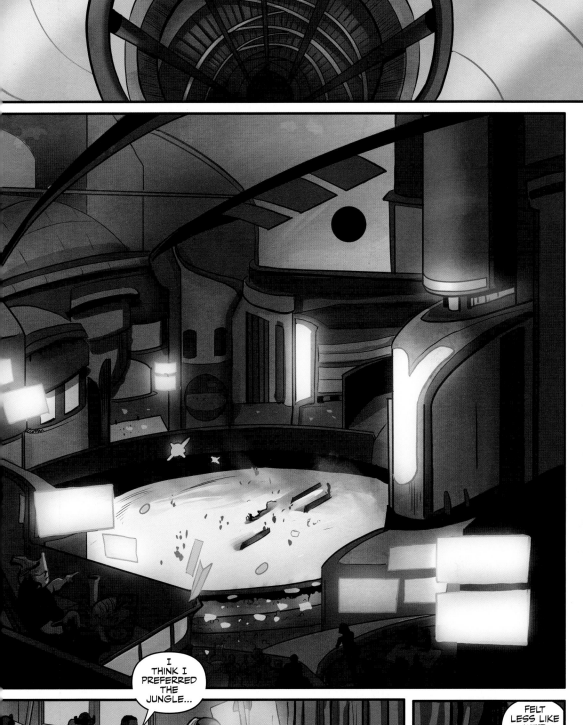

I THINK I PREFERRED THE JUNGLE...

FELT LESS LIKE WE'D BE TORN APART.

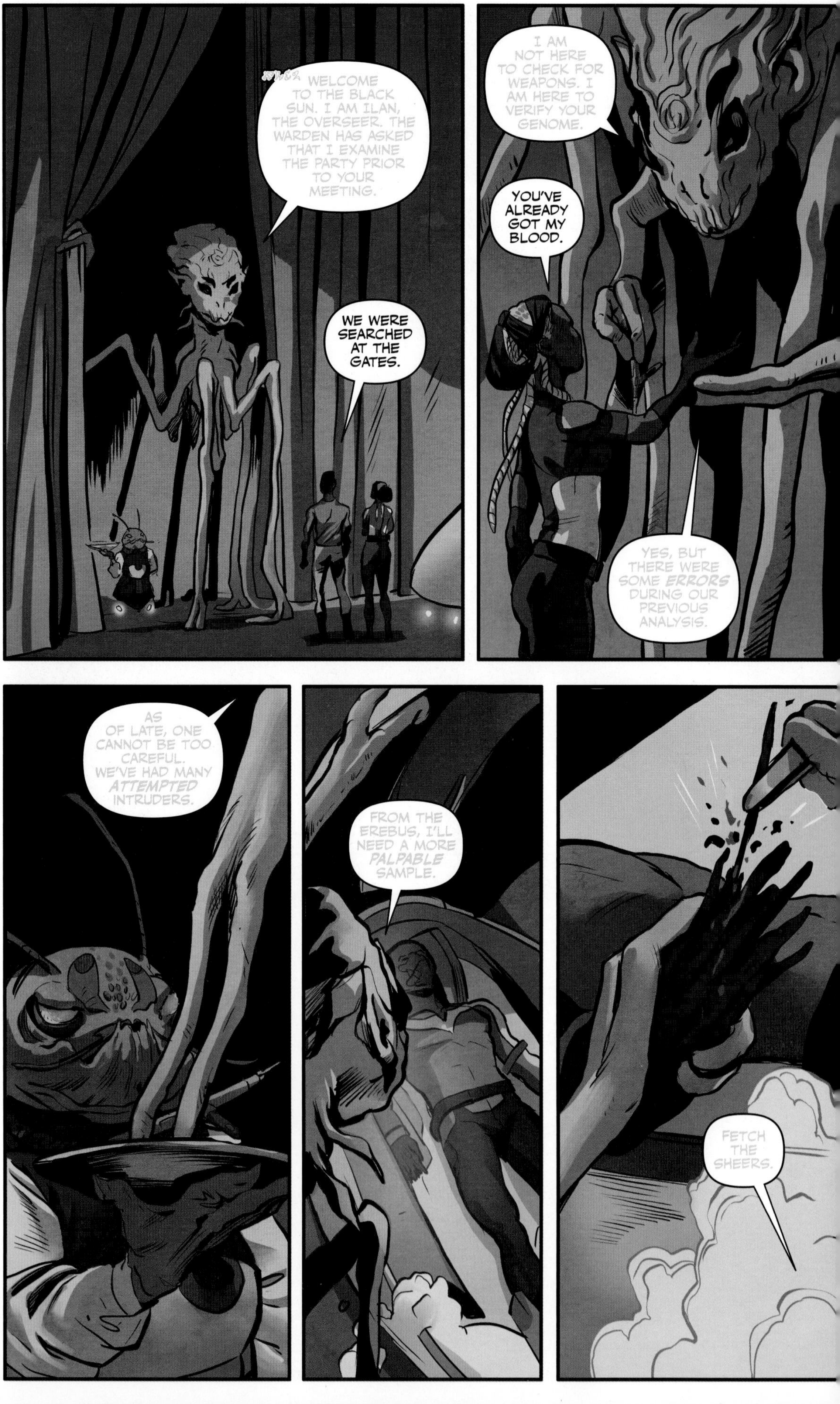
WELCOME TO THE BLACK SUN. I AM ILAN, THE OVERSEER. THE WARDEN HAS ASKED THAT I EXAMINE THE PARTY PRIOR TO YOUR MEETING.
WE WERE SEARCHED AT THE GATES.
I AM NOT HERE TO CHECK FOR WEAPONS. I AM HERE TO VERIFY YOUR GENOME.
YOU'VE ALREADY GOT MY BLOOD.
YES, BUT THERE WERE SOME ERRORS DURING OUR PREVIOUS ANALYSIS.
AS OF LATE, ONE CANNOT BE TOO CAREFUL. WE'VE HAD MANY ATTEMPTED INTRUDERS.
FROM THE EREBUS, I'LL NEED A MORE PALPABLE SAMPLE.
FETCH THE SHEERS.

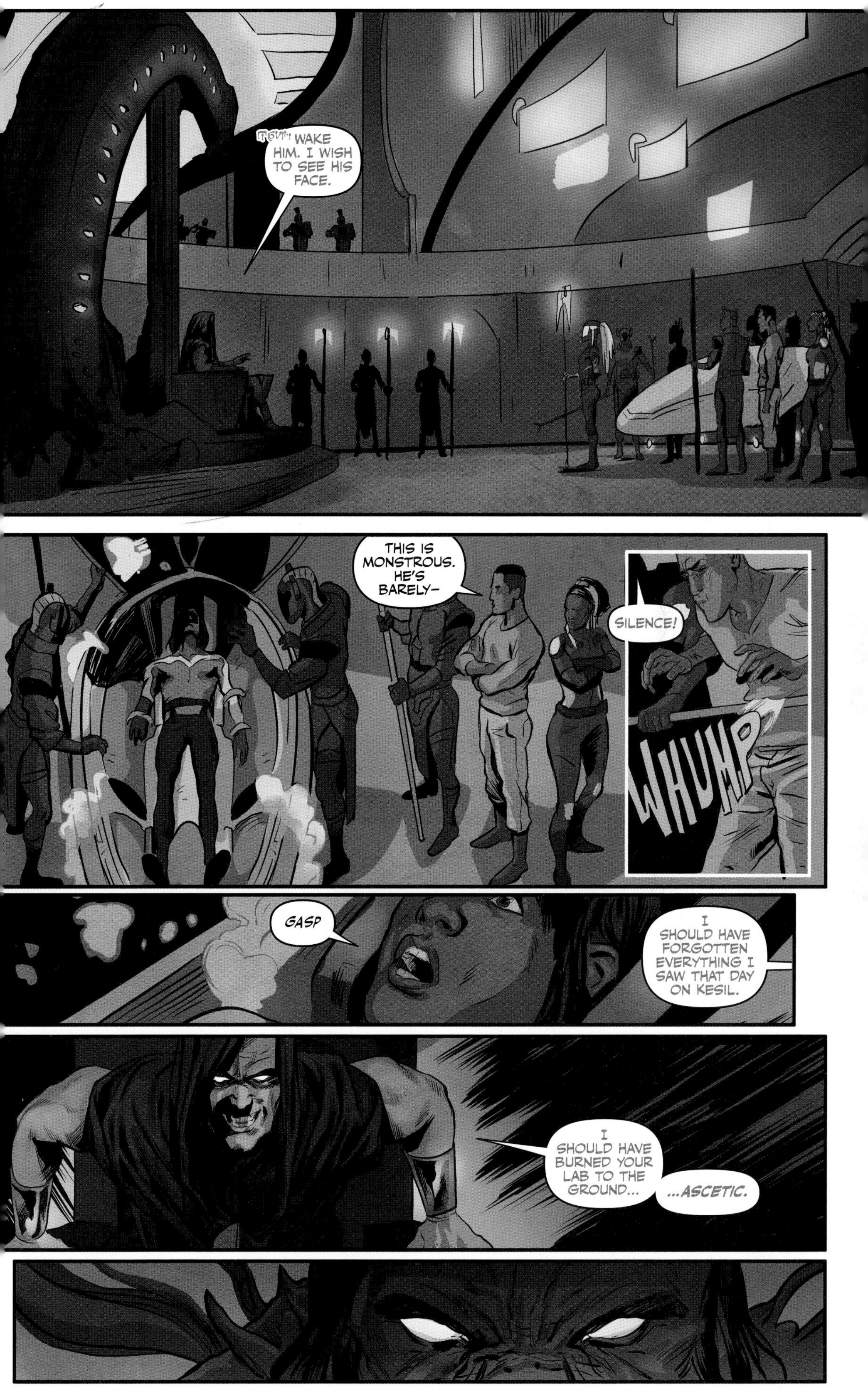
WAKE HIM. I WISH TO SEE HIS FACE.
THIS IS MONSTROUS. HE'S BARELY–
SILENCE!
WHUMP
GASP
I SHOULD HAVE FORGOTTEN EVERYTHING I SAW THAT DAY ON KESIL.
I SHOULD HAVE BURNED YOUR LAB TO THE GROUND...
...ASCETIC.

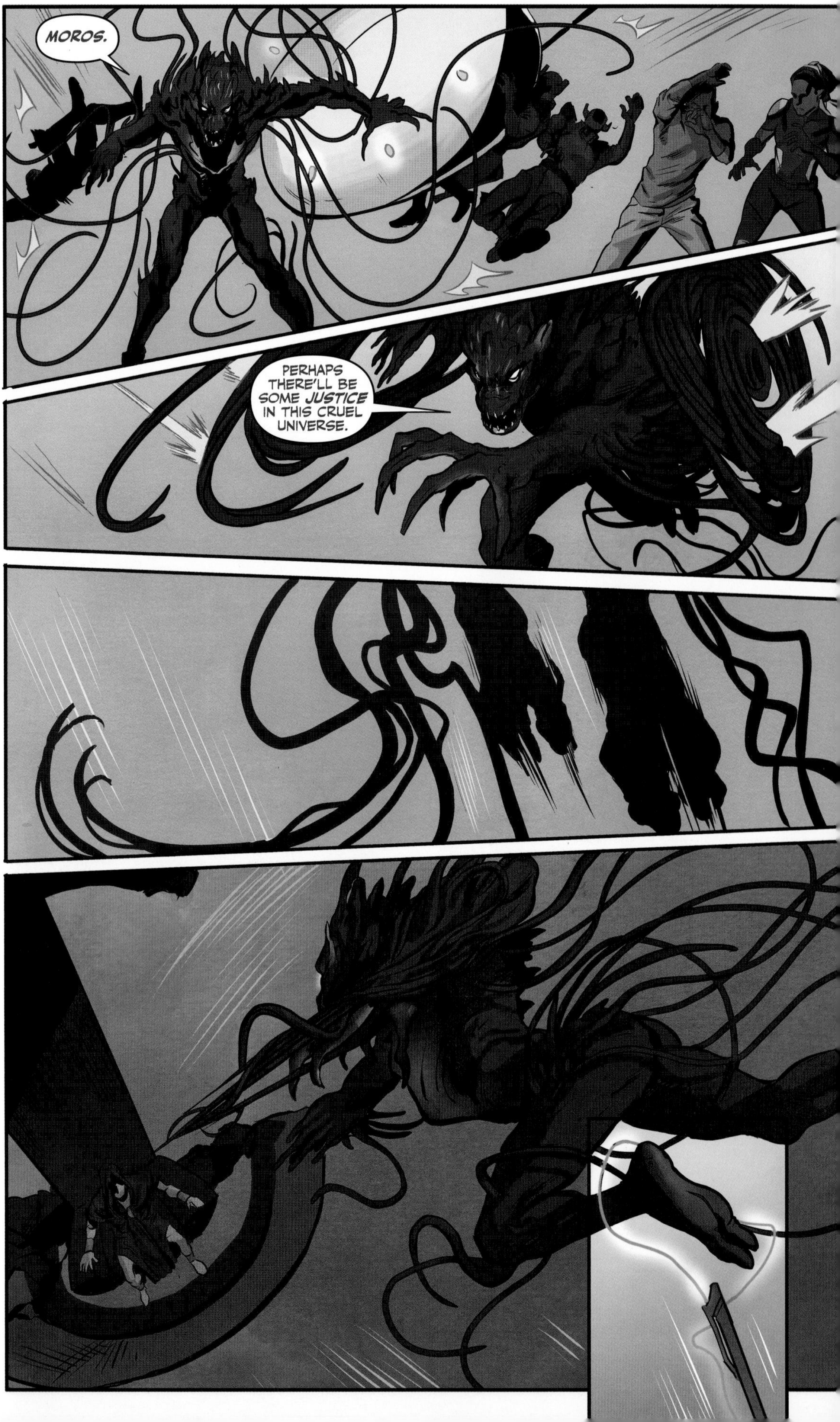
MOROS.
PERHAPS THERE'LL BE SOME *JUSTICE* IN THIS CRUEL UNIVERSE.

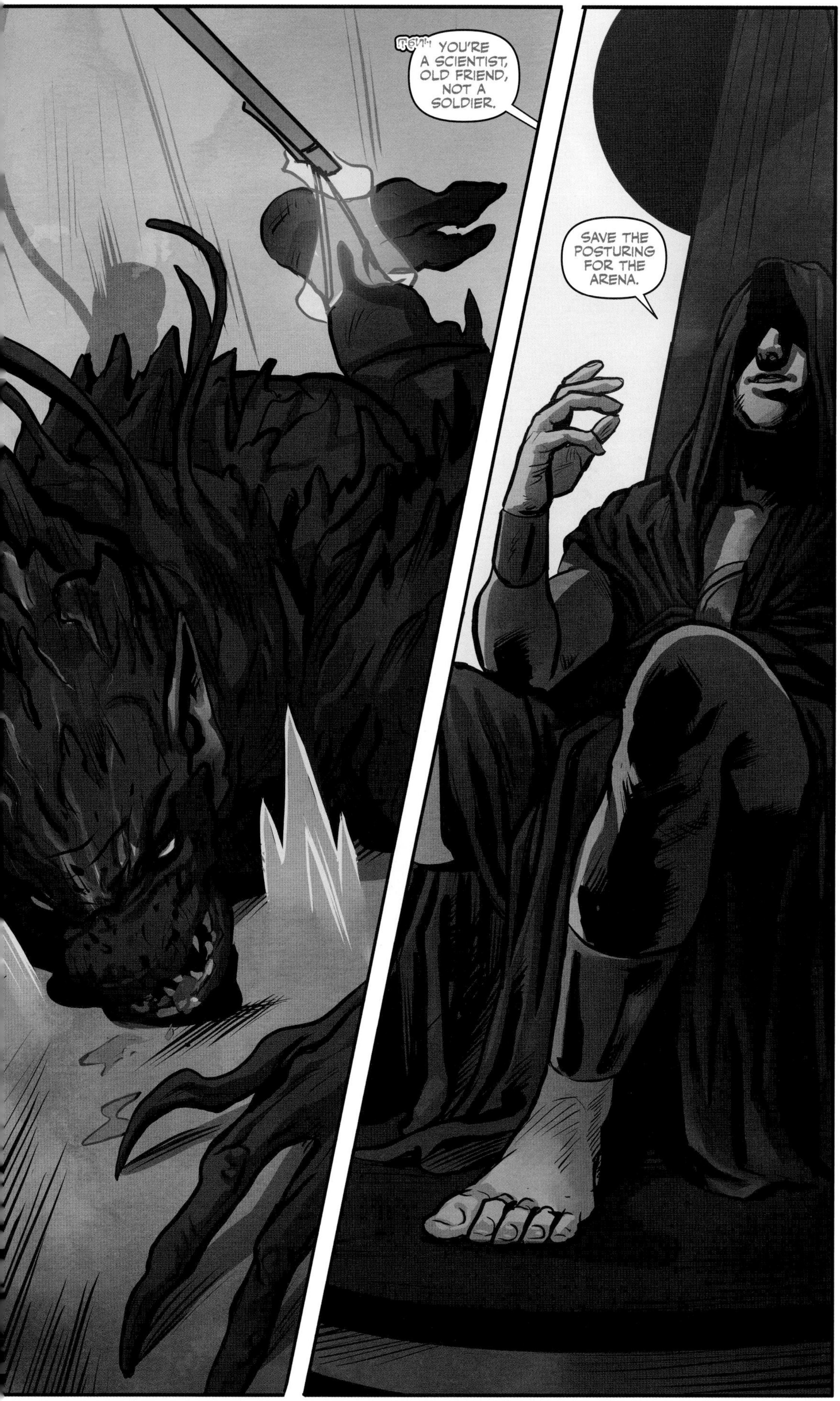
YOU'RE A SCIENTIST, OLD FRIEND, NOT A SOLDIER.
SAVE THE POSTURING FOR THE ARENA.

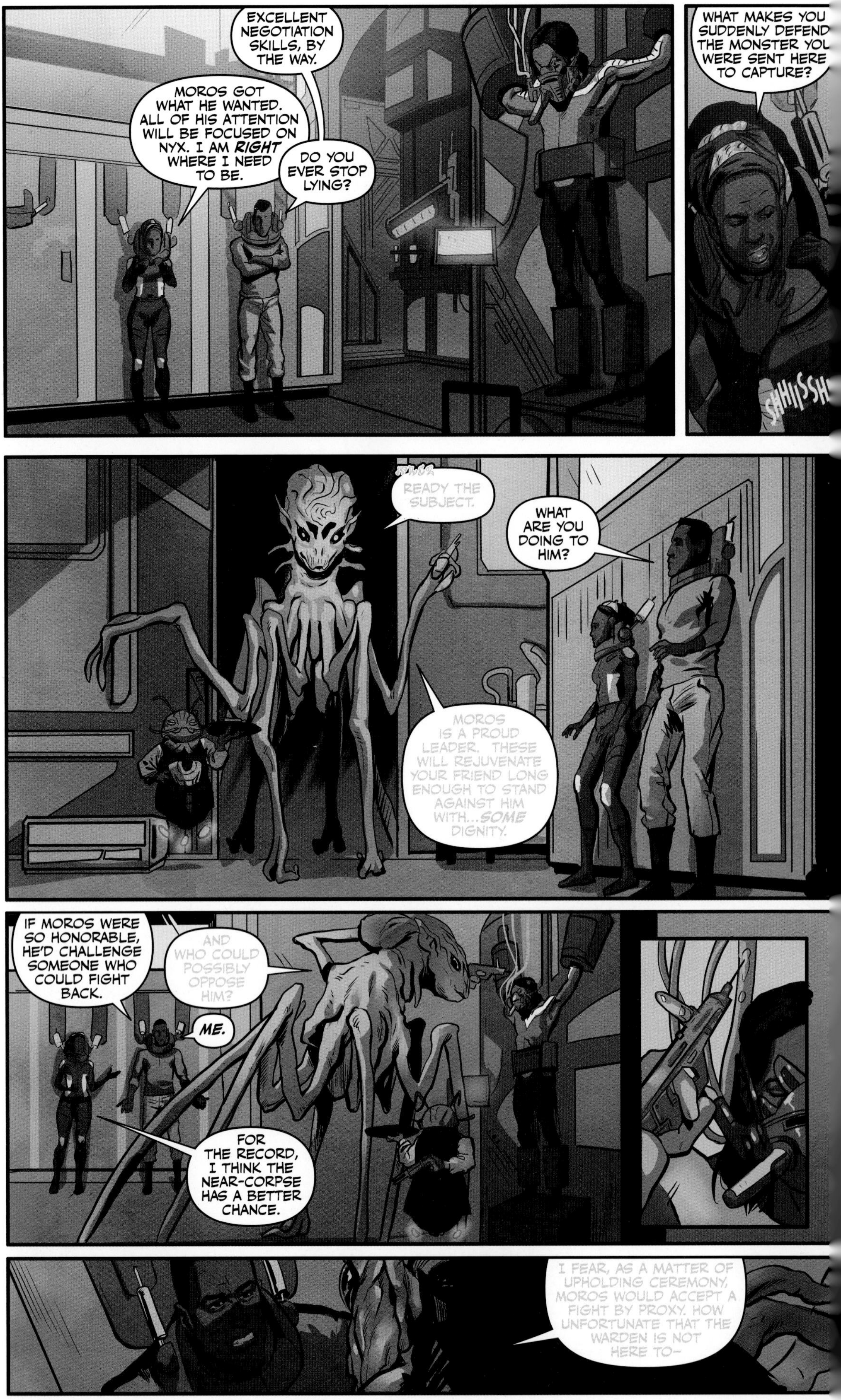
EXCELLENT NEGOTIATION SKILLS, BY THE WAY.
MOROS GOT WHAT HE WANTED. ALL OF HIS ATTENTION WILL BE FOCUSED ON NYX. I AM *RIGHT* WHERE I NEED TO BE.
DO YOU EVER STOP LYING?
WHAT MAKES YOU SUDDENLY DEFEND THE MONSTER YOU WERE SENT HERE TO CAPTURE?
SHHIISSH
READY THE SUBJECT.
WHAT ARE YOU DOING TO HIM?
MOROS IS A PROUD LEADER. THESE WILL REJUVENATE YOUR FRIEND LONG ENOUGH TO STAND AGAINST HIM WITH...*SOME* DIGNITY.
IF MOROS WERE SO HONORABLE, HE'D CHALLENGE SOMEONE WHO COULD FIGHT BACK.
AND WHO COULD POSSIBLY OPPOSE HIM?
ME.
FOR THE RECORD, I THINK THE NEAR-CORPSE HAS A BETTER CHANCE.
I FEAR, AS A MATTER OF UPHOLDING CEREMONY, MOROS WOULD ACCEPT A FIGHT BY PROXY. HOW UNFORTUNATE THAT THE WARDEN IS NOT HERE TO—

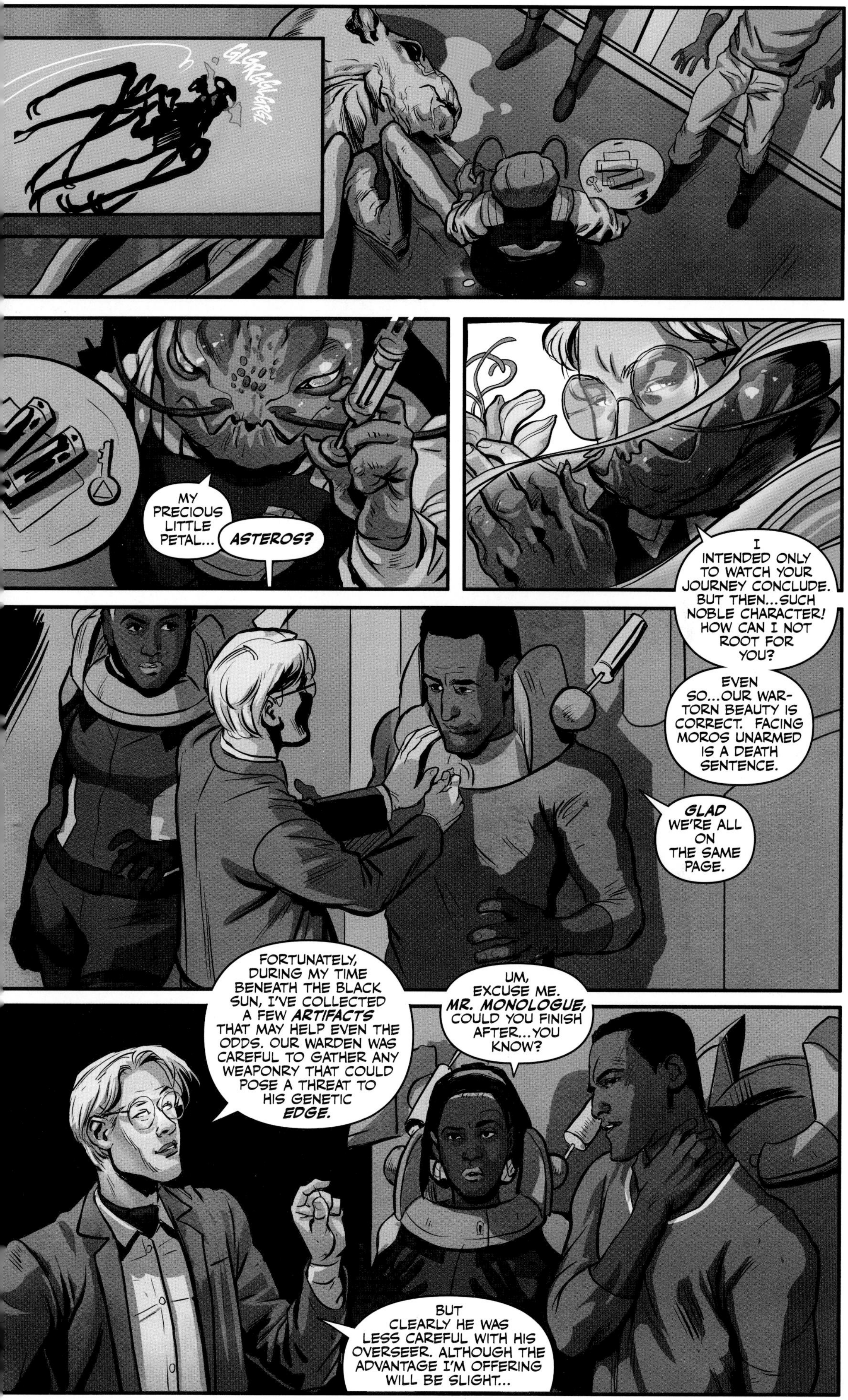
GLGRGGLGRGL
MY PRECIOUS LITTLE PETAL...
ASTEROS?
I INTENDED ONLY TO WATCH YOUR JOURNEY CONCLUDE. BUT THEN...SUCH NOBLE CHARACTER! HOW CAN I NOT ROOT FOR YOU?
EVEN SO...OUR WAR-TORN BEAUTY IS CORRECT. FACING MOROS UNARMED IS A DEATH SENTENCE.
GLAD WE'RE ALL ON THE SAME PAGE.
FORTUNATELY, DURING MY TIME BENEATH THE BLACK SUN, I'VE COLLECTED A FEW ARTIFACTS THAT MAY HELP EVEN THE ODDS. OUR WARDEN WAS CAREFUL TO GATHER ANY WEAPONRY THAT COULD POSE A THREAT TO HIS GENETIC EDGE.
UM, EXCUSE ME. MR. MONOLOGUE, COULD YOU FINISH AFTER...YOU KNOW?
BUT CLEARLY HE WAS LESS CAREFUL WITH HIS OVERSEER. ALTHOUGH THE ADVANTAGE I'M OFFERING WILL BE SLIGHT...

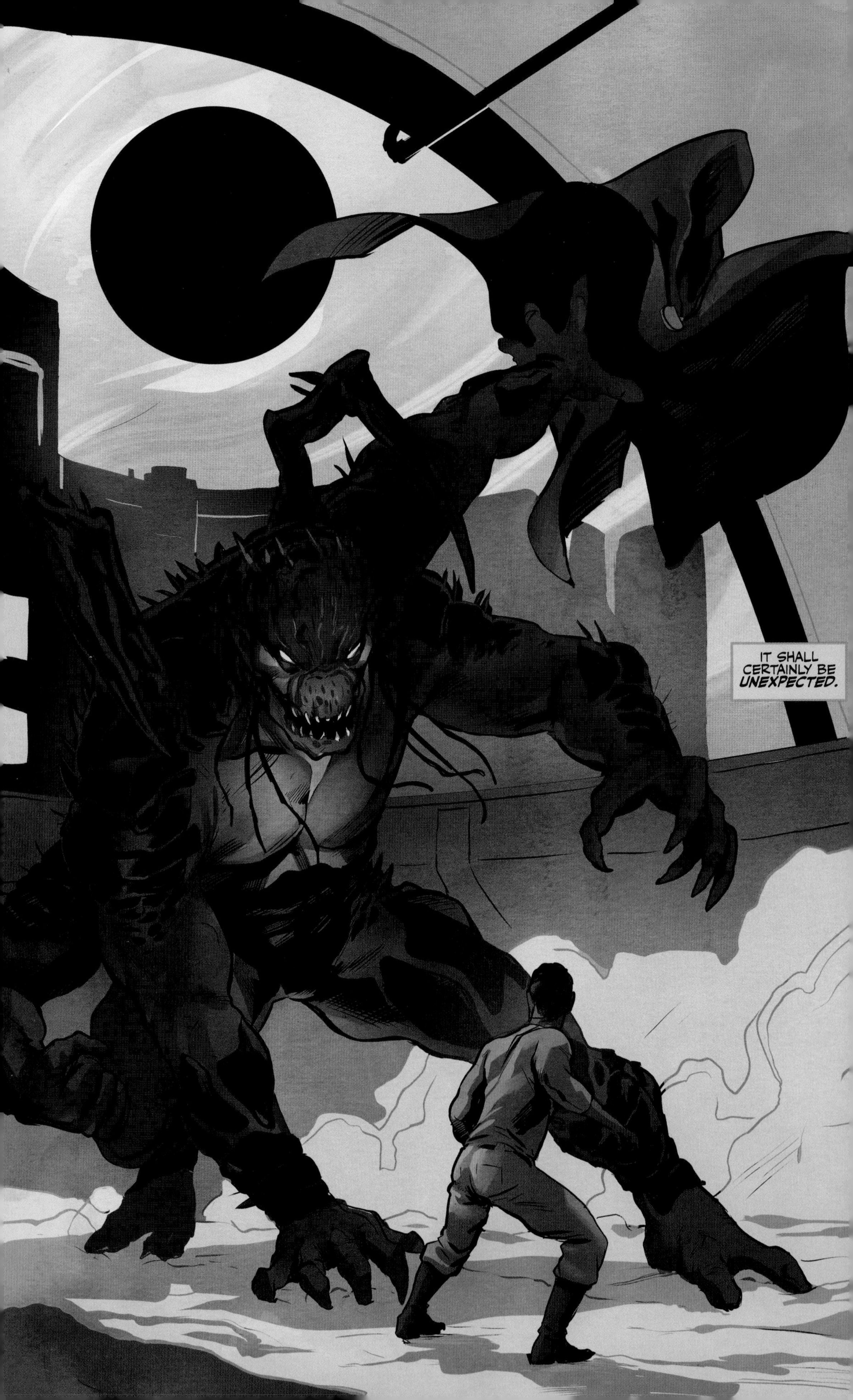
IT SHALL CERTAINLY BE UNEXPECTED.

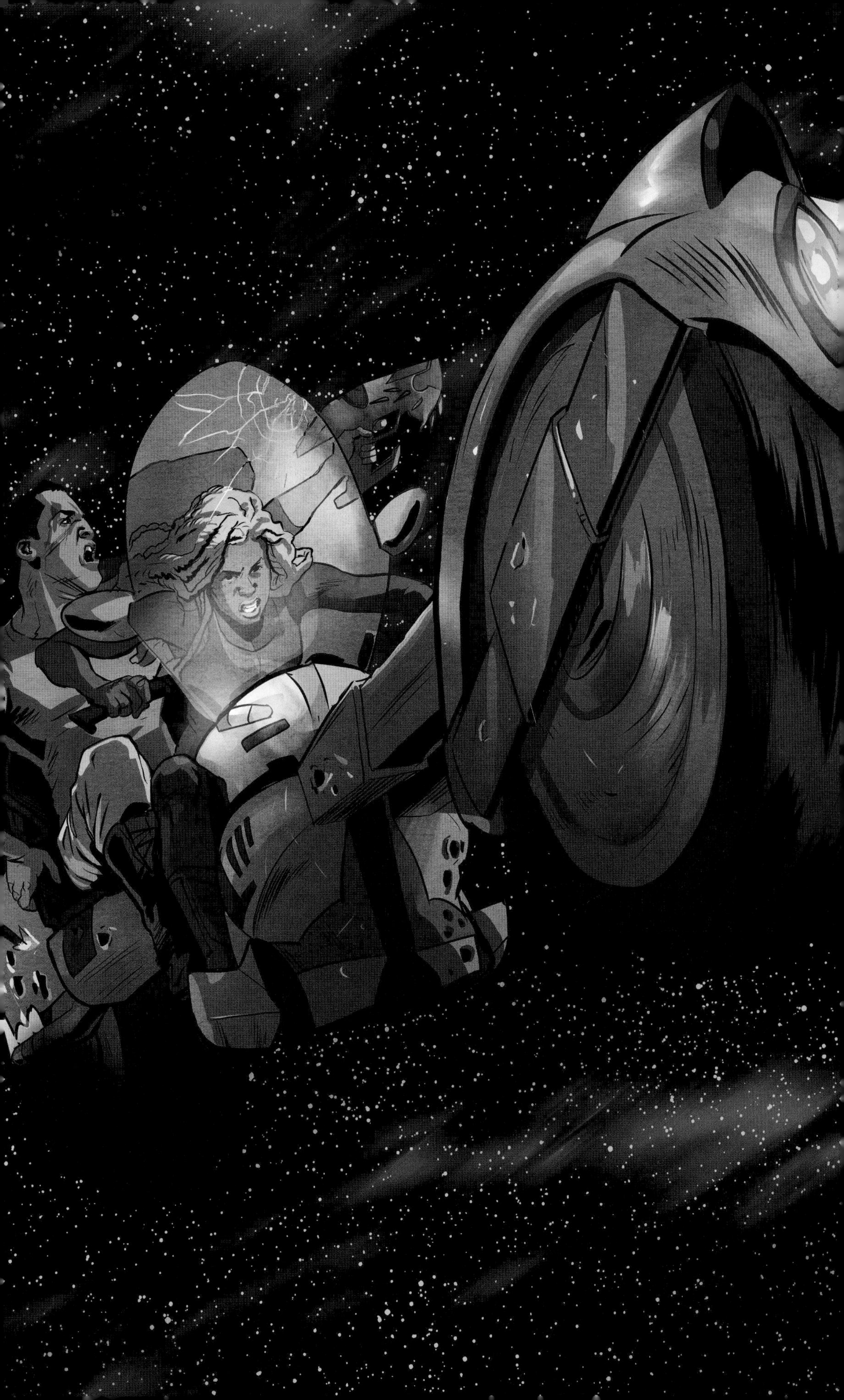

CHAPTER 5

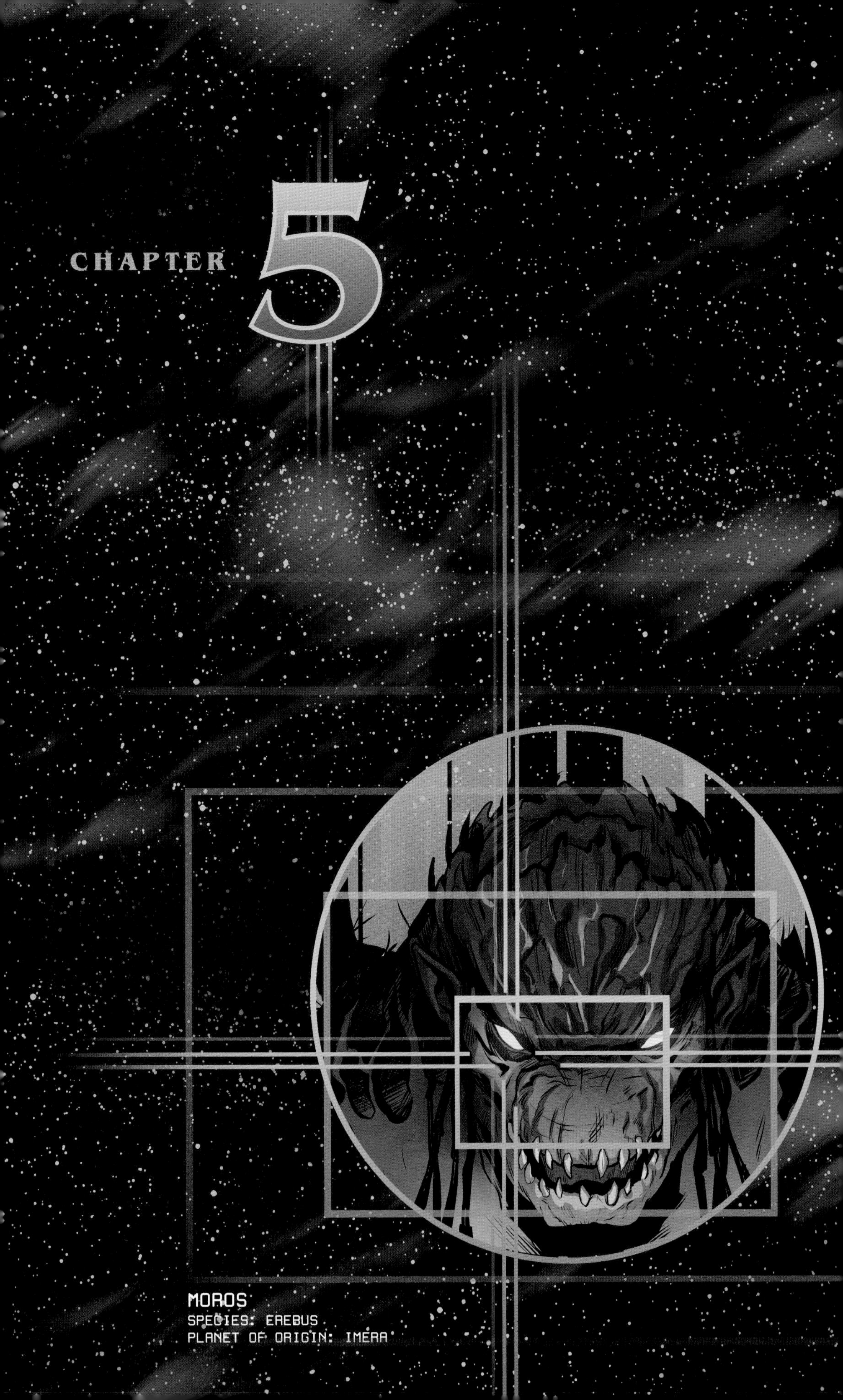
MOROS
SPECIES: EREBUS
PLANET OF ORIGIN: IMERA

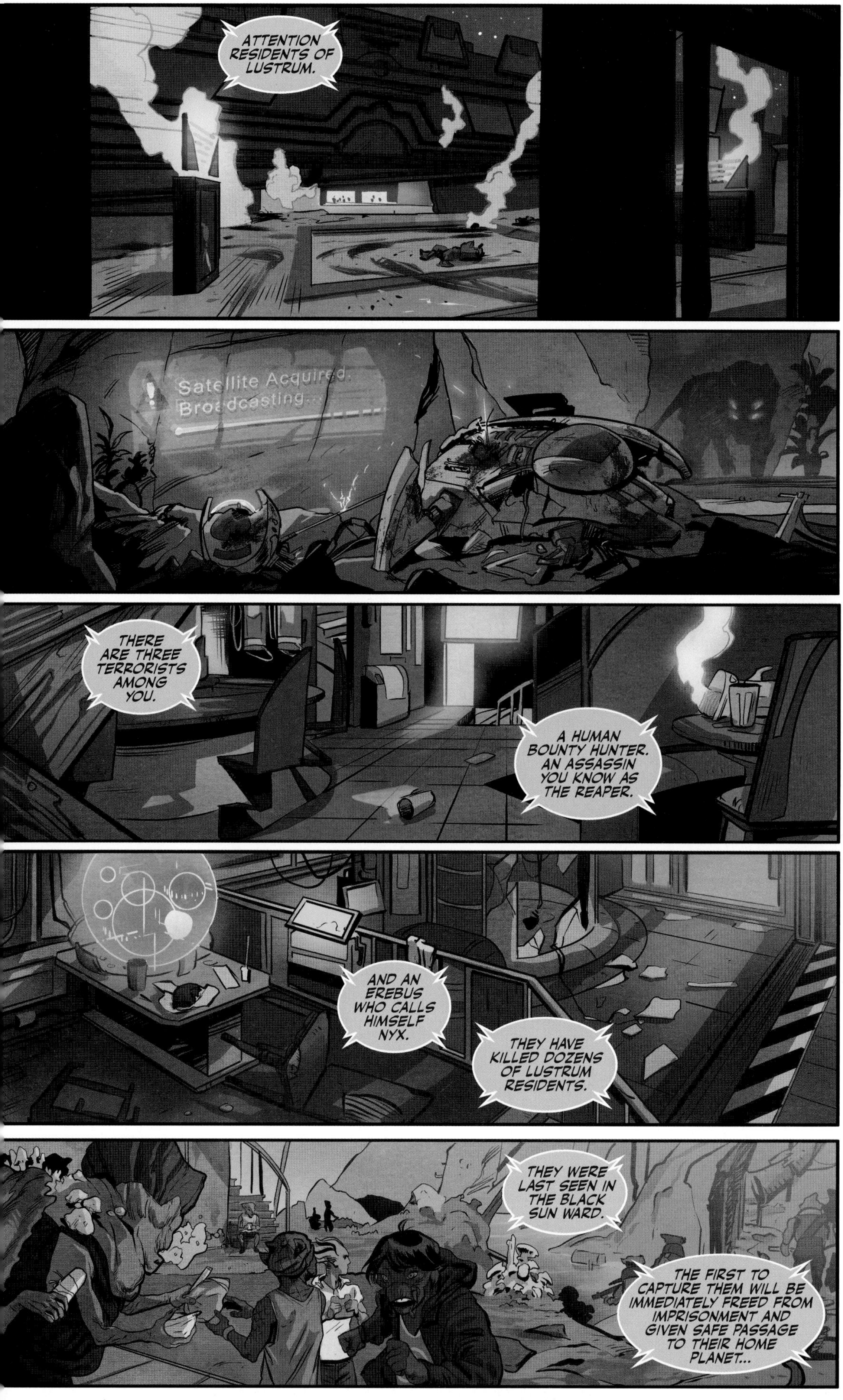
ATTENTION RESIDENTS OF LUSTRUM.
Satellite Acquired.
Broadcasting...
THERE ARE THREE TERRORISTS AMONG YOU.
A HUMAN BOUNTY HUNTER. AN ASSASSIN YOU KNOW AS THE REAPER.
AND AN EREBUS WHO CALLS HIMSELF NYX.
THEY HAVE KILLED DOZENS OF LUSTRUM RESIDENTS.
THEY WERE LAST SEEN IN THE BLACK SUN WARD.
THE FIRST TO CAPTURE THEM WILL BE IMMEDIATELY FREED FROM IMPRISONMENT AND GIVEN SAFE PASSAGE TO THEIR HOME PLANET...

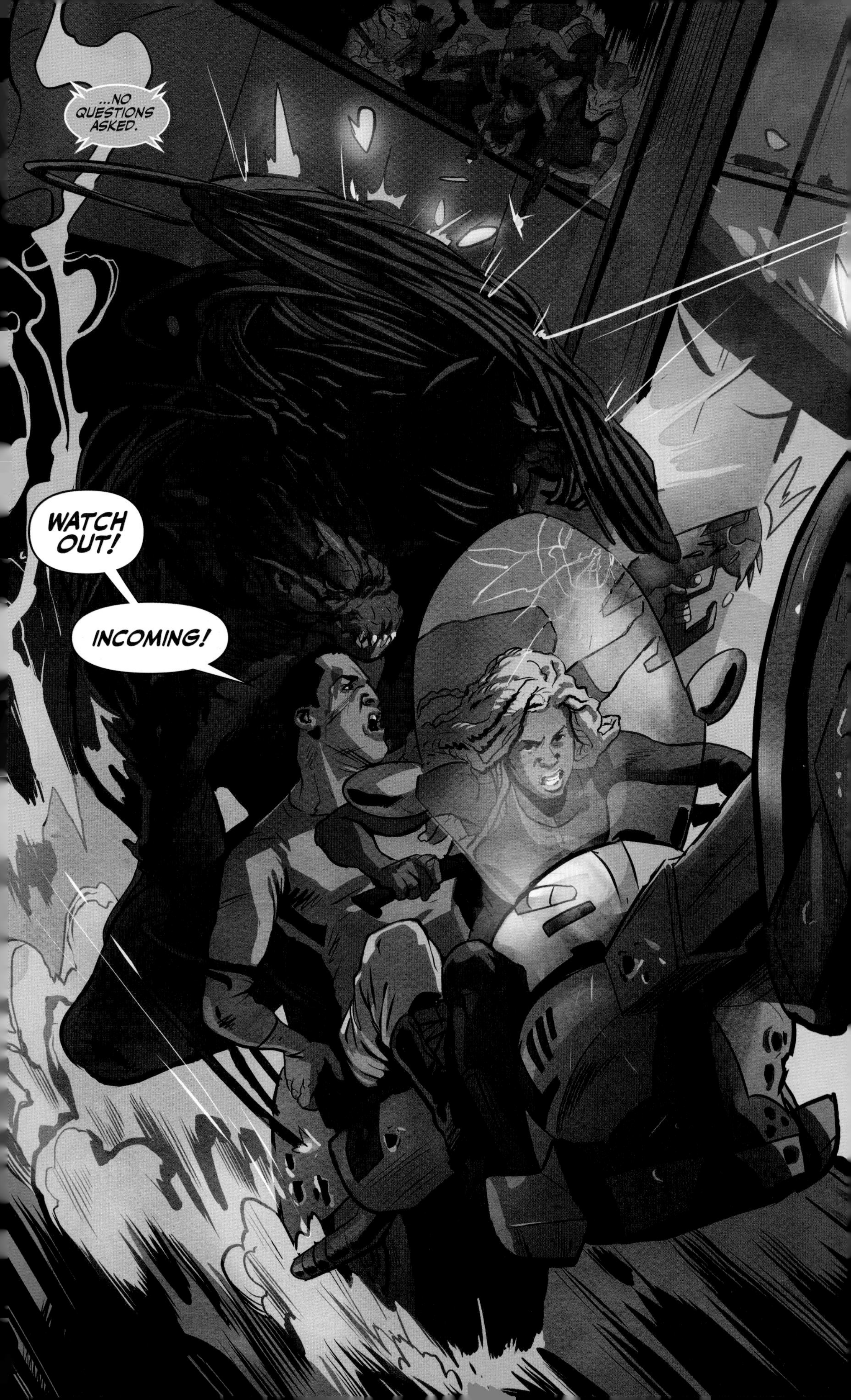
...NO QUESTIONS ASKED.
WATCH OUT!
INCOMING!

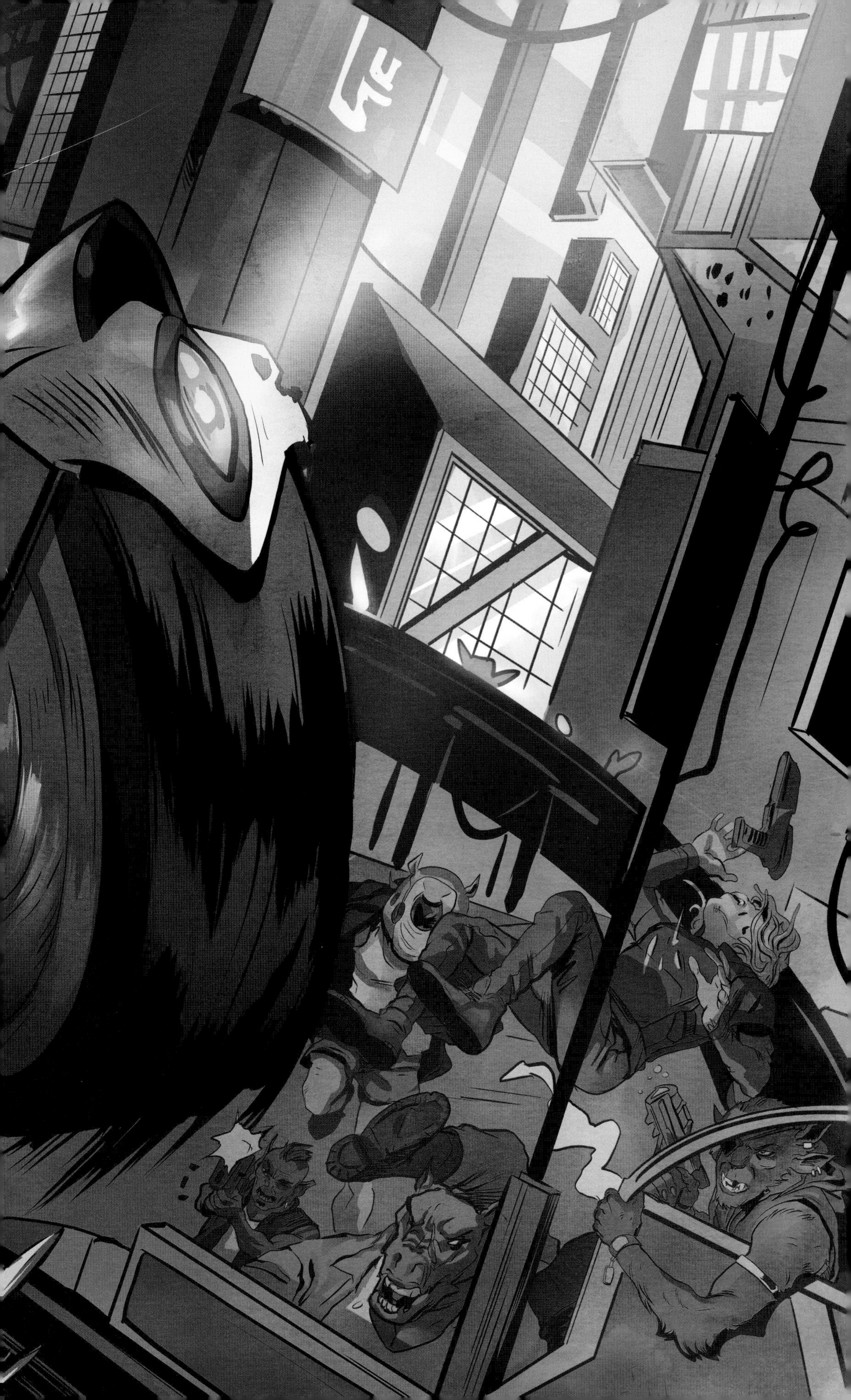

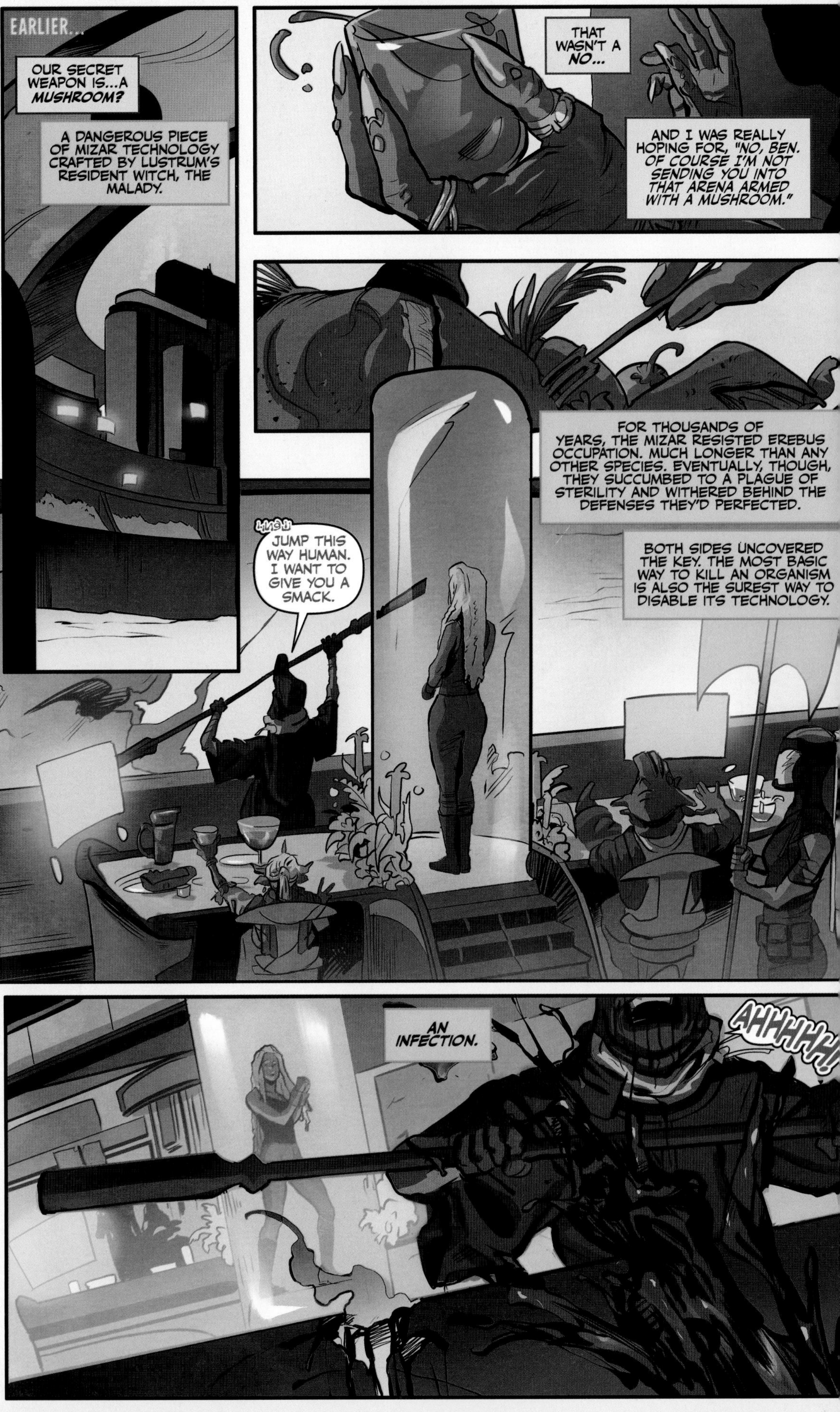
EARLIER...
OUR SECRET WEAPON IS...A MUSHROOM?
A DANGEROUS PIECE OF MIZAR TECHNOLOGY CRAFTED BY LUSTRUM'S RESIDENT WITCH, THE MALADY.
THAT WASN'T A NO...
AND I WAS REALLY HOPING FOR, "NO, BEN. OF COURSE I'M NOT SENDING YOU INTO THAT ARENA ARMED WITH A MUSHROOM."
FOR THOUSANDS OF YEARS, THE MIZAR RESISTED EREBUS OCCUPATION. MUCH LONGER THAN ANY OTHER SPECIES. EVENTUALLY, THOUGH, THEY SUCCUMBED TO A PLAGUE OF STERILITY AND WITHERED BEHIND THE DEFENSES THEY'D PERFECTED.
JUMP THIS WAY HUMAN. I WANT TO GIVE YOU A SMACK.
BOTH SIDES UNCOVERED THE KEY. THE MOST BASIC WAY TO KILL AN ORGANISM IS ALSO THE SUREST WAY TO DISABLE ITS TECHNOLOGY.
AN INFECTION.
AHHHHH!

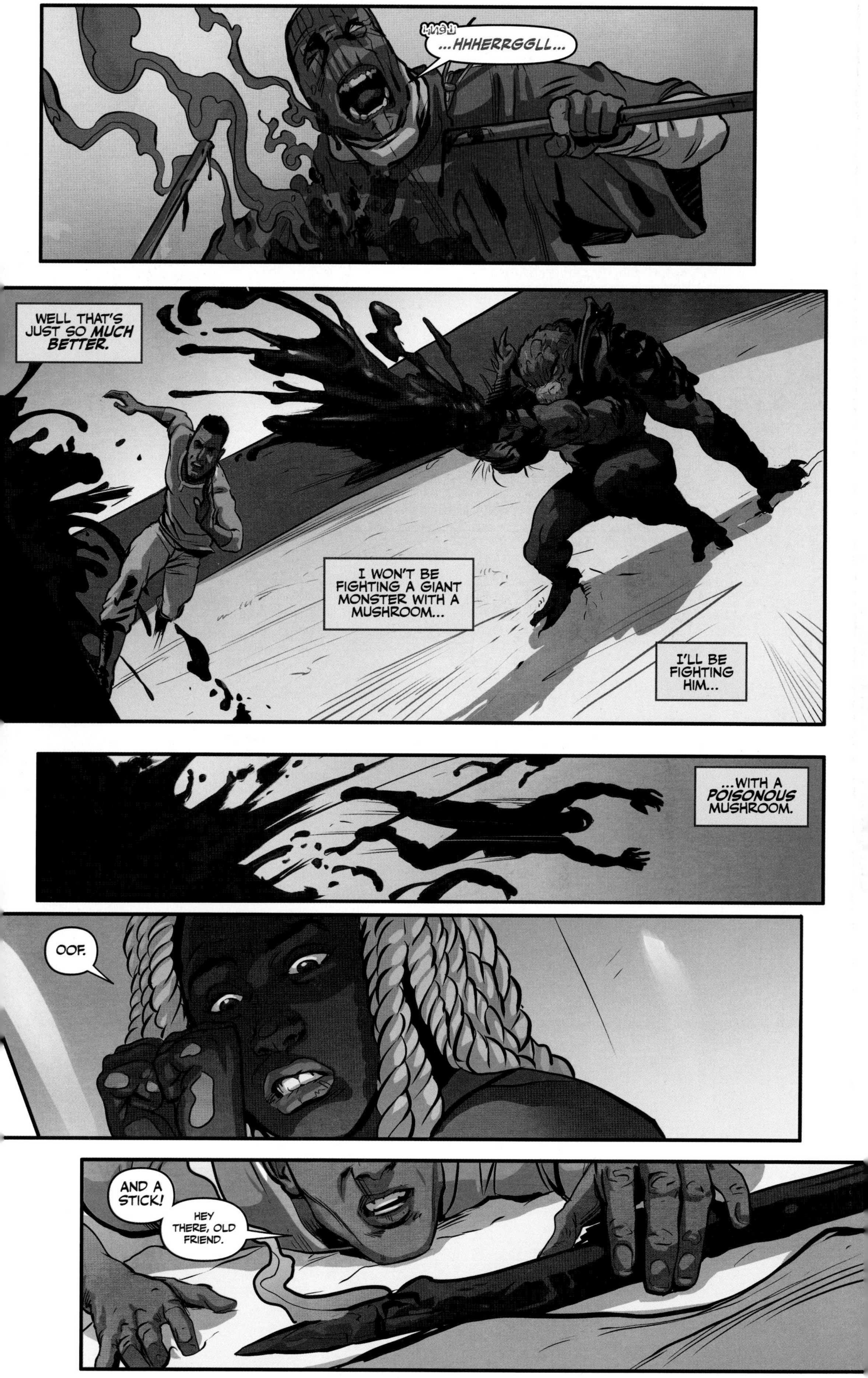
...HHHERRGGLL...
WELL THAT'S JUST SO MUCH BETTER.
I WON'T BE FIGHTING A GIANT MONSTER WITH A MUSHROOM...
I'LL BE FIGHTING HIM...
...WITH A POISONOUS MUSHROOM.
OOF.
AND A STICK!
HEY THERE, OLD FRIEND.

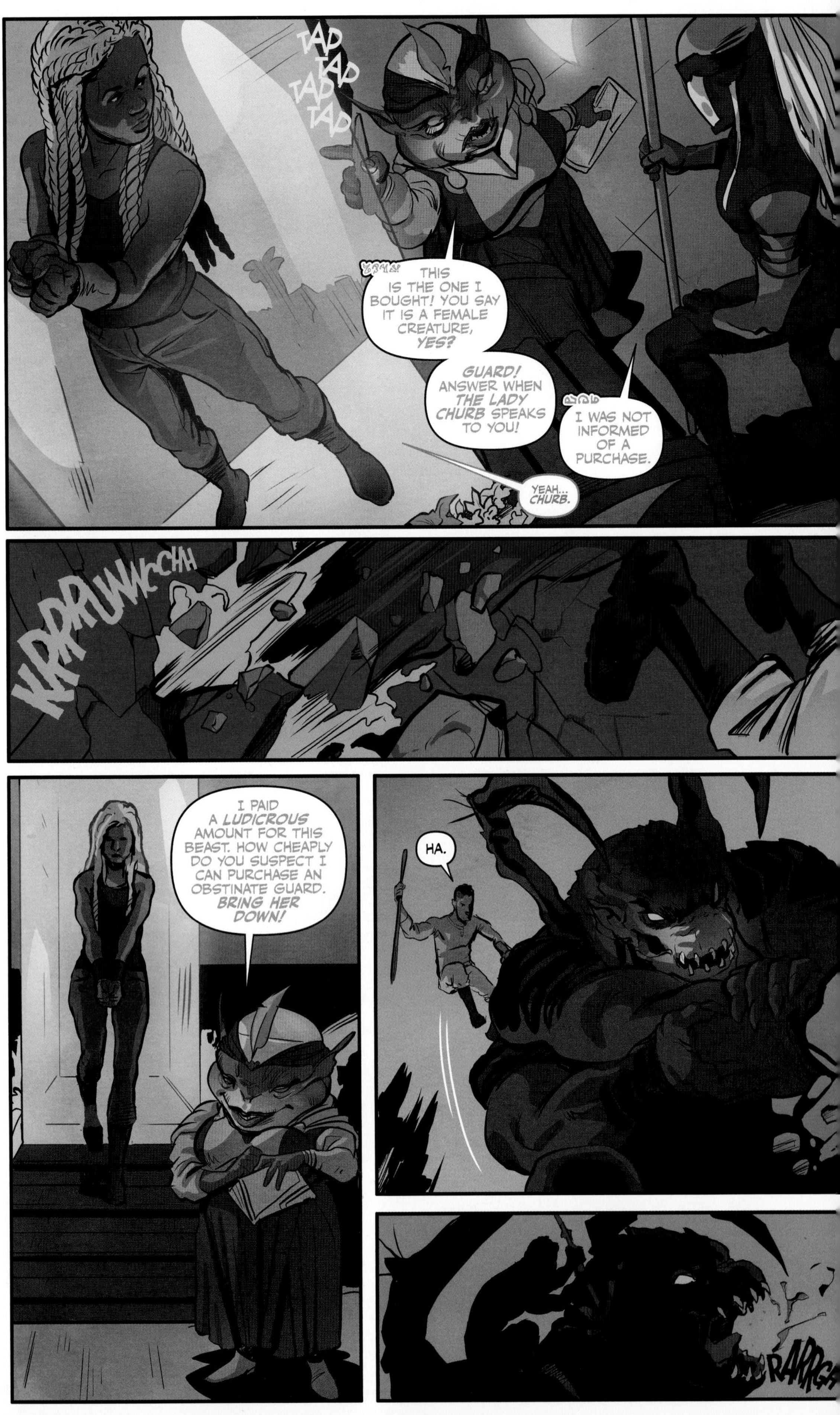
TAP TAP TAP TAP
THIS IS THE ONE I BOUGHT! YOU SAY IT IS A FEMALE CREATURE, YES?
GUARD! ANSWER WHEN THE LADY CHURB SPEAKS TO YOU!
I WAS NOT INFORMED OF A PURCHASE.
YEAH... CHURB.
KRRRUNCCHH
I PAID A LUDICROUS AMOUNT FOR THIS BEAST. HOW CHEAPLY DO YOU SUSPECT I CAN PURCHASE AN OBSTINATE GUARD. BRING HER DOWN!
HA.
RARRGA

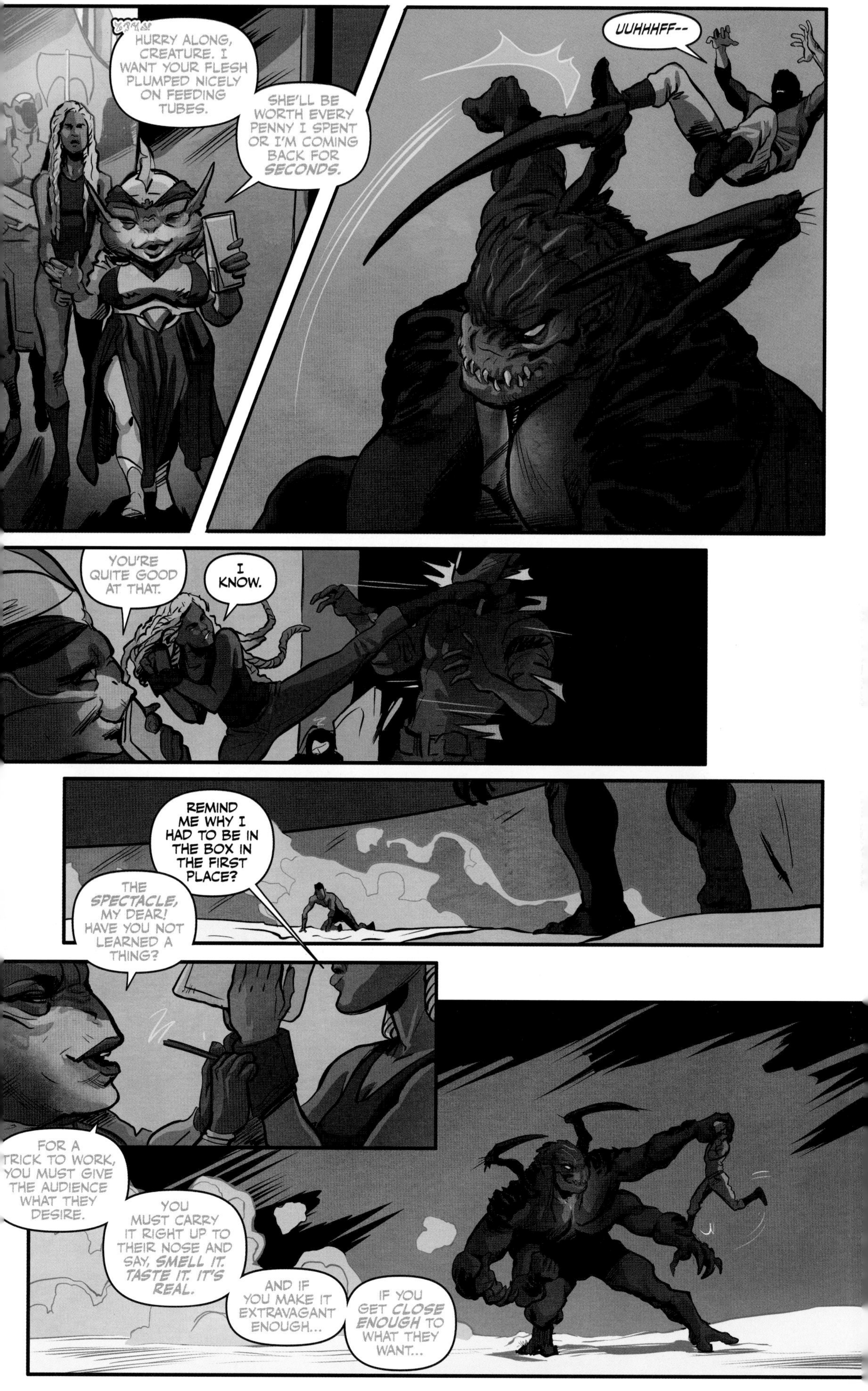
HURRY ALONG, CREATURE. I WANT YOUR FLESH PLUMPED NICELY ON FEEDING TUBES.
SHE'LL BE WORTH EVERY PENNY I SPENT OR I'M COMING BACK FOR SECONDS.
UUHHHFF--
YOU'RE QUITE GOOD AT THAT.
I KNOW.
REMIND ME WHY I HAD TO BE IN THE BOX IN THE FIRST PLACE?
THE SPECTACLE, MY DEAR! HAVE YOU NOT LEARNED A THING?
FOR A TRICK TO WORK, YOU MUST GIVE THE AUDIENCE WHAT THEY DESIRE.
YOU MUST CARRY IT RIGHT UP TO THEIR NOSE AND SAY, SMELL IT. TASTE IT. IT'S REAL.
AND IF YOU MAKE IT EXTRAVAGANT ENOUGH...
IF YOU GET CLOSE ENOUGH TO WHAT THEY WANT...

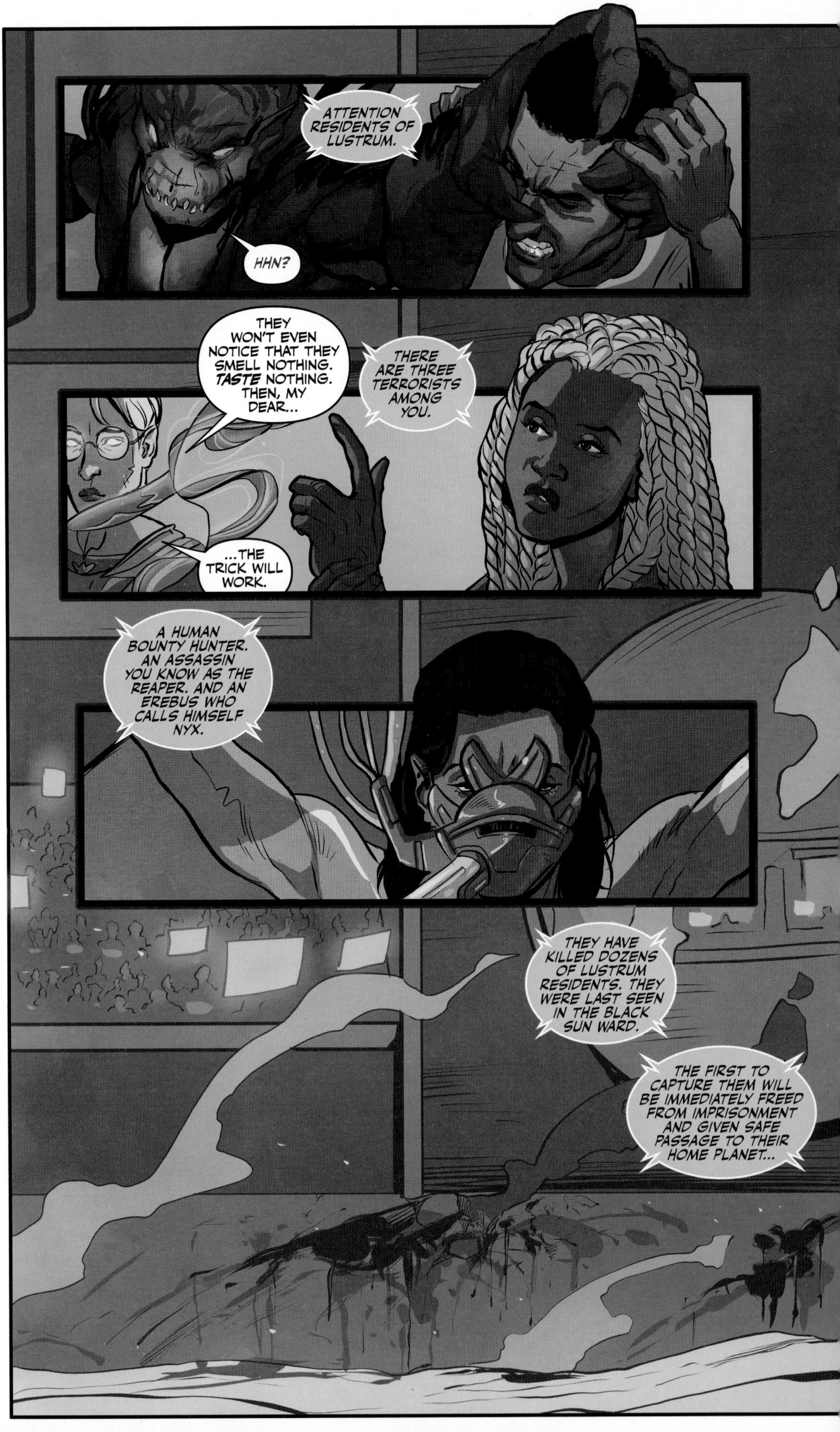
ATTENTION RESIDENTS OF LUSTRUM.
HHN?
THEY WON'T EVEN NOTICE THAT THEY SMELL NOTHING. *TASTE* NOTHING. THEN, MY DEAR...
THERE ARE THREE TERRORISTS AMONG YOU.
...THE TRICK WILL WORK.
A HUMAN BOUNTY HUNTER. AN ASSASSIN YOU KNOW AS THE REAPER. AND AN EREBUS WHO CALLS HIMSELF NYX.
THEY HAVE KILLED DOZENS OF LUSTRUM RESIDENTS. THEY WERE LAST SEEN IN THE BLACK SUN WARD.
THE FIRST TO CAPTURE THEM WILL BE IMMEDIATELY FREED FROM IMPRISONMENT AND GIVEN SAFE PASSAGE TO THEIR HOME PLANET...

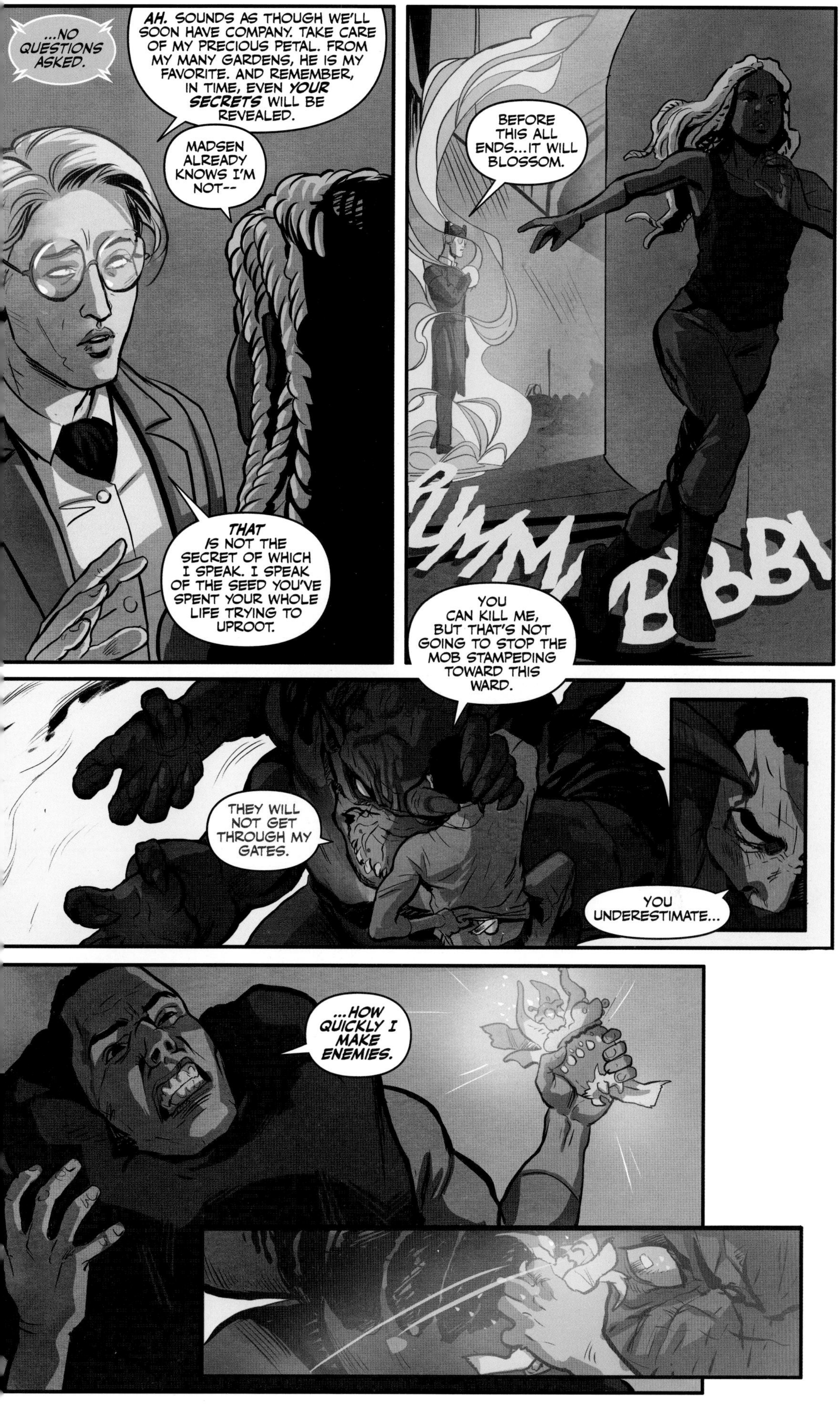
...NO QUESTIONS ASKED.
AH. SOUNDS AS THOUGH WE'LL SOON HAVE COMPANY. TAKE CARE OF MY PRECIOUS PETAL. FROM MY MANY GARDENS, HE IS MY FAVORITE. AND REMEMBER, IN TIME, EVEN YOUR SECRETS WILL BE REVEALED.
MADSEN ALREADY KNOWS I'M NOT--
THAT IS NOT THE SECRET OF WHICH I SPEAK. I SPEAK OF THE SEED YOU'VE SPENT YOUR WHOLE LIFE TRYING TO UPROOT.
BEFORE THIS ALL ENDS...IT WILL BLOSSOM.
YOU CAN KILL ME, BUT THAT'S NOT GOING TO STOP THE MOB STAMPEDING TOWARD THIS WARD.
THEY WILL NOT GET THROUGH MY GATES.
YOU UNDERESTIMATE...
...HOW QUICKLY I MAKE ENEMIES.

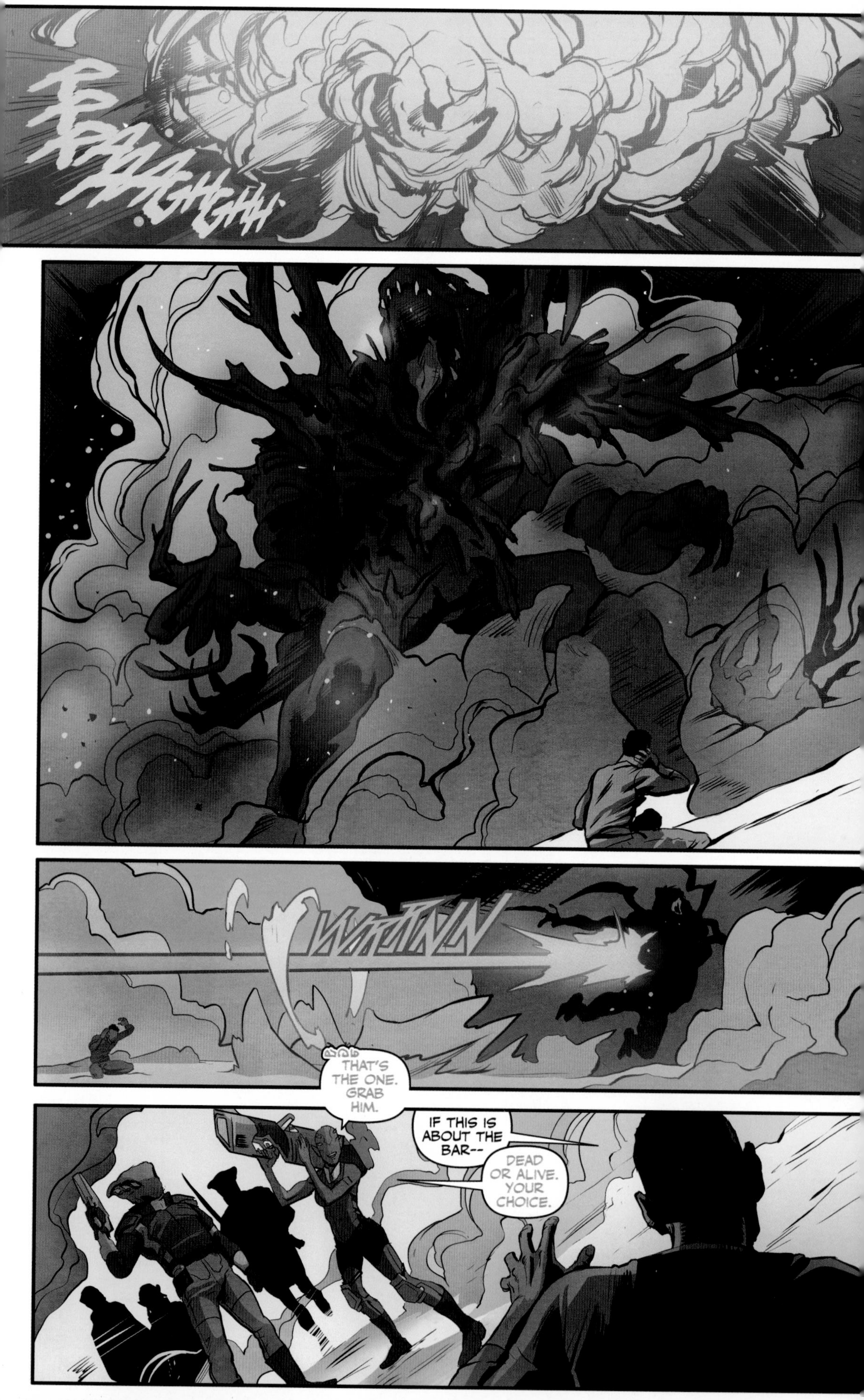
THAT'S THE ONE. GRAB HIM.
IF THIS IS ABOUT THE BAR--
DEAD OR ALIVE. YOUR CHOICE.

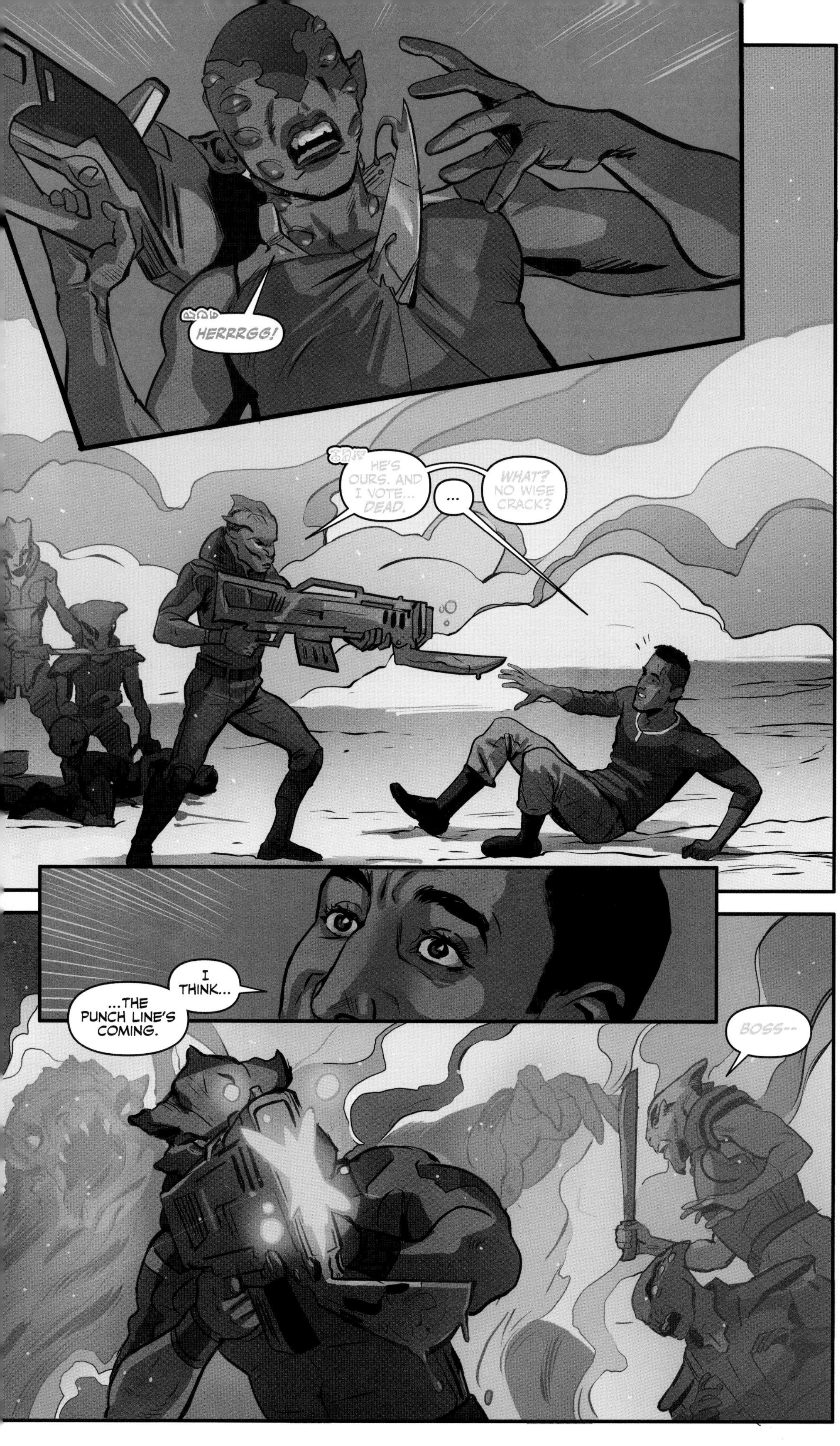
HERRRGG!
HE'S OURS. AND I VOTE... DEAD.
...
WHAT? NO WISE CRACK?
I THINK...
...THE PUNCH LINE'S COMING.
BOSS--

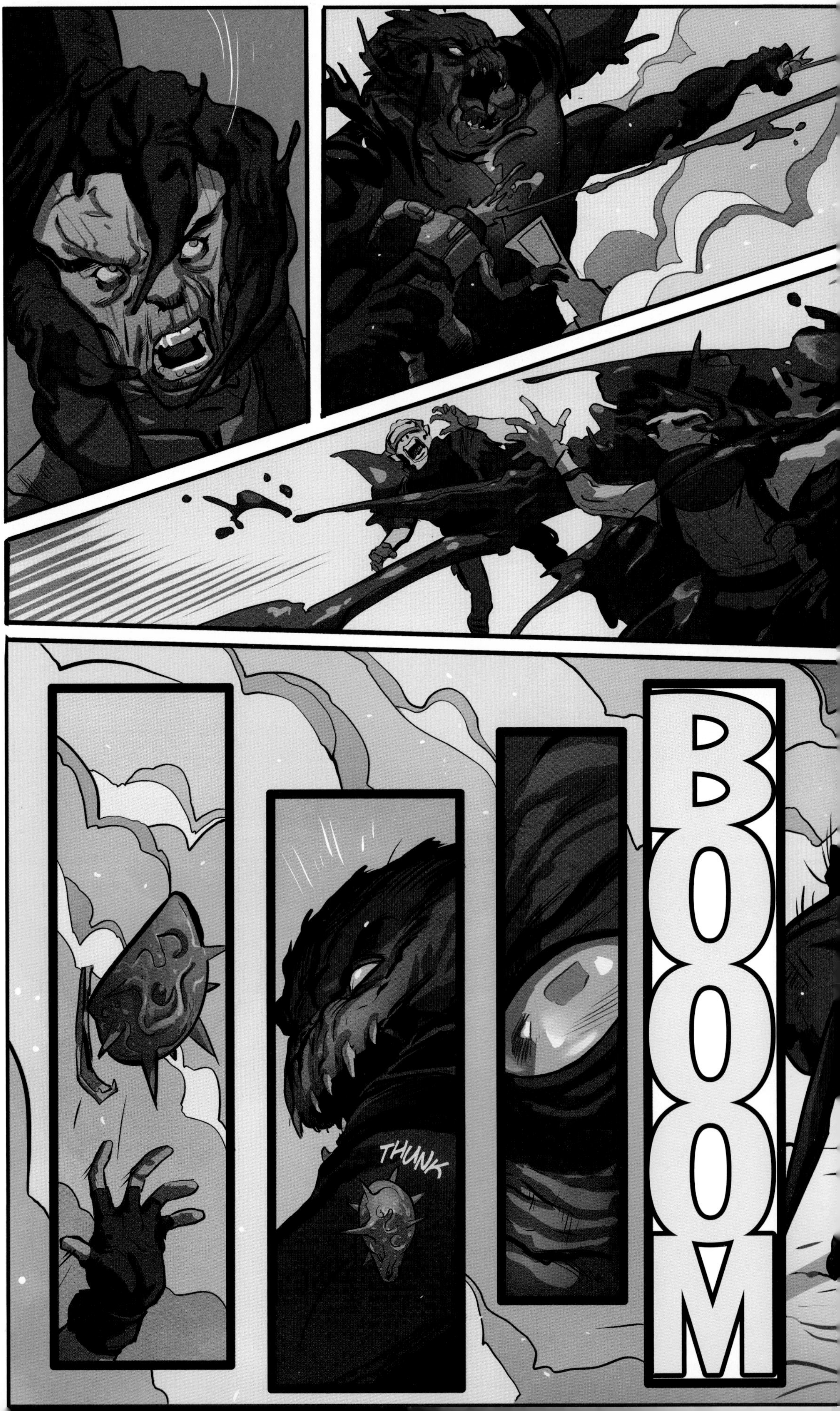
THUNK
BOOOOM

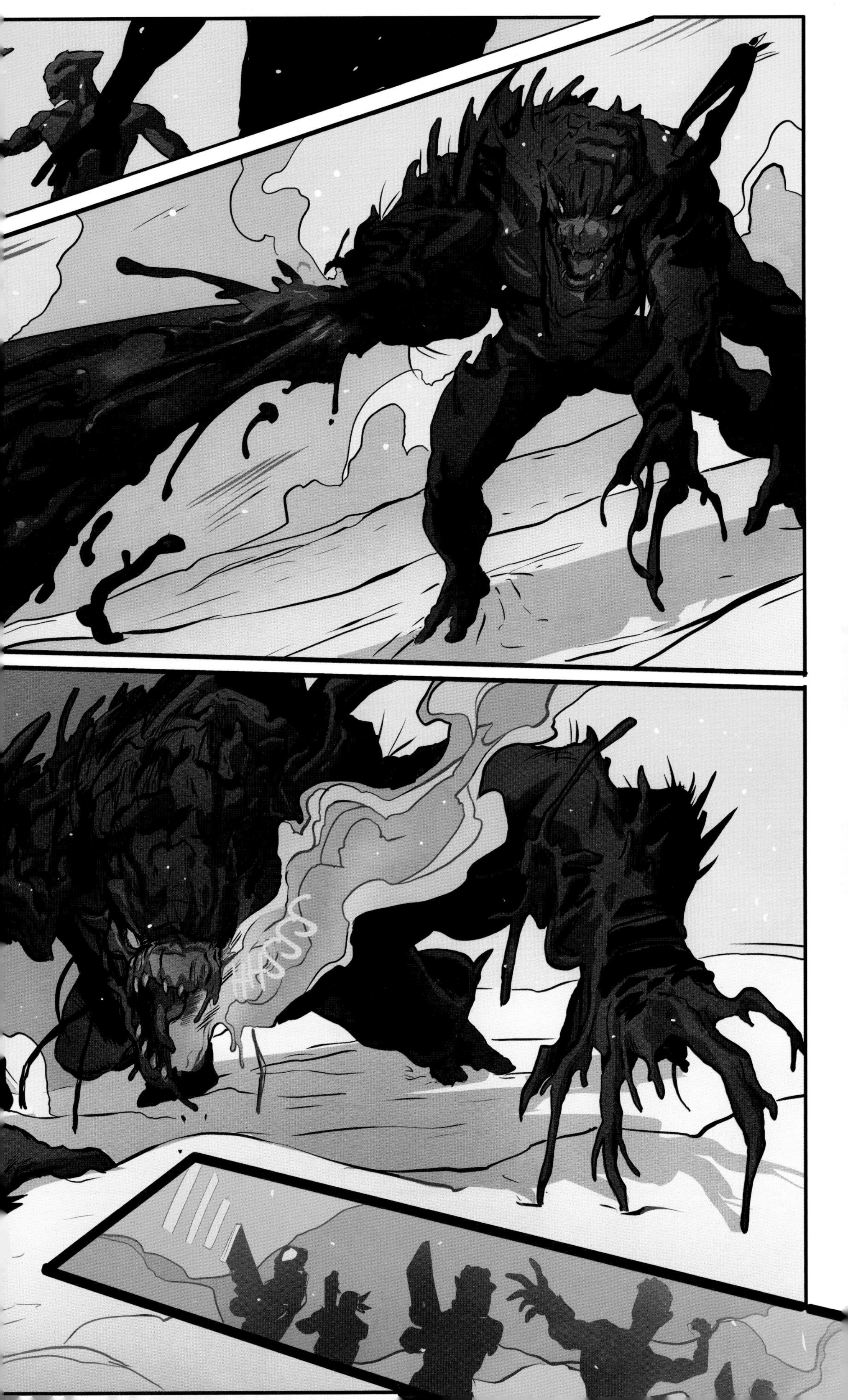
HSSS

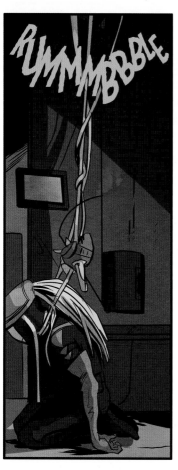

RUMMMBBBLE

RUMMMBBBLE

HURRY.

THAT'S FAR ENOUGH.

DO YOU HEAR WHAT'S HAPPENING? WE NEED TO GET TO THE MIDNIGHT GATES.

I WILL NOT ABANDON HIM.

HE STEPPED INTO THAT ARENA TO FACE A THREAT YOU CANNOT POSSIBLY COMPREHEND. GIVEN THE CHOICE...

...I'D RATHER DIE BESIDE SOMEONE WITH INTEGRITY.

THAT'S VERY NOBLE AND ALL...

...BUT THE ARENA IS THIS DIRECTION.

FORGET THE EREBUS! WHERE'S THE HUMAN?

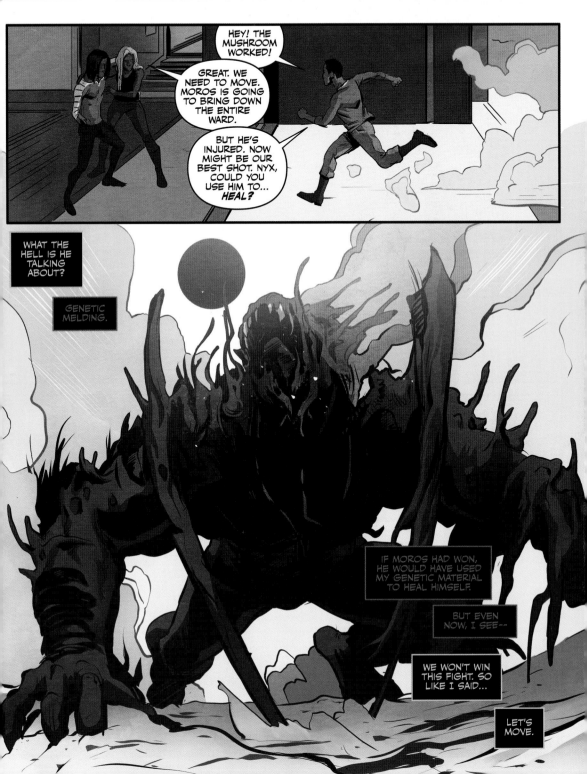

HEY! THE MUSHROOM WORKED!

GREAT. WE NEED TO MOVE. MOROS IS GOING TO BRING DOWN THE ENTIRE WARD.

BUT HE'S INJURED. NOW MIGHT BE OUR BEST SHOT. NYX, COULD YOU USE HIM TO... *HEAL?*

WHAT THE HELL IS HE TALKING ABOUT?

GENETIC MELDING.

IF MOROS HAD WON, HE WOULD HAVE USED MY GENETIC MATERIAL TO HEAL HIMSELF.

BUT EVEN NOW, I SEE--

WE WON'T WIN THIS FIGHT. SO LIKE I SAID...

LET'S MOVE.

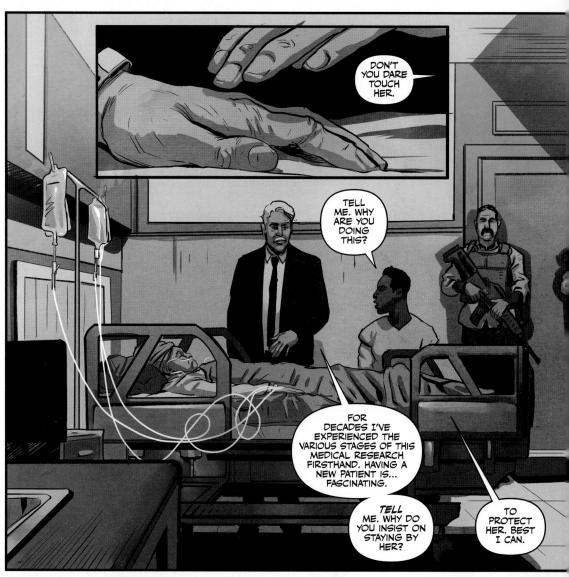

DON'T YOU DARE TOUCH HER.

TELL ME. WHY ARE YOU DOING THIS?

FOR DECADES I'VE EXPERIENCED THE VARIOUS STAGES OF THIS MEDICAL RESEARCH FIRSTHAND. HAVING A NEW PATIENT IS... FASCINATING.

TELL ME. WHY DO YOU INSIST ON STAYING BY HER?

TO PROTECT HER. BEST I CAN.

PRECISELY. SHE IS ONE PERSON. I PROTECT SEVEN *BILLION.*

CSSSZZZCHHK... COALITION CRAFT HAS TOUCHED DOWN.

THIS IS *PROTECTION?* ABDUCTING US AND BRINGING US TO THIS...THIS... *PRISON?*

SIR, THE COALITION--

I'M NOT DEAF.

KEEP AN EYE ON HER. IF SHE ACTS UP, FEEL FREE TO PLACE HER IN A SUSPENSION CHAMBER. AND MRS. BROOKS...

...IN MOMENTS, THE WORLD MAY GET ITS FIRST GLIMPSE OF LIFE WITHOUT MY PROTECTION. I CAN PROMISE...

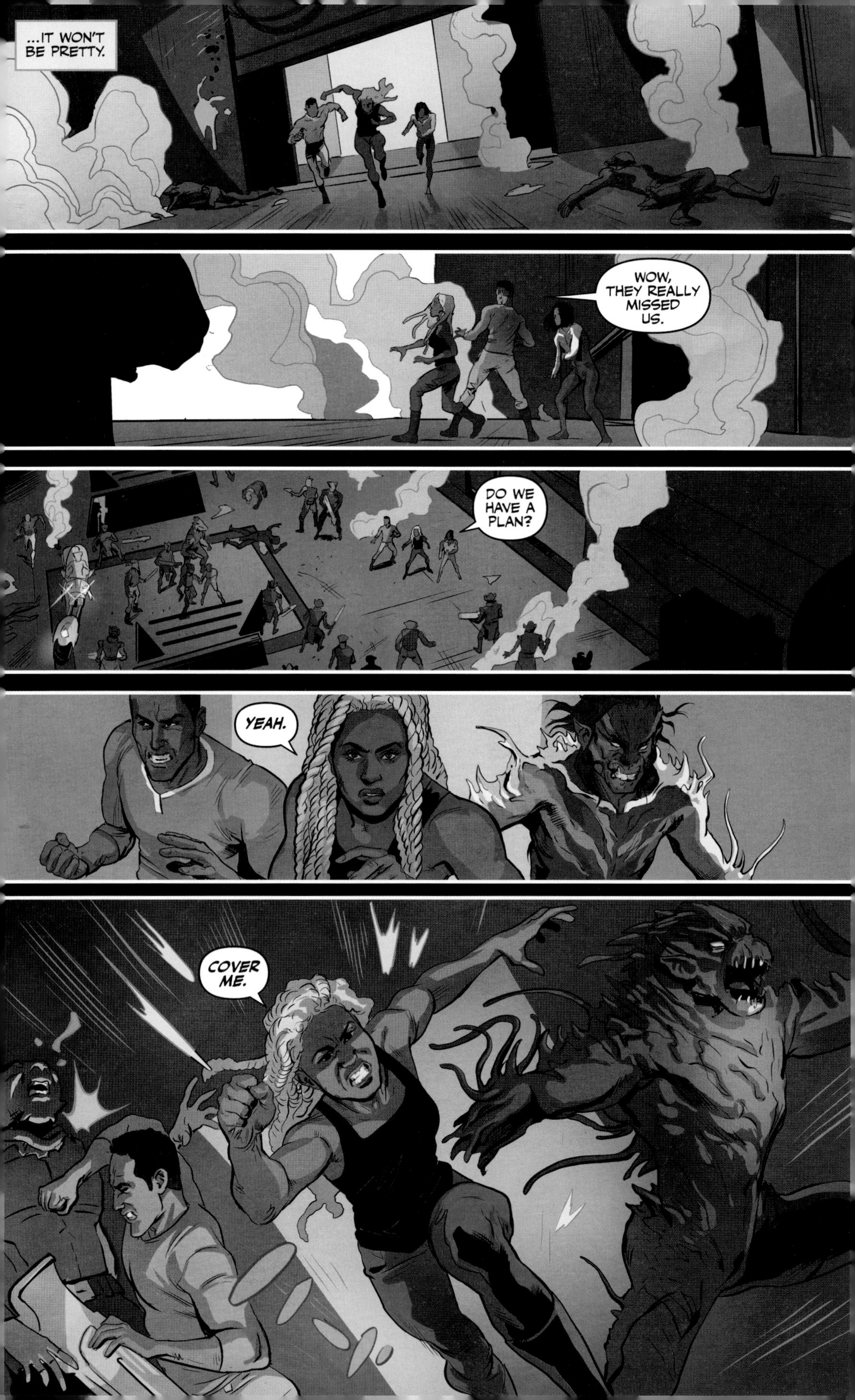
...IT WON'T BE PRETTY.
WOW, THEY REALLY MISSED US.
DO WE HAVE A PLAN?
YEAH.
COVER ME.

HEY, IDIOT. I NEED A GUNNER.

WHERE WE HEADED?

THE CITY CENTER! TO ENTER THE STATUE OF ANAX.

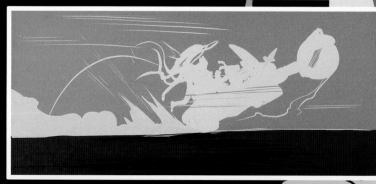

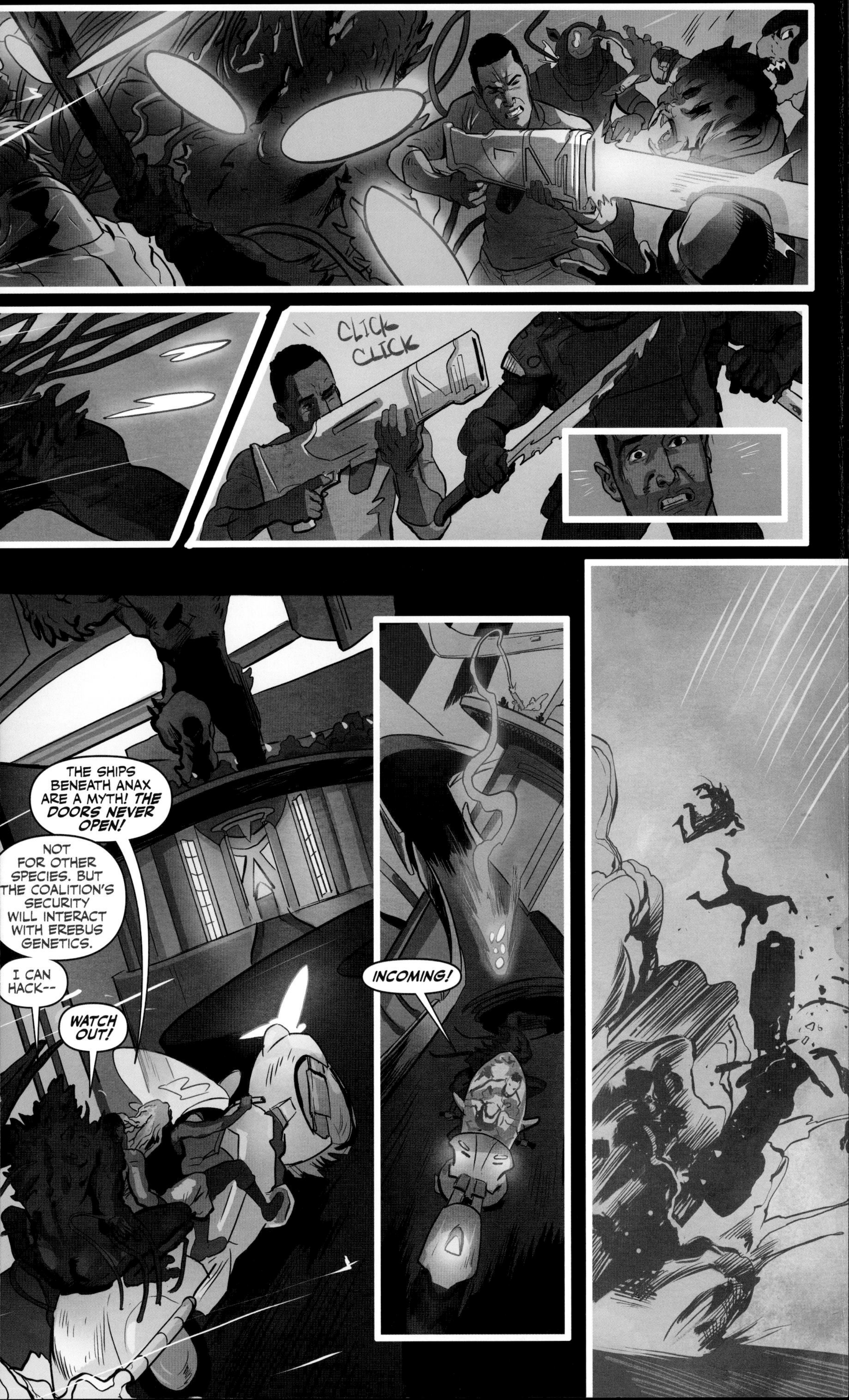
CLICK
CLICK
THE SHIPS BENEATH ANAX ARE A MYTH! THE DOORS NEVER OPEN!
NOT FOR OTHER SPECIES. BUT THE COALITION'S SECURITY WILL INTERACT WITH EREBUS GENETICS.
I CAN HACK--
WATCH OUT!
INCOMING!

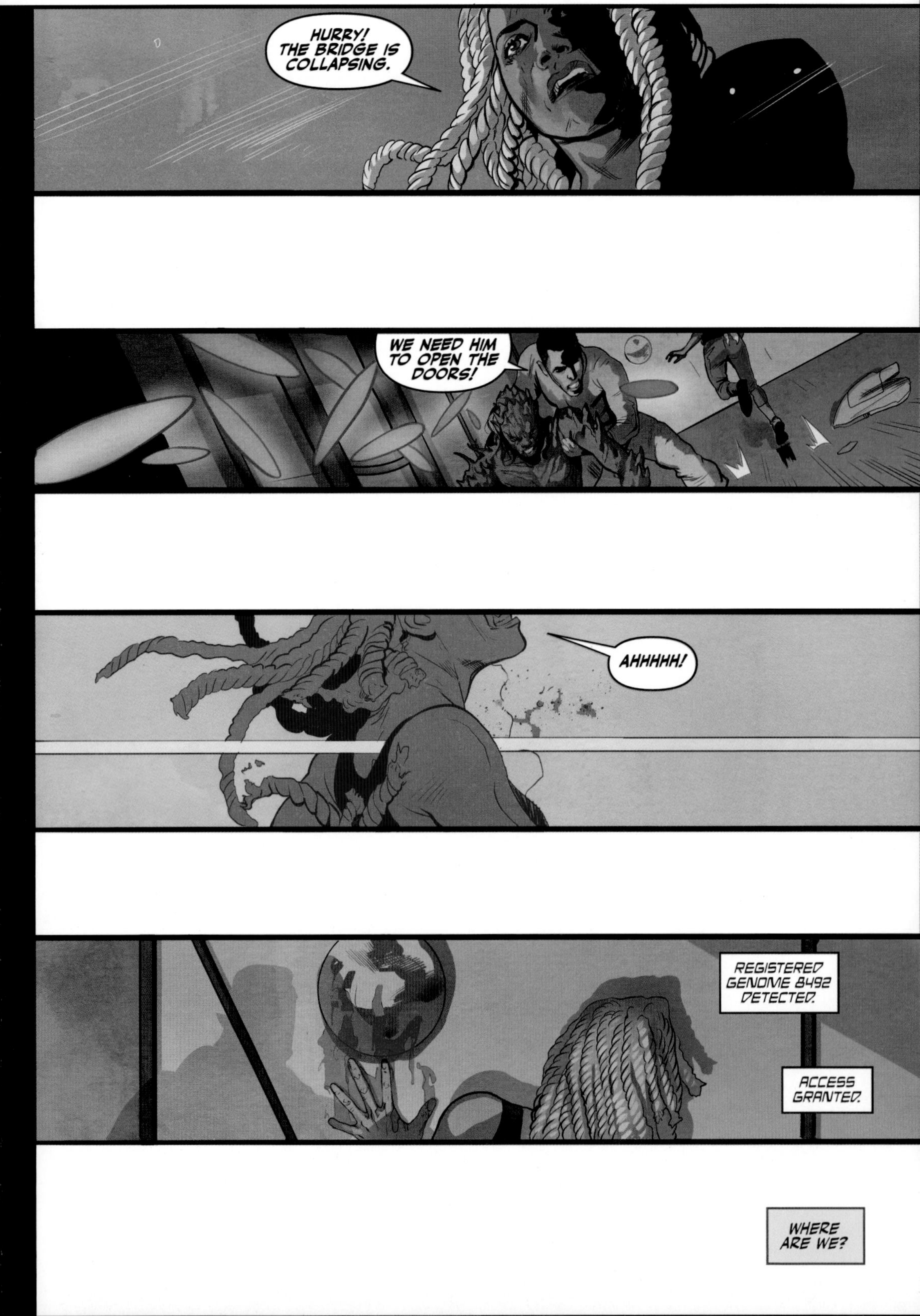
HURRY! THE BRIDGE IS COLLAPSING.
WE NEED HIM TO OPEN THE DOORS!
AHHHHH!
REGISTERED GENOME 8492 DETECTED.
ACCESS GRANTED.
WHERE ARE WE?

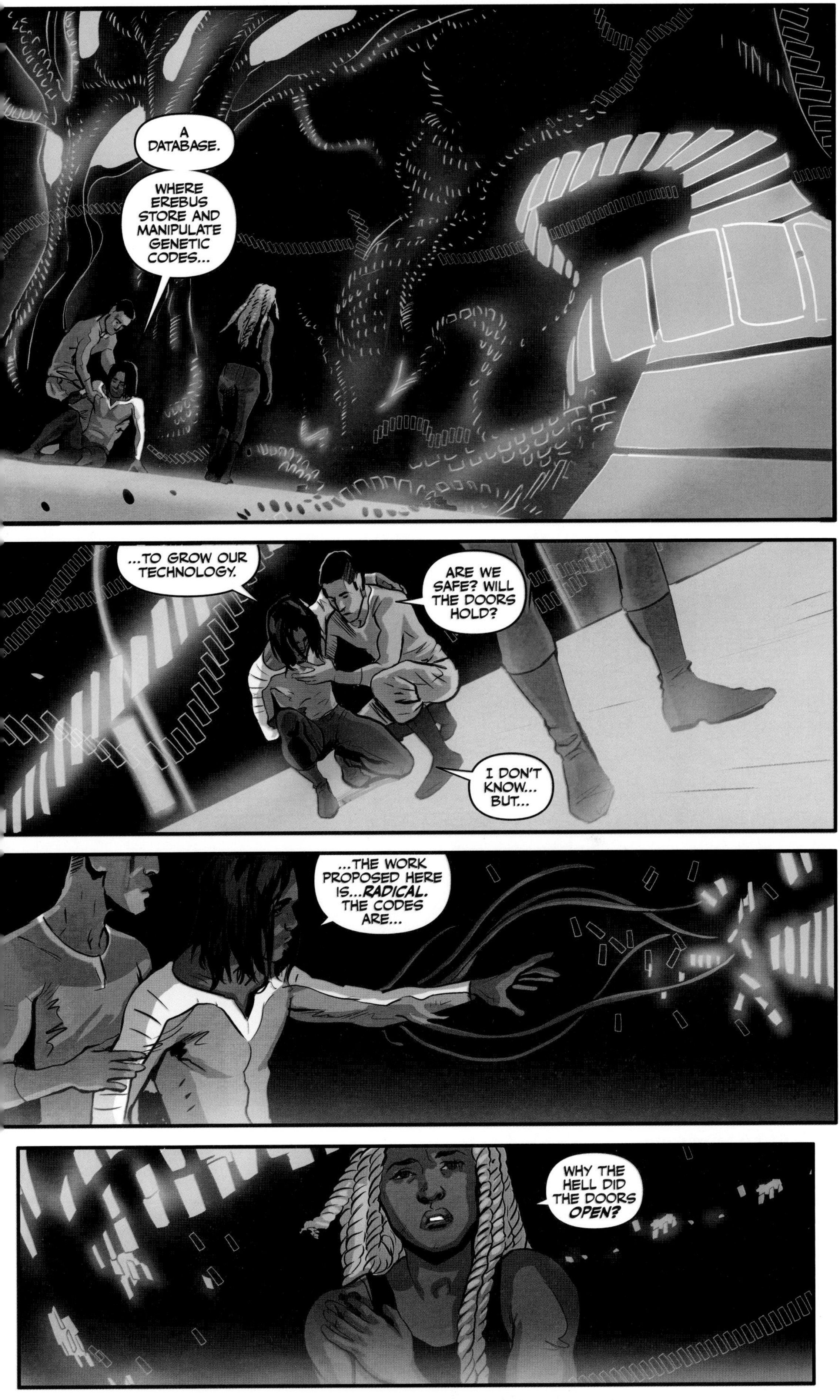
A DATABASE.
WHERE EREBUS STORE AND MANIPULATE GENETIC CODES...
...TO GROW OUR TECHNOLOGY.
ARE WE SAFE? WILL THE DOORS HOLD?
I DON'T KNOW... BUT...
...THE WORK PROPOSED HERE IS...*RADICAL.* THE CODES ARE...
WHY THE HELL DID THE DOORS *OPEN?*

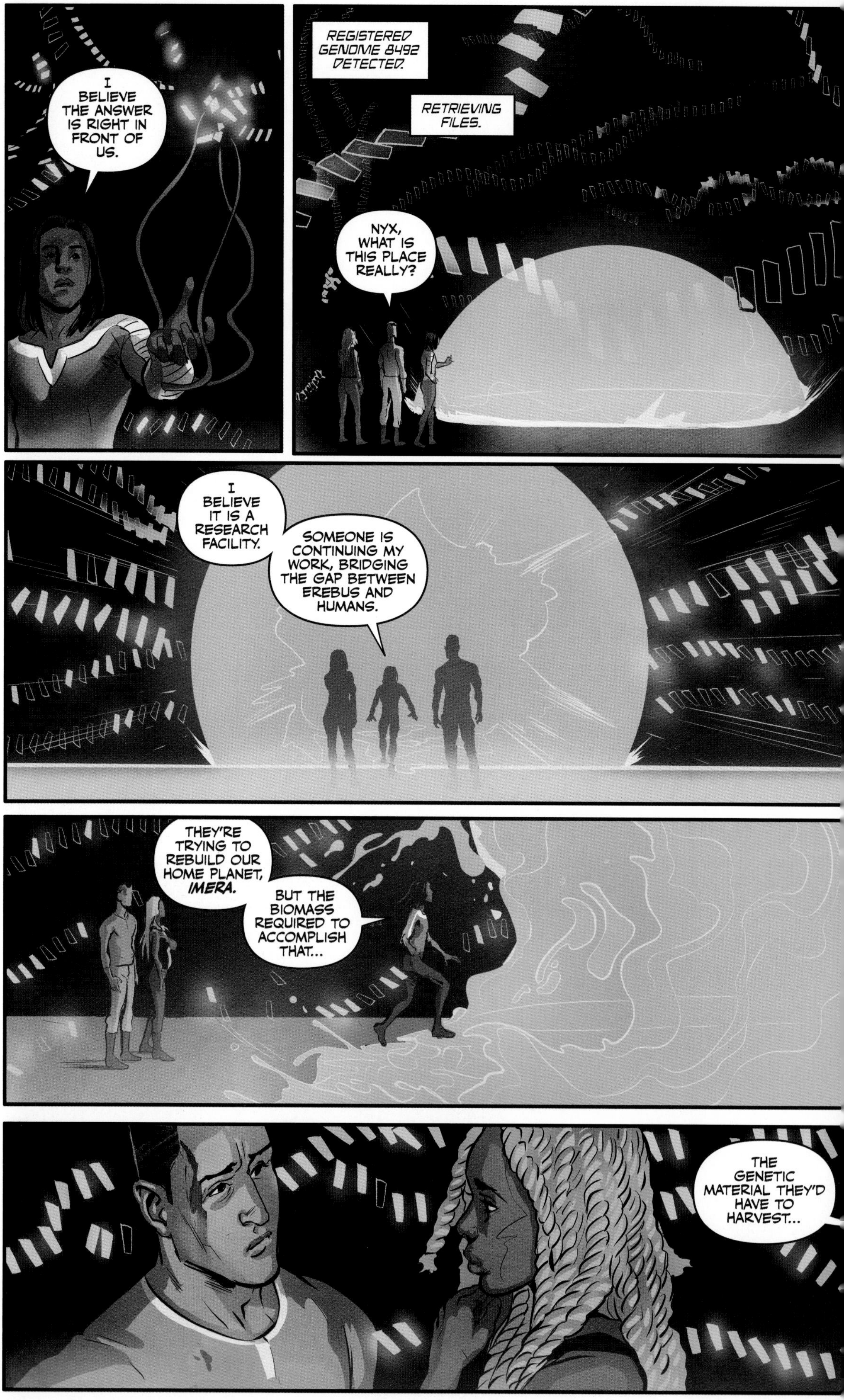
I BELIEVE THE ANSWER IS RIGHT IN FRONT OF US.
REGISTERED GENOME 8492 DETECTED.
RETRIEVING FILES.
NYX, WHAT IS THIS PLACE REALLY?
I BELIEVE IT IS A RESEARCH FACILITY.
SOMEONE IS CONTINUING MY WORK, BRIDGING THE GAP BETWEEN EREBUS AND HUMANS.
THEY'RE TRYING TO REBUILD OUR HOME PLANET, *IMERA.*
BUT THE BIOMASS REQUIRED TO ACCOMPLISH THAT...
THE GENETIC MATERIAL THEY'D HAVE TO HARVEST...

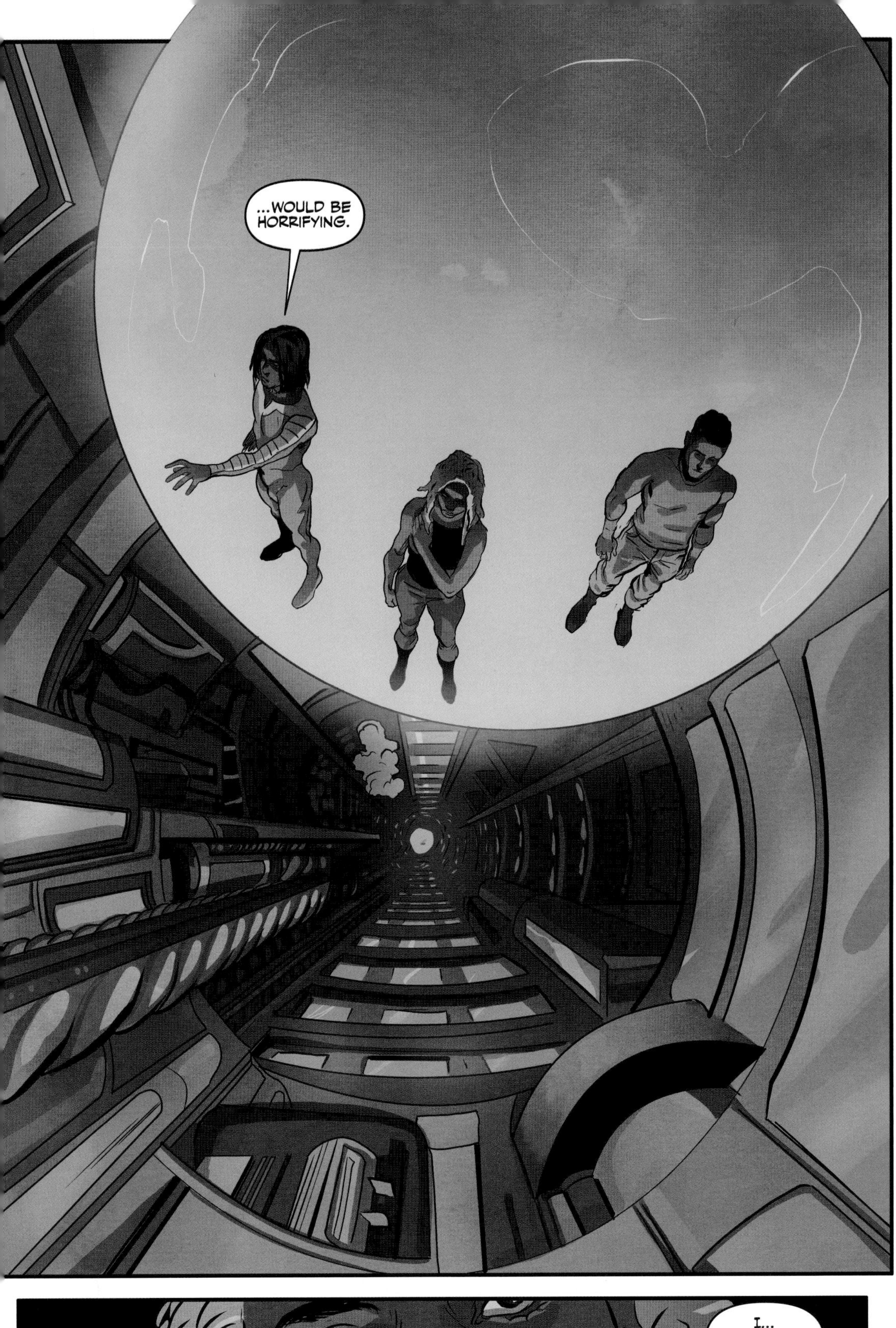
...WOULD BE HORRIFYING.

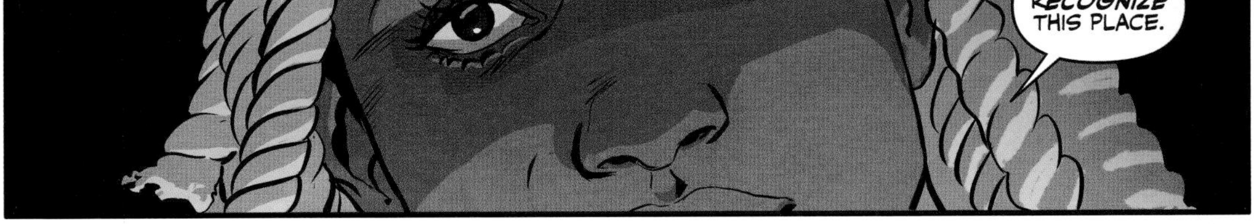
I... RECOGNIZE THIS PLACE.

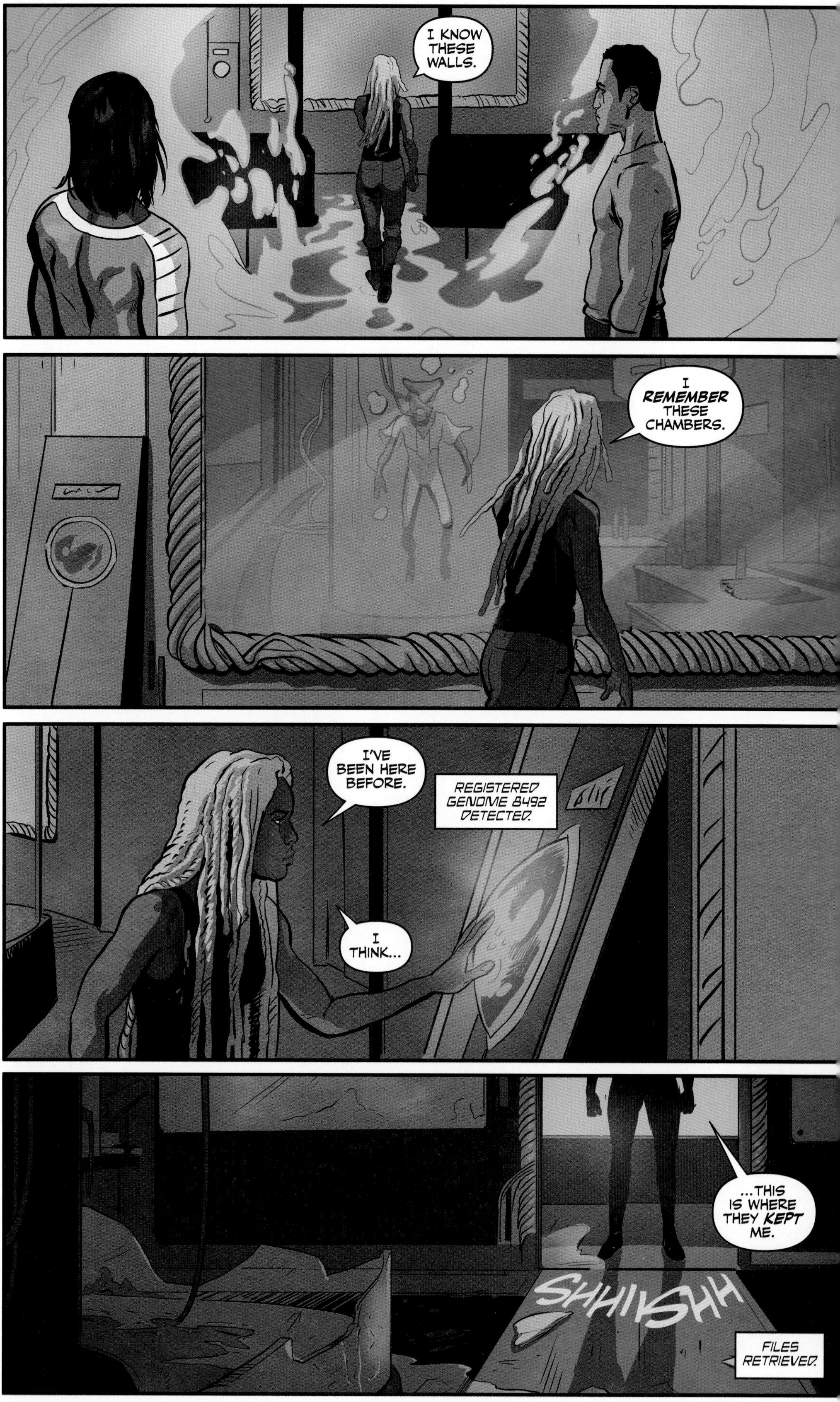

I KNOW THESE WALLS.
I REMEMBER THESE CHAMBERS.
I'VE BEEN HERE BEFORE.
REGISTERED GENOME 8492 DETECTED.
I THINK...
...THIS IS WHERE THEY KEPT ME.
SHHHSHH
FILES RETRIEVED.

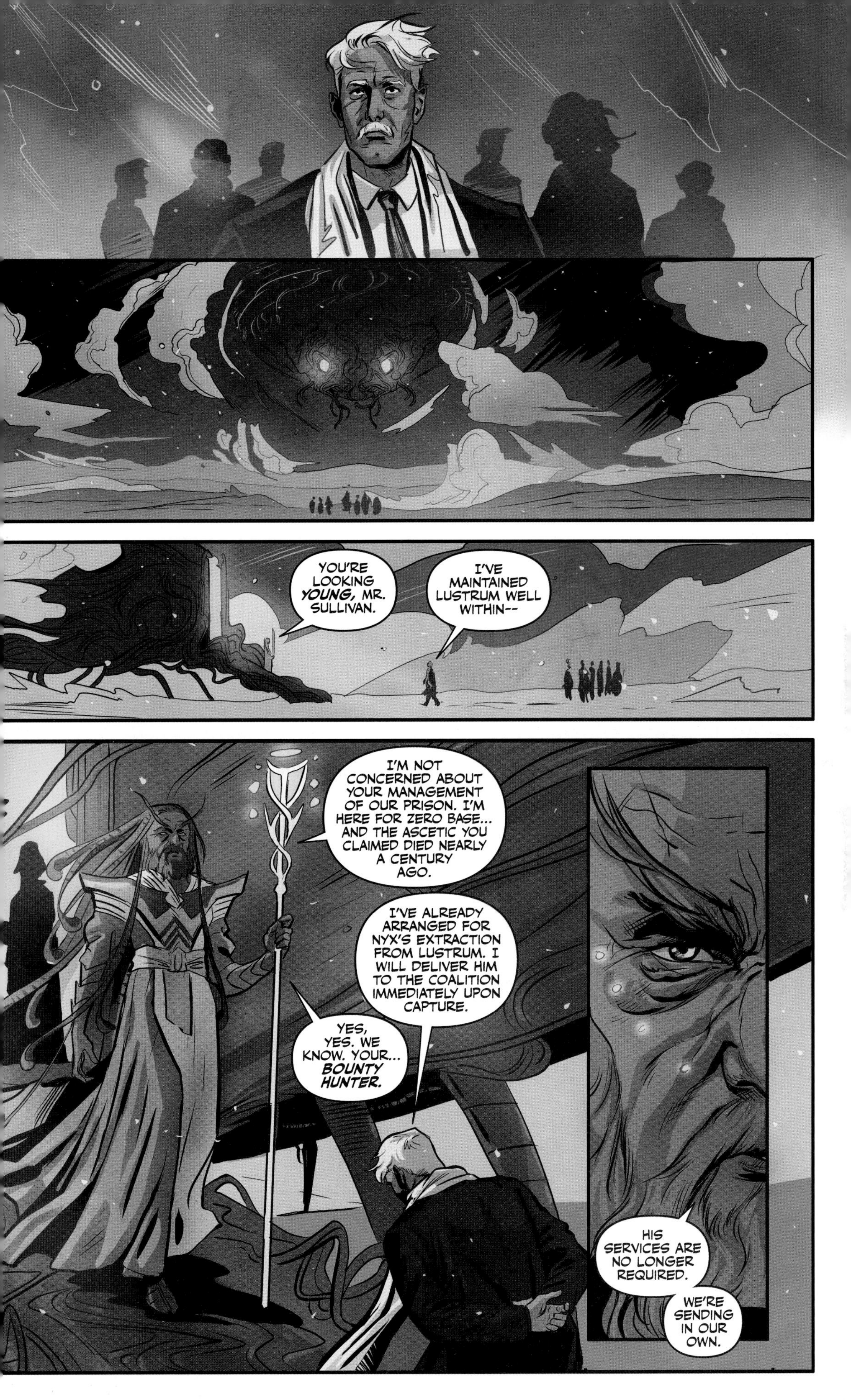
YOU'RE LOOKING YOUNG, MR. SULLIVAN.
I'VE MAINTAINED LUSTRUM WELL WITHIN--
I'M NOT CONCERNED ABOUT YOUR MANAGEMENT OF OUR PRISON. I'M HERE FOR ZERO BASE... AND THE ASCETIC YOU CLAIMED DIED NEARLY A CENTURY AGO.
I'VE ALREADY ARRANGED FOR NYX'S EXTRACTION FROM LUSTRUM. I WILL DELIVER HIM TO THE COALITION IMMEDIATELY UPON CAPTURE.
YES, YES. WE KNOW. YOUR... BOUNTY HUNTER.
HIS SERVICES ARE NO LONGER REQUIRED.
WE'RE SENDING IN OUR OWN.

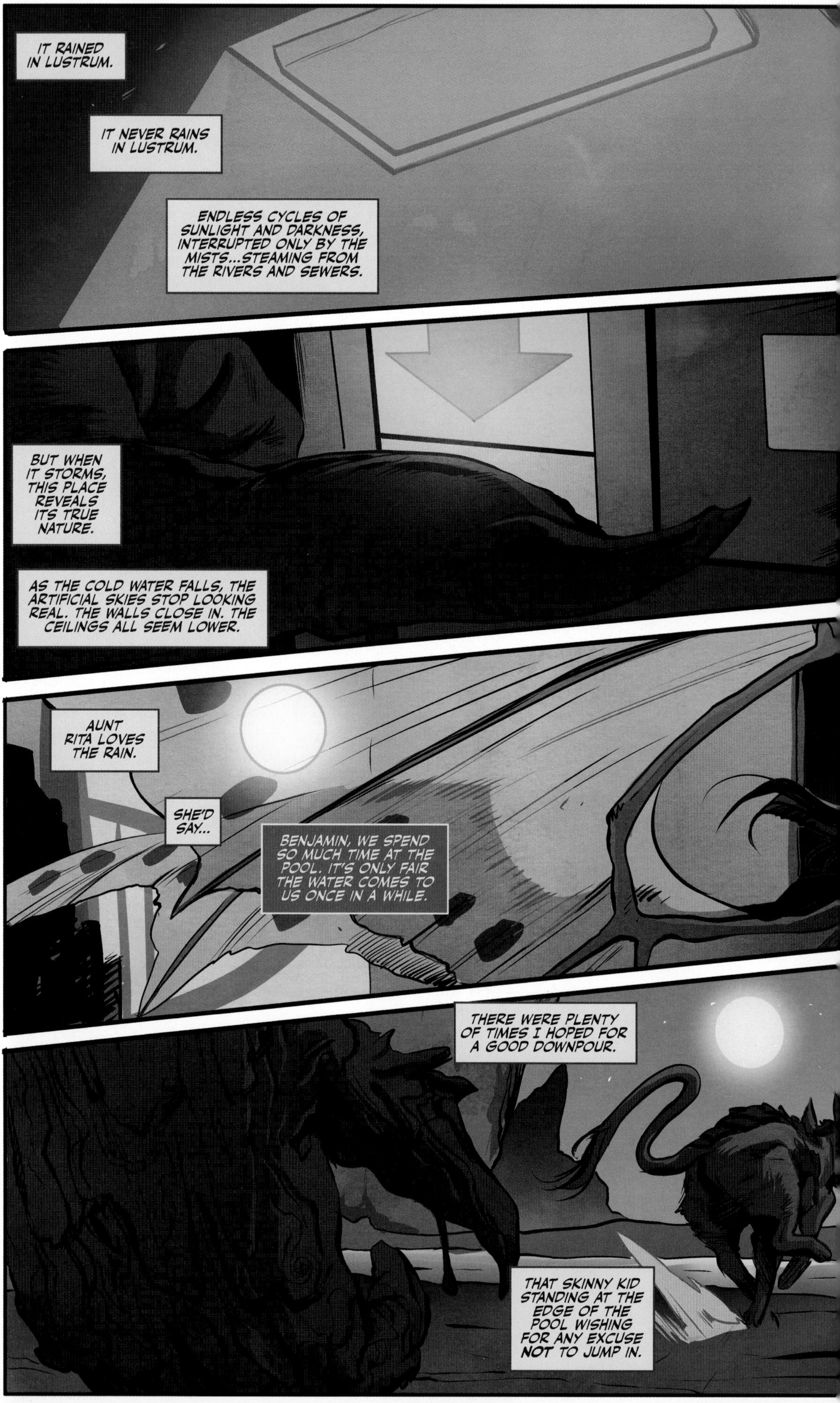
IT RAINED IN LUSTRUM.
IT NEVER RAINS IN LUSTRUM.
ENDLESS CYCLES OF SUNLIGHT AND DARKNESS, INTERRUPTED ONLY BY THE MISTS...STEAMING FROM THE RIVERS AND SEWERS.
BUT WHEN IT STORMS, THIS PLACE REVEALS ITS TRUE NATURE.
AS THE COLD WATER FALLS, THE ARTIFICIAL SKIES STOP LOOKING REAL. THE WALLS CLOSE IN. THE CEILINGS ALL SEEM LOWER.
AUNT RITA LOVES THE RAIN.
SHE'D SAY...
BENJAMIN, WE SPEND SO MUCH TIME AT THE POOL. IT'S ONLY FAIR THE WATER COMES TO US ONCE IN A WHILE.
THERE WERE PLENTY OF TIMES I HOPED FOR A GOOD DOWNPOUR.
THAT SKINNY KID STANDING AT THE EDGE OF THE POOL WISHING FOR ANY EXCUSE NOT TO JUMP IN.

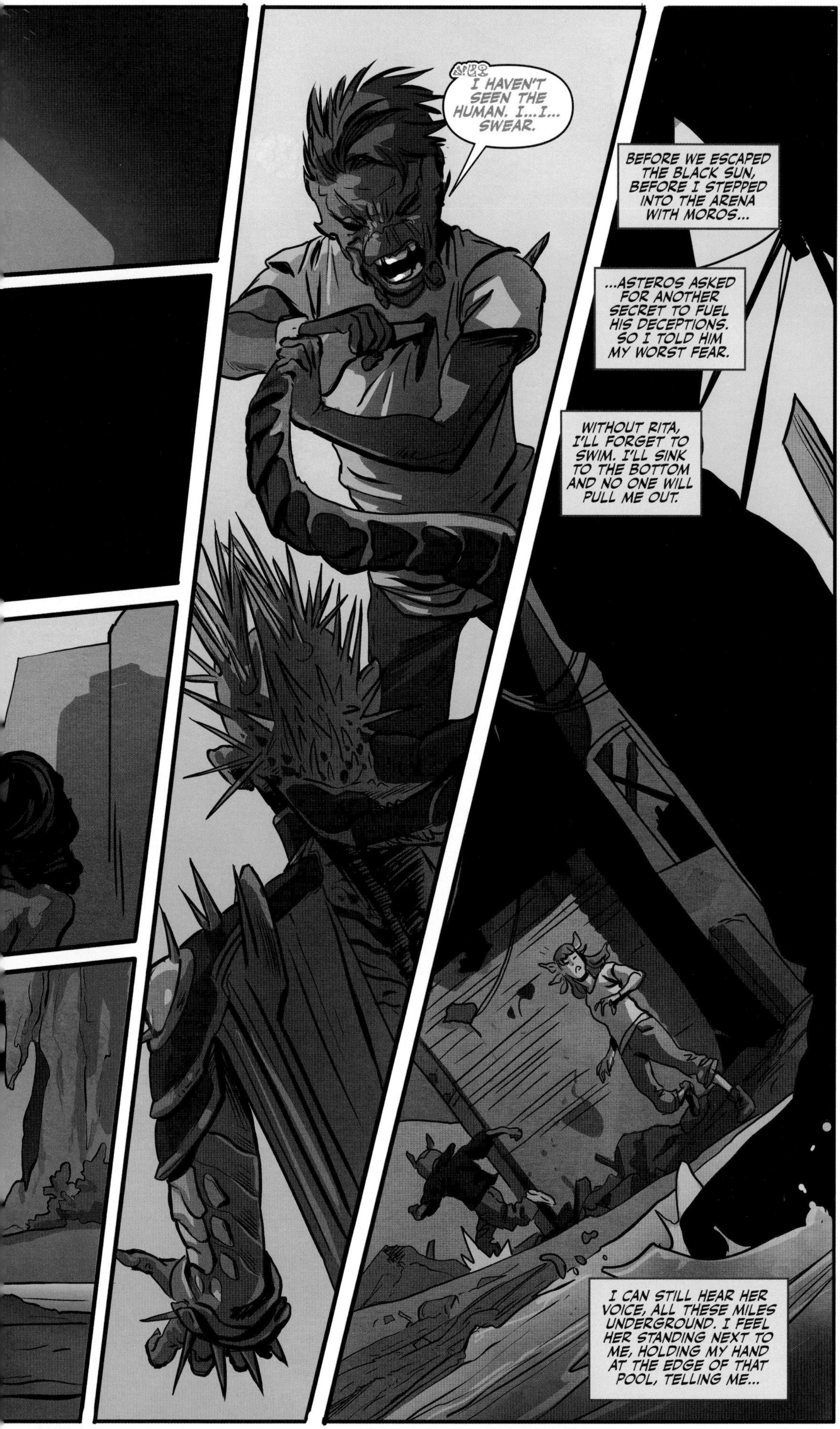
I HAVEN'T SEEN THE HUMAN. I...I... SWEAR.
BEFORE WE ESCAPED THE BLACK SUN, BEFORE I STEPPED INTO THE ARENA WITH MOROS...
...ASTEROS ASKED FOR ANOTHER SECRET TO FUEL HIS DECEPTIONS. SO I TOLD HIM MY WORST FEAR.
WITHOUT RITA, I'LL FORGET TO SWIM. I'LL SINK TO THE BOTTOM AND NO ONE WILL PULL ME OUT.
I CAN STILL HEAR HER VOICE, ALL THESE MILES UNDERGROUND. I FEEL HER STANDING NEXT TO ME, HOLDING MY HAND AT THE EDGE OF THAT POOL, TELLING ME...

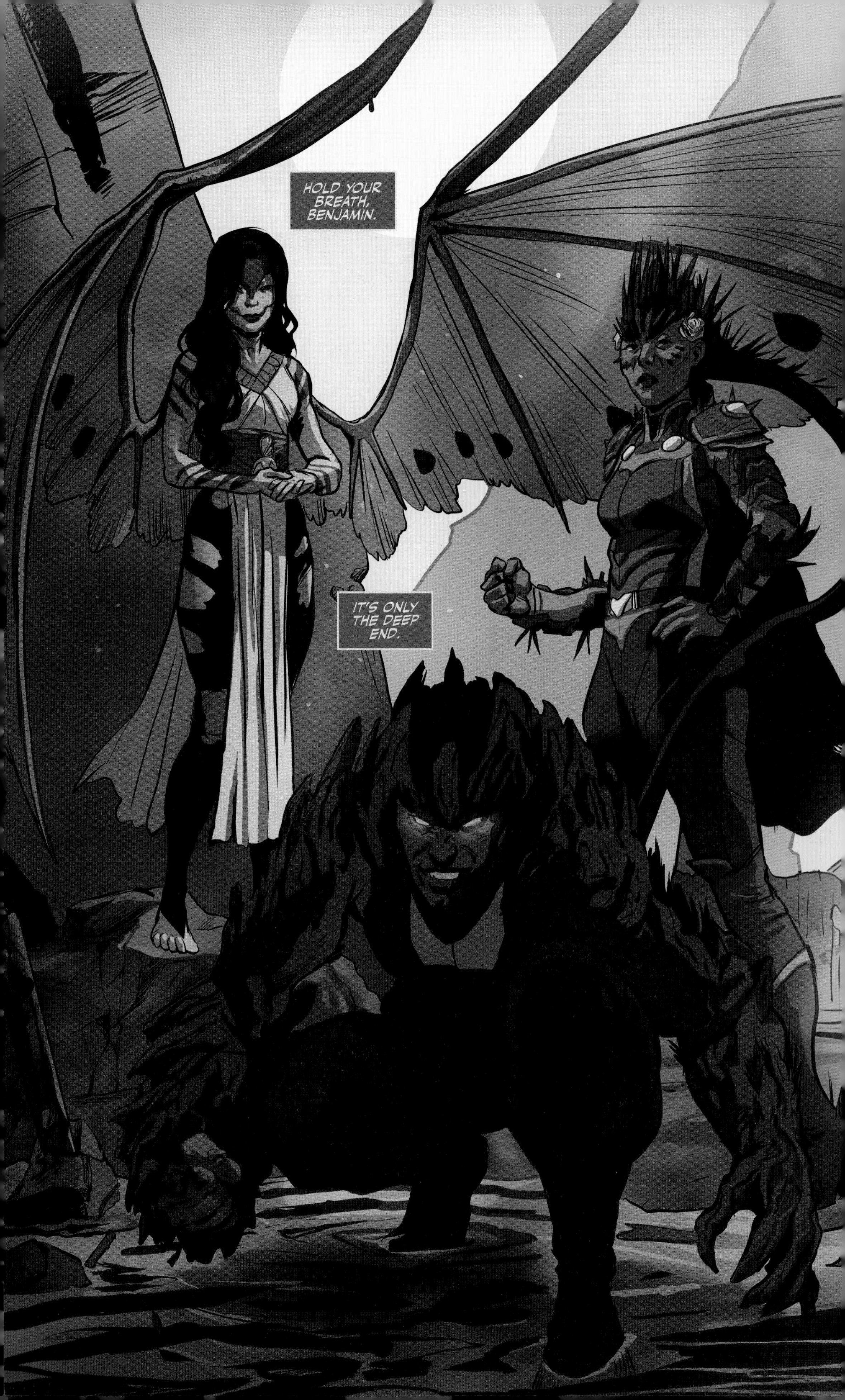
HOLD YOUR BREATH, BENJAMIN.
IT'S ONLY THE DEEP END.

COVER GALLERY
ALIEN
BOUNTY HUNTER

FEATURING THE ART OF NICK ROBLES

ISSUE ONE COVER

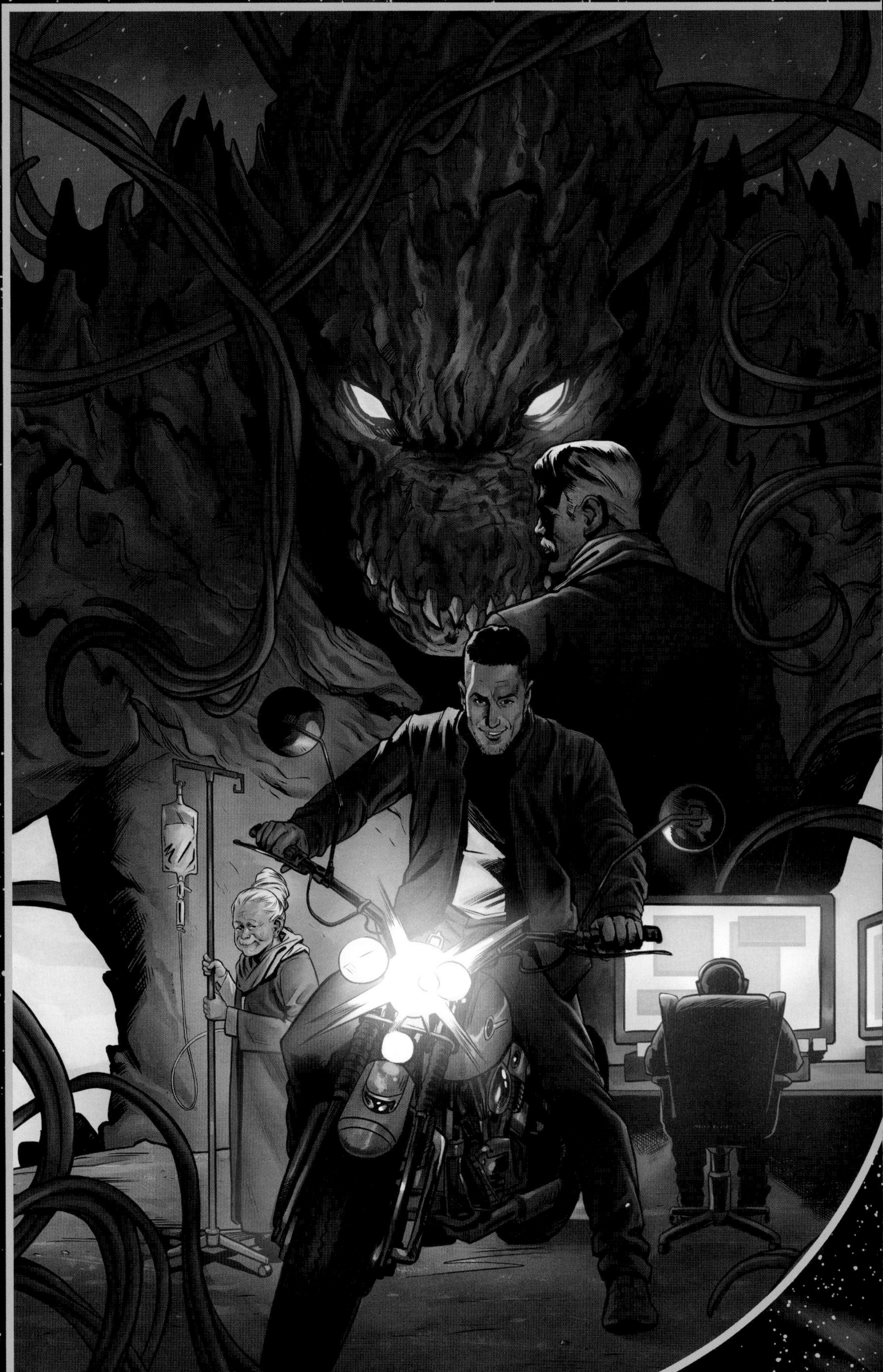

ARTIST
NICK ROBLES

SSUE TWO COVER

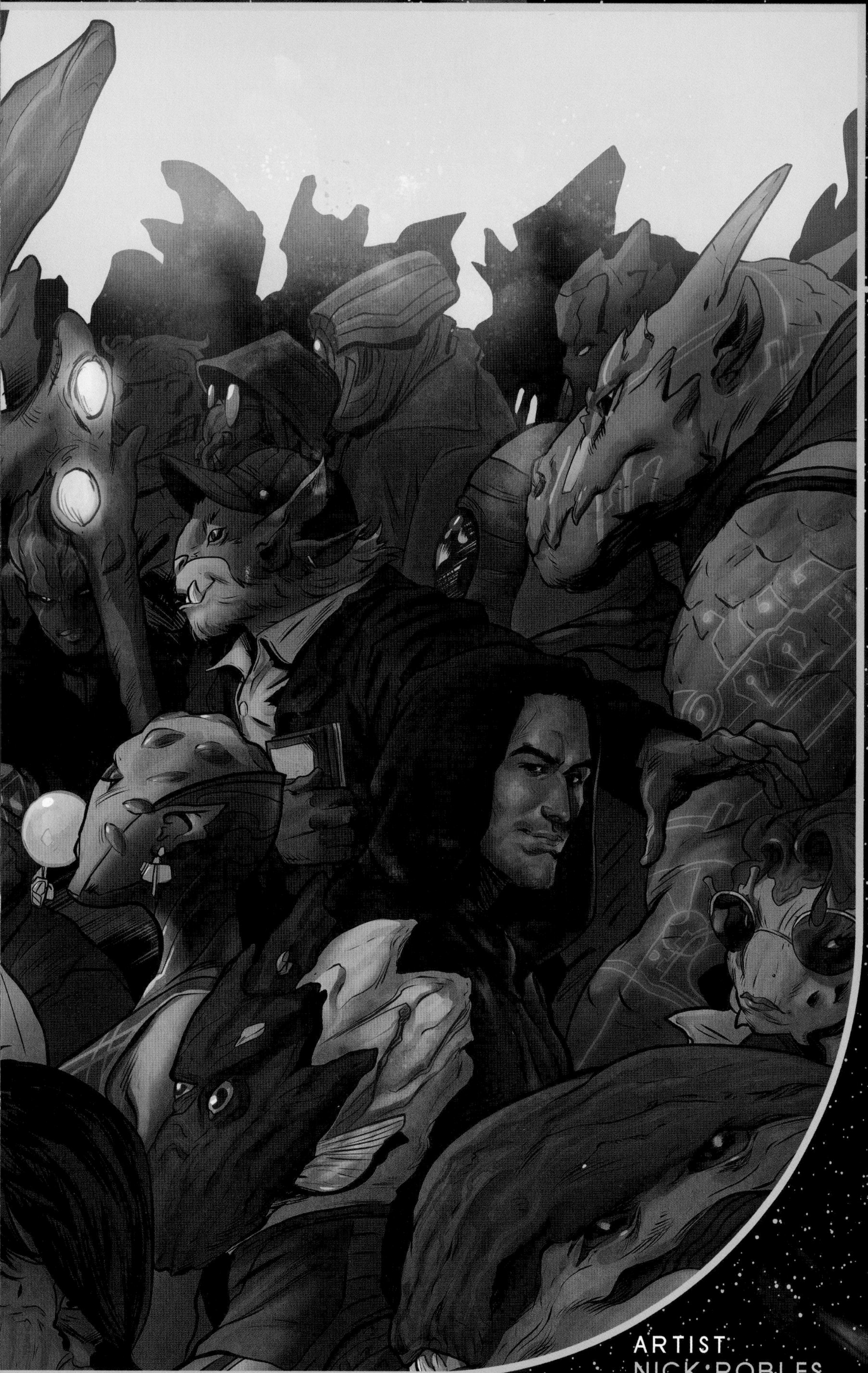

ARTIST
NICK ROBLES

ISSUE THREE COVER

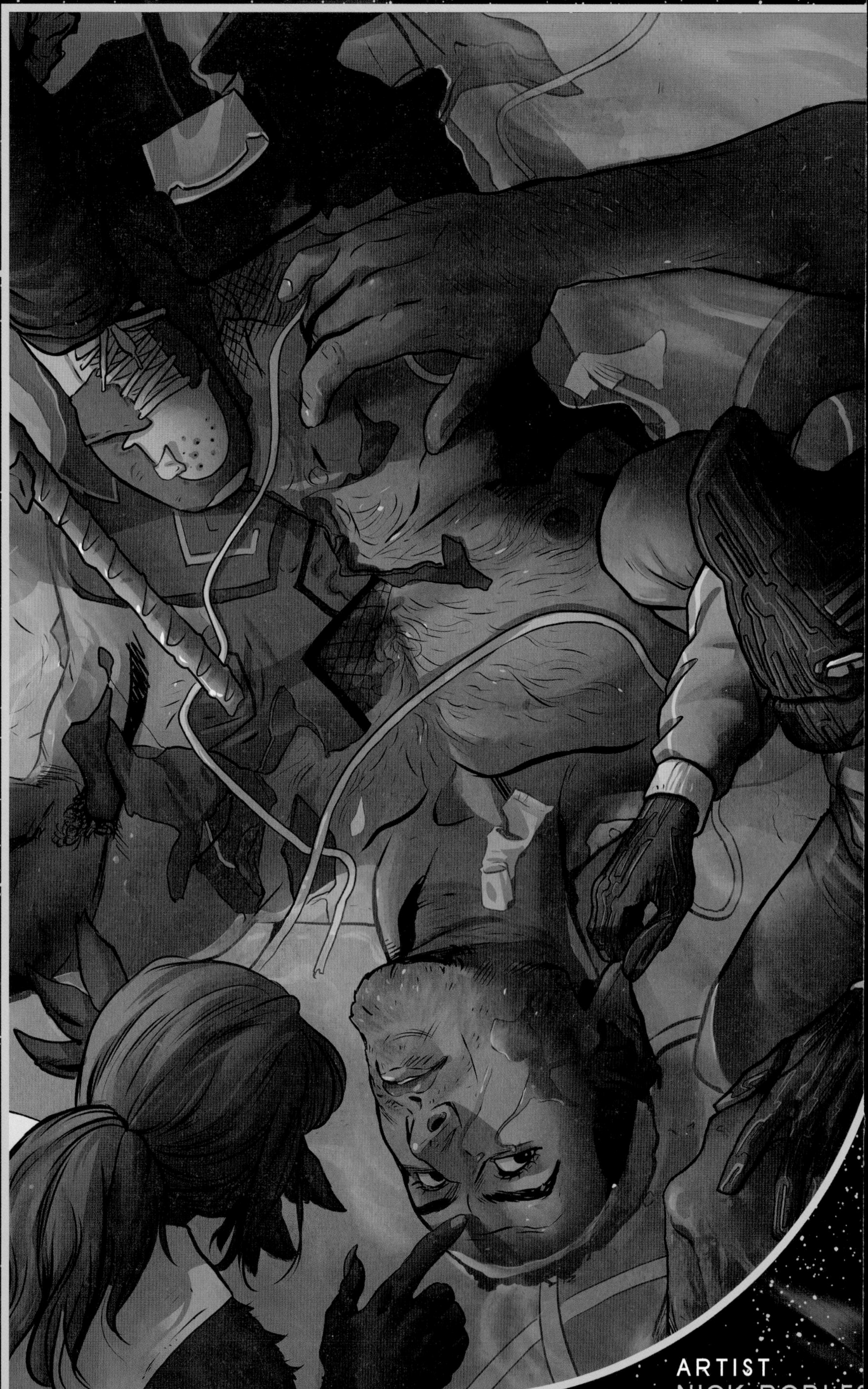

ARTIST
NICK ROBLES